A game of cat and witch

MONSTROUS SHIFTERS BOOK ONE

RUBY RUNE

This book is a work of fiction. The names, characters, and events in this book are the products of the author's imagination or are used fictitiously. Any similarities to real people, places, or events are entirely coincidental.

Published by Ruby Rune on 10/05/2026

1st edition 2026

ISBN: 978-1-7646627-0-3

Kindle Paperback ISBN: 978-1-7646627-1-0

Developmental & Copy Editing: Steph Rawlins at Rawls Reads Editing

Proofreading: Zee at The Blue Couch Edits

Cover design and typography: Design By Kage

Cover illustration and character art: Alilyushka

Artwork: talitasami

Formatting: Demi Clorissa

To all the girls who want to be chased through a maze and railed by a monster.
This is for you.

Note about the Monstrous Shifters Series:

Thank you so much for reading my debut novel. It genuinely means the world to me that you decided to pick this up and give this delightfully unhinged book a try. Please be warned there are lots of claws, fangs, and shadows in places they definitely shouldn't be. A Game of Cat and Witch is the first book in a series of interconnected standalones with an overarching plot. There will be some questions left open. There will be more sex to be had. But most of all, I hope you have an amazing time.

So buckle the fuck up, you're going for a ride ;)

Content Warnings:

Dub con/non con
Graphic sexual scenes
Sexual assault (on page)
Physical violence
Anxiety/Panic attacks
Dismembered bodies
Trauma
Death of a loved one (not on page)
Death of a parent (not on page)
Graphic violence
Slut shaming
Excessive drinking
Murder and attempted murder

For a full list of trigger warnings please visit:
rubyruneauthor.com

Prologue

Avery

In her life, Avery Alarch had made many stupid decisions. This one was monumentally, catastrophically, write-it-in-the-history-books-as-a-cautionary-tale levels of stupid. She followed the stone path through the quadrangle as the dusky sun plunged the University of Caerwyn into a fiery haze. Enforcers stood guard at the entrance of the building, their rifles blazing with the red core of magic imbued within them. Students meandered around, lazing in the last dregs of the sun before winter. They sprawled across the campus in clusters that Avery would never be part of again; some studied, while another group was passing around a bottle that was definitely not allowed on campus. None of them knew what she was about to attempt. None of them would attempt it, because they weren't fucking stupid. However, none of them were desperate enough either. Their familiars came easily, while hers evaded her like a rabid squirrel.

If they did happen to know, they would probably pour in droves to her show. *"Come one, come all: watch this useless witch attempt forbidden magic. It's sure to be the comedy of the century!"*

The enforcers nodded her through, and she continued along the path that led into the belly of the forest. Trees dropped their crimson leaves in a colorful rain, and yellow wolf's milk flowers dotted the floor. The limbs of the oaks twisted into the setting sky, their trunks wider than ten men but still offering little protection against the bite of the October wind. It was as cold as a witch's tit. *Thanks for nothing, trees.*

Her blazer took the brunt of it, the thick fabric flapping against the assault of the weather. Her nose stung; the tip blushed from the chill. It was something her sisters always teased her about; her face turned pink from the slightest change or comment. Both of them had somehow practiced the mask of pale statues, but she displayed every emotion like a billboard in Times Square.

She readjusted her leather bag, hiking it back onto her shoulder. Candles, her grimoire, and her expectations of how this would actually go—which were abysmal, deplorable, pathetic, and every other adjective that belonged in the thesaurus—weighed down the bag.

Arches crumbled around her, relics of a lost time. A statue of their goddess Cerituen still stood. Someone or something had cut away at the statue next to her, leaving just the plinth. No one seemed to know why, or they just ignored its existence entirely.

This was the only private place on the island. Caerwyn was small but populated, like a sardine can of magical prowess. There was the university and a town with a pub and shops that were destined to be your legacy if you failed to become a proper witch. Generally, one person a generation failed to summon a familiar, and lucky her, she was going to be that person. It seemed to run in the family. The last person to fail was her Aunt Alys, who was currently serving a sentence in Anoddun, for goddess knows what, no one would ever tell her.

For some reason, few people came to these woods. Students labeled it creepy. They were obviously not versed in the beauty that forests held. *And*, they were cowards.

The sound of crashing waves was a familiar calling. Rocks marbled the edge of the forest, the floor turning from crunching leaves to mossy stone. It was the only logical place to do a ritual, away from the prying eyes of others. Perhaps this was part of her failure. She hated being observed by anyone, and whenever she had attempted a summoning before their watching eyes, they became witnesses to her incompetence, solidifying her position as an underachiever, born loser, good-for-nothing witch. Perhaps she would win the university award for "Most likely not to succeed."

Wind whipped through the branches, their crack roaring with the sounds of waves bashing against the cliffs. The weather had significantly picked up. Maybe it was a warning from Cerituen that she should heed. That's what she *would* do if she weren't about to be expelled from Caerwyn and confined to this island for the rest of her days.

In this case, the goddess could go *kindly*—in case she really was listening—fuck herself. Avery's father always told her she was a dog with a bone when she wanted something. She would show Cerituen how much she wanted this. How desperate she had become to be a witch. How could she not be when her only other option was to be expelled? What job would she be able to get? The one pub on this tiny island? Listening to balding witches complain about their wives and kids, even though they hadn't picked up a dish in the sink for the last twenty years? She secretly always rooted for the wives getting so fed up that they killed their partners, took their money, and moved so they could sip cocktails in the Bahamas' witch enclave. Now that was an idea she could get behind.

Maybe life wasn't so bleak, after all. If only she could leave the island.

She dropped her bag to the forest floor, the wax candles rolling out like they were running away from a monster.

"Ugh, come on," she muttered, exhaling a sigh and picking them up one by one. She placed them in a circle, trying to remember if the spacing mattered. Probably? Everything in magic seemed to matter, which was honestly exhausting.

Seven candles (*normal*), seven animal bones (*don't ask*), seven sticks of sage (*from the corner shop, next to the chocolate bars*), and seven wolf's milk flowers (*an odd choice but luckily one that grew abundantly on the island*) lay in front of her in an arranged pattern. For the love of the fucking goddess, she hoped this worked.

Fumbling in the pockets of her uniform, she fished out a matchbox. Before she lit the candles, she let the sun dip below the horizon, the twilight settling in before she struck the match. Clutching it in her palm, she hesitated, almost to save herself the disappointment. If she walked away now, she wouldn't have to feel like a failure again. She simply wouldn't try; she could return to her bed with its Sparky blankets and sleep the rest of the night away, blissfully unconscious for eight hours.

But morning would always come.

Instead, she pushed that feeling down as it gnawed its way through her chest, trying to find something to latch onto, like an army of parasitic anxiety bugs. If only she could bug bomb herself. If only it were so easy to rid herself of the feeling. Even on the days when anxiety quietened down to the back of her mind, the bugs would rear their ugly heads again if Avery had the slightest doubt.

She struck the match, and the night came alive around her in red hues. Heat rolled off the tiny flame as she touched it to the candles one by one, sealing her fate in wax. The old language flowed through her—as best it could, she still butchered the pronunciations—as she channeled the earth around her, pulling its essence into a summoning circle. The smell of decaying leaves invaded her senses as the frigid wind picked up at the call of her voice.

The lines carved themselves into the platform, glowing red on the outer ring, the magic running like a river of blood, illuminating more of the circle. Each stream rushed toward her, following its engraved path of symbols and weak, intricate patterns like lava between rocks.

She swallowed, those damn anxiety bugs pumping adrenaline through her veins, her heart thumping so hard she thought it might bruise. Was she really doing this? Was she really so desperate that forbidden magic was what she had to resort to?

Yes. Yes, she was.

She'd rather be dead than not have magic. Did anyone know how convenient it was to be a witch? You could turn off the light without leaving your bed. You could make the kitchen your personal chef. The possibilities were endless, and she'd be damned if she let such a fantastic opportunity pass her by. It was kind of ironic the lengths she was going to be lazy, though.

Okay, it was more than that. It was status. Acceptance. It meant she could leave this stupid island she had spent her entire life on. If she got a familiar, if she joined one of the houses, she could finally *fucking* leave.

The forest suddenly pressed in on her, the tall walls of pines and oaks closing in. Her limbs shook like branches in the wind. Her breath caught in her chest, panic lacing her veins with its poison, and all she wanted to do was run. She turned, following the magic making its way up the stone to the statue of the goddess above. Her eyes, once stone, now glowed an unsightly red, as if she were casting divine judgment upon her.

Avery swallowed, her stomach twisted with nausea, and she felt the bile climbing its way up her throat until it burned.

She turned away from the statue. Out of sight, out of mind. Kneeling, she touched her hand to the middle of the circle. It could be her imagination, but she swore to the goddess she felt a hum underneath her fingertips, like that of a cat's purr. Or perhaps they were close to falling off from frostbite. It was hard to tell.

Wind whipped through the branches as she continued the incantations, her voice competing with their cracking and the waves roaring against the cliffs.

She pulled a dagger from her bag, ready to complete the final step. A drop of her blood was all it took. It would take all her problems away. She could graduate, she could become a healer like her father, and go about her normal life. Only, something in her knew that wouldn't happen, that this would change something fundamental. That perhaps, she would fuck up more spectacularly.

She had come too far to turn back.

Chanting the words, she called upon the forest to bring her a familiar. Please be something powerful, she had gone to all this trouble. A dragon. A griffin. A pegasus. Not a toad. Anything but a toad. The way they licked their eyeballs with their tongues freaked her out.

The ritual demanded her blood. She stared at the hungry circle, the forest threatening to swallow her if she didn't heed its needs. It was far more than forbidden to use blood magic; it was sacrilege. Even the thought of blood made her sick. But her fucks were flying away faster than the island's migrating geese.

So she gave it. She dragged the knife over her wrist, wincing, as sharp pain shot up her arm—because using your palm was stupid; she needed that hand—almost letting out a whimper. But she would be damned if she let the goddess have any doubt that she was strong enough for this, that she deserved this.

The pungent scent of magic suffocated her nostrils as the circle ate her blood up hungrily, the symbols of the old language now glowing brighter than they ever had.

The last thing she saw before it went dark was the bloodred moon.

A deep voice slithered through her mind.

"Witch."

One

Avery

The night before the ritual...

Avery's mother always said it was her who should have been eaten in the womb. That the twin Avery ate would have been a more successful student. Today, Avery was inclined to believe her because she was about to be expelled.

The watered-down whiskey tingled as it met her lips, leaving a fiery trail of cinnamon sliding over her throat and settling warm in her chest. Drinking wasn't the healthiest of coping mechanisms, but for now, it would do.

As the warmth of the alcohol spread through her limbs, her dorm room became a little hazier. The dark wood of the furniture blended with the sunset, and the crackle of the fireplace was the only sound apart from the maddened rise and fall of Maya's breathing across from her. The valedictorian sprawled out on Avery's bed, her usually pristine uniform loose and in crumples. She had one sock on and one off; she had given up on propriety three drinks ago. Even her bra lay lonely on the chair after she flung it away mid-rant, declaring it was as useless as the men in the reality TV show they were watching.

"Boooo," Maya slurred, throwing chocolate almonds at the flickering projector. She'd paused it because she had become so angry that her favorite couple had just broken up. "He couldn't resist putting his dick in a new arrival for twenty-four hours after he had publicly declared that he loved the girl?"

Avery caught the almond midair and popped it into her mouth. "Men."

The human TV show was inane enough to leave you clinging to waning brain cells at the end of it. But it was a pleasant distraction from the reality she found herself in.

Thunder rolled outside the window, flickering the projector on and off; the electricity at the university was at the weather's mercy. You would think, as witches, they could solve that problem, but no, instead they spent their energy on more useless things, like watching reality TV. It was kind of addictive, though.

"Gimme some more of that," Maya said, stirring. She made a half-hearted grab toward the bottle in Avery's hand.

Avery held it straight up out of her reach, with a surprisingly quick motion for a tipsy person. "No, no more for you. I don't want to clean up your vomit off my floor again."

"That was one time!"

"Was it, though?" Avery raised a pointed eyebrow at her because it was definitely more than once. The piece of bleached wood stood out like a sore thumb from their celebration a year ago. One that she now knew was entirely premature.

"Fiiiine." Maya flopped back against the pillows, staring at the ceiling. "I should probably stop drinking now, anyway. Two days isn't enough time to sober up for class."

The very thing Avery had been drinking to forget slapped her in the face like a flaccid cock. Two days to summon a familiar or probably be expelled. It was literally the only requirement for their final year. She was going to kiss her magical education goodbye.

Maya's face crumpled as soon as she said it, a hand flying to her mouth. "Sorry, I didn't mean to..."

"It's fine," Avery said, waving her off. "It's something you should be proud of. You worked your ass off."

"Yeahhh, but so did you." Maya shook her head in disbelief. "I can't believe Julian fucking Ainsworth got a familiar before you. The man is as dumb as a doorknob."

Avery let out a bitter laugh, taking another swig from the bottle. A delightful burn coated her throat.

Maya propped herself up on one elbow, her dark braided hair falling messily over her face. "You were, like, at least five points ahead of him in the final theory test."

Maya attempted to brush a piece of hair away and failed miserably. "He and his new familiar can go. Fuck. Themselves," she said, punctuating each word by poking her finger through a circle she'd made with her other hand.

It was hilarious seeing Maya like this. She was usually so reserved and determined not to say a bad thing about anyone, but drunk Maya had opinions. Loud ones.

The sound of wings beat overhead, the force of them enough to rattle the windows.

Maya sighed. "Ugh, I hate dragon riders; they really need to introduce a no-fly policy past midnight. The number of times I've woken up from one of those dumb beasts..."

"What if you got one of those dumb beasts?"

"Nah, I'm way too cool for a dragon. That's why I got a crow."

As if on cue, the black shadow perched on Avery's

window let out an ear-screeching caw. Avery snorted at Maya's statement. Dragons were known as the most powerful familiars you could summon; anyone would be lucky enough to have one. Crows, foxes, cats, bats, horses, etcetera, etcetera, were all considered normal. They gave you power, but it was nothing compared to the mythical beasts. The only person to summon anything mythical in their year was Julian fucking Ainsworth and his griffin. They say familiars look like their owners, and both looked like pompous pricks.

Maya had summoned her crow a year ago, as soon as we were allowed to perform the ritual. It was a given that she was the first to get a familiar. In theory, it was easy. You drew a summoning circle, set up the candles, read the incantations, and offered the goddess a token in exchange for a familiar; out popped a crow, and Bob's your witchy uncle.

However, Bob was not *her* uncle, nor was he helpful at all in summoning a fucking familiar. Maya had done it all perfectly. The rest of her class followed over the following months. It was now a fucking petting zoo and Avery still had manifested nothing but perpetual disappointment.

Jealousy festered within her. It was a wound that wouldn't heal. She tried not to give a fuck, but unfortunately, she gave too many; she was a slut for them. She was happy for Maya to be the first. But selfishly, she would like to be a little happy too.

Maya sighed again, stumbling as she made her way out of the bed, half sliding, half crawling like a cat that missed its jump, hanging onto the duvet for dear life. "I should go back to my dorm before the wicked witch notices me gone. The woman has a second sense for me, I swear to the goddess."

The wicked witch was wicked indeed. Their housemother was the epitome of what humans thought of witches... well, how their movies displayed them anyway. Warts growing on a protruding nose, wrinkles forming lines where they shouldn't, hairs on her chinny, chin chin. It was a crude depiction, even though humans were well aware of how witches actually looked. And usually, they looked normal. The only giveaway that they weren't human was a magical signature that set off alarms if they crossed the wards without permission in the human territories.

Witch enclaves were designed to keep witches in and humans out. Step through the barrier without clearance, and as Avery had discovered when her cabin fever became particularly bad, you were magically flung back. Still, better than being burned alive at the stake, which humans had done at one point.

Even shifters had more rights than witches. The humans let them walk around and travel wherever they wanted, and it was said that they could turn into *literal* monsters—but she wasn't sure if that was a myth or not. Back in the distant past, shifters played nicer with the humans, working with them rather than against them. Witches, on the other hand, preferred to stay in their hidden enclaves, only interacting when it benefited them. Turns out the humans took that personally. They shouldn't; most witches just wanted to stay near the ley lines that ran under the enclaves, where they were most powerful.

However, Avery didn't care, and she really wanted to taste some chicken nuggets. Tragically, there was not one chicken shop on the whole island. Maybe see a few of the world's wonders too. Anything but the same university and town skyline.

Maya paused, one foot touching the floor. "There's still time for you to summon a familiar, you know."

Avery's hand tightened around the bottle. She wanted to believe her, she really did. The subtle hope still simmered like embers in her chest long after she had doused it. The small child in her refused to believe that her dream was long over.

Hope was cruel. So she shoved that little light as far down as she could, locking it in a dark box and starving it of oxygen where the fire couldn't rage inside her.

She took another swig of the bottle, the contents of it almost empty. Fourth-year started in two days. She had two days to somehow produce a familiar out of her ass and present it to the university council. A seemingly impossible task, when she had tried and failed so many times before. And as her close, personal friend, Charlotte Lucas, from *Pride and Prejudice* once said: I'm twenty-seven years old (twenty-two actually), I have no money (true) and no prospects (if she didn't get a familiar), I'm already a burden on my parents (parent), and I'm frightened (the truest of all).

"Avery—" Before Maya could finish, a massive thump shook the ceiling. They both scrambled back against the bed as roof tiles clattered overhead, sliding down and shattering on the balcony with dramatic clangs.

"What was that?" Maya said, suddenly far more sober. She clutched a pillow to her chest, as if it would protect her from whatever had just landed on the roof.

"I'm not sure," Avery said honestly. The whiskey had dulled her senses far enough to get off the bed and investigate the noise. She may be smart, but she was still an idiot. She took careful steps toward the arched doors and saw there was nothing to see but the moon rising over the silhouette of the campus's spires snarling over buildings reaching far up into the sky.

"Avery? Get back here," Maya whispered desperately.

And for a brief moment, Avery saw the shimmer of iridescent scales against the orange light. Her heart jumped as a knock rang out through the room.

"Shit." She kept her voice low. "Hide the whiskey, it's Wren."

In her drunken stupor, Maya sprang into action with the

grace of a newborn foal. Her body hit the floor with a thud before she scrambled under the bed to plant the whiskey far out of sight. In doing so, she hit her head on the slats and clanged the bottle against the bed frame. To top it off, the crow let out an alarmed squawk, its collar jingling as it did. Wren was going to kill her.

Another knock, more insistent this time.

"Coming!" Avery's voice cracked at the high pitch of someone trying to have a semblance of normalcy in it. Smoothing her uniform and her hair, she cracked open the door to find her eldest sister, her eyes as fiery as her dragon perched on the roof.

"Hey!" Avery said with a hiccup.

Wren looked past her, her eyes landing immediately on Maya's disheveled state, the faint smell of cinnamon not yet aired out. Her expression was unreadable, but blessed be the fucking goddess, she said nothing. Although with Wren, it was hard to tell. Avery was convinced the university's beautician had magically altered her to stay that way, something Wren vehemently denied at every dinner Avery brought it up at.

"What are you doing?" Wren asked, her tone flat.

"Nothing," Avery said too quickly. "What are you doing?"

Wren was absolutely, utterly not convinced by her answer. Avery was convincing no one, let alone her sister. She was dressed in her full enforcer regalia, the fitted maroon blazer tight against her muscled form. A rifle was slung across her back, the red crystal embedded within it giving a small hum.

Another shot of jealousy ripped through Avery as she eyed the golden patches, which signaled that Wren was a High Commander. She had no desire to become an enforcer, but at this point, she would take it. It was almost like looking in a mirror of what she could be. Although, Avery didn't really look much like her sister. Where Avery had hair like cinnamon, Wren's hair was black, a symptom of her cold, cold heart. A terrible disease, really. Tragic.

The main difference between them, though, was that Wren looked as if a giant stick was up her ass, especially since she assumed the position of High Commander, and it was now shoved even further. Their mother had that effect on people, though, and it wasn't surprising her smile had faded after spending more than a minute with the devil like Wren did.

Finally, Wren broke the tension.

"The High Councilor would like to speak to you."

"You mean, Mother would like to speak to me?"

Wren raised an eyebrow, a warning not to challenge her. She had enough ammunition in this room alone to get Avery expelled. Avery wondered what she would become besides the pub pouring bitch. A barista, perhaps in one of two coffee shops on the island? Potentially a seller of the forbidden toe pictures? Maybe she could become homeless! What a treat. Her small world was truly her oyster. The only good thing about being expelled was that she could have some proper time to plan her escape. Although she had tried her damn hardest to do that, but every time she somehow made it to the ferry, she was irritatingly, magically, sling-shotted back to Caerwyn Island. Was it too much to ask that a simple witch would like to get a taste of some chicken nuggets?

Her toxic trait was her confidence in thinking she could swim her way to the mainland of Wales, that somehow the only thing standing between her and the coast was unwavering determination, and her deluded hope that maybe the witch boundary magic didn't work in the water. She probably could do it; swimming was her primary hobby, if the magic didn't pull her back first. The only thing standing between her and attempting a swim to freedom was the idea of being trapped in the jaws of a shark, and no, she didn't care that the percentage was as low as her dead grandmother's bosoms. With her luck in the last year, it would happen.

"Wow, I didn't know you could do that." Avery pointed to her own wiggling eyebrows. "With, you know, the work you've had done."

She was really pushing it now.

Wren only pinched the bridge of her nose, probably regretting her decision to personally fetch her. It was likely Mother's idea. Wren would rather fetch a turd out of a toilet than doing this right now.

"Please don't be difficult. She said it's urgent."

In reality, they both knew Avery was stalling. Seeing her mother was never a pleasant experience, and especially now, when she was the only one in her class not to summon a familiar. She was almost sure this was her mother's way of solidifying the idea that she was the family's failure, a letdown of generational proportions. Just like her aunt. Her mother was absolutely going to expel her. At least she had it in her cold, dark heart to tell her in person, instead of sending a pigeon or something. Something so cute shouldn't be burdened with such messages of misery.

Wren stared her down. "Are you going to go to the chambers or will Sparky have to carry you?" If Avery didn't come willingly, she was sure Wren would have incapacitated her and taken her anyway. They had such a lovely sisterly bond.

Maya yelped as the massive dragon dropped its head down from the roof, its golden eye the size of a dinner plate, peering through the balcony doors. Wren had bonded the gigantic lizard three years ago, and Avery still hadn't gotten used to the beast. As much as Wren declared Sparky a *whittle baby*, Avery always gave him a wide berth.

Walking it was.

As if he sensed her hesitance, Sparky blew out a breath toward her, fogging up the glass. His black body shook in a way that Avery was fairly sure meant he was laughing at her. Even Wren's dragon was an asshole.

"I'll walk. I prefer my feet attached securely to the ground."

Wren only shrugged. "Your loss, enjoy the stairs."

It was Avery's turn to roll her eyes. They weren't that bad.

Two

Avery

THE STAIRS REALLY WERE THAT BAD.

At least two years had passed since Avery had climbed the stairs to the council tower, and she had completely forgotten how steep the walk was between here and the main campus. There had to be at least a thousand steps on this goddess-forsaken path. That mixed with nausea from both the alcohol and a pit of nervousness that would not go away. Her head swirled, and the tree-lined steps blurred as saliva pooled in her mouth and her stomach churned.

Halfway up the stairs, her body decided to expel the alcohol she had so lovingly bestowed upon it and spray the trunk of a poor pine tree that had done nothing but be in the wrong place, wrong time. To make it even worse, the moon had completely disappeared, and her phone had died. So with no light, an overwhelming urge to brush her teeth, and a whole lot of misplaced confidence in her footing, she somehow made it up the stairs with minimal scraping.

When she reached the top gate, the air was noticeably thinner. Her breath came in ragged pants, forming little ghosts in the cool wind. The dense forest canopy had given way to a manicured garden that surrounded a path of stone and arches. Flowers bloomed the same blazing maroon as the ivy that coated the council tower. The scent of it always confused her. The garden should have carried the smell of a florist; instead, it smelled of decaying leaves and damp earth. It hadn't changed at all in two years.

She leaned against the iron posts, catching her breath. For a swimmer, stairs shouldn't be her worst enemy, but in her eyes, they were worse than shifters, and given that they were a witch's mortal enemy, it was saying a lot.

The council tower was easily the most ominous building on campus. Built on a sheer cliff-side of jagged, mossy rocks, it was a thin, entirely menacing building that seemed to be shrouded in fog, no matter the weather. It was visible practically everywhere you went in Caerwyn. At the top sat a belfry. A sound that rang in only the most dire of situations. One that maybe she should ring now, as seeing her mother was really reserved for the most dire of things.

An enforcer eyed her from the last arch encasing an iron gate that did very little to actually secure the building, given beds of flowers surrounded it rather than a fence. With a nod, he opened the squeaking gate, the noise preparing her for the grating voice of her mother being disappointed in her yet again. Giving him a curt smile, she walked past with every inch of confidence she could muster, which was abysmal, akin to a mouse that had challenged a cat.

Wren leaned against the stone building, looking minuscule in comparison to the statue of their goddess, Cerituen, that was carved into the building next to her. Cerituen looked about as lifelike as Wren. Their stony features were a mirror image of each other. Her marble form looked so real, the way the fabric draped across her eyes and her body, even her expression, Avery wouldn't be surprised if her lips started moving.

The stone bore three carved symbols: a sword, an open

book, and a pair of wings. The sword was for the enforcers of House of Rhyfel, the book was for the scholars of the House of Doethur, and the wings were for the healers of House of Seren.

The three houses, the three symbols of witchhood, the three vestiges that granted you a sliver of her power.

After graduation, Avery aimed to join House Seren. Her father raised her to be a healer. She was never one to fight. Her sister used to try to spar with her for practice, yet she now knew that Wren had really just wanted to use her as a punching bag. She had an enormous amount of rage as a child, but now she had settled it into a practiced mask, just as their mother did. It had made sense that she had ended up as an enforcer. Avery's little sister, Gwyn, also had the same problem, yet she preferred to whack girls with lacrosse sticks instead.

Her father was the only one like her. He was dead, and she was dead inside. The family resemblance was palpable.

How he and her mother had gotten along at all baffled her. They were the worst possible match the council could have made. Still, she was grateful her father had been around long enough to leave his gentleness. She missed him dearly. His stories about the outside world had inspired her to follow in his footsteps. Healers, along with enforcers, were one of the few who could visit human territories, working in their hospitals and clinics under diplomatic immunity. Because nothing says *trust me with your appendectomy* more than a witch with no formal medical training.

But at least they weren't putting shifters in hospitals, could you imagine?

Something about the shifters was alluring, though. Recently, there'd been a surge in human literature on a website you could only access through a series of archived forums. Many humans had written about getting freaky with a shifter.

She had stumbled upon this site during a random, *totally* unrelated search at three a.m. She wondered if humans and shifters really did mingle like that. They were different species, so they couldn't procreate, but she guessed it didn't stop them from trying. She was ashamed to admit that she had too much time on her hands that night, and she had devoured at least five different novellas describing in intimate detail how one could be pleasantly overpowered by the monsters. The glutton in her tried to search for a witch-shifter pairing story, but that was too far for authors. It was true depravity, and she liked it. Maybe that was why the goddess was punishing her.

"Took you long enough," Wren said, tightening her ponytail.

There were plenty of retorts on Avery's tongue, but she didn't want to give her sister the satisfaction of showing her she was indeed out of breath. Instead, she pursed her lips, showing Wren that the little sister was, in fact, the bigger person here. The amount of satisfaction she got from pissing off her family should really be studied. She was an enigma, a statistical anomaly, a case study in petty behavior.

Wren and Avery walked side by side up the last twisting set of stone stairs that made it harder to hide the shaking of her breath through her nostrils. Would it kill them to put in an elevator? Apparently, it was noticeable enough to have Wren side-eyeing her more than a few times.

"Had a bit much?" she said.

"Shut up, Wren." So much for being the bigger person.

When they reached the door to their mother's office, Wren gave a quick knock against the oak in a peculiar pattern, letting the devil know they were there. After a moment, the door opened on its own, beckoning them into her lair.

Their mother's office was as harsh as she was. Bookshelves lined the walls, each book meticulously color coordinated. A terrible way to organize your books, but she digressed. Her mother's black pegasus familiar was nowhere to be seen. It was probably ominously hovering somewhere, trying to scare children. The furniture was anything but plush and inviting. This school had an obsession with hard chairs. With all the money they had, you would think they wouldn't have a problem putting a cushion or two somewhere. Humans supplied most of witches' income by paying handsomely for enforcers or healers. One of either rank was worth fifty humans, and even then, they had abilities that were priceless. Avery wasn't sure what that made her, though. Hated and powerless? Without a familiar, she would never fit in anywhere. Too witch for the humans, too human for the witches.

Her mother sat behind her desk, leaning back into a tall chair that appeared more like a throne. Her angular features met the aesthetic of the room. She was gorgeous for her age. Avery would give her that. Although she suspected her mother had gone through the same procedure, which put the stick up Wren's ass. Her dark hair was slicked back in a bun, without a split end in sight. Avery's fingers ran through her own hair, the loose waves falling in an unruly mess. She felt a threatening need to pick the scab that healed whenever she was not around her mother and sisters. Instead, she picked at her nails.

"Thank you for coming on short notice, Avery." Her mother's tone was cold, its timbre as maternal as a praying mantis.

Avery didn't say anything. She was quiet as a traumatized mouse.

"Do you know why you're here?"

"Haven't the foggiest," Avery lied. She knew exactly why she was there.

Her mother slid a piece of paper toward her, her expulsion hand signed in fresh ink at the bottom by the chancellor. She knew it was coming, but still, tears blurred at the edges of

Avery's vision, the bookshelves swaying a touch bit more than they were before.

"Oh, for goddess's sake, Avery, don't cry," her mother chided.

They were already falling, burning a path down her cold cheeks. She generally wasn't so sensitive, but this past year had been a lot. "Sorry," she murmured, wiping them away with the sleeves of her blazer. "I can't help it."

"Just like you can't help your inability to summon even a rat," her mother tutted.

Avery should bill her for this conversation. It was tacking on another meal to a restaurant of trauma. Unfortunately, it was true. She was an utter failure according to her mother, the university, and hell, probably the whole world at this point. She had even disappointed the singular plant by her windowsill. Its drooping, yellowing leaves yearned for a drop of water. She hadn't bothered to take care of it because the rest of her life was falling apart.

"I've been trying."

"Trying is not a word in the vocabulary of Caerwyn, Avery." Her mother leaned forward in her chair, its spires twisting into a snarl that matched her terrifying energy. "You either do, or you don't."

"Let me try again," Avery begged. She was not above getting down on her knees and pleading. Although her knees might suffer for it; being the ripe age of twenty-two had done numbers on her joints.

Her mother sighed. "Why, to fail again? Embarrass this family further like your aunt did?"

She'd always heard about her Aunt Alys, and how terrible she was, but she'd never met her to see that for herself. For some reason, she hadn't been able to summon a familiar either.

Shame scorched Avery's cheeks; the familiar feeling

engraved itself in her body like a brand she constantly carried. *Failure* may as well be tattooed across her forehead. She knew she was running out of time, that it would come to this.

"I just need one more day," Avery begged.

Her mother looked unconvinced, eyes narrowed. It was almost a challenge, almost like she was waiting for her to fail, like she wanted her to.

"*Please*, Mother."

She relented. "Fine, you get one more day. After that, I will file this expulsion, and you will cease to be a part of this prestigious institution." She took a deep breath, as if chiding her child was a strenuous activity, when for her it was more of a hobby. Avery's hobbies were swimming and scanning the internet for increasingly harder riddles and freaky shifter porn, apparently. She wouldn't be surprised if her mother dabbled in killing innocent animals as a hobby.

"I won't let you down, Councilor." Avery used her mother's official title, not bothering with the familiarities of addressing her. In reality, this was as far as their relationship went. Apart from the occasional and awkward mandatory family dinners, there wasn't a single drop of interest in being a mother. There never really was. Before, when Avery had been an exemplary student, if she wasn't as good as Wren or Gwyn, she was still a failure.

Her mother's phone vibrated on the table, her glare finally breaking away to look at who texted her. She looked at Wren and gave her a nod. "We have something to attend to. See yourself out, Avery."

When the door shut behind her, like the well-adjusted, mature adult she was, Avery mimicked *"See yourself out, Avery"* like a cantankerous four-year-old as the tears streamed down her face.

One more day. That was all she had to summon a familiar. Something she had failed to do for the last year. She had tried everything: obscure phases of the moon, following ley lines, fucking getting down on her knees and begging for the grace of the goddess to grant her a rat. She wondered if one would give her special powers. A cheese connoisseur? A world-famous French chef, perhaps? So many possibilities.

Part of her wanted to collapse into it, to become the very thing that her mother envisioned for her. It would be easy, *so easy* to climb back into her bed for another day, to hide under the covers and watch the world go by.

"*Fuck* that," she whispered to herself.

THE LIBRARY GREETED HER WITH ITS FAMILIAR warmth. Stained-glass windows showered the double-story hall in puddles of crimson. The domed ceiling displayed an intricate artwork of their goddess spearing a bull shifter through the heart, as she should. Although Avery must say the artist did a fine job on his muscles. *Damn that website.*

Before she headed to her usual spot, she poured herself a cup of tea from the library kitchen and tried not to let it spill as she headed to the back of the library. She passed groups of students, mostly sitting together studying, or at least trying to study. *Trying* being a very optimistic word for it. A fourth-year student from her class sat in a nook. He pretended to look at an open book while another student sat on his knees underneath the desk. Avery looked away quickly, her cheeks heating. It had been a while since she'd had any sort of debauchery. She tried not to think about the memory that was like an incessant fly in desperate need of swatting. Where the shifters got her wet, the memory of the dubious choices she had made over the years got her drier than the Sahara now. Maybe she should pray to the goddess for some good dick. Anything would be better than a balls-deep loser who didn't know where the clit was.

When she reached the back of the library, she took her seat. Shelves on each side surrounded the table, with a small gap between them to make an entryway. It was secluded, cozy, and she was hardly ever bothered apart from the occasional visit of the librarian or her white owl, who sometimes came to peer at what she was doing.

She had spent an ungoddessly amount of time in this section, poring over the books about familiar bonds and how to summon them. For most witches, it was easy. Some had to try a few times; maybe they read a word or two wrong, but they always got a familiar. For some reason, biological, psychological, metaphysical, and spiritual, she was inept. It happened from time to time when a witch failed to manifest their familiar. Witch culture saw it as a sign from the goddess that the culprit was not meant to be a witch. Avery, however, did not believe that the goddess was even real. Had she ever seen her? Had anyone ever brought forward tangible proof that she exists? If she did exist, she was a bitch—respectfully, of course. People and animals died in such a horrific manner that she couldn't believe a benevolent goddess would ever allow such things to happen. The Tomes said it was for balance. Avery said it was for sadistic pleasure. What other things would you have to do with an immortal life?

In some ways, she understood, though. There was that one time where she removed the ladder from the pool in her Sims game and let them drown just for the fuck of it. Perhaps they had more in common than she thought.

The owl hooted over her shoulder, its talons gripping her as it found a painful perch on her collarbone.

"Shoo!" Avery waved her hand at it. It did nothing but flap its wings unceremoniously. "Don't you have better places to be?" she asked it, as if she expected it to talk back. If a familiar could talk, she wondered what they would say. A theater played out inside her mind of an owl. One of them was intelligent, a true savant of literature; it would say something like *"I find your lack of knowledge disturbing."* The other one would bob its head up and down and screech. The librarian's owl was always a stickybeak, literally always getting up in her business and distracting her. It was its full-time job.

Using her collarbone as a launchpad, it flung itself off her shoulder and onto the towering bookshelf. It hooted from the top, almost beckoning her to follow. Or was it all an elaborate plot to take her eyeballs from their sockets once she reached the top of the shelf?

She sighed and climbed the nearby ladder, the rickety wood straining under her weight. *Please don't collapse. Please don't collapse.*

When she made it to the top, dust bunnies hopped around collecting dust for their nests. They were strange little creatures, so unbearably cute. An old book lay on its side, where a few bunnies grazed on top of it like a sprawling field. She wondered if they had little dust ranches, where one wore a cowboy hat and sat down with his wife on their dusty porch swing at the end of the day and said, *"It ain't much, but it's honest work."* The thought brought a smile to her face as she reached her hand out to examine the book.

One of them hissed at her. *Bitch.* She took everything she said back, and she took it back with pride. May their nests never be filled with dust. May their children never experience a bountiful dust harvest.

She curled the book into her arm and made her way down the ladder. As she dropped it on the table, the owl once again came to join her, nudging its little black beak between the pages, trying to use it as some sort of chew toy.

The book was old; the edges were yellowed, its spine cracked from years of use. It would have been hand-bound, a rarity in books nowadays. She hadn't seen it before in the library, which seemed impossible given that she had pretty much read everything in this section. There was always the chance that someone had mislabeled something or put it somewhere else. Maybe if the owl didn't spend so long harassing its students, perhaps it would do its actual full-time job, which was organizing the damn books, or technically giving the librarian the power to organize the books, which she didn't do either.

His beak was trying to turn the pages, using his little talons to scratch as if that would change anything at all. The owl was far more animated than usual, and now that she looked at it, its feathers were darker than usual, its eyes a different shade. She was probably just drunk, though—actually, she was still *very* drunk. She put the owl out of its misery and opened the page it was trying to get to.

Her heart skipped when she deciphered the title written in the old language. "*Familiar Bonding Ritual.*" It took her about ten minutes to translate the language because linguistic classes were never her strong suit, and unfortunately for her, the witches would never allow the sacred old language to be Googleable, so she had to rely on her good ole noggin to decipher what it was actually going on about, and that noggin was fighting for its life, given she had doused it in alcohol a mere few hours earlier.

The moon puddled through the stained glass windows, throwing dappled red lights onto the table in front of her as she worked through the ritual. For a moment, she thought it was just her being stupid, but it turned out the words actually spelled out a riddle.

A smile curved at her lips. She *fucking* loved riddles. She didn't do drugs, but if she did, riddles would be the crack she would be whoring herself out for.

Her fingers traced the yellowing pages, the text indenting

the page as if it had been written by ink and quill. Given how old the book looked, it probably would have been. She highly doubted a twelfth-century witch peasant would have had access to an HP OfficeJet Pro.

The old language was tricky, the spelling archaic.

She recognized most of the words. *Seith*—seven. Seven wicks of flame—candles, obvious. Seven ivory prisons of the servants—bones, most probably of animals. She kept bird skulls in her room for arts and crafts when she felt morbidly inspired. Her latest piece of art was an egret skull hanging with dried daisies that said, "I Egret many of my choices." The witches' choice of artwork on Caerwyn was usually delightfully depressing. The works were beautiful, yes, but somber. So she took it upon herself to make her own depressing artwork, because at least they were a bit more whimsical.

Her finger followed the next line. Seven green tongues. That stumped her for a moment. Serpents? Literal tongues? She rubbed her temples, something she often did while trying to solve them.

"Sage?" she questioned no one but the owl. "Sage!" That made sense; they literally looked like green tongues. A rush of satisfaction coursed through her.

The next word she was unfamiliar with. It didn't help that some of it had smudged. Curse the twelfth-century witch peasants and their grimy, grubby hands. She tried to sound it out. "*Seith cusan...g...wyn...y bleidd.*"

Seven kisses of the white wolf? It had to be white. *Gwyn* was her sister's name, which meant white, holy, blessed. Even though she was literally none of those things, she was an incarnation of the devil herself, beating unsuspecting students with a lacrosse stick.

It had to be some sort of ingredient. She racked her brain, shuffling through her mental catalog of ritual herbs. Wolfsbane was purple, so that was out. Wolf's milk was a yellow flower on the outside, but it had white sap-like stuff inside, hence the "Milk" part. Luckily, the translation was not literal, and she did not need to go harass a pregnant wolf. An unbidden thought crashed through her mind of that damn website where the main character had milked a wolf shifter. Goddess, how far she had fallen. Wolf's milk—the plant kind—was endemic to the island, and she could easily find it in the forest.

It seemed like a standard ritual, bar a few ingredients. Until one unriddled word stopped her. *Gweli.* Blood.

Blood magic was forbidden.

The only thing she hadn't tried was forbidden magic, something that would get her expelled, anyway.

However, desperate times called for desperate measures, and she was one desperate bitch.

Three

Felix

Present Day

What the fuck.

It took a minute to orient himself. Darkness surrounded him. Had he gone blind? Had he had a stroke? Grogginess weighed down his limbs as if he had just woken up from a nap that had gone too long. He took a step, and it felt like wading through mud, even though nothing physical blocked his path. If this had anything to do with Ciro and one of his stupid pranks, he was not in the mood.

What the fuck.

He waited a few moments for the joke to drop, but it didn't come. There was only a void of nothingness, nothing to see, nothing to touch, an immaterial existence. Everywhere he turned, there was darkness, and just his luck, somehow this plane of existence had weather. Small drops of water fell at first, dusting the floor, but before long, a heavy downpour unleashed itself upon him.

Drops battered his clothes. He *despised* getting wet.

One moment, he was drinking in his courtyard in London, delightfully warm and with a sense of peace for the first time in months. It was his only day off from hunting witches, and here he was, getting ripped across the fabric of space and time, clothes soaked, hair clinging to his skull, and no recollection of where he actually was. Goose bumps skittered across him, the cold seeping into his bones. *Fantastic.*

He took a step forward, the sound echoing through the empty space.

A sound sliced through the rain, and a whooshing noise raced past his ears. It was loud enough that he instinctively covered them. The noise built and built until he felt the pressure compound enough that it might crack his skull. His body knew before his mind did and primed itself to fight; the hairs on his arm raised as if there was danger. His claws lengthened, and shadows wrapped their way up his arm, imbuing it with power. He had to be careful not to imbue too much, otherwise the monster in him would be let out of its cage far too early. He liked to be in full control for his fun first.

The darkness rippled, the danger revealing itself. There was only one creature that could perform a summoning ritual.

"*Witch*," he hissed.

Of fucking course it was a witch. The intricate symbols now forming on the floor a few feet away solidified it; the world flooded with a bloody hue. The symbols danced around her as if they themselves were worshipping the very ground the witch walked on. *Disgusting*. A woman materialized in the middle, wearing a red academy uniform of some sort. A student. How the hell had a student summoned him? If she weren't a witch, she would have been pretty. Long hair, freckled pale skin, and deep blue eyes. He would have been enamored. *Except* she *was* a witch, and now he had to murder her. Such a waste. She looked around as if she were lost, stumbling through the darkness like she didn't know how she got here. He didn't believe in the innocent act for a second. He snarled at himself mostly, hating that somehow he was stuck in here with a witch. She flinched at the sound.

"Ceritueh?" she called out to her false goddess, voice quivering.

He said nothing. Maybe if she thought nothing was there, she would drop the spell. Whatever the spell was. They were excellent actors, witches. This one in particular was a cunning little one. Her body seemed genuinely scared, her pulse was fluttering like a hummingbird, her long limbs shaking. She wouldn't have summoned him by accident. He took another step toward her, now standing directly in front of her.

Part of him wanted to play with her. Witches made for excellent prey. The other, more rational part of him would like to get the fuck out of here and go back to drowning himself in a bottle of whiskey, on a rare sunny day in London. He was sunbathing, despite the air's coolness. He had a whole weekend planned, too. And now, instead of getting vitamin D, he was getting fucked by this ritual.

The other part of him wanted to slit her throat on sight. An ingrained habit. But first, he wanted to know what she wanted, and how the fuck she had summoned him here. Still, she couldn't see him.

She took one hesitant step toward him as if drawn by some invisible force. They were almost touching, his skin crawling and reaching for hers at the same time. He didn't think he had ever been this close to a witch without being covered in her blood. Luckily, he never had to play nice with the witches like some shifters did; he was simply contracted to end them if they stepped out of line, which they often did. Why the humans let them cross in the first place was beyond him. If it were up to him, they would stay near their ley lines and never leave.

"What do you want, witch?" he asked.

He tried to make his voice sound as godly as possible. Maybe she would think she was having some sort of religious vision.

Her head swiveled, eyes wide, looking around like a mouse who had caught the scent of a cat.

"A familiar." Her voice quivered.

A burst of hysterics bubbled in his throat. He couldn't help it. She wanted a shifter as a familiar? She wanted *him*? Over his fucking dead body.

The way she knitted her eyebrows as if she was confused only made him laugh harder. The little witch had picked the wrong creature.

Witches used familiars like personal batteries to power their magic, magic that they had used to tear shifters apart in the many wars between their species. Familiars were animals, not shifters. He had no interest in becoming a battery, but even if he did, the whole thing was impossible; this witch was delusional if she thought she could bond him. How she summoned him in the first place was an entirely different question.

He moved toward her in the darkness, his footsteps lighter now, echoing through the void. She couldn't track his movement, even when he was only an arm's length away from her. Something inside screamed to touch her, to run his claws through that long hair. He shoved it down to the deepest part of himself, locking it in its cage.

As amusing as this was, he had had enough. The witch was clearly going to try something, and he wanted no part in it. She flinched as he moved behind her, and a traitorous part of him swelled low within him. He was close enough now to scent her, and to his horror, it was intoxicating. It was like the honeysuckles that only bloomed deep in the forest, sweet and citrusy all at the same time. Involuntarily, he licked his tongue over his fangs, wanting to sink them into her slender neck.

He took a step back. *Fucking witches.*

"I—" she hesitated.

"*What's the matter, little witch?*" He leaned in next to her ear for dramatic effect, and she flinched away again at the sound in the smoke around them. The witch was not as tough as she made herself out to be.

"*Cat got your tongue?*" It wouldn't have made sense to anyone but him, but at least he amused himself. He shouldn't even be speaking with her. Shouldn't be *here* with her.

She fluttered her eyes shut. Concentrating on something. She opened her mouth to speak, another language flowing from her tongue. An incantation. She really was trying to bond him.

Absolutely the fuck not.

Light erupted between them. A ribbon-like thread, golden and pulsing with magic, materialized from her chest.

No.

No, no, no.

Dread coiled tight in his stomach. The thread stood still for a moment, hovering between them. Before he could react, it moved like a serpent in water; the thread found him, piercing through his rib cage like a spear. He felt it test him, he felt it inside him, the serpent circling inside of him looking for its final meal. Somehow, this witch was bonding him.

"*What are you doing?*" he snarled, all pretense of amusement gone. He grabbed the thread, but his fingers passed through it.

"*What the fuck did you DO?*"

She didn't react, didn't even hear him as he yelled at the top of his lungs.

"*BREAK IT,*" he roared.

He lunged forward, grabbing at her, but like the thread,

his hands passed right through her. The thread stretched but didn't snap.

"Break it right now, witch!"

Her chanting only increased, louder, the voice swirling around his head as if it were inside him. The thread pulsed brighter. Something was changing. The darkness around them began to fracture, the night sky becoming visible, a bloodred moon flooding them. He felt the thread binding itself to him; he felt it in his veins, like a poison.

"Let me go." His voice came out strangled. "*Whatever spell you cast, I don't care. Let. Me. Go.*"

He was almost driven to beg, to get on his knees and plead, something he had never done for anyone. He couldn't be bonded to a witch. His mind searched for an answer, racking his brain for any solution. His body cracked at the seams as he pushed it toward an unyielding wall. It held steady, refusing to do the very thing that was natural to him. Panic clawed at his throat, real, chest-crushing, panic.

The monster within him grew restless and yearned to be let out of its cage. It was always a gamble; sometimes it would tear him apart for days after, and he'd be bed-bound, his body punishing him for losing control. But right now, he needed the monster.

His shadow form took over, towering above the small witch who was oblivious to the beast in front of her. Limbs and tendrils of shadow grew outward, and with them, his mind darkened until he lost himself within it. His shadow monster let out a deafening roar, giant claws slashing at the threads that refused to break as more erupted from the tether between them. The gold ribbons swirled like magical vines, twisting and pulling at his armor of shadows. But it was a losing battle. The main thread between them glowed, blindingly so.

The thread snapped taut. Something that shouldn't be

possible, pulling them closer. He could feel her now, her fear, her confusion, her rapid heartbeat pounding in his head in time with his own. He felt the edges of her fear claw with his own. He let out a bellowing roar that only fell on deaf ears.

Fuck, *fuck*.

The little witch had bonded him.

Four

Avery

Dawn shone down on Avery as she pried her eyes open. Sticks poked into her back as she coughed, her mouth dry and hoarse like she had just licked the forest floor. Strangely, she sometimes wanted to eat the dirt—courtesy of her iron deficiency—but it didn't taste as good as she thought it would. Sitting up, she wiped the dirt from her face as her head swam. She must have fallen asleep in the forest; it wasn't the first time. She always had the strangest dreams out in nature. In this one, she'd successfully bonded with a familiar, and she swore it spoke to her. How strange. Using her hand to pry herself off the floor, she stood, her head swaying and vision blurring with the sudden movement.

Her heart dropped.

The remnants of the ritual lay strewn across the floor. She trembled. Dried blood still stuck to the gleaming ritual bones. The candles lay in melted pools of wax, the herbs scattered or burned away.

And in the middle—*holy shit.*

In the middle lay a cat. There was a cat asleep amongst the

remnants, its black fur dusted in ash and soot. It wasn't a dream. Not a fucking dream.

She'd actually done it. She had summoned a familiar.

Hope swelled in her chest like a million butterflies caged and smothered for far too long. But this time, she set them free. Versions of her life where she succeeded were finally allowed through the wall she had built around them. She could finally graduate. She could finally leave. She could be a healer. Well, after she finished a year of training. And *then* she would leave.

Moving closer to the cat, she inspected how its chest rose and fell with the sound of the nearby crashing waves. She was grateful, truly, but out of all the familiars the goddess could have sent her, especially because this had been a forbidden ritual, she got a fucking house cat? It truly would be the goddess's sense of humor, wouldn't it?

The icy light shone in her eyes, stinging from a night spent near the seawater. She scooped the cat up in her blazer. The fabric was dusted in salt, and the cat's wilted body hung in her arms. The bond hummed in her chest, its presence a foreign pulsing which meant that somehow, she really had summoned a familiar. A smile stretched along her face. *Fuck everyone who had ever doubted her. She had done it.*

Mud caked her boots as she dragged them through the entrance of Caerwyn University, the iron gates welcoming her with a haunting symphony of metal creaking. She walked past dozy enforcers and shivered, her limp familiar, swaddled in her blazer like a newborn child. Its fur, although grimy, had a softness to it that was comforting. She peered under the blazer to check it was still breathing, to reassure herself that she hadn't somehow killed it.

The first dregs of sun peeked over the spires, drenching the campus in a golden hue. Tall spires and towers of stone were swallowed in the red ivy, its leaves turning shades of orange and red to mark the start of autumn. Her boots clicked against the stone streets as leaves tumbled around the campus, their paths carving a cold wind. The October chill had already settled in, and it was enough to release her from the shackles of little sleep. Following the stone path through the quadrangle, the arched doors of the dorms loomed in the distance. More sleepy enforcers guarded the entrance, their rifles glowing red.

Great job, guys. Not that they ever protected them from anything, there hadn't been anything amiss on Caerwyn apart from the occasional streaking student. It was quite amusing watching highly trained guards running after a drunk, flopping dick and piling on top of them.

Lacrosse players rubbed their eyes as they headed out to the field, and she thanked the goddess that it was not her little sister's team. Maybe she should be less harsh on the goddess. She did give her a familiar, after all.

Gwyn would have asked her a million questions she wasn't ready to answer, because Gwyn was a nosy bitch. The rest of them didn't notice as she slipped past them to the dorms. She gave the enforcers a totally normal, nonchalant nod as she carried a hidden package in her blazer that wasn't suspicious at all.

The morning poured through the giant stone window frames of her dorm building, letting in the cool air. Their intricate elegance had taken precedence over the practicality of warmth. A few students lingered in the foyer, pouring cups of steaming coffee.

The cat hardly stirred in her arms as she walked. Its warm breath made puffs against the chill. She had wrapped it in her blazer, half to cover it from questioning, the other half to keep it warm, not that all its fur wouldn't have done that for him.

Callum, an enforcer who had graduated last year, stood at the bottom of the stairs. His familiar, a white fox, lay at his heels sleeping as soundly as the cat did in her arms. Callum sent her a small smile, looking at his feet rather than meeting her eyes. Her mind went to the obvious answer of him hating her, but he was just shy; he had always been like that ever since they kissed in her first year of university. Her friends—at the time, they were bitches now—shoved them into a closet together where they shared a gentle peck.

"Morning, Avery." His auburn hair was windswept and framed his face nicely. If she were to get into a relationship, it would be with someone like him. Handsome, kind, gentle. But right now, a relationship was the furthest thing she could consider.

She sent him a smile back, heading for the stairs before he could stop her for a chat like he usually did.

"Hey, wait!"

Bollocks.

She turned on her heel. "What's up?"

"I was wondering if you wanted to have dinner sometime?" he said, placing a hand behind his head and scratching at his hair awkwardly.

She sent him a raised eyebrow. "Oh, um, are you sure?"

"Yeah, why wouldn't I be?"

"You aren't afraid to be seen going on a date with the resident failure?" *No need to remind him. This would be the first action you'd gotten in a year!*

He chuckled. "No, Avery, I fully believe in your ability to summon a familiar." He paused, his face falling wistful. "It makes sense you haven't been able to, with everything that happened and all."

Callum had been there through it all. He had seen her fall apart after her father's death. He had tried to reach out to her throughout the year, but she had mostly shut down every interaction. Why he was trying again now was beyond her. It was not that she didn't like the attention. She did. Especially when she had the likeness of an ugly beetle to other students. But it felt strange and somewhat nice that he still wanted her.

"Yeah, sure," she said. "I'll send you a text when I'm free."

"Cool," he said, with an adorable puppy-dog smile. For a moment, they just stood there awkwardly, basking in the oddness of it all. Just when she was about to leave again, he pointed out the thing that had started squirming inside her jacket. She squeezed hard against it, willing it to stop. The cat responded in kind by digging a set of claws through her shirt and piercing her stomach. She had to stop the visual wince on her face from reaching Callum's enforcer-like perception.

"What's in your blazer?" he asked.

Fuck.

"Oh, just a bunch of books, you know." *No, he didn't know, Avery.* What books fucking squirmed?

"Books," he repeated, giving her the look. "Well, I am an enforcer, so I'll need you to open your blazer, Miss Alarch, in the name of the school's safety."

She froze, her heartbeat thundering in her ears. It's not like there was anything wrong with summoning a familiar. It was expected. Why she hid it was an entirely different story. One she didn't want to explain yet. One she didn't know how to explain yet. She was the type that needed about three to five business days to process what the fuck just happened.

"No?" he pressed.

Like a child, she shook her head. She had no explanation for what squirmed beneath her blazer. He put a hand over his heart in a mock gesture. "Fine, keep your secrets. You're free to go, Miss Alarch," he said, and smiled.

Thank the goddess. He was just playing around. She almost forgot that not everyone was a hard-ass like her sister. She gave him a grateful smile and climbed the stairs to her dorm.

By the time she reached the top, she was embarrassingly

out of breath. She supposed that lying in bed and mourning her dad for a year would do that. She still did swim, but not nearly as much as she used to. Instead, she had focused all of her energy on studying and trying to summon a familiar. Her body was only catching back up. With one hand, she opened the wooden door to her dorm, holding the sleeping cat in the other. After the squirming, it now hardly stirred with the jarring movement or the sound the hinges made as the door shut behind them.

The dorm was silent, but the weight of the day was deafening. She set the blazer down on her bed with the sleeping cat still inside. The rise and fall of its small chest was a steady rhythm, unlike her heart, which had been pounding since the summoning. Kneeling, she ran her hand over the small creature, almost in disbelief that it was real. The fur was soft under her fingers.

Until it wasn't. Fingers ran over fur matted with mud, the scents of damp earth and sea wafting under her nose. Some of the debris crumbled away under her touch, along with the salt matting the fur, but the more she looked, the more she found.

Guilt opened a cavern in her chest. The cat was filthy. What had she done?

She shivered. Dammit, she had left the window open, and it was as cold as her mother. Leaving the cat to sleep on the bed, she crossed the room and kneeled by the fireplace. One day, hopefully soon, she would be able to light this with a flick of a finger, but their bond wasn't formed enough yet for her to summon her familiar's magic on a whim. Neither would she feel good about pulling energy from something that was already unconscious. So, it was the old-fashioned way instead.

She piled sticks under kindling, and the fireplace roared to life. It drenched the otherwise dark room in an orange hue, the soft crackling singing along with the birds outside. The smell of woodsmoke was like a comforting embrace, and it constantly lingered in her dorm from how much she used it.

The clock ticking in the corner reminded her of the time. It was the day before fourth-year started, and she hadn't even begun to get ready yet. She left the small cat on the bed to have a shower and quickly changed into a clean uniform. By the time she was dressed, the cat was still asleep. She cringed at the amount of dirt left on it, but the last thing she wanted was to disturb it. She had gone a year without a familiar. She could go another day.

RAIN DRIZZLED ON THE STONE FOOTPATHS, AND students lingered in the quadrangle where orientation markets had been set up. The students at Caerwyn amused themselves with many things—clubs, sports, parties. Avery used to be involved in all of them, but since her father passed and her inability to summon a familiar became evident, all of it fell away.

She passed the lacrosse players back from their training. The women's and men's teams were talking among themselves, including her sister, Gwyn, the captain of the women's team. She was talking to Julian fucking Ainsworth, the captain of the men's team. Gwyn tossed her long black hair behind her, smiling at something he said.

Goddess, he was a slimy cunt. A part of her wanted to go up to them, to protect her sister from making the same mistake she did.

Before she could make a decision, she heard her name.

"Avery!" She swiveled her head to see Maya standing next to the swim team tent, where some of her old teammates huddled from the rain.

They were once among her closest friends. Then she

became a social pariah for not having summoned a familiar, and given who her mother was, she was expected to be among the first. It was a long fall down to the bottom, and it had been plastered with half-assed pranks and vitriolic rumors. She was shunned with the same iciness as a medieval wench who had been bedded out of wedlock. Blasphemous.

Reluctantly, she moved her feet toward the group of girls and the familiars huddled around them, giving them a tight smile as they evaded all contact with thy wench. Avery didn't bother to make small talk, knowing it would lead to nothing but awkwardness. If they were plants, she wouldn't ignore them; she would fertilize and water them so they would grow the fuck up, if she didn't let them die like her own house plant. Maya was the only one who had stuck by her.

She wondered if it would change now she had a familiar, albeit a house cat. Even though a cat wasn't particularly powerful, she and the cat would do many wonderful things together. Mostly out of spite. A silent guilt gnawed at her heart like little rats did with a big block of cheese. Despite it being an incredible achievement and a necessary milestone, she had done something forbidden. *Cheated* in getting a familiar. Although she supposed that witches cheated in many things, and technically, it wasn't the first forbidden thing she had done. After all, she had been drinking in her dorm room last night. She supposed it wasn't nearly as up there as literally using blood magic.

Still, if it were the only choice between a life of being a glorified prisoner on this island and one of freedom, she would have done it again and again.

Maya pulled her away by the arm before she had to stand there for too long, the girls muttering about some transfer students from the other witch provinces she couldn't care less about. She found it entirely unfair that they could travel as students and she could not. Her mother had denied her when she applied because she would just widen the sphere of embarrassment for her family.

"I keep trying to talk them into letting you back on the team," Maya said.

"Please don't. I'd rather shit in my hands and clap than swim with them again."

"You're so dramatic."

"I don't think I'm dramatic enough, actually, given the way they have treated me."

Maya sighed, rolling her shoulders back. "Fine, no swim team for you. At least swim with me in the morning again. I miss my training buddy."

"I don't swim anymore, Maya, you know that."

She still did, just not with a team; now she only swam for herself. It still felt like the only safe place, the one thing that was hers, that she could control when her life was spiraling.

But maybe, just maybe, things were starting to look up.

Five

Felix

He woke in a haze. A haze of delicious scents of cinnamon and wood fire invaded his senses. His eyes flew open—too bright, fuck, way too bright—before his cat vision adjusted.

Looking around, he realized he was in some sort of university dorm room.

That *little* witch.

His fur bristled along his back, his muscles coiling and tensing to strike. She had brought him here. Wherever here was. Rain pattered outside the window, hitting the pane in a peaceful rhythm. But nothing about this was fucking peaceful. The gray sun was high, the room drenched in light despite the curtains. Given the angle of it, it had to be sometime in the afternoon. Was it the same day? How long had he been out?

He studied the room. The dorm screamed wealth from every corner, the furniture embellished with golden features standing out against the dark woods. The desk was lavish, its craftsmanship the finest one could own. Witches always seemed to live lavishly due to all the money the human government paid them. His body dragged as he stood on the bed, his paws sinking into the plush mattress. That was his first red flag; whoever slept on such a soft mattress was, in his opinion, a psychopath.

A fireplace crackled and startled him. No one was here.

But that witch *had* been here. Her scent was over everything. Which should be obvious given that this was likely her dorm room. Still, it grated on him that the witch had somehow brought him here. How his unconscious body had flopped in her arms. It sent shivers down his spine at being carried like some *pet*.

Above the fireplace was a coat of arms on a banner. He stilled.

CAERWYN UNIVERSITY.

Caerwyn University was somewhere in the Celtic Sea. There was absolutely no way this witch had dragged him hundreds of miles from London. It was impossible. What the fuck had she done? Maybe it was just decoration, and they were somehow still in London? To his knowledge, a witch wouldn't be able to pull something off like this. What did they want with him? And why in all fuck was he in a dorm room instead of a prison?

Panic clawed at his bones. He needed to call Ciro. He needed his other form. His muscles were primed to shift, but nothing happened.

He tried again. And again. *Fuck.* It was because he used his monster form; it always locked him to his cat form for a while. For now, it would have to do.

The bed dipped as he jumped to the desk, landing light on his feet. Her desk was messy, strewn with textbooks and leather-bound grimoires with titles such as *Summoning a Familiar 101* and *Healing for Dummy Witches*. Nothing that screamed *I kidnap shifters for fun.* On the desk lay a phone and a laptop. Why had she left her phone behind?

He pawed her phone, careful at first to sense if it was a

trap. But no—just a phone. The screen lit up with a picture of her smiling brightly with another witch. He needed to get to Maps to figure out where the fuck he was. He swiped up, but instead of it opening the passcode, it opened the camera and took photos of his black fur and mismatched eyes at an extremely unflattering angle.

Curse having no opposable thumbs.

His tail lashed behind him as he tried again. The same thing happened.

He took in a deep breath for strength, as he was so close to losing his shit it wasn't even funny.

On the third try, it worked, and the passcode screen came up. With one extended toe bean, he pawed in the most obvious one he could think of: 0000.

It unlocked. *No fucking way.*

What kind of criminal mastermind had that for a passcode? Was this amateur hour? Unless this all really was some elaborate joke, none of this made any sense.

He opened the phone and clicked carefully on the Maps. The blue dot indicating his location came up. And lo and fucking behold, he was on Caerwyn Island. His mind stalled in disbelief for a second. You couldn't just walk onto Caerwyn, let alone pull an unconscious shifter through its wards. The kind of magic required to do that was far above his pay grade.

How the fuck had a student witch managed this?

Stacks of spare notebooks and what looked like a journal lay in the top drawer. He itched to flip through it, to learn the secrets of this witch, privacy morals be damned. He would call Ciro in a moment. First, he needed to find a weapon that wasn't his own weak self. His monster had drained him.

He searched the rest of the drawers, finding mundane items like pens and a stray chip that had seen better days, nothing slightly usable. Next, he went to her wardrobe.

Perhaps she kept a weapon in here. He filtered through the drawers of clothes. There were shirts, tartan skirts, and, oh, Jesus Christ. With his paw, he picked up the hem of a pair of skimpy underwear. Its white lace was so sheer, he could see the drawers beneath it.

A primal sound tore through his throat. He bared his fangs at the thing like it had teeth of its own. The faint smell of cinnamon clung to the item, and his traitorous body pleaded with him to huff them like some deranged dog. His tongue traced his fangs, the urge overwhelming.

As if the bond had heard it, it awoke within his chest. Warmth spread across his body, the thread incessantly humming like the witch was close, or not close enough. It invaded every part of him. No. No. *Fuck no*. With a growl of frustration, he flung the underwear across the room. Fucking witches. It was like she had enchanted her room to entice him. There was nothing here; calling for help was his next best option.

Before he could go back to the desk, the door opened. He looked around wildly. The nearest hiding place was—her underwear drawer. Oh, for fuck's sake. The irony was not lost on him. Neither was the humiliation. This was what his life had come to. No time to question it. He jumped in, but ended up standing in his evidence, so he flattened himself among the silky thongs at the back corner of the drawers within the shadow and tried to block out the torturous scent.

The witch walked through the door. She dropped her leather bag, a bag of kibble, and a mat with 'Pawsitively Hungry' in cute letters on the floor, then flopped onto the bed face-down with the grace of a sack of potatoes, a muffled sigh escaping her. *Because it was so hard being a witch with everything handed to her.* If he could roll his eyes, they would have fallen out of his fucking sockets.

He watched her flop her hand around on the bed like a

dying fish, patting blindly at the duvet. What was she doing? Probably looking for her new *pet*.

When her hand found nothing but sheets, she propped herself up by the elbow, those blue eyes scanning the room.

Suddenly, she moved with a frantic energy. The burgundy duvet was ripped from the bed and flung aside. When he wasn't there, she started looking under the bed, shoving furniture, straining against the wooden bed. This is the witch who had summoned him? Pathetic. Ten minutes of pointless effort left her panting on the floor, having checked every spot but this one. Hair tangled between her fingers as she ran her hands through it, almost in a way to soothe herself, the echoes of her anxiety coursing through him.

"Here, kitty kitty," she started to coo.

Once again, if he could roll his eyes, he fucking would have.

And then her deep blue eyes found his peeking out of the drawer.

Shit.

Smiling, she trudged over to her drawer of underwear and pulled it and him out with a *thump*.

She let out a relieved breath. "There you are!" she cooed at him. "Were you in my underwear drawer, you little pervert?"

He hissed, a clear warning, and if that wasn't enough, he dug his claws into her underwear, but she only held steady, completely unaware of the monster literally in her drawer. Humiliation simmered across his chest. Being looked at by a witch like a pet was almost enough to make him shift right there and then, just to stick a claw in her and rip out her throat. She obviously thought he was her familiar, or she was just very, very stupid.

But he couldn't kill her yet. He needed information on why this had happened. Then he would kill her. Slowly. So, he stayed in the drawer corner, calculating the many ways he would make her suffer for this.

And she would suffer. Every witch deserved to. As much as he was a monster to them, they had done far worse to his kind.

And then the witch did the unthinkable. She hoisted him up and out of the drawers, a pair of her underwear tangled in his tail coming with him like a silk-wrapped present. *He was definitely, absolutely, going to kill her for this.* She held him so close to her chest that he could hear her heartbeat thumping in time with his own. The bond sang in response, a pleased hum that made him want to claw his own chest open.

She pulled him just far away enough from her that their eyes locked for a moment. Her innocent eyes were full of relief. His were likely full of rage.

Her voice pulled him from his thoughts. "I think I'll call you Lucky."

HAH. Just how wrong she was. If she knew what he really was, she would be down on her knees begging him for a mercy he wouldn't give.

For some reason, she had taken his being in her presence as kindness and stuck a hand out as if to pat him. Was she dumb? Had she not seen him hissing? Over his dead fucking body. This witch would not touch him. Once again, her scent overwhelmed him, as if her hand was casting a spell on his senses. He needed her away from him.

She moved her hand closer. He was going to lose it. So, he did the only logical thing he could think of to do in that situation.

He bit her finger, his fangs sinking down to the bone.

Six

Avery

HE BIT HER FUCKING FINGER.

She screamed. He didn't let go, only sinking his teeth deeper. She wasn't in the business of animal abuse; in fact, she found it deplorable. However, she had never wanted to fling a cat across the room more than she wanted to now.

When he finally released her, his sandpaper tongue swept across his bloodied canines as if he'd just finished a delicious snack. And that snack was fucking *her*.

She jerked her hand away, breath coming ragged. Pain blazed up her arm, a searing agony that made her vision blur. She pressed her lips together to keep from crying out again. How deep did he send his fangs? *I wish I could heal myself right now.* She knew how to, in theory, but in practice, pulling magic from your familiar was something else entirely.

"Why?" she asked through gritted teeth. She couldn't mask the hurt in her voice. A familiar wasn't supposed to harm their witches. A simmering wrath boiled in her stomach, but it didn't feel like her own.

"*I don't like to be touched.*" His tone was infuriatingly calm.

"You could have said something!" She winced as another shooting pain ran up her arm.

He cocked his head, ears pricked in a way that looked innocent. *Bastard.*

"*I taught you a lesson that needed to be learned, little witch.*"

Wait. *Wait. Was the familiar talking?* Familiars didn't talk. Was the pain making her hallucinate?

"How are you talking?" Her voice wobbled, half from the pain, half from the shock of hearing his voice in her head once more. Something like amusement glinted in her familiar's eyes.

He tilted his head. "*Meow?*"

Did she imagine it? Was her familiar gaslighting her? She narrowed her eyes at him.

"Don't play with me, Lucky. I know you can talk."

"*It's Felix.*"

"I knew it! You can talk." Lying, asshole, bastard, cunt-nugget—if she wasn't in pain, she could have come up with a more creative insult. Her mother always told her it was deplorable—that's why she did it so much. Instead, she settled on, "How are you talking?"

"*The same way you are listening.*"

"That does—that doesn't even make sense." She gestured with her bleeding hand for emphasis and immediately regretted it as fresh pain shot up her arm.

"*You're the one who summoned me, witch. You should know how the hell I'm speaking into your mind.*"

"But...familiars don't talk."

Something like a pained strangle came out of him. "*Well... this one does.*"

Guilt turned her stomach. It must have been the forbidden part of the ritual. Maybe he was more powerful than just a house cat? In everything they had learned about familiars, the tutors never said that a familiar talking was possible. She narrowed her eyes even more to shitty slits, assessing him with the same suspicion as he did her. She supposed, in the witch world, nothing was impossible. What reason would one of the goddess's servants have to lie to her? And, even if Lucky was an asshole that didn't like to be touched, Cerituen blessed her with a familiar for a reason.

She was really trying to convince herself here. It wasn't working.

Blood dripped onto the floorboards, dark drops that pooled between the cracks. She pressed her other hand over the wound, but it did nothing to stop the flow. The pain had evolved from agony to a deep, pulsing throb that matched her heartbeat.

"*You're bleeding on the floor.*"

She whipped her head toward the cat. "You bit me!"

"*And you ignored my warning.*" He stretched out by the fire, completely unbothered. "*I told you I don't like to be touched.*"

"After you bit me!"

"*Semantics.*"

Semantics. Fucking semantics. She wanted to scream. Or cry. Maybe she'd do both. Instead, she stumbled to the bathroom, leaving a trail of red behind her. Her reflection in the mirror looked pale. The bite marks were deep, two perfect punctures on either side of her index finger.

Running it under cold water made her hiss. The stream turned pink, then red, swirling down the drain. She counted to thirty, then forty, willing it to stop. When she pulled her hand back, fresh blood immediately beaded at the surface. This was it. She was going to get sepsis and die. That was what Google always told her it would be. Who knows where that cat's mouth had been in the godly realm, if it had been anywhere as filthy as his personality, she was so *fucked*.

"Why isn't it stopping?" she hissed under her breath, low enough that he couldn't hear.

She rummaged through the cabinet with her good hand. Bandages. She needed bandages. Her fingers knocked over bottles of tinctures and healing salves until she found the small tin she kept for emergencies. Never thought the emergency would be her own familiar.

The gauze was harder to manage with one hand. She tried to wrap it around her finger, but it kept slipping, the white fabric immediately soaking through with red. Her hand shook. Whether from pain or shock, or anger, she couldn't tell.

"*Because you're doing it wrong.*"

She froze. The cat sat in the doorway, watching her while his tail flicked against the rug.

"Please enlighten me." Her voice dripped with sarcasm.

"Do they not teach you basic first aid? You need to apply pressure first."

"I know that." She pressed the gauze against the wound, her jaw tight.

"*Clearly not well enough.*"

How did a cat know so much about patching up wounds?

Heat crept up her neck. Here she was, bleeding because of him, and he had the audacity to criticize her. She wanted to throw something at his smug cat face.

Minutes passed in silence while she held the gauze to her finger. When she pulled it away, the bleeding had finally slowed to a sluggish trickle. She managed to wrap the bandage around her finger this time, though it looked sloppy. The white fabric already had spots of red seeping through, but at least it was something.

"There." Her middle finger had been the one that had been affected, and she flipped him off to show him. "Happy?"

"*You should clean the blood off the floor before it stains.*"

Her fist clenched at her side. The good one. "You are the worst familiar in the history of familiars."

THE DORM WAS SILENT. THE CAT CURLED UP NEXT to the fireplace, its matted fur illuminated by the flickering orange light. Guilt coiled in her gut. *Lucky* was still an asshole, but she had a duty of care to this familiar. He must be so uncomfortable in his own skin. Maybe that was why he was being so rude.

She had spent the night researching familiars on her laptop, including asking, *Why is my familiar an asshole*, and found nothing to explain any of it. Nowhere did anyone say anything about them being able to talk to you. It was unheard of. She had tried to ask him about it, but he was extremely reluctant to give out any information. It was like trying to talk to a furry brick wall.

But researching was an excuse. She needed to present him as her familiar tomorrow. To the class, to her mother, who was probably sending the enforcers soon to escort her out of the university to some shitty apartment in town. A familiar was supposed to be the highlight of a witch's life, the moment where all their hard work paid off, but when she thought about it, it was like a giant weight had been placed on her chest, refusing to let up.

Staying light on her feet, she tiptoed over to the fireplace and kneeled next to the cat. She went to pat him, but before she made contact, she stopped, remembering he hated to be touched. She wondered if a familiar had ever hated its witch so much. A sadness throbbed through her, and she felt tears threatening to fall. It seemed every road to being a witch would be a hard one. It seemed most witches climbed a hill, where she was climbing an Everest—which, in her opinion, was a really dumb thing to do. He slept soundly, more soundly than any familiar should when he just bit his witch. Did he feel no guilt? She was *this* close to a mental breakdown.

The cat was still filthy. She had given him a day to clean himself cat-style, but he seemed to have no interest. He needed to be clean before she presented him tomorrow. A bath it was, even though she knew she would receive many more bites and scratches, and some verbal abuse, too. *Fantastic.* A small part of her reveled in getting back at him, though. He'd bitten her. Now he'd get dunked. Revenge would be wet and soapy.

Before he could react, she lunged forward, scooping him into her arms, ignoring his startled yowls and claws digging against her bare skin.

"*Witch*!" he yelled into her mind. "*Put me down, or you will regret it.*"

She held Lucky—she refused to call him Felix—tight against her chest as he fought desperately against her grip, thrashing, twisting, and clawing his way to freedom, but she only held him tighter.

"*I swear to God, let me go, or I will murder you.*"

She ignored him and kicked the bathroom door shut behind her and locked it, all the while trying to contain the monstrosity of a cat in her arms. After many scratches, she let him go, and he bolted to the corner of the bathroom. Its bright eyes stared up at her, and for the first time, she noticed they were different colors, one brown, the other green. She left it in the corner to sulk.

The taps groaned as she turned the handle, and the steam rose from the water as it started to fill the bathtub. For good measure, she poured a small amount of chamomile into the bath. Not that she was sure the cat would appreciate any of this, but it didn't hurt to try.

The bathtub was large enough that washing him would have been too awkward to lean over the side, and her back seemed to fall out of place with the slightest twinge, so standing wasn't an option. She peeled off her bandage and her clothes and let them fall to a heap on the floor, leaving on only her underwear. Using her good hand, she tested the water and found it adequate for what she thought a cat would like.

"I'm sorry," she muttered toward the cat, cornering him and scooping him up in her arms. She hesitantly took the first step in the bath. He scratched her chest, leaving thin, weeping slices as he yowled with displeasure. The warm water lapped around her calf. It was a touch too hot for her freezing toe, but after a minute of standing, her body adjusted. As she submerged herself in the water, he went quiet.

It was too late to go back. For better or worse, they were in this together. Slowly, she lowered Lucky into the water. She cringed as a mix of her blood and mud seeped into the clear water, the mix of damp earth and chamomile steaming the room.

Using her hand, she scooped water from the bath and brushed away the caked mud on its fur. With each stroke, the water dirtied, and her guilt climbed. For some reason, he let her.

Until he didn't.

The cat let out another yowl loud enough to rattle in her ears. Water splashed up the walls of the bath. Her familiar immediately tried to scramble out, claws scrabbling against porcelain, but she caught him and held him close, her arms getting caught in the bloody crossfire.

"*This is your final warning, witch,*" he growled. "*Let. Me. Out.*"

She ignored him again and his unbridled rage. His sleek black fur was already flattening, and those eyes glared up at her with the kind of outrage that made her think, just for a heartbeat, that maybe she'd made a mistake.

Oh. *Fuck.*

Smoke tendrils began steaming from his form.

She'd definitely, absolutely made a mistake.

Her stomach dropped.

The witch lights along the walls sputtered and dimmed until the bathroom was swallowed in shadow. Still holding him, she scrambled back with her legs toward the back of the bath, pressing herself against the lip as much as she could to get away from whatever was transpiring before her.

The small, sodden body in her arms grew heavy. Limbs lengthened under her grip, bone and muscle that hadn't been there moments ago. Shadow became warm, bare flesh.

The haze thinned.

She wasn't holding a cat anymore.

Above her was a man. A very naked, very wet, very pissed-off man who kneeled over her in the tub. Water rippled around them; his frame was tall enough that his knees bent awkwardly in the confined space. Wet hair as black as the cat's fur adorned his head, and he had the same eyes; one was a stunning honey color, the other a mossy emerald. They were far more unsettling in a human face. Water rivulets mixed with dirt dripped off his dark hair and glistened across muscles that were tattooed with black ink in swirling patterns. Bits of grime still clung to the caverns of his collarbones. Cuts and fresh wounds marred his body.

Her jaw must have slackened in shock. The man took her chin between his fingers and tilted her face up to meet his.

Her breath caught, fingers still resting against his skin from where she'd been holding him, her palm flat against the bulging muscles of his chest. She pulled them back as if they'd shocked her, but he caught her wrist before she could retreat; her pulse fluttered under his grip.

"Witch." His voice seethed. She could hear it aloud now. It was a dangerous voice, low and far too close to her. She gasped as she noticed the twitch of two cat-like ears crowned on his head. The ghost of a tail wrapped around her leg.

This was no man. This was no familiar. But it was his voice, Lucky's voice.

"I warned you, witch."

Her immediate instinct was to get out. *Now.* Adrenaline flooded her system. She twisted, shoving hard against him.

He smiled, the faint glint of fangs catching the dim light as if her resistance amused him.

Before she could even register the movement, his hand was in her hair with his fingers curling tight at the nape of her neck. He pushed her back down into the tub, the water rising high enough that her mouth hovered just above the surface, forcing her to drag in shallow, panicked breaths.

His body was an unyielding wall. Every time she fought, he pressed her further into the tub. Water entered her mouth, and she spluttered it out, her legs trapped against the porcelain, his own braced hard to pin them in place. Her arms were wrenched above her head, his grip locking them there until her elbows bit into the cold curve of the bath. She was pinned in every sense. Her body was splayed beneath him, nowhere to hide, her underwear soaked—not the fun kind—and sheer, and almost every inch of her lay bare under his gaze.

For some reason, the first coherent thought that formed in her mind was that this was the first time a man had seen her naked in a year. Well, basically naked.

How sad.

"Stay put," he murmured, his gaze traveling the length of her as the word vibrated through his chest against hers.

She kept her chin lifted enough to breathe, heart hammering so hard it made the water ripple. Every time she tried to move, his hold adjusted, firm, inescapable, but never quite enough to push her under. She felt the steady pulse of him against her, calm in a way that told her he didn't need to strain.

The realization hit her all at once.

"Shifter," she breathed out.

She was sharing a bath with a shifter. Taking a shuddering breath, the thought pounded against her chest. No. No! He couldn't be. She started to shake her head. This couldn't be happening. Witches and shifters couldn't bond. What had she done? She couldn't have.

"Very good, little witch." His voice was exactly as it had been in her head.

Terror clawed up her throat, and she went to scream again. Before she could, he shoved a hand across her face, so hard she tasted blood as her lips banged against her teeth. A *tut, tut* sound crawled around her head, chiding her as if she were a wayward child.

He moved close to her face, his breath tingling against her nose as he spoke, "Do not scream again, witch, otherwise I will slit your throat."

She nodded slowly, not wanting to test his words. He looked as if he would enjoy it. He slipped his hand away and hovered it above her face. To make a point, his fingers elongated into claws. They curled at the tip, their sharpness evident. Tears burned at the sides of her eyes as she stared at the nails that could end her existence in the blink of an eye. She bit her tongue to keep from crying out, but a strangled whimper escaped.

Feline ears perked at the sound, tilting his head in a creature-like manner as his glare ran over her bloodied lips before meeting back up at her eyes.

His gaze raked her body. Every urge screamed at her to cover herself somehow. But there was nowhere to hide. His hold loosened ever so slightly, and she seized the opportunity to thrash. Water sloshed in the tub, sending more over the edge.

His hand slipped from her wrists, and a sliver of hope shone through her; she could run. She started to move before his hand moved unnaturally fast to wrap around her throat. Her meager courage dwindled and died. She was a mouse caught in his trap.

Her gasp was swallowed by the rush of water shifting around them. In a single motion, he hauled her higher, forcing her back over the curved lip of the bath. The cool air of the room skimmed her wet skin, and she felt it tightening at the sudden change of temperature.

One of his legs slid between hers, lifting her up by her core. He braced her against the bath, using the leverage to arch her body further over the bath rim until her spine protested. Her head tipped back, vision swimming with spots of light.

His eyes locked on hers, assessing her.

"Careful, little witch," he murmured, his thumb pressing just enough to make her heartbeat thunder in her ears. "You won't win that game."

A strangled breath escaped her as she clawed at the shifter's arms. Maybe this memory would be useful one day, maybe she could write the first witch-shifter porn. She was losing her vision. He was going to kill her. Maybe that was a good thing. This would all be over. One less useless witch in the world. It was better that way.

But she didn't want to die. Like a possum that had determined in its peanut brain that it was the best course of action, she played dead.

Seven

Felix

Shit. She was losing consciousness. He needed this fucking witch alive. She gave up far too quickly. It was disappointing. A cat liked to play with its prey, after all. And what wonderful prey she made.

Normally, with witches, a bounty would come through from the human government because a witch had broken one of their rules. Often, that rule involved using unauthorized magic on humans or breaking through the wards. Most witches followed the rules, but the ones who didn't, they were *his.* It wouldn't heal the hole that the witches had left when they killed his father, but each one he killed helped.

Before he could decide to let the little witch go, she slumped in his hold, twitching and jerking dramatically from the lack of oxygen.

A groan escaped him as he let her down gently into the water, making sure she didn't slip beneath. He hated that he had to be careful with one of them. She deserved none of his kindness, not that there was any left, and especially not for a witch. Two fingers pressed against the veins in her throat, checking for a pulse. It thundered hard against her neck, indicating that, fortunately or unfortunately, she was still alive.

Maybe this was good. It gave him time to think. He thought he couldn't shift so soon after his monster form, but the way she had manhandled him into the bath was the last straw, and his ego couldn't take it. He wasn't going to spend one more second letting her treat him like a pet.

The constellation of freckles on her body caught his attention as the water lapped at his knees. Some were sparse, some were in groups. Her body reminded him of an artist's canvas, two small peaks surrounded by a pale night sky. His gaze traced her belly button before he found the place where her thighs met. Sheer lace mocked him; he shouldn't be looking, but he couldn't tear his eyes away either.

His cock twitched; he wanted to touch her. Shifting always made everything more intense: his hunger, his arousal, the sensations of this witch against his body tenfold in this form.

"Fuck," he growled, directing his eyes away from this goddamn witch. The sight of him choking her as she writhed underneath him had awakened something in him that hadn't stirred in years. Most women fell at his feet, which was nice, easy. But the ones he had to chase, *literally* chase, were his favorite.

Regardless of the way his body reacted to her, he would never defile himself with a witch. Why was he even still touching her? He hated every moment of this.

Another wave of need pulsed through him despite his hatred. He looked to the ceiling to collect himself for just a moment. *Stupid bond. That's all this is, some stupid bonding spell she had put on him.* She stirred underneath him. That wasn't right. An unconscious person shouldn't stir.

He glanced down. One of her eyes cracked open, just a sliver, but enough to be noticeable. Their stares met, and she slammed her lid shut as if they hadn't just made eye contact for a full second. A part of him found it amusing that in the face of the most dangerous thing to a witch, her grand strategy was to play dead.

"I know you're awake, little witch," he said, grabbing her face between his sharp claws. How easy it would be to break her delicate bones. The witch glared at him as if he had actually woken her up from a deep slumber, and that his presence was an inconvenience rather than a scare. *She was a feisty one.*

In a moment of weakness, his body loosened, and she spat in his face. The glob of spit landed between his eyeballs, temporarily blinding him as the witch shoved against his chest and scrambled out of the tub.

The *fucking* audacity. *He* was the one to usually spit in girls' faces—sexually, and consensually, of course.

He could have caught her. One quick grab and it would have been over. But the rush of her breaking free sent a hot jolt through him. He *loved* the chase. A feral snarl tore from his throat as he went after her.

Giving her a head start, after just a few seconds, he stepped out of the tub with unhurried feline grace. Water slid in rivulets down his torso, pooling at his feet before he followed her like a bloodhound.

"Run all you want, little witch, just remember I hunt better than you hide," he said, licking his fangs.

He caught her in the lounge before she could make it to the door. A shadow snaked out, the tendril clamping around her ankle, and he yanked. She hit the floor with a muffled thump, a hitched inhale tearing from her lungs. Satisfaction coursed through him while something else hummed in his chest; he couldn't tell whether it was the bond or the monster within him waking once again.

In an instant, he was over her. His legs locked around hers, pinning them hard against the carpet. One hand wrenched her arms behind her back, and the other pressed her head to the floor, forcing her cheek into the rug. Her breath came shallow beneath him, the heat of her skin burning through his wet grip.

If this were anyone else from his den, this would be ideal. It would be so easy. One shift of his hips, one thrust, and he could bury himself between her thighs. Oh god, how he wanted to. A shiver of disgust convulsed through him. *What the fuck* was he thinking? That was the last thing he wanted. This witch needed to suffer, and it would be *him* who made her suffer.

The thought almost hurt. But then, she stilled. Completely limp under him. Her head lolled to the side. Was she pretending again? Fainting this time like a scared goat? Felix jostled her shoulders, searching for any sign of dishonesty. But no, this time he had really knocked her out; she must have hit her head as she fell. She lay splayed out on the floor. These witches were so pathetically delicate. He swore under his breath. At least this time, it *actually* bought him some time to figure out what to do with the little witch.

Rolling his eyes, he got up off her. He conjured himself some pants made of shadows, it would have to do until he could find something real. Felix was a talented magic user. Unlike the witch in front of them, shifter magic wasn't tied to ley lines or familiars; it was born inside of them. But it was a double-edged sword, a consuming wildfire that many shifters lost themselves to.

Hauling her onto his shoulder, he grabbed her ass to keep her from sliding as her naked body slid against him, despising every moment her skin made contact with his. Unfortunately, it was necessary. This was *not* how he thought he would be spending his weekend.

He slid her off his shoulder, and she slumped on the floor next to her bed. His shadows slipped from his palm as he held it up to the witch, and tied them like a collar around her throat; a magical leash that meant she couldn't do anything but sit like a *good whittle puppy.* Felix didn't mind shifters of other types, but for some reason, he had always had a disdain for the dogs. They smelled like a wet blanket and were far too eager.

The shadows glided through the air with an ease that made him pause; it was as easy as breathing. Normally, he had to concentrate to not let his power explode, like the lid on an overflowing pot, constantly threatening to boil over. This was far too easy. *Why* was it this easy?

Shadows wrapped themselves around her ankles before they snaked their way to her wrists and stomach, pinning her to the bed. Some of them obeyed him; others had a mind of their own, slithering possessively around her.

The shadows were simple enough and would serve what he needed. She wouldn't be strong enough to break it. With no familiar, she was even less powerful than a newborn shifter —and he sure as hell wasn't her familiar. They writhed and purred as they settled across her body, as if they were enjoying it.

Sighing, he resolved to sit on the chair across from her to wait for her to regain consciousness and formulate a plan. He had to get out of here, but unfortunately, he had no idea how the fuck to get off a warded island in the first place. The wards were easy, although they were probably far stronger here due to the ley lines; however, the island part was a bit of a problem. Sure, he could find a way off. But there was a small inkling inside of him that told him he needed to stay, if only to figure out how she had done this in the first place.

The little witch twitched under his shadows. Her head lolled to the side, the damp strands of her hair clinging to her freckled face. His eyes followed the marks he had left on her neck, still red from where he had choked her. A flicker of regret went through him before he killed it. A bead of water dropped from her hair onto the swell of her breasts, and it traveled down to the dip in her waist, the curve of her hips, down to the apex of her thighs, still shimmering with the gleam of bathwater. Involuntarily, his cock twitched again. Why the hell was his body reacting like this?

Disgust coiled in his gut.

Witch. She was a witch. And he was as hard as a rock for her.

Fucking bond.

Eight

Avery

At first, she thought she'd had another strange dream. A dream about her cat turning into a shifter and trying to murder her.

Until her eyes fluttered open.

A man with cat ears poking out of his hair sat before her on her burgundy Chesterfield armchair. There was no denying who was in front of her.

The chair he sat in was comically small compared to his body of long, corded muscles. He tensed under her gaze. That didn't bother her, but what *did* bother her was the way his pants moved as if they were swirling with dark patterns. Strange, almost beautiful. *Focus, Avery.*

"My eyes are up here, little witch." The sound of his voice jerked her out of her trance. His tail thumped against the soft fabric of the armchair in a way that suggested he was not nearly as relaxed as he seemed. Her eyes found his; the mismatched stare and large cat ears twisted toward her.

Instinctively, she tried to move away from the danger. But she realized in horror that she was bound by some sort of shadow ropes. They were firm and soft like fur as they slithered across her, caressing her in places she would rather not be caressed—never mind that they felt good. One of them had found itself far too close to her *holes.* She tried to move, but they wouldn't budge. A sudden spike of fear jolted through her, urging her to run, to scream, to be anywhere other than tied to...her bed? Yep, she was tied to her bed. Her one place of solace had turned into a betrayal. If the bed were sentient, she would have had a strong word with it. Maybe she still would.

"Shifter," she breathed out.

"Astute observation, witch." His voice was dangerous, but alluring like a bug to the nectar of a Venus flytrap. "What do you want?" he asked.

Warmth flushed her cheeks. Was he sassing her? Narrowing her eyes at him, she sassed him right back. "What do I want?"

"Are you a parrot? That's what I said."

She only stared at him for a moment, almost in disbelief that *he* was asking *her* what *she* wanted. She wanted a familiar, she wanted to graduate, she wanted him to put on some damn pants. What she *didn't* want was a shifter as a familiar.

"*What do you want?*" he repeated in the old language.

"What?" The language caught her off guard. How did he know the witches' sacred tongue?

"Oh, sorry, I thought you might respond in the old language because you didn't answer my question." He sneered.

"You know the old language?"

"How uneducated do you think we are? Just answer the question, witch."

Avery had once been told that shifters were incapable of jokes, and they were only ever serious. This almost proved that theory. Did this one have a sense of humor? What else about the shifters was a lie? Also, they *were* uneducated. It wasn't rude to ask.

"In the old language or in English?"

He pinched the bridge of his nose in a way that she knew she was getting under his skin. Watch out, bitches, even tied up, she could be annoying. Perhaps she could annoy him enough to let her go?

"Answer the question, or I'll kill you. Is that language clear enough for you?"

A lump formed in her throat. "Crystal." She looked down at her bound legs. This situation was quite a pickle, and she didn't quite care for pickles. "I wanted to summon a familiar."

"That much is obvious," he said. "Let me rephrase the question, then. How did you summon me?"

Leaning forward, she tested the holds again, almost yelping as one started to kiss her ass, *literally*. "You think I meant to bind a shifter?"

"I really have no idea about your intentions, hence why I am asking."

Rude. So incredibly rude. Although she supposed it made sense, if she had been kidnapped—catnapped?—across time and space and bound to a shifter, she might have felt the same way. Why she wasn't freaking out more was beyond her. She was probably dissociating, something her mind did often during stressful situations. She imagined the little gremlin in her mind cheerleading, 'two four six eight, time to dissociate!' at the first drop of adrenaline. The shifter growled, beckoning back her attention.

In her dissociated brain, all she could think was, were all these shifters ridiculously, distractingly handsome? Sharp cheekbones. Strong jawline. Dark lashes framed his eyes, which would make most women jealous. Thick hair that didn't look like it had a chance of balding in the next twenty years. His mouth, in particular, was devilishly lush. She wondered what it could do? Hurt her feelings, probably. But his eyes, goddess, his eyes, were the most striking of all.

A feeling pooled low in her, one that she most certainly ignored. *No, Avery, you cannot under any circumstances find a shifter attractive! They were witches' mortal enemies for goddess's sake, if not for that, this particular shifter had you bound to a bed.* Best not to think about the fact that she had read this very same scenario only a few days back, although it ended much differently than she was expecting this one to go. A blush crept across her cheeks as more shadows explored her body. Why did they start to feel good?

"Do I need to speak in the old tongue again?"

The sound of his deep voice jostled her from her thoughts, almost as pleasurable as a hand between her legs. "That won't be necessary." She didn't want to admit it had sounded nice sliding over his tongue. She wondered if his tongue was barbed like a normal house cat's. *Nope. Not going there.*

"There was a book in the library that had this riddle in it, and then I solved it and then some..." She rambled when she was nervous. "And then I did the ritual in the book, and it involved some blood, and then somehow you appeared instead of a familiar and..." The words tumbled out of her with no sign of stopping.

"You used blood magic? Isn't that forbidden in your witch society?" he interrupted.

"Mmhmm," she replied quietly, as if confirming it softly would make the deed less forbidden. Where would the doing of the deed with a shifter sit on the forbidden scale? *Goddess, Avery, stop.* If she got out of this alive, she would definitely be writing that fanfiction.

A dark chuckle came from his sinful lips. "Naughty witch."

Irritation flared through her; he was playing with her. Unfortunately, that heat had spread. Stupid handsome shifter. She had to tread carefully; he could kill her in an instant if she did something wrong. If she screamed, the enforcers would come. But she would be long dead by then, and he would likely kill them too. It was a delicate situation which she approached like a politician rather than the raging whoremonal university student she was.

"Bite me, shifter."

Not quite what she had intended.

"Got quite a mouth on you, don't you?" He smirked. "Someone should teach you what to do with it."

Wetness pooled between the apex of her thighs. *No, no, no. I will not let a shifter make me feel this way*, Avery vowed. *I am a woman who is in control of her emotions.* Her eyes, however, were not in her control, and made their way back to his shadow pants.

Fangs glinted in the witch lights as he smiled, looking down on her. She didn't speak, keeping her lips firmly sealed to keep from screaming. Even from where she was sitting, he was absolutely massive. She never thought of herself as small, but in front of him, she was tiny.

Instead of giving him the satisfaction, she stared directly into his abs, specifically, the deep V that dipped below his pants. It wasn't where she wanted to be looking, but some part of her could not face the reality of him. Of the shifter she had summoned. He was supposed to be lucky. He was supposed to be the answer to all her problems. Instead, it had just become one giant, complicated clusterfuck of a problem.

Reality became clear to her, though. There was nothing she could do. She was truly, utterly trapped. At the mercy of a shifter *and* most definitely not in control of her emotions. The warmth dissipated, replaced by tears burning at her eyes, forming hot streams on her face as they fell. It almost seemed to amuse him further, his smile widening at her distress. Embarrassment brandished her; she couldn't stop the tears, she never could. Even something as small as accidentally crushing an ant under her finger was enough to bring her to tears, something she would need to curb if she wanted to be a healer.

The shifter moved from the chair and circled her with a predatory grace, as if she was his prey—let's face it, she was—then kneeled before her.

"Are you going to kill me?" she said through choked sobs.

"Perhaps," he said, and that only made her sob harder. "Look at me, little witch," he said, almost gently.

She didn't comply. Instead, she shut her eyes like a petulant child, ignoring the request.

Shadows kissed her, dancing gently just out of touching range, scraping the fine hairs on her face. If this were a different situation, she would have enjoyed being tied down, but this really, truly, sucked.

"I said, look at me." The shifter's voice was harsher this time, commanding. Another spike of fear swept through her, sending a prickling pain skittering across her skin at the power in his voice. Who was this man? Even for a shifter, he seemed to wield a crackling power that she couldn't turn away from. The shadows tilted her chin up, forcing her to once again look him in the eye. The moment their eyes met, the slits dilated, making him seem more human. She wanted to turn away, close her eyes, but the shadows held steady.

"Good girl." Features softening, his mouth forming into a lazy smile. "That wasn't so hard, was it?"

A sick shiver twisted through her at his words of praise. It disturbed her more than anything had so far. Another sob escaped. He rolled his eyes. "Good god, witch, pull yourself together," he said, "I'm not going to kill you—yet."

Yet. Yet! As if that were comforting! Somehow, though, she found the strength to hold her dignity together, which was already abysmal, and sucked the tears back into her eyeballs.

Settling on the floor across from her, he was still somehow taller than her, so she had to look up just to meet his eyes. The shifter leaned back on his hands, his tail flicking against the wooden floor in an irritated manner, cat ears twitching alongside it. For some weird reason, he had human ears too. Avery didn't think that this was the appropriate time to ask about it, though.

"Please release me from these...uh...things." The shadows wriggled around her, caressing but holding firm.

"I don't trust witches."

She looked down at the many shadow ties that latched her to the bed. "Evidently," she said, sarcasm dripping from her tongue.

"Now," he began. "You're going to break the bond, or whatever the fuck you've done between us, little witch." His tongue played with his fangs, as if he were enjoying this.

She kept her mouth shut. As far as she knew, a bond between a familiar and its witch was permanent. But Felix was no familiar.

"And if I refuse?" The question emerged far more vulnerable than she intended.

"Then I'll kill you," he said with no hesitation, as if stating a simple fact.

If even a lashing of defiance remained, it was now thoroughly doused by the reality in which she found herself. Panic clawed at her, threatening to consume her. She swallowed hard, as if to physically force it down. She couldn't die. She had so much to live for. Well, that part was not true. She had very little to live for, actually. Only reading as many fanfics as she could, leaving the island, and god dammit, she wouldn't let a shifter take that away from her.

The shadows loosened slightly around the back of her hands. Enough that she could move them. She tested the strength of the tendrils. He didn't seem to notice as she wriggled her hands behind her back.

A plan. She needed a plan.

"I will only help you if you unbind me first, shifter."

He just laughed. Unfortunately for her, it was a nice laugh. What would she even do if he let her go? What she *should* do is turn him in. That meant that she would turn herself in, too. And only the goddess knew what they would do with such a filthy traitor. The dungeons, perhaps? Public stoning? Behavioral euthanasia? So many creative ways to die.

This was truly a clusterfuck. How had she found herself here? How would she find her way out of this? If he let her live, how the hell was she going to first of all hide this shifter, second of all unbind him, and third and most impossible get him off the island when she herself hadn't managed to do that? Questions assaulted her mind, with no answers in sight.

"Let me go." She wriggled against the holds, trying her hardest to escape them. It was futile.

Felix rose high above her. One of his shadows moved, tangling between her hair, almost as if it was brushing through the strands with its tendrils. Gentle at first, testing. Then he fisted her hair and yanked. She cried out from the sudden pain, her head snapping back, though he was careful not to break her neck. As if that made it better somehow. A smile curved his lips as he held her head inches from his, forcing her to meet his eyes.

"I don't take orders from a witch," he spat out, his voice deeper and more demonic than before. His eyes darkened, and more tendrils raced from his body. She was covered in them now, these writhing beings. His feral smile widened, pleased by their doing. She didn't know this shifter, but something was happening within him. Like he was losing control. Shadows tightened against her flesh.

"*Mine.*" A demonic voice bled into her mind.

Dear fucking goddess. He was going to kill her. He was turning into a monster and was going to kill her. More shadows curved around them both like a dark cocoon; his eyes blazed brightly. One slipped around her neck.

"Felix?" She squeezed out, wasting a precious breath. But they didn't give, only compressing her until she thought a bone might snap.

Then all at once, his shadows faltered, eyelids rapidly blinking before he fell on the floor with a thump, making far more noise than she would like. Did he just pass out?

"Felix," she hissed at him, flicking his nose to make sure he wasn't playing with her.

The goddess truly hated her.

She needed time. Time to figure this out. Not only had the shadows that held her dissipated, but the ones that had made up his pants had gone too. Leaving him not only passed out, but naked. It was really hard not to look at the impressive length of him.

This was good, she told herself. If she locked him in the bathroom and tied him up—not her usual style, but in her defense, he had done it first with his weird shadow creatures. It would give her time.

There was no way she could carry him. Couldn't he have passed out as a damn cat? She'd have to drag him. Using all the strength she could muster, she hooked her arms around his chest and pulled him across the floor. She tried to ignore the scent of him. He smelled of the forest, like pine needles and crisp winter air. Part of her wanted to huff it in, the other part of her actually focused on dragging this six-foot-six naked monster across the ground. Another part of her hoped he got a splinter in his ass.

His ear flicked her nose as she dragged him across the floor, her breath heaving with the effort. Goddess, she needed to get fit again. They were both going to be sent to the dungeons she was sure this school had.

She dropped the shifter on the ground of the bathroom, his head hitting the tiles a bit harder than it should have. *Oops.*

His *thing* wouldn't stop staring her in the face. So she decided to dress him and *then* tie him up. Because she had basic human decency, which he severely lacked. Shifters were just as brutal as she had always been told.

Dressed and tied, she locked the bathroom door and waited for the beast to awaken.

NINE

FELIX

A SPLITTING HEADACHE COAXED HIM AWAKE.

Once again, he had woken up somewhere he should not be. The first thing he noticed was the cold tiles against his top half, while his bottom half was nice and toasty. Rage boiled under his skin. Did that fucking witch dress him while he was unconscious? *Right*—he was going to murder her.

He had used too much magic, letting himself lose control. Usually, he would have passed out much earlier, but the monster in him screamed to touch her, to feel her. It had kept him conscious to watch; it had taken over, and he let it. Shame flooded him. That wouldn't happen again.

He tried to move himself from the floor. But as soon as he did, he realized there were ropes crudely tied around his ankles and wrists. That little witch. She was more cunning than he gave her credit for. A growl rumbled through his chest. The ropes wouldn't stop him; they were more insulting than effective.

His ears pricked at movement outside the door, the scent of her hitting him the next second, that cinnamon perfume he had already attached to her. She was here. The ropes snapped easily as he strained against them. Using the bathtub as support, he stood, his head swimming as it hit the chandelier. *Who needs a fucking chandelier in a bathroom?*

The mirror showed his reflection, its ornate gold framing his humiliation. The witch had put a too-small maroon sweater on him. The university logo with the three houses plastered on the front, with Caerwyn Swim Team written across the chest. Turning in the mirror, his eyes slid to the maroon shorts that matched the sweater. She had cut a crude hole and pulled his tail through it. He was definitely, absolutely, *without a fucking question,* going to murder her.

Stumbling through the bathroom, he clung to the wall for support, the cool tiles grounding him in the space while his head pounded. Felix grabbed the handle and tried to open the door. It was locked. Closing his eyes, he quickly exhaled, trying not to lose his shit and get himself caught. He was teetering on a very fine line. Back in the den, Ciro, his best friend and leader of his den, had tried to teach him to count to ten *before* acting on his anger; it worked sometimes, other times it didn't. The sound of the witch shuffling on the other side was just the icing on the goddamn cake; he could practically hear her heart thumping against the door like a rapid drumbeat.

Breaking down the door would be easy. But he also did not want an enforcer to hear the noise and come running. Negotiation it was. It wasn't his strong suit; decapitation was his preferred method.

"Witch?" he called out, remaining surprisingly calm despite the utter rage boiling within him.

A squeak of surprise answered him, as if she had been pressing her ear right up against the door.

"Open the door, witch, or I'll—" he said, claws scraping against the wood.

"You'll what? Call the *pawlice*?" Her smug, muffled voice

came through the door. "Well, well, well. How the tables have turned, shifter."

A muscle ticked in his jaw. It was most definitely not the same situation to any degree, but he would let her think she had the power in this conversation. When he got out, though, he would teach her a lesson for thinking she could cage a shifter.

He pounded on the door. "Let. Me. Out."

"I will only let you out once we have come to a deal that doesn't involve dismembering each other, like mature, well-adjusted adults," she said, trying her very best to sound assertive.

"You're the one who locked me in a bathroom."

"You said you would kill me!"

"That's what you think of me?" He feigned the sound of hurt in his voice.

"Yes."

"Fair enough." He sighed. He had said he was going to kill her. Many times. "Well then?"

"Well what?" she asked, as if she had lost the very purpose of the conversation.

Was she a goldfish?

Rolling his eyes, he asked, "What deal do you propose?"

"I need you to pretend to be my familiar."

A short laugh snorted out of him. She wasn't serious? He waited for the joke to drop, for her to propose an actual alternative. It never came.

"Not happening," he stated flatly, resting his forehead against the door to cool the headache forming once again.

"Why not?" she asked.

"I don't whore myself out like your familiars do."

She scoffed. "They don't. And you don't have a choice." Her trying to be confident was cute, like the dragon hatchlings at his den that puffed up their chests and snorted boogers of fire when they didn't get sweets.

His ears flattened against his head, tail thumping against the tiles. "I have plenty of choices, and none of them involve playing your pet."

"I'll call the enforcers on you." It was an empty threat, and they both knew it.

"And incriminate yourself in the process?"

A knock sounded at the door. They both froze.

Felix spoke in a hushed tone, his body tensing. Had she called the enforcers already? "Who is that?"

"I don't know! I don't have who's behind-the-door sentience," she whispered back.

"Avery! Open up." A woman's voice. *Now that was a voice that held authority.*

"Tell her to leave," he spoke into her mind.

"One second, just getting out of the shower!" she squeaked loud enough for the woman to hear, her voice breaking slightly. Whispering again, she warned him, *"Don't* say anything."

Footsteps faded away from the bathroom, the sound of the door opening piquing his hearing. Carefully, he sat on the floor, his back against the door as he listened.

"What do you want?" the little witch said, her tone fiercer than it had been with him.

"Lovely to see you too, sis," the voice answered, dripping in sarcasm. *The little witch had a sister?* He filed that information away for later.

The voice spoke again. "Mother is asking if you summoned a familiar yet."

"Nope," she said, popping the 'p.' "That's all?"

"Yep," the sister replied. What a riveting conversation. He had never heard such a loving, sisterly bond in his life.

There was silence for a moment, and what Felix expected

was the closing of a door and for the little witch to come crawling back. An unbidden thought crashed through him of the little witch crawling to him on her knees. *Not a time for a boner, Felix.*

"Soo, enforcer sister," the little witch chimed, her voice far cheerier and higher-pitched than before.

His cock went flaccid, his body tensing in its place. *Her sister was an enforcer then. Just fucking great.* As if this couldn't get more complicated than it already was. What was the little witch playing at?

"What would you do if there were a shifter on campus?" she asked, trying to be inconspicuous.

"Why do you ask?" The sister's voice was controlled, not giving anything away.

The witch, on the other hand. "No reason," she said suspiciously.

He rubbed his hand against his head. Jesus Christ, he was going to die. Either she was being so painfully obvious and alerting her sister that he was in the bathroom. Or she was just stupid. Honestly, it was hard to tell.

"First of all, there wouldn't be." The sister deadpanned. Felix almost snorted. *There was, but carry on.* "But if there was one, we would kill it and anyone who helped get it here," she continued.

Was this some thinly veiled threat she was trying to cook up? If so, she was doing a terrible job at it.

"Right, well, thanks for that. You can leave. I have assignments and all that," she said, fumbling over her words.

"The year hasn't even started yet," her sister pointed out.

"Yeah...I know that. Just catching up is all."

Painful. This was absolutely painful to listen to.

"Right. Well. You won't have anything to catch up to if you don't summon a familiar by tomorrow morning."

"I know that, tell Mother—I mean, *High Councilor*, that I send my regards." She seethed at her sister.

"I'm not doing that," her sister said.

He sighed quietly. Her mother was the High Councilor? Eleri fucking Alarch? As if it couldn't get any worse. Was her dad going to be the Chancellor or something? If he were caught by anyone, it would have the same outcome—his head on a spike. But this made it infinitely harder to slip around unnoticed.

The door shut, and footsteps trailed back over to the bathroom. By the sounds of it, she slid her back down the door, her butt landing on the floor with a thump.

"What do you want in exchange for being my familiar?" she said, her voice quieter as if she was truly coming to terms with how helpless she was.

"The bond broken, and to get off this godforsaken island, *without* having to play your pet," he stated simply. He didn't want to be anywhere near this witch or this place any longer.

The little witch interrupted his train of thought. "I don't know how to break the bond."

"If there is a will, there is a way."

"There's definitely a fucking will, trust me." She sighed. "If we both just sit here with our asses in our hands, then we're both dead."

"Seems like a you problem." He was being slightly childish now; it was most definitely his problem as well. But some small part of him enjoyed taunting her. He imagined her cheeks heating and flushing with frustration.

He couldn't see her face, but he felt the way she was throwing daggers through the door. A smile tugged at his lips.

"It's also a *you* problem if you want to live," she shot back. He liked the feisty side of her. He wanted more. The monster in him stirred, sending a pleasing hum through him. Felix wondered if it traveled down the bond. The little witch squirmed against the door. *So it did.*

"I'd rather die than pretend to be a familiar." It was mostly true. He would play a familiar if it served him. Begrudgingly.

She scoffed. "Seems dramatic."

"It really isn't."

"You don't have anything else to live for? A wife? Living to see another sunset? *Anything?*"

He thought about it for a second. Other than his brothers back at the den, he didn't really have much. Women came and went; the only consistent ones in his life were his mother and his sister Eimi. Eimi called him a slut, but he preferred the term *Catanova.* But he always made sure the women he slept with were taken care of. They always came first, and hopefully multiple times, and walked away satisfied. If he had an Uber rating for being a good ride, it would be five stars.

He cleared his throat. "Nothing of the sort, kitten."

"Don't call me that."

"Don't call you what?"

"*That.*"

"I won't call you *that.*"

"You're impossible!" She let out a frustrated groan that only widened the smile on his face.

"Thank you."

"Wasn't a compliment," she grumbled.

The other side of the door went silent for a moment. He was enjoying this far too much. The strange feeling in his chest had grown; he couldn't tell where the monster or the bond began, and she ended. He could feel her on the other side of their golden tether, mulling over ideas like one takes a sip of wine to taste the flavors—something he always thought was pretentious; wine all tasted the same. Clamping down on the connection, he tried to sever it from his own feelings. He hated how foreign it felt, how, even on the other side of the door, he could feel her every expression, every crease on her forehead as she thought of a solution to their predicament. And what a predicament it was.

"*Please* pretend to be my familiar," she pleaded.

Something about the way she said *please* made his cock jump. He loved it when a woman begged for him.

"After all that thinking, that's what you came up with? Begging?" He was curious where she was taking this.

Her voice sounded strained as she spoke. "It's the best idea I have. It's going to take time to figure out how to break the bond."

He thought for a moment. "Then we get off the island and go back to my den. They will figure it out there."

It wasn't the worst idea. He was influential enough to convince the den not to kill her in the name of figuring out how to unbind them. But something else still gnawed at him, too. How was it possible that she had found a ritual to bind a shifter to her like a familiar? It *shouldn't* be possible. Although now that he thought about it, if he did play her familiar, he could gain access to places no shifter had ever gone. There could be useful information hiding within the depths of this school, and more especially about how she had found a book that could summon a shifter. A cold feeling drenched over him. If a witch with no familiar could summon a shifter as powerful as him...what if they all did? What if they already were?

"Are you insane?" she said, responding to his plan.

"Quite."

"The wards will incinerate you," she pointed out.

A smirk formed on his lips. He wouldn't be incinerated. There was an art to crossing through wards, one that he had perfected. However, because they were on a fucking island in the middle of the Celtic Sea, that would be a problem. Shivers ran down his spine as he thought about that much water in one place.

"Lucky?" she said, a pleading tone in her voice. He bristled at the sound of his pet name.

"It's *Felix,*" he corrected.

"Fine. Felix." She sighed. "Please, just give me some time to figure out how to break the bond and get us off the island. But I need you to pretend to be my familiar."

He shut his eyes and leaned his head back against the door —a sensitive lump was on his head. *Did she drop him when she pulled him in here?* As far as plans went, well, it was the only option. He might as well see if he could get off this island alive, even if it meant dragging her back to his den and hoping they didn't kill her first.

He knew their history, and so did she. Shifters and witches had never gotten along. Tolerating each other was a bullshit way to put it. They often just stayed out of each other's way, apart from his bounty hunting. Because when they didn't, someone ended up dead. There had been many wars, some with no clear cause, and many reasons for them to hate each other, but really, it just came from instinct. A natural-born desire to eradicate one another.

After the last war, humans decided they didn't love all the death and destruction, which was fair, so when they had the technology to do so, they banded together to try to take us out to have some peace. As they outnumbered shifters and witches ten to one, they almost succeeded in killing both species. Shifters made a deal with the humans, and now, we were at their beck and call. Witches, being witches, did not—hence why they were restricted to their little enclaves until they got a deal of their own to hire out their magical powers. They always put their pride before survival.

Humans trusted shifters far more; they needed them, and have since deployed shifters as a special military, filling in gaps where humans couldn't. There was also the sideline in bounty hunting like he specialized in. Otherwise, shifters kept to themselves and to their own land, slipping in and out between the territories.

Unfortunately, the human world realized it still needed witches. They possessed powers such as healing and certain types of magic that were just not available to shifters. It was a delicate game they all played; the peace among all three hung by a thread.

That thread was looking pretty fucking frayed right now.

"How long?" he asked her.

"A few weeks, maybe more."

It was an awful idea, but it was the only one they had, and as much as he hated playing pet, he had to get off this island. Alive.

"Fine."

His sensitive hearing picked up the skip in her chest as he said it.

"Really?!"

"Yes, now open this fucking door before I change my mind."

In the split second before he could react and readjust his body, the door opened, and his back hit the floor with a thud. A bright blue-eyed witch stared him down, trying not to laugh at his splayed posture on the floor.

She went to help him up.

"Do not. Touch me."

She held her hands up in surrender.

Felix dusted off his knees and his bruised ego as he stood.

The witch took a step back from him and then held out her pinky finger expectantly, a human custom to swear an oath to one another that she must have picked up from some human TV show. He only looked at the pinky finger and then back up at her, not moving a muscle.

"Truce?"

"For now."

Sighing, she took her hand away. "Right, no touching, got it."

Ten

Avery

There was no known way to break a bond, and no known way to get off the island. She would need a dozen lifetimes to figure out how to do that. But a few weeks alive was better than dead today. She needed to figure out something, and between the shifter and the university, one would be the death of her.

Tiredness racked her body as she slugged herself into the bathroom, locking the door behind her. It had been a fucking day.

She turned on the witch lights, their gentle hum a blessing to her ears. The small bathroom was illuminated under the warmth of the lights, the copper fixtures so shiny they were almost blinding. Her favorite part of the room was the circular window above the bath; it was just high enough so that when she was taking a shower at night, she could watch the stars go by as she lost hours to the water. It was the only place in the academy she felt truly safe.

However, there was no safety tonight. Her bedroom held a shifter, her sister was suspicious—her fault—and her plan was a steaming pile of horse shit.

So not only did she need to find out how to unbind a shifter, she needed to find out a way to get him off the island, *and* come to the horrifying acceptance that she would end up never leaving the island. Or dead from treason of bonding a shifter.

Just *fucking* fantastic.

Stripping off her robe, she let it drop to the floor and kicked it into the wicker hamper. Stepping into the bath, she turned on the shower, cursing as the cold spray hit her already frigid skin before it finally warmed. Under the stream, everything fell away. If there was a pure form of magic, it had to be water. The source of all life. Even the goddess made them from it. Something powerful enough to drown you, yet gentle enough to cleanse you, that was true magic. The silver moon shone through the window as she looked out through it, losing herself to the stars. Warm water drummed against her skin, almost loud enough to drown out all the noises of the world. Except the single creak of a door still made it past.

She stilled, instinctively folding her arms to cover her breasts from the silent intruder. Yet, when she looked into the darkness beyond the bathroom, there was nothing. She swore she had locked the door, but all she could see was just a sliver of her barely lit dorm. Thinking she was hearing things, she ignored the noise and went back to her shower, letting the water run over her face.

The noise came again, louder this time. The bathroom door creaked open like it had been pushed. Then she saw him, sitting so still she almost missed him. A cat stood at the threshold of the door.

Felix was watching her in the shower.

It took her a moment to realize that in the shock of it all, she had left herself entirely uncovered this time. Her arms dangling by her side like useless limp noodles, leaving her as stark as the day she was born. His eyes raked it all in.

"It's rude to stare, little witch," a voice said into her mind. Not *a* voice. His voice. The feeling of it slithering through her head wouldn't be something she would get used to quickly. The goddess-honest audacity of this shifter astounded her. Her? She was the one who was staring?

"Get out," she hissed at the cat.

"Make me."

He very well fucking knew she couldn't get out of this shower without giving him a full show.

"Can you not?"

"Not what, witch?"

She'd officially lost her mind. She was arguing with a shifter while butt-naked. Maybe she hit her head and died, and this was some version of hell. Out of all the things that had happened today, this felt like the worst. She moved to cover herself with the shower curtain, the water still drenching her and sticking her body to the thin fabric. Felix's eyes dropped down for a second before meeting hers again. *That little shit.*

"Do not—" She gestured wildly with her hands. "Watch me in the shower." She fumbled for words that didn't sound ridiculous. A low rumble came through their connection, something that sounded awfully like a laugh.

"You wanted me to be your familiar. I go where you go," he teased.

That was so wrong on so many levels. This wasn't what she meant, and he knew that.

"That doesn't mean you can just watch me while I'm naked."

"I'm naked too, if that helps."

It really didn't. If a cat could look smug, he did. She let out an exasperated sigh. If she wasn't dead, this had to be some sort of fucked-up dream that she would wake up from any second now. She closed her eyes. There were too many knots in her mind, too many strings of problems that she didn't know where to start to untangle.

Using the shower curtain to cover herself, Avery leaned forward toward the towel rack, yanked the towel off it, wrapped it around herself, and slammed the door in the pervy cat's face. One problem sorted. Sort of.

She dried herself off and brushed her hair in silence, reveling in the small moment of peace that life had afforded her.

A scratch sounded at the door. Then silence. Then another series of increasingly urgent scratches. Was he seriously fucking scratching at the door to get in? Avery's mouth parted, and then clamped shut again before she stalked over to the door and opened it, expecting to find a small cat staring up at her. Instead, she found nothing. Felix licked his paws on her chest of drawers, the complete picture of nonchalance.

"Something bothering you, witch?" he said.

This was going to be a long few weeks.

Avery didn't get much sleep that night, and neither did Felix, she guessed. He had stayed on the armchair in his cat form in front of the fire, readjusting every few minutes. It was a tense sort of calm, one where neither of them was comfortable in the other's presence. They were, after all, natural enemies who had been shoved into a dorm room and forced to work together. Every so often, she would open her eyes, only to find him staring back at her.

Morning light poured through the curtains, illuminating the room. Dust motes drifted through the air, dust bunnies darting out to snatch them mid-flight. A bunny crossed over Felix's paws, and he went to swipe at it before stopping short, letting the magical creature run away with a few of his hairs that had found their way to the ground.

"What are they?" he questioned, paw still hovering.

"You don't have dust bunnies in...wherever you're from?"

"No, we don't have magical dust bunnies in London."

The shifter was from London? She had pulled him from that far? She supposed it wasn't the most far-fetched thing in the world, given that she had pulled a shifter into a bond. Did the bond have to choose such an asshole, though? Surely there were nicer shifters.

"Were you there when I, you know, summoned you?" she asked, playing with the threads in the duvet.

"I was having a cocktail in my courtyard before you so rudely interrupted me."

"Sorry," she said sincerely. It must have been a rude awakening. She imagined him sipping on a piña colada with a little umbrella. The thought shouldn't have brought a smile to her face.

"What are you smiling at, witch?" He scowled.

And just like that, the grumpy cat put her in a sour mood again. A scowl formed in its place.

"Classes start today," she told him.

"And?"

"*And*"—you sassy bitch, she didn't add that—"I am due to present my familiar today, otherwise I'll get expelled."

The cat sat silently for a moment, contemplating. "*Fine.*"

She sucked in a breath. Thank the goddess, he hadn't changed his mind. One day at a time.

Avery got dressed in the bathroom, this time putting a chair up against the door so he couldn't open it with whatever shadow magic he had. It wouldn't stop a shifter, but it made her feel better.

From what she knew, unlike witches, shifters were born with their magic; they could use it from birth, and often they were incredibly powerful. There was a caveat to that, though; they burned out quickly if not careful. It took an immense amount of control and concentration for a shifter to channel their magic without letting it flare up and become incapacitated for days. She heard that sometimes when they truly lost control of their emotions, they supposedly turned into literal monsters. *Never mind* that she had heard that from the fanfiction, and that they had done *other stuff.*

Felix jumped down from the armchair. *"After your classes, we begin hunting for a cure to our... infection."*

Out of all the insults that have been hurled toward Avery, that one was potentially the worst so far. An infection. The way he said it made it sound like she was some sort of venereal disease. *Asshole.* If she were an infection, she would be far more interesting than gonorrhea.

Once she had gotten dressed and her bag packed, she opened the door to the hallway, the cool air rushing in. Other students in her year level meandered through the dorm hall, making their way to the first day of class. Felix's ears flattened as he sniffed the air that wafted in. Slowly but surely, he took a few steps toward the open door, one paw in front of the other. When he reached the door, he stood on the threshold. Avery went to move her foot toward the back end of him, giving him a small nudge out the door.

He hissed at her. *"Don't rush me, witch."*

Avery rolled her eyes.

A single paw touched the threshold, then, by some miracle, the cat committed to walking through. She shut the door behind him so he couldn't change his mind.

Felix looked around cautiously, sticking to the wall as they walked beside each other. She had thought all shifters were brave, or at least they were cocky enough never to be fearful. But it seemed he was cautious. And he should be; he was surrounded by enemies.

The more they walked, the more relaxed he got, except for when he walked past an enforcer, and all the hairs on his body stood up.

Maybe. Somehow. This would work out. Although deep down she knew she was just delaying the inevitable, once she broke the bond—if that was even possible—and put this behind her, she would have nothing. No one. She would be truly ostracized. Loneliness was a feeling she was already used to, even in a family, even with a single friend. She still felt the soul-crushing weight of having no one in her corner but herself.

Her father had been. Until he died. Which Avery thought was quite rude of him, to be honest. Even though it had only been a year, his face slipped from her mind. The wrinkles that crinkled at the edges of his blue eyes disappeared, replaced by her mind's rendition of what she thought they might look like, like an artist painting from memory. When she looked at the photos, it was almost like looking at a stranger. At least his soul remained, the essence of who he was, which was kind and gentle, always stuck with her.

The walk across campus was torture. Each step brought them closer to the lecture hall, closer to dozens of witches who would sense something was wrong. Who would know? They had to know. Her heart pounded in her chest. Maybe this was a terrible idea. Maybe she should just turn herself in right now. She wondered if they would kill her on the spot or whether they would ship her off to Anoddun, the magical version of Alcatraz. Shivers raced down her spine at the thought.

Rain misted across the quadrangle, turning the fallen leaves into a treacherous carpet of red and gold. First-year students giggled in groups and admired the senior students' familiars that sauntered past them: a fox here, a raven there, even a small dragon circling overhead.

Avery hung back until they'd all moved on.

"Your heart is pounding," Felix observed. *"I can hear it from down here."*

"Shut up," she muttered under her breath, earning a curious glance from a third-year student.

They passed the statue of Cerituen in the courtyard, her stone face eternally judging, and guilt twisted in her stomach. What would the goddess think of what she'd done? Binding a shifter, her mortal enemy, and parading him through her sacred halls when witches had died to get rid of them?

"You look like you're about to vomit."

"I might."

"Please don't. I'd rather not have to be bathed again."

Despite everything, a nervous laugh bubbled up in her throat. She quickly stifled it, but not before Felix made a rumbling sound, one that could have been a purr or could have been a laugh. Were they getting along? *No*, it was far too early for that.

The entrance to the great hall loomed ahead. Towering arches gave way to spires, the intricate patterns blurring together as the cool rain fell against her skin. Enforcers eyed them up and down, one of them readjusting the grip on his rifle, which made Avery's heart almost explode. But they did nothing, only stood there like ever-present statues.

When she was a child, Avery had once asked her mother why they were always there. She had only replied, "*To protect us.*" From what Avery had never seen. There hadn't been a single incident on the island that warranted their intervention...until now, she supposed. Most of the enforcers just waited to be deployed to a post as elite human security, patrolling luxury compounds. Witches had no purpose anymore except to be a pawn to the highest bidder. It was quite depressing, really. The culture of witches was beautiful, but Avery thought, we had come so far from how we were meant to live, or what we were truly striving for. Instead of being a coven, we were pitted against one another, shamed for not being the best among our peers. From what she had read, it hadn't been like that. Something had changed amongst witches for the worse.

The enforcers opened the arched doors for them, Felix's ears flattening as he went past. She could almost feel the amount of self-control it was taking him not to hiss at the enforcer. Before they entered the grand hall, they took the set of stone stairs to the right, climbing them to the professor's office.

She knocked on the door three times and stepped back, waiting for it to open.

ELEVEN

FELIX

A DULL, SHIMMERING GLOW WEBBED THE DOOR THAT the little witch knocked on. It was a protective security ward, this specific one, he presumed, surrounded the campus. There was also an *almost* impenetrable one around the island.

Slipping through the wards was second nature to him now. It would be a piece of cake. He assessed the one at the door. Yep. Standard variety witch ward. But before he could react, before he could use his magic to slip through it, she opened the door and shoved him, pushing him through the web of light.

Perhaps because of the bond, perhaps because they'd gotten fucking *lucky*, the ward had regarded him as a regular familiar. The fact that even the wards thought he was a familiar vexed him immensely, *and* not even a single enforcer had batted an eyelid. Humiliating. He would come back later to destroy this ward on principle.

An older witch beckoned them in. A professor, he guessed, based on his attire. Circular-rimmed glasses fell down his nose, a long salt and pepper mustache, and beard. The man couldn't be more cliché if he tried.

The professor looked the witch up and down before his eyes landed on Felix. If the professor noticed anything off about Felix, his face gave nothing away, just a stern line drawn into his mouth. Behind him, a phoenix picked at its flaming feathers, and one of them floated down gently before turning into ash before it hit the polished wooden floors.

"Well." The professor's voice was gruff, likely from the years of smoking, if the stank of his office was anything to go on. He moved behind his desk, but didn't sit, only bracing his hands against the table.

"What do we have here, Miss Alarch?" he said, looking down his nose.

"I've summoned a familiar," she said nervously, her hands fiddling with each other behind her back. "Sir," she tacked on.

Felix watched her, almost palpitating now, his chest tightening along with hers. Perhaps they wouldn't even last the day before they got caught. But the real question was: *Why the fuck did he find her nervousness so cute?* Felix physically shook his head to rid himself of the unbidden thought that most definitely wasn't fucking welcome in his head.

"I wasn't sure you'd be able to do it," the professor quipped, his tone far too condescending for Felix's liking.

The witch's face flushed red as she struggled to maintain eye contact. "Thank you, sir."

Thank you? *Thank you?* Felix let out a low growl, and the professor arched an eyebrow. He wanted to rip it off his face. Why would she say thank you to such a brazen insult? Felix would never stand for it.

Shame surged down the bond. Shame that wasn't his.

Feeling her emotions wasn't something he would like to get used to. Feelings in general were quite foreign to him; shoving them into a dark hole and beating them into submission was his preferred method.

Instead of letting the little witch's emotion overwhelm

him, he focused on something much simpler, like the witch professor in front of him, head on a platter. He imagined it in vivid detail, his instincts starting to kick in as his claws extended onto the dark wood. It had been a while since he had taken such simple pleasure in killing a witch, one that was far overdue. Simpler times.

In the last year, he had taken out a dozen witches who had been under diplomatic immunity. The last one had turned a human woman into a toad because she had said the wrong thing around a particularly angry witch. He wouldn't mind adding a few more to that tally.

"What a fine familiar you've summoned." The professor's booming voice shook Felix out of his trance, his ears flattening against his head. "A cat will do you well."

She only smiled back at him.

"Put a collar on him, and you can attend class, Miss Alarch," the professor said.

Collar?

These witches wanted to collar him?

Over his dead fucking body. Or theirs. Preferably theirs.

The professor pulled out a black collar from under his desk, which had a nametag in the shape of a heart on it, ready for engraving. To Felix's horror, the professor held his hand up to the collar, running his fingers along it to adjust it to be cat-sized. The hair on his back rose at the sight of it.

"Have you thought of a name for him?" The professor's eyes didn't leave what he was doing.

"Lucky," she replied with no hesitation, the ghost of a smile forming on her face.

"You're going to pay for that, witch," he hissed into her mind.

From this angle, it looked like she was chewing her cheek as if not to laugh. This was no laughing matter. This was an atrocity. A collar. Leashed to a witch.

"Lovely choice," the professor said with a strained smile as he engraved the name into the heart.

It was almost enough to tip Felix over the edge, to make him shift on the spot and rip both their hearts out of their chests for the sheer audacity of it.

The professor shuffled some papers around. "Make sure to tell your mother as well; she will be pleased to see you've finally gotten a familiar."

She took the collar from the professor and moved to put it on him. His back arched, hair standing straight up in an almost mohawk-like fashion.

"Don't you dare, witch," he said into her mind.

But he couldn't do anything in front of this professor. She knew it too and took advantage of the poor cat he was. *Traitor.*

She slipped the collar over his head to his displeased rumble. He truly was a pet now, and this collar signaled it to the world. How his brothers would *laugh.* They had no idea the sacrifice he was making for them right now.

The professor dismissed them, and they walked down the steps to the entrance of the lecture hall, that damned collar announcing him with every step—*jingle, jingle, jingle.* Each note added to a murderous rage that simmered under the surface. At the bottom, the witch hesitated outside the threshold, fingers twitching at her side. Her peers stared as they passed her. First to her, then down to him, snickers and disbelief left in their wake.

"Having second thoughts, witch?" Felix asked.

She spoke under her breath. "About a thousand of them."

Out of all the witches he had met, none of them was quite as anxious as she was. Most witches he met were cunning, salivating at the thought of killing him. This one seemed like she would tremble killing a fly.

"You've made your bed, witch, now you have to lie in it."

She rolled her eyes. "Inspirational."

"I try."

She pushed the arched door open, its handles creaking with the effort. She held the door open for him, as she should, as shifters were far superior to witches, despite the fucking collar that jingled an entirely different song.

The grand hall was layered with rows of wooden benches fitted with desks made of the same bark. Stained glass windows threw light around the room, drenching it in red. It was fitting for the witches, as bloodshed seemed to be their answer for everything. Witch lights hummed and hovered above them. Small familiars lay about in the classroom, the sound of jingling collars grating on his ears. At least the big ones weren't here.

There was chatter among the students, but slowly, all the sounds in the room died, and all eyes focused on them. The witch put her head down, avoiding eye contact with the snickering or bewildered students. There were at least a hundred of them in the hall, their small familiars hovering around. The big ones were tethered outside. Thank God, because he didn't feel like becoming dragon chow today. A ferret he could take in a fight in his cat form, but dragons could barbecue him in one roar. A strange urge overtook Felix. He was levelheaded—mostly—but the way they looked at her made a coil tighten in his chest, one that threatened to snap if any one of them made a move against her. *Fucking bond.* He shouldn't care what they said about her; actually, he should relish in their whispers and insults. But *he* wanted to be the one to insult her, to make her mad. None of these cockwombles could ever come up with an insult worthy of the little witch.

They ascended the aisle until they reached the back. She took a seat next to a friendly-looking classmate whose crow gave Felix a wary look that made him want to spit on it. But he wasn't a llama, and likely couldn't get away with it, so he held back.

Perhaps I will spit on her. The thought brought hundreds of images flashing through his mind of the little witch on her knees. *No. No. Absolutely fucking not.* Only if she asked. *No, Felix, still not then.*

His heart jumped as the girl squealed, giving Felix the fright of his nine lives, but it was enough to release him from the shackles of his impure thoughts.

"Oh, my goddess! You summoned a familiar!" she said in an annoyingly high-pitched voice. Felix had the urge to send out a shadow and smother her. "When? How?"

"Yesterday," the little witch said. "Yep, turns out I was just saying one of the words wrong the whole time." It almost looked painful for the lie to flow from her tongue.

"Those old language words are such a pain, aren't they?" the witch said awkwardly. "Can I?" she asked. Felix tensed as the friend reached out slowly toward him.

"No!" The witch's response came fast. The other witch jerked her hand back, confusion flashing across her face. "Sorry, I mean, he's still adjusting. He doesn't like strangers," she said in a panic.

Felix proved her point by hissing, showing a flash of white fangs. It wasn't an act. He would bite; he had done it before, and he would do it again. He loved the taste of witch's blood on his tongue. Probably too much. *I want to taste hers again.*

NO.

Nope.

The friend's crow squawked in alarm, flapping its wings and sending a gust of air over them.

"Oh. Right. Of course." The friend settled back in her seat, still smiling, but the warmth had dimmed slightly.

More students filtered in, and with them came the stares. Some curious, some disbelieving, some outright hostile. Realistically, they should be happy that their peer had succeeded. Perhaps for some reason, they thought she was a threat, or they resented her when they'd written her off already. Humans and witches were far too predictable, but he asked her anyway.

"Why are they staring at you, little witch?"

She didn't reply, but her mouth set into a hard line to indicate she was listening. It occurred to him she probably didn't know how to speak down the bond. He hadn't known it was something he could do either with a witch; usually, it was something reserved for shifters within the same den, but for some reason, it had worked in the same way with her. Unfortunately, he would have to teach her. A wrongness bled within him. He shouldn't be teaching a witch anything to do with shifters. Mind speak was reserved for families within dens, for mates, but in this case, it seemed necessary.

"If you want to speak to me, imagine you are speaking to me in your mind," he explained to her like he would a child shifter back at his den.

She pondered what he said for a moment. *"Can you hear me?"*

He shivered as the bond hummed at the connection, enjoying her angelic voice sliding over his mind. *It's just the bond*; *it means nothing.*

To distract himself—or to hear her voice again—he teased her, *"How did you imagine me in your mind? A cat? Human? Naked purrhaps?"*

A blush rose to the tip of her cheeks; she was so deliciously fun to tease. He watched as pink spread down her slender neck, fangs pulsating with the need to bite her. Mark her.

"I imagined you as a ghost after I'd murdered you," she sent back.

Any sort of heat that remained was thoroughly doused in ice water.

"Rude." Felix licked his paw, his tongue running over the

fur—a habit he'd picked up when he was trying not to let his rage overtake his rational mind.

"They are staring because we used to be friends until they shunned me for being familiarless and now they probably don't know what to do. They thought I would have been expelled," she said bitterly.

"That's awful." Felix faked sincerity, but it was enough to earn a sparkle of hope from the little witch's eyes as he looked at her. *"Every witch is a waste of space. They shouldn't have made you feel so special."*

Her face fell. If he weren't in his cat form right now, he would be grinning ear to ear. She was so easy to rile up. Despite the slightly dire circumstances, it was the most fun he had had in a while. The back of his mind warned him that it was becoming *too* fun, and Felix was an addict of fun. It was the only way to relieve stress from his job. He dabbled in many addictions, and he should be afraid of the little witch becoming one of them.

The professor who had suggested to collar him—and was now inscribed on his kill list—cleared his throat as his dark crimson robes swept behind him. His phoenix familiar flew in after him, finding a perch next to the lectern as he approached.

"Welcome to your final year!" His voice carried across the space. There was something about him, apart from just being a witch, that had Felix's teeth setting on edge. He continued, "You stand here today because the goddess has found you worthy. Because you proved yourself capable of the bond that separates witch from mortal."

The little witch sank down in her seat, crossing her hands over her chest.

"This year, you will train in all three houses." He left the lectern, putting his hands behind his back. "You will be tested." He stopped, looking right at the space where she was. "And should you fail, you will not graduate. You will not join your peers." He held out his arm, beckoning forth the massive phoenix. "Caerwyn has no room for weakness, not anymore."

Felix didn't care for the way the professor looked at the witch, his nostrils flaring as if he were a dragon, claws digging into the wood of the desk he sat on.

"When you graduate, you will be placed in a house you are best suited to, and you may be deployed to a human territory or in service to the university."

For the rest of the class, the professor set out the witches' fourth-year schedule. Their days were to be split up into physical training, healing, and history, which, Felix thought, was likely where their witch propaganda would be smushed into their little pea brains. It was what caused all the problems in his territory. Their ego was always the death of them.

The little witch was starting to nod off. Her palm held up her head as her lush lips parted.

"Are you dreaming about me, witch?"

It jolted her awake. "Shut up!" she said aloud to him. The whole room turned to look at her. She sank into her seat even lower, the blush once again creeping across her freckled face.

Oops.

Twelve

Avery

After her mortifying outburst in class, Avery wanted to hide in her dorm and recover from the morning. Bed was always the answer.

But no, Felix demanded, very rudely she might add, that she take him to see the book she had used to summon him, and to see whether there was an undo to her unfortunate doing of summoning the rude familiar.

They walked through the arched doors of the library. She relaxed, and Felix looked at her inquisitively. The walls of books upon books gave way to the grand vaulted ceilings that had become her second home, to study, yes, but also to hide, because there weren't any problems a library of books couldn't solve. Avery knew that if anyone ever used the line, "I want to build you a library," she would instantly fall in love. They kept walking until they came across the dusty corner where she had found the forbidden book.

Before her eyes, the little black cat in front of her gave way to a towering shifter, his ears flattening against his head as he stretched his annoyingly defined biceps above his head, the collar nowhere in sight. It took everything in her not to say, *"Biggggg stretch."*

She tried to look away, she really did. But her eyes were as glued to him as a horse straight from the factory. Swirling tattoos disappeared under his black shirt, one that gripped the planes of his muscles far too well. It was almost distracting enough to forget the fact that he had shifted in front of her, in a public place.

"What are you doing?" Avery hissed under her breath.

"It's fine, witch, I can hear anyone coming from a mile away."

It most definitely was not fine. What if they got caught? Her hindbrain told her it didn't matter because he was just so lovely to look at. Stupid prehistoric brain.

"Why can't you just stay a cat?" she pressed.

He gave the same look as a pissed-off cat. "Try shoving yourself in a tiny glass box all day and see how you feel. It becomes uncomfortable after a while."

She huffed and crossed her arms. "Fine. Just promise me you'll shift back as soon as you hear someone coming."

He held out his pinky to her. Hesitantly, she took it with her own. In a split second, he yanked on it until their faces were mere inches apart, enough that she could feel his hot breath fanning her face and her heart rattling around like a cracked-out bird in a cage.

"Pinky swear," he said in a fake-cute voice before letting her go abruptly enough that she stumbled back into her chair, her ass hitting the wood harder than she would have liked.

Oh, so he can touch her whenever he wants, but she wasn't allowed to touch him. *Bastard cat.*

"Why did you put it back in the library?" he said, changing the subject, while Avery's heart was still lodged in her throat.

"What?"

"*Why did you put—*" he recited in the old language.

"Stop with the old language! It's sacred to us!" She also hated the way it sounded delicious sliding off his tongue.

He smirked. "Shame, it's a beautiful language."

"I didn't want to get fees," she admitted, somewhat painfully. Her book return success rate was immaculate, not even a forbidden book could mess that up.

"How would you have gotten fees on a book you stole?"

She sighed. "You don't understand—the librarian's owl sees everything; it was the one that helped me find it."

Felix raised a brow. "The owl pointed it out to you?"

She furrowed her own. "Yes, why?"

"Interesting," he said. "Who does the owl belong to?"

"The librarian."

"Hmm." Her eyes flicked to his neck, a flutter forming in her stomach at the way his throat bobbed up and down. "Where's the book then?" he asked.

Narrowing her eyes at him, she walked past and started climbing the ladder to the top, where the book should have been. Instead, she found an empty shelf and a dust-free rectangle. Even the dust bunnies had moved out. She looked around at him, confused, then glared.

"It's not—Are you staring at my ass?" She looked down at him from the ladder, folding her skirt against her skin to obscure his view.

"What if I were?"

"Well..." She wasn't sure what she would do; she hated even more to admit that she kind of liked it. "Stop it."

He looked her in the eye with a lazy smirk plastered on his face. *Asshole*.

"The book isn't there."

His smirk fell away. "Well, it didn't just fucking grow legs and walk away, did it?"

Avery searched the rows of books high and low, searching for any sign of the giant forbidden text that, honestly, should stick out like a cat among mice. There was no sign of it. Her memory wasn't fantastic, but she knew she had placed it right back where she found it.

I bet those dust bunnies ate it just to spite me.

Did someone take it? She raked her mind for answers. If they knew, then why hadn't they turned her in yet? None of it made sense. All of it made her brain hurt. She loved a good mystery, that was why she loved riddles so much. But there was nothing to go off, no definitive logical answer to this puzzle that was forming.

"Do you think the librarian could have taken it?" Felix questioned.

Avery shook her head. In all her years here, she had only ever seen the librarian move once from her chair. The librarian was ancient. Her wrinkles had wrinkles. She didn't want the witch beauty treatments they sold to the rich humans. The only time that she had seen her moving was only a few feet away from her chair, and it took her almost a full day to get back. She had always been on death's doorstep, but out of pure spite, she survived day after day.

She wasn't ruling it out. It could be a farce. Maybe it was just some horrid skin suit she wore around the students while she astro-projected her spirit around the library. Shivers skittered over her spine at the thought of it. The librarian hadn't been crossed off the list.

She pondered who else it could be. "I think someone planted the book for me to find."

"You're only now catching on? I expected better," he said, trailing the books with a finger.

Avery's hands balled into fists at her side, nails digging into her palms. "Fine, shifter, who do you think it is?"

"Shouldn't you be consulting your crystal ball?"

She rolled her eyes. "Shouldn't you be eating children?"

"Really?" he deadpanned. "What stories have you been reading about shifters?"

Definitely not shifter porn. Not at all. She crossed her arms, trying to hide the blush creeping along her face. "We don't use crystal balls."

"And we don't eat children. Seems like we have both been told porkies." Felix's tail thumped the edge of the bookshelf.

It was annoying how good he was at getting under her skin, and it was annoying how good he looked while he did it. She hadn't had the *attention* of, well, anyone, in over a year—apart from fictional men. And she had never been in the presence of someone so frustratingly handsome. He was defying everything shifters were supposed to be. Witches talked about them as if they were ugly, bloodsucking beasts. Humans didn't seem to mind them; in fact, they didn't mind them at all, given the things she had read about them. They had far more respect than witches ever did, and quite frankly, they had done nothing to deserve it. Why were witches confined to their islands unless they had a visa, while shifters got to roam free? When she asked her mother about it, she'd said humans and shifters unjustly hated witches. That the shifters had conned the humans into making them glorified prisoners for their own agendas.

She envied the shifters for their freedom.

She yearned to see the world for herself, to see something different from the metaphorical four walls of the island. A healer was a start to leave, but the one thing she took away from the professor's lecture today, which she'd half-slept through from exhaustion, was that she would be 'deployed.' The word stuck with her. She wouldn't have a say in where she wanted to go; she'd be told.

Still, it would have to be better than her current culinary and tourist limitations. She wanted to try something different from the cafeteria food or the meager restaurants that littered the island. She didn't care that they supposedly hired the best witch chefs; she wanted to make up her own mind about what was good and what was bad. She wanted to stand in the shadow of Stonehenge and smell the oil paint at the Louvre, not just scroll past them on a screen. Her days were a monotonous blur of the same.

It was pretentious motivation, and she should be grateful for what she had. But gratefulness didn't get her closer to chicken nuggets, so fuck it.

Out of the corner of her eye, she spotted movement.

An army of dust bunnies appeared from under a bookshelf, carrying a tome like servants carrying a royal carriage. Somehow, their little bodies made of light fluff could carry the thick leather-bound pages with surprising ease. Felix shot her a look to make sure he was seeing the same thing she was and hadn't started randomly hallucinating.

Avery kneeled to meet the small creature's height, which was minuscule. Had they been the ones to hide the tomes? *Little bastards.*

But when she got a closer look, the book was unique. This leather was worn smooth, the crimson coloring faded to a lifeless brown. The gold embroidered markings looked similar at first glance, but the old language was different, older somehow, the symbols more intricate and harder to parse. But she still recognized it for what it was: a book of riddles.

She picked up the tome from the dust bunnies that hopped back under the bookshelf. Except for one. It stayed, rearing on its hind paws, asking for a pat, which Avery complied with, using her pinky finger to give the small being a scratch on the head.

Avery blew off the remaining dust from the book before putting it on the table in front of them. She opened the first page, the leather creaking and cracking. It had been a while since it had been opened.

"Well?" Felix said, leaning in as she flicked through the pages.

She shook her head. Each one was blank, except for one verse in the center. A smile formed on her lips. Regardless of what it meant and why the dust bunnies had given it to her, one riddle was enough to excite the inner child in her. A riddle was a problem she could solve. Unlike the rest of whatever clusterfuck her life was going on.

Her fingers traced the words. Did the goddess want her to solve it? The very idea seemed preposterous. But a bunch of bunnies had just marched it to her—it had to mean something.

"Why are you smiling like that?" Felix asked.

"Because I love riddles."

"Oh, yeah?" He had the same grin as a Cheshire cat plastered on his face. "I have a head but no face. I have no legs, yet I stand tall. I can be hard, but I have no bones. I am often hidden beneath a hood. What am I?"

Avery couldn't help herself.

"PENIS!" she said it loud enough that the whole library could have heard before she slapped a hand over her mouth, her cheeks warming at the outburst.

"You're disgusting," she said through muffled fingers.

A dark chuckle made her blush for a whole different kind of reason. His fangs glinted in the witch lights. How would you kiss with those swords in your mouth?

Avery's blush deepened as the thought of Felix kissing her played out like a lewd movie in her mind. A dappling of heat spread through her core as she pressed her thighs together to stop it from spreading further. She refused to be turned on by a shifter; there were plenty of fine witches who would indulge her once this was over. Perhaps she should take Callum, the sweet enforcer, up on the date. She needed a release that her own hands couldn't satisfy any longer.

She ignored the shifter who was still chuckling to himself about his terrible riddle. She turned to the book to concentrate on something other than him. Was this the goddess's will? But why? Why would the goddess want her to be bound to her enemy? Or maybe the dust bunnies just knew she liked a riddle.

The enemy cut through the noise of her thoughts. "How will a book of riddles help us?"

"I don't know how it will help." She only knew that her gut was pulling her toward it. And not just because she wanted to solve the riddle.

"Fantastic," Felix said sarcastically.

"I think the goddess wants us to solve it."

He narrowed his eyes at Avery. "Are you well, like, mentally?"

"Not when you're around," she bit back.

Felix smirked. "I tend to have that effect on people. Or they drop their panties for me, it's one or the other, really."

Dropping the book on the table, she flipped him off, only for his smirk to twist into a devilish grin. She ignored him and tried to translate the first line of the riddle.

"To be freed is what you seek," she said in the old language.

Her breath caught in her throat; Felix's eyes widened as they locked on hers.

"I think you might be onto something, little witch," he said in the old language. It sounded otherworldly coming off his tongue; he spoke it so fluently. Even better than her, and she had had countless classes dedicated to just the language.

She was always taught that shifters couldn't understand their language. She tried racking her brain for anything else she remembered being taught about shifters. They were dangerous, incomprehensibly powerful magical beings that could shift into animals. Involuntarily, she laughed.

Felix gave her a look. "What's so funny, witch?"

That pushed her over the edge into full-blown hysterics. For the first time in a while, she laughed. Really, truly, laughed. The shifter looked at her like she was a woman possessed. He probably thought she was, and that only made her laugh harder. This whole situation was absurd. It was like the start of a bad joke. Shadows slithered out from him, wrapping themselves around her chest and squeezing. Not enough to take her breath away, but enough to stop her from laughing and focus on breathing instead.

"I'll ask you one more time. What is so funny?" he said, punctuating each word.

A small giggle escaped. She couldn't help it. "It's just, when you think of a shifter, you think of a dragon razing a city, or a griffin terrorizing a village. You don't think of a tiny cat."

"I'm not tiny," he retorted, crossing his arms.

"You kind of are."

He rolled his eyes. "My tiny form could kill you."

"Death by a thousand surface-level scratches. Sounds like a horrible way to go."

A shadow slipped around her neck and yanked her forward, close enough to him that she felt his warm breath against her, the heat in her core returning like a catching wildfire. The shadow tightened against her neck, cutting off her air supply. "Does this feel surface-level to you?"

She didn't know what stupid part of her possessed her to taunt him further, but she did. "Doesn't…" She breathed in a strangled breath. "Count."

Felix rose slowly, not taking his eyes off her as the shadows continued to writhe across her. His eyes darkened as he leaned on the table, claws lengthening and digging into the wood. A shadow forced its way through the small gap between buttons, tickling the fine hairs on the skin of her stomach. What she should have felt was fear. Maybe it was the lack of oxygen, but the shadows started to feel *good.*

A small involuntary moan left her mouth as one made its way to her breast, lightly grazing the hardened buds of her nipple. *She shouldn't be enjoying this.* Yet the wetness pooled between her thighs anyway.

Splinters started to pop up from the wood as Felix dug further into her favorite table. He looked as if he wasn't even breathing, his eyes transfixed on hers as they met in a feverish dance of predator and prey. His nostrils flared. As if the moan hadn't been enough to signal to him that she was reveling in the touch she had been starved of for so long, he could smell her too.

His shadows faltered, no longer as strong as they were a few minutes ago. Another moment passed, and they fell. He slumped back in the chair, his hands shaking as Avery's ragged breathing filled the space.

He looked crazed and starved as he said, "I need food."

Thirteen

Felix

The library had left them nothing but more questions. Felix, now back in cat form, the collar jingling, padded beside her to the dining hall. He gazed at the rows of witches all dressed in their pretentious red uniforms. Some had their familiars sitting in chairs, others were lying at their feet. A female witch closest to the front had a fox on the chair next to her. The bright orange fox had a white bib with "cute as fox" written on it, wrapped around its neck like a baby, while it happily awaited the witch to feed it a piece of steak.

Kill me now.

Other witches talked amongst themselves, their familiars obviously too large to fit in the dining hall.

A witch walked past them out of the dining hall, holding his head high. He just would be the type of guy to have a couple of buttons undone. His sooty wolf lagged not far behind, eyeing them with curiosity, at least at first. Suddenly, the wolf stopped in its tracks. The witch paid them no attention, but the wolf's nostrils flared as it lowered its head, amber eyes dilating as if it had found its prey. Before Felix could react, it lunged toward his rear and tried to sniff his ass to get a better scent. He hated dogs but one that close to his ass was just *too* far.

Twisting away, a hiss ripped from his throat as he bristled his fur to make himself look twice his size. There was nothing he could do in this form unless he wanted to give himself away. The wolf froze, and cocking its head, it studied him. It knew something was wrong. Of course, it knew. For a familiar, it was surprisingly quite smart. He primed his body to shift, ready to run if that's what it came to.

The little witch put her body between them, even as the wolf snarled toward him, baring and gnashing its teeth at her.

What are you doing? She was going to get herself killed. Not that he cared about her in any way, shape, or form, but who knew what the bond might do if she died. Who knew what kind of magic she fucking used on him?

Felix rushed between her legs, hissing and flattening his ears.

"Fenris!" the witch shouted out from somewhere behind them. "Heel."

Like an obedient pup, the wolf immediately sat down. It had the gall to look innocent, even wagging its tail a bit when his witch paid it the slightest bit of attention. It was truly disgusting. And to think that was what was expected of him. Maybe dying wouldn't be the worst thing in the world if it meant he had to show his belly to the enemy. He wouldn't die humiliated.

"I'm so sorry about that," the witch said, his voice as smooth as his polished loafers. "Fenris is... protective." The witch scratched the back of his head in a way that was meant to be attractive, but made Felix want to upchuck a furball on his shiny shoes.

She smiled. "It's no problem." She waved him off as if she hadn't almost become a chew toy.

The witch's attention lingered on her a second too long,

looking her body up and down in a way that made Felix want to do the kind thing like releasing his eyes from their sockets. And God help him, the way he smiled at her hovered at the back of his mind, like an unreachable itch. A low growl rumbled through him. He clamped down on it, but it was too late. She looked toward him, concern knitting her eyebrows.

Fuck.

What was happening to him? This stupid mutt and his stupid witch were far too close for his liking. His fur raised as blood roared in his ears, begging him to shift and rip their dumb heads off. Except, the only dumb one right now was him.

This was the bond. It had to be. It thrummed between them, her anxiety buzzing through him as if she had kicked a bee's nest and sent them after him. His mind wrestled with his body, instinct winning over logic. But his body didn't care. If the witch took even a step closer, he would lose control.

"See you round, Avery." The witch said it like a promise, and somehow, by the grace of God, Felix kept it together until he sidestepped them and walked off.

The little witch gave him another concerned look.

Using his paw, he signaled to keep going.

Scents of meats and spiced wine filled the air as they wound around the tables. Saliva pooled in his mouth. It had been days since he had last eaten. His stomach rumbled at the thought of it. A juicy chicken leg was not far away, and there was nothing better than ripping a piece of meat off the bones. Maybe it was a leftover from their ancestors, a piece of carnal history he would be eternally grateful for.

The further they walked, the more her unease slithered down the bond. As they passed familiars, each animal turned its head. Some sniffed the air, others hid, and some even growled. They all knew he was different somehow, a threat.

The witches seemed curious, then turned away. Dumb witches.

The little witch chose a seat at the very back, away from the proximity of others. It was far enough away that no one could notice them.

"Why are they reacting like that?" she said, speaking into his mind.

"They know greatness when they see it."

It was a deflection, and she knew it. Rolling her eyes, she dumped her leather bag next to her. The thud of it was enough to surprise him. There must have been at least ten books in there, stuffed in like a clown car. It was the epitome of pretentiousness. A laptop or a phone carried the world of knowledge at her fingertips, and she had both, yet she carried around troves of books instead. This whole place was pretentious.

"Stay," she said, getting up to go get some food.

His fur bristled. This was truly a humiliation ritual. What the hell had he done to deserve this?

Students continued their dull chatter, their heavy silver forks clanging against gold-lined bowls. They feasted on soups and breads, meats and fruits, all sorts of delicacies that made his stomach rumble. She slid a tray onto the table, the plates piled high, the scent wafting under his nose like a poisoned temptress. Saliva pooled in his mouth from his traitorous body. He wanted nothing more than to refuse anything given to him by a witch, but with the way his body growled, at that point, he would have eaten the ass out of a low-flying duck.

The little witch picked up a bowl of something he hadn't seen before and set it in front of him.

Kibble. Cat kibble. Mystery meat packaged into hard rocks. She'd brought it back from the familiars' food buffet section of the dining room. Kibble, bird seed, whole goats for the dragons, and other shit, he supposed.

Absolutely the fuck not.

"Is this a joke?" he spoke into her mind.

She flinched in her seat, still not used to the intrusion of his voice. Her eyes went wide as they met his, realizing he was completely serious. Shaking her head, she pushed the bowl closer toward him, as if it would somehow change his mind and coax him to eat the abomination she had put in front of him.

He pushed the bowl to the side of the table. Close enough that it lingered just on the edge.

"Give me the meat, witch."

She shook her head fervently, as if he had asked for her left limb instead. "It's what all familiars eat," she whispered, looking around as if not to get caught talking to herself, too nervous to remember to speak into his mind. Not only was she a witch, but she was now a liar, too. That fox had been hand-fed meat just before. Not just meat. Steak! He put a paw on her plate, pulling it toward him. She pulled it back just as easily. Curse this tiny body. It would have been easy to take it back in any other situation, but using his powers here was too risky.

"You could at least say please."

"Shifters do not say please to a witch." He would never compromise his morals for a morsel of rotisserie chicken.

Instead, he used his powers of annoyance. Letting go of the plate, he walked over to the bowl of kibble that he had pushed to the edge of the table. The witch followed him with her eyes, realizing too late what he was about to do.

"Don't," she whispered.

With a simple nudge, the bowl fell off the table. She lunged for it, but was a second too slow before the bowl shattered on the floor, sending kibble scattering. So much for keeping a low profile. But he wouldn't live like this. Not when meats were within reach. And just for good measure, he pushed a glass of water off as well. To really drive the point home.

They stared at each other. He glared. She glared. Dozens of witches watched the glare-off. She heard giggling.

Finally, with an exasperated breath, she pushed her plate of meat before him, opting to take a large swig of her red wine instead.

Felix purred. A small victory. The first of many.

He chowed into the scrumptious thigh meat with the fever of a man who hadn't eaten in years. The little witch had a disgusted frown on her face that only went deeper when he started to crunch on the bones. It only made him do it louder.

THE FIREPLACE CRACKLED AS THEY SAT IN AN awkward silence across from each other in the dorm. All Felix wanted right now was a glass of whiskey in a chair that wasn't built for a tiny witch. He draped his long legs over the Chesterfield chair, having pulled it as close to the fireplace as was safe. He always loved the warmth.

The witch sat in her reading nook, thumbing through the pages of the book which had mysteriously appeared on the backs of magical rabbits. She had spent hours trying to translate the cursive slop that vaguely resembled the old language. How was this his life right now? He missed his pub, watching rugby with his brothers, and sunning himself on the rooftop when the London skies allowed it. He missed having sex. It had already been a week since he had been buried inside someone, and that was far too many days to go without. If this went on any longer, he would have to hide himself in the bathroom and get himself off. *The horror.*

Silver light streamed through the window as the willow rattled softly against the panes, casting patterns that danced over her freckled skin. He watched her stir with a morbid sort of curiosity. He watched as she bit the end of her pen between her luscious lips, and just for a moment, he wished it were his cock. She was wearing her pajamas—shorts and a thin cami. The way it hugged her body made his attention linger. He had to admit, it was a nice sight to behold. The moon illuminated another sliver of light onto the smooth line of her stomach. It was a cold night, even with the fire, and he was particularly taken with the way her nipples puckered through her shirt. A low, involuntary purr vibrated in his chest before he could stop it, and the bond thrummed in answer.

The way the little witch had moaned for him surfaced in his mind. Would it be the worst thing in the world to use her body while he was here? He shook his head to rid himself of the thought. No, he would *never* do that. Not after what they did to him. To his father.

The bond was fucking with his head.

Witches were disgusting, he told himself, as he dragged his eyes away, jaw tight, trying to mask the anger in his voice with boredom. "Has the magical bunny book told you anything about breaking this bond yet?"

With one hand, she shut the book forcefully enough to move strands of her long hair away from her face. "I told you, the *book* has a riddle in it that I think the goddess wants us to solve."

"Yeah? And I'm the Queen of England, huzzah." Felix quipped.

She rolled her eyes. "I'd like to hear if you have a better idea."

"I don't."

Felix rested his head on his palm as he looked over at the studious witch. "Let's see it then."

She moved from the bed and kneeled to the side of the armchair, passing him the book. He tried not to think about how much he liked the sight of her on her knees. He thumbed through the pages until he reached the riddle.

She translated the old words, smudged together in a barely legible script of loops and curls. If the goddess wrote it, she had terrible handwriting. Or the bunnies had gotten to it first.

He studied it for a moment, but deciphering metaphors was never really his thing; he preferred people to say what they fucking meant. So instead, he handed it back to her, trying not to look at the line that disappeared beneath her shirt. "Haven't the foggiest."

She gave him a *look*. "Helpful."

"Have you tried Googling it?"

"You think the answer to a magical riddle would be on Google?"

"Perhaps," he purred.

"Perhaps not. The sacred text isn't on Google. And if the riddle is, that takes the fun out of it. You should know that."

"Know what?" he questioned, head cocking.

She smiled. "That it's not about the reward, it's about the chase, the thrill."

"*Touché*, little witch."

Moving from her knees, she crossed her legs and studied the book some more, repeating the riddle out loud in the old language. *"Freedom is the thing you seek, to come to me and speak. A crown I carry, but not a queen I am. Still, I sit upon a high-seat of red and green."*

"Your pronunciation is terrible."

"Shut up," she retorted.

"A tree?" She thought on it for a second, "Yes! I think that's the answer."

A smile of pure childish delight lit up her face, enough for the edges of Felix's mouth to tug upward before he smothered it behind a hand, literally wiping it off his face. She was infectious in more ways than one.

A nail tapped against her chin as she spoke. "It must be the oak tree in the forest."

"That narrows it down," he said sarcastically.

"It does actually, there's a particular tree in the forest—"

"Witch?" Felix interrupted.

"What?"

"When."

"When what?" she repeated.

"When did I ask?"

"*Asshole.*" She seethed.

She closed the book with a slap and carried it to her bed. Furiously, she plaited her hair and ignored him. He stretched uncomfortably in the damn chair.

Perhaps that was a bit mean; she was trying to help them break the bond, after all. He could stand to be nicer to her. After all the witches he had met, she had been the least *witch* out of all of them. Although his sample size was quite small, considering every witch he had met had ended with their blood drained from their body and their head mysteriously missing. This was the first time he had really spent any time around one with a head still attached. He didn't hate it as much as he thought. It was still awful, though. At least that was what he told himself.

He wouldn't apologize to her; that was just too far. He leaned his head back against his hand, looking bored. "Tell me about the tree, if it is important."

She looked at him from her bed, side-eyeing him like a pissed-off cat before sighing and turning toward him.

"There is an oak tree in the forest, it's far larger than any of the others, and it has been referenced in our history from the beginning of the three tomes. If it was going to be any tree, it would be that one."

Felix clicked his tongue. "When do we leave?"

FOURTEEN

AVERY

RAIN BATTERED THE TWO OF THEM AS THEY LEFT the confines of the campus and walked into the forest of Caerwyn.

Felix couldn't hide the scowl on his face even in cat form.

Serves him right. The rain didn't bother Avery; she enjoyed it on most occasions, albeit tonight it was like frigid bullets as it whipped past them, like the sky was angry at them. It very well could be. She wasn't convinced that it was the goddess who had handed this riddle to her, but it was the only theory she had to go off.

When they were deep enough in the forest, Felix shifted out of his cat form. Wet hair clung to his face, and even the fluff on his ears looked sad and soggy. Avery almost felt bad for him. Almost.

At just past midnight, they reached the tree in question. Crooked branches twisted high into the sky, further than the eye could see. The oak tree swayed in the wind, its orange leaves clinging on until it got cold enough to shed. Avery almost wished she could do that. Shed herself every year. But all her leaves stuck to her, every evergreen failure, every joy refusing to fall from her tree.

The wind rustled the trees, sending scents of mossy wood that seemed much stronger than they were before. Her nose wrinkled. There was an undertone of something else, something that almost reminded her of when magic was cast.

"Now what?" Felix asked, his soggy ears twitching.

The rain had died down enough so Avery could safely pull out the book, her fingers shaking from the cold as she opened her phone for a flashlight.

She repeated the riddle out loud in the old language. Her pronunciation was still atrocious, but she tried.

Nothing happened. Not even a leaf fell.

The silence mocked her. What was she expecting? Fireworks congratulating her for getting it right? Anything to confirm her theory would have been preferable to the deafening silence. Maybe she had gotten it wrong.

They waited in the cold until Avery's teeth started to chatter.

"Stop that," Felix snapped.

"I can't help it, I'm freezing," she said, wrapping her arms around herself. That did absolutely nothing to ward off the chill. It was so cold she could dial a rotary phone with her nipples.

Felix only rolled his eyes and sent his shadows to her. She froze like a deer in headlights, thinking he was about to strangle her again. But instead, the shadows knitted until they formed a sweater. A strange, shadowy, moving sweater that felt like silk. *No wonder he made his clothes out of this stuff; it was fucking comfy, no overstimulating fibers in sight.* To his credit, it helped the bite of the cold. It was a bit sad to say it was the nicest thing someone had done for her in a while.

"Thank you," she said, her teeth chattering significantly less.

The more they waited, though, the more the shadows decided to start copping a feel, tendrils sliding and circling her breasts. Was he doing this on purpose? She stifled a moan. She never thought she would have to worry about a pervy shadow sweater, but here she was.

When the cold started to bite again, despite the sweater, she admitted defeat. This obviously wasn't the answer. It hurt her ego more than she cared to admit. She *never* got a riddle wrong.

Then, only a few steps away from the tree, they heard it.

A cackling sound sliced through the branches.

They stopped in their tracks, slowly turning to face the noise.

"Felix?" Avery asked, still trembling.

"I see it, witch."

They stared at the face now carved out of the wood of the trunk. A young woman with flowing hair of bark stared them down.

"Come closer," the voice hissed.

Avery went to take a step forward before Felix shot his arm out, gripped her wrist, and pulled her behind him, putting himself between the talking tree and her.

"What are you doing?" Avery whispered.

"Not walking blind into something that could be dangerous," he snapped back.

Avery hadn't even thought of it being a trap, too preoccupied with solving the riddle. The real puzzle was why he'd saved her.

"I don't bite," the tree crooned at them. To be fair to Felix, it absolutely sounded like the kind of voice that would bite.

Felix could have let go of her wrist by now, but for some reason, his touch lingered. The heat of his fingers wrapping around her cold wrist was a comfort she hadn't expected. It felt nice to be protected. His broad shoulders obscured her vision of the tree. Absentmindedly, she snuggled into his back, a solid wall of *him*.

The tree's mouth stretched into a smile, splitting the bark like a pair of wooden chapped lips. Avery didn't like the sight of it at all.

"You have done well to answer my riddle," the tree said, its voice otherworldly.

"Who are you?" Avery demanded in a small voice.

Felix's fingers tightened even more, warning her off saying anything further.

"Never mind that," the tree said. But Avery minded it very much. Was it the goddess? Had she heard Avery call her a bitch in her head? *Fuck*.

"To get what you seek"—the tree's wooden eyes gleamed with mischief—"a kiss must be freely given, and the tree a witness to your bond."

Felix stiffened beside her.

"Absolutely not," Felix said.

"No!" Avery snapped out of her shock. They looked at each other, then back to the tree. "There must be something else we can do."

The tree shook its head, a few leaves falling off its branches to the ground. "I'm afraid not. The tree wants what the tree wants." It let out a mournful sigh, as if the pair had made it sad. Why did it want them to kiss? That seemed like the very opposite of breaking the bond.

Felix finally let go of her. Her hand dropped, immediately missing the contact as soon as it left. He crossed his arms over his chest, and Avery couldn't help but notice the way they strained against his shadowy T-shirt. As far as shifters went, he wasn't terrible-looking.

She supposed a kiss wouldn't be the end of the world, especially if the goddess or some other strange entity that had taken over this tree wanted it—then it had to mean something, right? She couldn't tell if it was her horny prehistoric brain doing the rationalizing.

"We're not doing that." His tail swished once before it curled itself around her leg. Felix didn't notice, but the tree's eyes fell toward the movement, and then back up, its smile creaking wider.

"I don't take orders from a talking tree," he said.

"If you do not kiss, then you will stay as you are, stagnant, and possibly six feet under, who's to say?" the tree said.

Felix growled, the rumble in his chest vibrating against her chest, as his cat ears flattened against his head. "Are you threatening us?"

The tree made a roaring laugh. "It is up to you to determine your fate, shifter. I am merely the messenger."

Felix's jaw set hard, lost in thought. He wasn't seriously considering this, was he? Warmth crept up Avery's neck, replacing the gnawing cold along with a knot twisting in her stomach that wound tighter with each passing second.

"Fine." He turned toward Avery, and she did everything in her power not to let out a squeal. She felt like a wounded deer, stalked by a hunter when his mismatched eyes looked into her own. This was not happening. She wasn't about to kiss a shifter because a tree told her to? Was she?

"Let's get this over with," he bit out.

She was.

Her mouth said something different, though. "What? No—"

"Would you rather stay bonded forever, witch?" His voice was strained. Like he was holding back.

Avery swallowed the lump in her throat, suddenly in dire need of a jug of water. She had doubts that something as simple as a kiss beneath a tree would break the bond. It was worth a try.

"I suppose not."

It wasn't like she hadn't been kissed before, or done much more filthy things than that. But for some reason, being in front of the shifter made her feel entirely inexperienced. It occurred to her she didn't even know how old he was. He didn't look younger than her, and he certainly wasn't graying.

"How old are you?" she blurted out awkwardly.

The question took him back for a second. "Thirty."

She breathed out a sigh of relief, as if somehow that made kissing him any better.

They stood there only for a moment, looking at each other. The rain had slowed to a drizzle, droplets catching along Felix's dark hair, one particularly stubborn drop falling on his long eyelashes. His eyes suddenly formed into slits, making him look more catlike than ever before. His gaze dropped to her lips, his ears standing at full attention toward her.

Avery felt her heart skip.

Slowly, gently, he took her chin between his thumb and forefinger, forcing her to look at him. It was a ghost of when they had first met, yet the first time had been much more violent.

"It doesn't mean anything," he said. His voice was a steadying beat amidst the wind that seemed to intensify by the second. The scent of him surrounded her, calming her frenzied heart more than it should.

"Obviously," she choked out.

Felix leaned in, hesitating. His warm breath fanned her face, thawing the frigid skin. His lips were only inches away. Avery squirmed, trying to keep her arms by her side.

"Stay still, witch," he quietly commanded.

"Do you think we shoul—" She didn't get to finish her sentence.

Felix's lips crashed into hers. Not gently, but fervently, as if he had been waiting for this. Heat rushed through her veins like a wildfire, threatening to consume her at this very moment. At first, she froze, like she had forgotten how to kiss, her mind short-circuiting at the delicious feel of his satin lips asking for entry into hers. She parted her lips for him. The bond flared to life between them like a dormant volcano. Felix's hand slipped from her chin to wrap around her neck, pulling her in closer but not close enough that their bodies met.

Her hands stayed by her side, still obeying his command even when her body begged her not to. They were simply useless as she lost herself between his lips. She didn't care at that moment that they were being watched by a tree with a face, or that he was a shifter. She cared only about the sweet pressure that made her dizzy. His mouth was like a drug, only one taste, and she was addicted. *Those humans were onto something.*

A noise escaped her, one that only encouraged the ravenous beast within him further, because he pulled away for only a second just to sweep his tongue across her bottom lip, his fangs grazing them ever so slightly, sending delicious shivers down her body, and something clenching deep within her.

They should have stopped there. Felix's tail wrapped around her bare leg again, the sensation pulling a hitching breath from her mouth, which Felix swallowed with his own. She felt him everywhere, not just physically, but deep within her, their emotions demanding that they collide together. Fear, frustration, *need.* The bond wanted it all. It wanted to be greedy. It wanted to *devour.*

Against her better judgment, she let a hand loose, let it explore where it wanted to. Hesitant, she touched his chest, wanting to feel more of him than just his lips.

Felix jumped back. The cold rushed between them like an avalanche as Avery forgot how to breathe. Felix's shoulders moved up and down, his nostrils flared, pupils dilated so much that his eyes appeared black.

Avery gasped as her hand went to touch her swollen lips, the flesh still tender.

The sound of wood creaking brought her out of her trance, one she wasn't ready to leave. Two branches came together to clap, the leaves creating an orange rain.

"Good, good!" The tree looked delighted. Felix, however, did not. "There is a key high in my canopy. Retrieve it for the next clue."

"Was the key up there the whole time?" Felix questioned, his tail swishing violently, something Avery noticed he did when he was more than irritated.

"Perhaps," the tree admitted.

Felix rolled his eyes before turning back to Avery. "I will get the key. Can you look out for me?"

Avery was still too stunned to speak, her fingers lightly feathering her lips. It was the best kiss she had ever had, and it wasn't even real. Well, it was real, far too real. But it had been because a talking tree had asked them to do it. What she should have felt was disgust. Regret. Anything but the burning desire to do it again.

"Witch," Felix snapped at her.

Their eyes met, and for a moment, Avery swore his softened the moment her eyes met his.

"Mmhmm!"

Felix lingered on her for a moment, his eyes darting to her swollen lips, sending another fresh wave of fire coursing through her. Was this the bond's doing? Or her? She supposed it didn't matter. Regardless of where it came from, it was still there.

With surprising grace, Felix shifted into his cat form and leapt onto the tree, digging his nails into the bark to climb higher and higher. The tree winced slightly as its gaze traveled up with him.

He leapt from branch to branch, until it was almost

impossible to see his small form bleeding into the night. A spectral shadow retrieved a golden key, blended amongst the hues of pale orange.

A smile played on Avery's lips. She had been right. The riddle had meant something; it was leading them somewhere. Down what path she had no idea.

"If we solve the riddles, will you unbond us?" she asked the tree.

The tree pondered her question for a moment, looking up to the shifter and then back down to her. "Sure." It dragged out the 'e,' as if it were actually completely unsure. "As the riddle said, if it is freedom you seek..."

She could have sworn the damn cryptic tree was glaring right back at her.

Felix's voice rang through her mind, interrupting their staring contest. "*Witch?*"

She hated that he kept calling her that. She had a name.

What sounded like a pitiful meow made its way down the tree. *"I can't get down."*

Fifteen

Felix

He was stuck.

The little witch didn't bother to use the bond to talk. "You're joking."

"Unfortunately, I am not." It was painful to admit. He was a great climber—getting back *down* the tree, though, was another matter entirely.

A laugh escaped her throat. He was already embarrassed enough, and now she was laughing about it? *"Keep laughing, witch, and I promise to make you regret it."*

She doubled over in stitches. "You'd," she wheezed. "You'd have to get down here first."

Yes, yes, a real fucking knee-slapper it was. A shifter of his caliber should not be stuck in a tree, but heights were still something he was grappling with. Sometimes he could descend just fine, other times not so much.

The tree started to laugh along with the witch, the branches shaking so hard that he clawed onto them for dear life so he didn't fall.

"Shut up," Felix hissed, although he wasn't sure if he was speaking to the tree or her. Both. It was both.

After a minute of guffaw after guffaw, she finally managed to quieten herself, wiping tears at the edges of her eyes.

"What do you want me to do about it?" she asked.

He hated to admit he liked the sound of her name slipping off his tongue. He liked the feeling of her tongue in general. *Stupid fucking bond. Stupid fucking tree.*

"Just...guide me down. I can't see where I'm going."

He couldn't shift when he was nervous. He looked at the ground for only a moment, and the forest floor swayed as if it would swallow him whole. Heights usually didn't bother him, but sometimes the little fear became a huge one. He focused back on the witch instead, for some reason, even though she was technically on the ground, it was entirely less frightening. She moved closer to the trunk, tilting her head back until she spotted him. It was at least sixty feet off the ground—maybe more. Either way, if he fell, he would get seriously injured. His shadows could catch him, but sometimes they had a mind of their own.

"I can see you!" she shouted up, even though he could hear her perfectly fine with his sensitive hearing.

"Can you just...go back down the way you came?" she asked.

"Don't you think I would have done that already if I could," he hissed.

She decided to use the moment to her advantage. "I will only help you down if you promise to be nice to me for twenty-four hours." She crossed her arms.

That little witch. He was about to spew profanities at her, metaphorically rip off her head for the audacity. Felix wasn't nice. There wasn't a nice bone in his body. His pride cracked in his chest, but he wouldn't make it down without her; his depth perception was shit, the one drawback of being a cat. He can't believe he had to ask a witch for help. She had left him no choice.

"Fine," he bit out. *"Will you help me down?"*

"What's the magic word?"

"Now."

She rolled her eyes. The tree started to shake, his grip loosening on the bark as his claws desperately clung to the branch. *"I will turn you into logs, you stupid tree!"*

She tapped her foot. The tree didn't slow down.

"Okay! Okay, stop," he pleaded.

The rustling of the trees came to a standstill. *"Little witch, would you help me out of this tree?"*

She smiled, smug. At least he hadn't said please. He could keep that small bit of dignity for himself. The rest had been devoured like a pig on a spit roast.

Her voice softened ever so slightly. "I can do that."

He hated everything about this. Hated relying on a witch. Hated that he was bound to one. Hated that he had to depend on the very thing he was trained to kill. He wanted to go back to a time before he had met her. And most especially before he had that kiss.

He shook the thought away, its gravity threatening to pull him back into the memory.

"To your left," she instructed. "There's a branch you can lower your paw onto."

Felix started to lower his back paw, but he couldn't reach it. He held the key in his mouth as he struggled to find a foothold.

"Just a bit lower!"

He didn't want to trust her, but he did. He lowered his paw down enough to find the branch and climb down to it, his claws leaving marks on the bark on the way down.

"You're doing great!"

"Don't patronize me, witch."

"Being nice, remember?" she said as if she were talking to a child, and indeed patronizing him even more. She held too much power.

He didn't reply.

She continued to guide him down the tree, one branch at a time. But he made a fatal mistake. He looked down at the ground.

It was still high enough for his vision to swim. Suddenly, everything went blurry, his head dizzying as the world around him tilted. Up? Down? He couldn't tell. Her instructions flew over his head as his grip started to slip. He clawed back into the branches, but it wasn't enough; his foot slipped, and he fell.

He was going to die.

And the last thing he had done was being *nice* to a witch. Although if it were any witch, he was glad it was this little one.

He fell, and fell, and fell, waiting for the ground to catch him.

Instead, he fell into a cloud of gentle arms. The little witch had caught him.

For a moment, they both stared into each other's eyes, shock plastered on both of their faces. She had caught him, *saved* him.

Reality crashed over him like a wave. *"Put me down,"* he demanded.

She obeyed, dropping him with no warning. He landed on his feet, shifting as soon as he hit the ground.

"I told you not to touch me," he hissed.

"What? I just saved you!" she said.

"Cats always land on their feet; there was no reason for it." There was very much a reason for it. But he wouldn't admit it. He would have been too high up. There was a very real chance that he would not land on his feet, at least without injury.

"Whatever," she said, turning away from him. "Next time I'll let your ungrateful ass splatter on a canvas and sell it to a modern art museum for millions."

For once, he let himself smile. Truly smile.

"Thank you," he said.

The little witch turned her head to look at him over her shoulder. "You're welcome."

"Ahh, young love," the tree said.

"Shut up," they said in unison.

FELIX STRETCHED OUT IN THE LITTLE WITCH'S BED, trying to ignore the scents of cinnamon that were all her. The key was cold in his palm as he studied it, the inscription catching the light. His brows furrowed. *What the fuck?*

A bright-eyed little witch moved from the chair, shutting her book and getting in his space. "What does it say?"

He groaned inwardly at the thought of saying it out loud. Why him? Why couldn't the goddess have taken literally anyone else?

Exhaling forcefully, he read out the riddle on the key. "Twisted lovers surround her, circling an aching hole that has yet to be filled."

He looked up at the little witch, whose skin was turning redder by the second. For the last line, he didn't break eye contact, just to see what she would do. "If you want to find what you seek, open her legs and slip inside her waiting labyrinth."

Her throat bobbed. "It's so uh...lewd."

"Mmhmm." Interesting. Maybe the little witch wasn't as innocent as he thought. She rubbed her temples, like she was churning the riddle over in her mind. He tried to do the same, but when he thought about an aching hole that was yet to be filled—*fucking hell.* She was corrupting his goddamn mind.

After a minute, she yawned, covering her mouth. "I need to shower and sleep. I can't think about anything right now."

Her gaze dropped to where he'd sprawled across her mattress. "Can you get off?"

Felix raised his eyebrows.

"*Gross*, not like that."

Regardless, he wasn't moving. His neck hadn't ached this much in years. "I am not sleeping on that thing again; my neck won't recover."

"If you sleep as a cat, what's the difference?"

Felix looks to the chair, pointing, "Hard." He pointed back to the bed beneath him. "Soft."

She glared at him, unconvinced.

"Just because I can sleep as a cat doesn't mean I don't have standards. You try sleeping on the chair."

She scoffed at him. "It's my bed, shifter."

"And you're sharing it with me."

"This is ridiculous."

"It's quite *diculous*, actually."

"That's not even a word!" she said, storming off into the bathroom. She shut the door loud enough for the wall to rattle ever so slightly. The corners of his mouth tilted up. He hadn't smiled this much in years. He was known to be stoic at home. His brothers would make it their daily mission to say something funny enough to actually get Felix to crack. It never worked. But for some reason, the witch had been the one to do it.

The groan of the shower handles turning piqued his hearing. He tried not to imagine what she was doing in there *—probably washing her hair, you idiot.* Still, his cock jumped at the thought of her naked and rubbing her hands all over her body.

He shoved a hand through his hair, exhaling sharply and pulling at the damp strands to try to distract himself. A few days. That was all it had been. A few days, and he was already falling apart. His head hit the back of the bed, jaw grinding hard enough to crack teeth. Sharp nails twitched at his hands and feet. His shadows came out too, like they had a mind of their own and undulated around him. Impatient, restless. He heard the little witch humming a tune in the shower, a reminder that she was in there, naked, wet—he didn't like the wet part; he preferred making women wet. That was all it took for his hand to drop, palming the hard line of his cock through his shadow pants.

He rubbed against the fabric, the friction already too fucking good. He'd spent his entire life hunting them, ripping out their throats with his teeth. But this one? This one he wanted to taste first, to lick the crook of her neck before sinking claws into her jugular. The memory of the kiss pulled him back in, the taste of her. He wanted more, he wanted so much fucking more.

Just pent up. Means nothing. The lie tasted bitter as he freed himself from his pants, biting back a groan at the first bare stroke. He was already leaking; days without release had him trembling at his own grip. He stroked slowly, savoring the feeling of his own hand. *I wish it were hers.*

His hand moved faster now, imagining it was her playing with his cock, breath ragged through clenched teeth. Part of him didn't care if the witch saw him like this. Part of him wanted her too.

Close. So close, but before he could tip over the edge, the door opened.

He froze.

Sixteen

Avery

Scalding water washed over her skin. She almost liked the way it burned, the way it prickled. It was her place to go when the world became too much, letting the water drum against her skin, its droplets the only sound allowed through her mind.

The metal squealed as she shut off the water, taking her time to step out of the bath. It wasn't funny how many times she had eaten shit stepping out of it.

Using the towel, she dried off her body and looked around the bathroom for her clothes.

Fuck.

Her clothes were out there. With him.

She sighed, wiping a hand at the fog on the mirror. She would have to go out there.

Taking a deep breath, she opened the door. At least she would be covered in a towel.

With false confidence, she wrenched open the door and strode past the elephant in the room. Well, cat.

She didn't even need to look at him. Instantly, she felt his eyes on her, his intense gaze driving into her. She didn't dare look. Making her way to the dresser, she started to rifle through her clothes, grabbing anything she could that would cover her body.

Her spine straightened on instinct. She hadn't heard him move. Heat rolled off her back, evaporating the tiny droplets into a fine mist. He was right behind her. She went as still as a rabbit looking down a hunter's gun. He didn't touch her, but his hands gripped the dresser in front of her, caging her in between him. His hands were abnormally large and were white-knuckling the dresser. The wood groaned underneath the strength of it. Veins strained underneath his skin, almost as if they were ready to pop.

"What are you doing, witch?" His breath fanned her back as he spoke, sending a shiver down her spine.

She gulped. "Trying to find some clothes."

"That much is obvious." His voice was lower, filled with gravel, as if it was strained. Was she affecting him this much? "You just conveniently forgot your clothes?"

She nodded, lost for words.

"Are you trying to seduce me?"

"No." That was the last thing she was trying to do. Against her will, dampness pooled in her core. Her body reacted to a man being so close. Not a man, a shifter. A monster. Her breath came in short pants. He took a deep inhale through his nose, almost as if he were sniffing her, sniffing the air. Oh goddess, could he?

A muttered fuck came through him, the wood groaning even harder underneath his fingers.

A swell of emotions rose through her. Against all better judgment, she spoke. "Is it working?" Her own voice was strained. *Dumb, stupid brain!* Something flushed up and down her body. The feeling wasn't new, but the intensity dialed up immensely from what she'd ever felt before.

His body slammed into hers, pinning her against the

dresser. She felt the hard length of him against her—two little pieces of material separating them. She let go of the towel, the top folds of it coming away, exposing her breasts to the cold air. Her nipples hardened, the feeling of the wood enough to cause a small moan to escape.

His nails lengthened into black points, impossibly sharp claws sinking into the dresser, splintering the wood as he pulled against it. Her breath caught, the sight slicing through the haze of lust. This was Felix, a shifter. Was he doing this to her? Was this some kind of shifter spell he had put her under? She needed to get away from him.

He shifted slightly beneath her, his hard length creating a delicious friction that made her grind back into him, clouding any thoughts she had before. The bond flourished in her chest, the feeling almost a purr.

"Little witch, what would your precious university say about you grinding into a shifter?" He chuckled as he spoke, the vibration sending another jolt straight to her core.

The sudden thump of something hitting the window caused him to jump back. Her body instantly missed his presence. The cold seeped in quickly, shaking her out of the trance of lust she had found herself in.

What the fuck was I doing?

Using the distraction, she quickly gathered her clothes and darted into the bathroom, slamming the door behind her. Whatever that noise was, she didn't care right now. Shame burned her cheeks. Her breath came in rushed and ragged. The fresh memory caused a stir of emotions to rip through her. Her eyes darted around the room. She was alone.

She put a palm against her heart, willing it to slow. Intrusive memories came back from mere minutes ago, but she swatted them away like they were a pesky fly. She refused to believe she had submitted to a shifter like that. A moment of weakness, that was all it was. It would *never* happen again.

Dressing herself in her pajamas, she realized in her rush that she hadn't picked up any underwear. She slapped a hand against her forehead. Why was she like this?

She willed herself to pull herself together before stepping out into the room again, facing the very thing that had just unraveled her. Their eyes instantly met across the room. His head cocked, and his eyes narrowed, looking her up and down before quickly looking away. That one look was enough to send a flare of heat through her once again. *Fuck*.

Felix cleared his throat. "A letter came for you."

The thump must have been a pigeon hitting the window, a white feather lay at the bottom of the sill as evidence.

She walked over to him. The closer she got, the more the bond hummed in her chest, wanting her closer. She ignored it and held out her hand.

"You didn't read it, did you?" she asked.

"Why would I do that?"

"Seems like something you would do."

"You wound me." He faked a broken heart. "I'm being nice, remember?"

She rolled her eyes and opened the letter, unraveling the ribbon just as she had become unraveled mere moments ago. Her mind wandered for a moment. Did he feel what she did? Lose control like she did? Or was it some deluded game? That was the most likely answer. He was a shifter after all. She wouldn't let him get to her again. Her eyes flicked up to him. He stood looking out the window, his tail swishing in long sweeps, almost as if he was annoyed. He was as lost in thought as she was.

She peeled her eyes away from him and read the letter.

Dinner at the tower tomorrow, 6 p.m.

The bottom of the page had her mother's councilor

stamp, as cold and impersonal as she was. Why she still sent pigeons when there were phones, or even her sister and that dragon, was beyond her. A simple text would have sufficed.

But where would that have gone if that bird hadn't startled them? She sighed and chucked the letter on top of the desk. Her mother had definitely heard about her getting a familiar, and she had yet to present him to her. It had been something she had been actively avoiding. Something in her told her that her mother would know immediately that Felix was a shifter. Avery was a terrible liar. She rubbed her hand against her head, the cool of her fingers a slight respite to the giant headache that was forming.

The headache spoke. "Where are you sleeping tonight, witch?"

Her face fell flat, any remaining warmth flapping, just like that pigeon off, into the aether. Fluttering her eyes shut, she prayed to the goddess for a modicum of strength to get through this hell she had found herself in. She just wanted to graduate. She just wanted to be normal. Why had she been handed this difficult life?

"On my bed, shifter. Where are you sleeping?" she said.

"On your bed."

The audacity of males. Of any species, apparently.

"We're not sleeping together."

His fangs showed through when he smiled. "Yet."

Another flood of heat went through her. Absolutely the fuck not. Over her dead body would she share a bed with a shifter. Especially after that little moment they had.

"I didn't mean it like that," she hissed, the pink of her cheeks a dead giveaway.

"But you thought of it, didn't you?" He took a step toward her, somehow making the small room around them even smaller. "Now, and before."

"That will never happen again, shifter."

"We will see, little witch. We will see."

He clucked his tongue. He was still on the bed and had no intention of moving anywhere. *Asshole.* And unfortunately for her, he had decided that the most appropriate clothing for the occasion was a pair of boxers.

"You're not just wearing that, are you?" she said, gesturing to the boxers that moved like the shadow fabric he often tended to wear.

"Why, don't like what you see?" A lazy grin stretched across his face.

"No."

"Liar." His grin never faltered. "Don't worry, you don't have to see me in these much longer—I sleep *naked*."

Avery closed her eyes and swallowed, trying to fight the rising desire threatening to take her over. Again. She hadn't been this horny and repressed since, well, ever. And as much as the man was the most handsome thing she had ever seen, she did not trust herself to sleep next to him naked.

"We can share the bed—*if* you stay a cat."

"Deal." His smile was diabolical.

She waited for him to shift, and to his credit, he did. She crawled into bed, as he sat at the foot of it, curled up in a ball, looking like a peaceful statue; the only sign he was still alive was the gentle rise and fall of his chest and the slight jingle of a collar.

"Goodnight."

For the first time in a while, she felt peaceful, too, as she drifted asleep.

SEVENTEEN

FELIX

THE LITTLE WITCH'S BREATHING HAD EVENED OUT. Felix had waited until she was asleep to shift back, and god, she had a great ass. Her ass was going to be a problem. It took everything in him not to start kneading it like it was dough and get on with the mission he had set himself.

It had been a few days since he'd disappeared from the den, and by now, his brothers would have been losing their minds. He wouldn't be surprised if they weren't knocking at the wards already, but he hoped they weren't dumb enough to try.

Picking up her phone from the bedside table, he dropped into the armchair in front of the fireplace and typed in his brother's number into the keypad from memory. They weren't technically brothers; they were just a close group of friends who were leaders in the den. All of them were quite different, actually. Their den was made up of many different shifters, dragons, crows, basilisks, cats, griffins, and pegasuses, mostly. A fairly standard spread of species. His closest brother was Ciro—the one he called now.

The line rang twice before he picked up.

"Hello?" Ciro's voice came through, gruff and pissed off. He had woken up a slumbering dragon—*oops.*

"It's me," Felix said, low, glancing over his shoulder to make sure the little witch wouldn't wake up.

"Felix? What the fuck? Where have you been? Have you been sleeping with that porcupine shifter again? I told you he was into some weird shit."

"What? No. I'm on Caerwyn."

Ciro went silent. "Come the fuck again?"

Felix laid it out for him: the ritual, the bond, the riddles to undo it.

"You don't think she's your—"

"No. It's not possible."

"Yeah, well, last week I thought a bond between a witch and a shifter was impossible too, but here we are."

"Look." Felix pinched the bridge of his nose. "Do you have any ideas, or are you just going to continue being useless?"

"If you were here, I'd punch you for that."

"You'd miss."

"Fuck you." But it was a relieved kind of fuck you, the kind that came from knowing that your brother was safe enough to be an asshole. "Actually, holy shit." The sound of rustling sheets came over the line.

"What?"

"Remember that case I was working on where shifters were going missing?"

"Yeah?"

"I haven't been able to find a lead for months; all of them are dead ends."

Realization poured over Felix, something cold settling in his chest. "Until now."

He was one of the missing shifters. *This* was where they could be ending up. But if that were true, why hadn't any of them reached out? A phone call, a message—anything. Unless they couldn't.

What frustrated him more than anything, more than this witch, more than this absurd bond, was a question without an answer. Something almost feral in him refused to let it lie. It was borderline obsessive. It was also why, at thirty, he'd clawed his way so high up the ranks.

His instinct was right, though. Witches had something to do with it, and now, it pissed him off enough that he intended to find out what *exactly* they were doing with them. He felt a tingle in his balls that it wouldn't be good.

"Exactly," Ciro said.

"Tell me everything."

"It's been happening for over thirty years; all of the shifters disappeared without a trace, and we haven't heard anything from them. In the last week alone, three more have gone missing from the London Conglomerate."

Felix's tail went still as he sat up straighter, the armchair creaking under his weight. "Fuck. How many in total?"

"At least thirty," Ciro exhaled. "The human government swears they have nothing to do with it. The witches are as uncooperative as usual."

"Do they have anything in common?"

"Apart from them being from London and above the age of eighteen, no, there's not. Every single lead I've had has gone cold. I fucking knew the witches had something to do with it." He paused. "The witch you're bonded to, do you think she's behind this?"

He glanced at the little witch on the bed, at the way a hint of drool made its way onto her pillow. "No."

"Are you sure that's not the bond talking?"

"Yes." Felix's voice was strained, clipped. It was a fair question, but it still made him want to throttle him for asking.

Ciro made a low whistling noise. "Touchy."

Felix ignored him. There was no way she had anything to do with this—someone else was pulling the strings. Were there other shifters on the island? Were they bound to witches like him? Whether it was the goddess or someone else entirely, he intended to find out who was behind this. It was already personal, but this was a war against the shifters. They needed to solve the fucking riddle so he could question the goddess. It sounded insane. It also sounded like the most solid lead he'd had all week, which said a lot about his week.

Felix stiffened as the little witch stirred, rolling over so her back—her very nice back—was to him.

The dry drag of a cigarette came through the line. "Someone on that island knows something; you need to find out if there are others and how the fuck they're making them disappear."

"I'll investigate."

"Be careful. Eimi would murder me if something happened to you. She's already been hounding at my door every goddamn hour for an update."

The corner of his mouth pulled up. The small cat shifter was his rambunctious sister, his *actual* sister. "Tell her I'm fine, but for the love of god, don't tell her where I am."

"Don't worry, I won't, she would storm the island herself."

The line went dead, and some of the tension unspooled in his chest. It was good to hear from someone familiar. It grounded him in the insanity that had been the past few days, and Ciro, as insufferable as he was, had been it. Felix rubbed his temples. *What a shit show.* There were too many variables, too many questions.

Felix decided to be logical, just like he would in any mission. He approached it the way he approached everything —methodically, before the frustration could eat him alive. The only lead he had was a fucking talking tree, which was laughable on so many levels. But it was a start.

She still slept soundly, and he decided that now would be the best time to try to find some answers. He crossed to the window, unlatched it, and shifted. The sandstone bricks offered enough ledge to navigate him down without breaking anything. He bled into the shadows of an oak tree, his magic near invisible, and slipped past the enforcers who were conversing amongst themselves.

"Transfer students are coming tomorrow," a red-haired enforcer said.

"Really? Where from?"

"Lloer, Abermôr, Talgarth"

"Lucky bastards. I didn't get to go anywhere until I graduated."

"Yeah, I know. I'm meant to meet them at the ferry tomorrow to escort them."

Interesting.

No time to stay and chit-chat, Felix had places to be. He peeled away from the tree, sticking to the shadows and—

"Hey!"

Fuck.

Felix froze, one paw hovering above the ground. He turned his head slowly to see the auburn-haired enforcer jogging toward him, his fox familiar running after him. He didn't move. Running away would likely be suspicious, as familiars only had one mode, and that was blindingly obedient to witches. The other enforcer's hand moved to his rifle, a subtle movement, but one Felix definitely noted. He only had one option.

"What are you doing here, little kitty?" the enforcer said. *Barf.* The indignity. He crouched to Felix's level while the fox circled him with obvious curiosity. "Bit late for a midnight stroll, don't you think?" He grabbed hold of Felix's collar and read the nameplate.

"You're Avery's new familiar, aren't you?"

Fuck.

He had no choice but to do the most degrading thing he had ever done in his life.

He meowed. Pitifully.

The enforcer's expression immediately softened. "Poor little guy, must have gotten lost."

Felix did his best to play the part of a helpless house cat. Including widening his eyes and tilting his head so they twinkled in the starlight. This would be a memory he would never forget; it would haunt him when he tried to sleep at night. How low he had fallen.

This is the part where you leave me alone now.

"Aww."

He reached out slowly. *Don't touch me, don't touch me, don't—no! No!*

The enforcer scooped him up. Felix twisted, squirmed, made himself as inconvenient as physically possible, but he only held tighter. Every instinct screamed at him to shift, to kill this fucking witch and his fucking grabby hands.

"Come on, buddy, let's get you back to your witch."

There was nothing Felix could do but dangle helplessly like a furry potato sack in his arms as the enforcer carried him upstairs back to the dorm where he had just been ten minutes ago. There had to be a better way to move around than parading as a lost familiar. If he wanted to go anywhere on this Island, he couldn't risk being caught so far from his witch.

The enforcer talked at him while he climbed the stairs. "You know, I'm glad Avery finally got a familiar. I was worried about her. We all were, after what she went through last year."

Felix's ears perked up.

"She tried to stay strong after her dad passed, but anyway, I'm glad she has you now. She needs someone she can trust."

A wheezing cough escaped Felix. He truly had no idea.

"Can you do me a favor?" he said, scratching Felix's head. He gritted his teeth so hard he thought they might snap. "Can you convince Avery to go on a date with me soon?"

That was it. He had to kill him. Absolutely the fuck not. He would not watch his witch go on a date with him; *she is mine. She is—*

A knock at the door interrupted his spiraling thoughts. They both waited for a moment. But there was only silence from the other side. "Guess she's asleep, huh, buddy?"

He was not his buddy.

The enforcer grabbed a bunch of keys from his belt and found the one to her door far too easily. The enforcer creaked the door open and put him down at the threshold. Felix turned around and glared at him from the ground. It wasn't threatening by any means, but it made him feel better. That was positively the worst thing to ever happen to him. He wouldn't let anyone manhandle him again. An idea formed in his mind as he stepped through the door.

The enforcer lingered in the doorway for a moment, his gaze catching on the little witch longer than he could tolerate. "Sleep well, Avery," he said.

God, he was creepy. Felix didn't like the protective feeling swelling in his chest. He wanted to remove the enforcer's eyes for looking at her like that. Just before he was going to hiss and scratch him, the enforcer moved away, quietly shutting the door behind him.

Felix listened as the footsteps faded away and then shifted back into his human form. He ran a hand through his hair, looking at the witch who was blissfully ignorant of what had just occurred.

For a moment, he just stood near the bed, watching the

rise and fall of her shoulders. The dappled silver moon threw light over her freckled skin, enticing him closer and closer.

It was a terrible idea, but he did it anyway.

He crawled into the bed with her, lying down carefully so he didn't wake her. The scent of cinnamon reached him. He hated that it was actually comforting to him now.

Unconsciously, she turned around. He stiffened. He shouldn't be doing this; he should shift back into a cat. But as he watched her, her lips parted, he had the strange urge to kiss her again. To fill the space between her lips with his own. Instead, he just let the warmth of her breath against his shoulder be enough. Because that was all it could be. Because that had to be enough. Their bond would be broken, and he would be free to go back to...however he had been before.

Gently, he shook his head. That was all this was, just the bond calling out for its other half. It wasn't really him. For a few minutes, he would indulge it. He would shift back into a cat when he was about to fall asleep. Just a few minutes. Something spread within his chest, a foreign feeling. Whether it was the bond or not at that moment, he didn't care.

She shifted again, this time her hand finding his wrist. Instinctively, he wanted to rip it away. For a few moments, he did nothing but let it linger. Feeling the gentle touch of another that wasn't during sex. When was the last time someone had touched him like this? When was the last time he had let someone touch him in such a way? *It means nothing. I just don't want to wake her.* He told himself. Even while his thumb started to trace hers. Even when he moved so close that there was hardly any space between them.

Just a few more minutes.

EIGHTEEN

AVERY

AVERY WOKE TO SOMETHING HARD POKING INTO HER back, and a heavy pressure draped around her body; even her legs were cocooned in a soft, silky fur. Her eyes fluttered open, and the morning light poured through the curtains as dust danced around. Despite the dead fire, she was pleasantly warm and surrounded by the rich scent of pines and winter. It would have been easy to go back to sleep, just a few more minutes.

A hand flexed in front of her, one that was not her own. She stilled. *Felix was wrapped around her.* She held her breath in case any movement disrupted the shifter—one wrong move and his claws could find her jugular. She looked down as his tail curled in and out of her legs like it had a mind of its own and was stroking her for its own pleasure.

The shifter pulled her closer until she was flush with him. His *thing* pressed between her butt. Last night, she hadn't noticed the size of it, too distracted by, well, him. She released her breath, a small gasp escaping from her throat as she moved up the shaft.

Then she felt it, a rumbling against her skin, like a gentle motor humming through the mattress and vibrating down to her bones. Was he *purring*?

A laugh escaped her, one she had to stifle with a hand. Because even though she knew it was wrong, she didn't want to wake him just yet. She wanted to wait here in this entanglement of limbs and *other things*, for just a little while longer. Every bit of anxiety was sapped away from her as his purr thrummed through her body. It was wrong on so many levels. Yet, nothing in the world could have pulled her away at that very moment.

But of course, she had to sneeze.

She tried to stifle it, but her body had other plans. The beast that slumbered stirred next to her. *Shit.* She couldn't even deny that she was asleep.

For a moment, he clutched her tighter before his body went rigid, mirroring her own. "This hasn't happened before." He sounded confused, and unfortunately, his morning sleepy voice was as sexy as he was, and was doing something very unfair to her body.

"It's a first for me too, buddy."

"Do not call me buddy." His breath fanned against her ear, sending goose bumps skittering over her skin.

Geez, someone was grumpy in the mornings.

"Okay, *shifter*, do you mind letting me go? It's weird."

He grumbled something sleepy and annoyed that she didn't quite catch, but he let her go. She should have felt relief, but instead, she wanted him to come right back. It was a strange dichotomy in her mind that the safest she had felt in a while was in the arms of a monster.

Like the very sky was mad at her for even thinking such a thing, rain started to patter outside the window, the sun having stuck around as long as a father out to buy milk. Avery untangled herself and went to ready herself for the day ahead. She made sure the bathroom door was locked *and* that she brought her clothes with her this time to get changed. There couldn't be a repeat of last night. Of any of it. The kiss, the dresser, the cuddling. The cuddling somehow was the worst of all three. She was getting too close to this shifter.

When she got back, the shifter had fallen back asleep. Limbs tangled within her sheets, legs splayed, lips slightly parted, and sprawled across the bed like it was his own. One hand rested behind his head, while the other dangled off the bed. Cats slept a lot, she knew that, and he had seemed to get none lately.

Light on her feet, she padded to the bed. For someone who was deep in enemy territory, he looked remarkably blissful. She moved closer. His ears twitched in his sleep, almost like he could hear her coming.

She stood over him, admiring the beautiful specimen that he was. Shifters were always beautiful, in many ways. The books the witches had described them as ugly monsters—yet in every picture she had seen, and most definitely the infuriatingly handsome one in front of her—they were nothing of the sort. It made sense that they were so striking; after all, the things in nature that were the most beautiful were often the deadliest.

Absent-mindedly, she reached her hand out toward him. Because apparently, she had little to no self-preservation and was lured to her death as easily as a moth to a flame. Maybe the moths found the flame beautiful, and she understood them now more than she ever had.

She didn't get far. The shifter opened one green eye, the pupil slimming to a slit.

Fuck.

With terrifying speed, his claws closed around her wrist, yanking her from standing to straddling him within a millisecond, close enough that their noses almost touched. Once again, the hard length of him pressed into the apex of her thighs. It took all of her willpower not to grind into the man who was currently holding her captive.

"What," he hissed, "are you doing?"

There was no good answer for it. She had simply wanted to touch him. The bond thrummed happily in her chest, relishing the contact between them. Could he feel the pull, too? His hand tightened around her wrist.

"I told you not to touch me." His gaze hardened before dropping to her lips and back up again.

"I'm sorry, I wanted to wake you up. We're going to be late."

"There are other ways to rouse me."

"You already seem...uh...roused."

His eyes darkened. For a second, she thought he might pull her closer. Pull her into another forbidden kiss that she absolutely, definitely did not want. But to her disappointment, he let go of her wrist, letting it drop onto the pillow next to his head.

He didn't move her, though—his ears twitched curiously, and she had absolutely no idea what she was supposed to do with that.

"Get off me, witch."

Embarrassment flooded her cheeks. Right. Despite the bond that flared between them, it was stupid to think he wanted anything to do with her beyond her usefulness in breaking it. And it was what she wanted too. As annoyingly attractive as he was, she would never betray her kind like that. He was the enemy, and she would do well to remember that.

She cleared her throat and climbed off the bed, careful to avoid touching any part of him.

A knock sounded at the door. She looked back at Felix, who had already shifted. Adjusting her uniform, she crossed the room and opened the door so someone who was far too bright-eyed and bushy-tailed for her at this time of the morning could enter.

"Callum, hey." She gave him a short smile. She used to think he was handsome, and he still was, but when he measured up next to Felix, there was no comparison.

"I found your familiar wandering around last night, and thought you might want to know I brought him back."

She looked back at Felix, hoping he could feel the many daggers she sent his way. *Was he stupid?*

"No witch, not stupid."

Oops. She hadn't meant to say that into his mind.

"Thank you for returning him."

"It's no problem."

She looked at her feet, the silence stretching between them. "Well! Thanks for coming by." She went to shut the door, but he stopped her, putting his hand on the door above her.

"I, uh—" He scratched his head. Again, something she would have found cute before, but now she was just annoyed by it. Or maybe she was just getting her period. Men particularly annoyed her in her luteal phase. "Remember that date you agreed to? I was wondering if I could take you out tomorrow night?"

Shit. She had agreed to it.

"Ugh!" she said, pretending like she was annoyed. "I wish I could, but I have dinner with my family then."

He cocked his head, giving her a suspicious look. "Isn't that tonight?"

"Oh, right...Yeah, it is." An awkward chuckle escaped her. "How did you know that?"

"Your sister told me about it, I'm on her squad, remember?"

"Yeah, of course," she blurted out. "Well, then tomorrow's great," she said through gritted teeth.

Suddenly, she felt murderous. A feral urge of violence wanting to swing a bat at the enforcer's head. Until she realized, it wasn't her emotions she was feeling, it was *his.* Speaking of the little devil, Felix wound between her legs and tried to take a swing at Callum's leg.

"Bad kitty!" Avery scolded him, trying to swallow down the palpable anger searing in her veins that he was causing.

Callum smiled brightly, ignoring the cat. For the first time in her life, she wanted to punch him. Instead, she mirrored his smile, hoping she didn't look as pained as she felt.

"Great! I'll pick you up at six?"

"Mmhmm!"

Mist clung to the university grounds as the class walked toward the lecture theater. The path curved around a large lake to a sprawling grass field ringed by an orchard of oaks and apple trees before curving back around to the quadrangle, where they were headed. Maya walked beside her, as Felix trailed her heels as a cat. Avery swallowed. Until now, it had been easy to pretend that Felix was her familiar, but today she would be expected to perform magic.

"Have you been practicing?" Maya asked casually.

"Yup!" Avery lied through her teeth.

Her friend was far too nice for her lying ass and reassured her anyway. "I bet you'll do great."

The rest of the way to class, they caught up. Maya told her the latest gossip, how she had missed out on the latest episode of their reality TV show, how one of the swimmer's boyfriends had cheated on her. Avery half listened, nodding her head a lot and saying, "That's crazy," at least five times. Maya could tell she was distracted, but luckily, didn't pry. And that was why she loved her, even on the days that Avery hardly felt like a person, Maya wouldn't chide her for it; she would let her float off in her own world and hold her hand while she did. There weren't many people who would let you exist without it being just for their benefit.

The lecture hall loomed as her stomach dropped below her ankles. Many of her peers had been training for months with their familiars, and while Avery understood the theory, channeling from a shifter, if it was even possible, would be something else entirely.

She supposed she had channeled blood magic. Would it be so far-fetched that she could try to channel from a shifter? Getting Felix on board with the idea would be an entirely different mountain to climb. And it was a mountain she wanted to climb, in more ways than one. Ugh. Could she go an entire day without thinking a dirty thought? It was starting to feel impossible.

The students filed into their seats, Avery and Maya taking their spots near the window. Students talked among themselves while the professor strode in, robes swishing against the wooden floors. Felix hopped onto the table, gave a lazy stretch, and knocked her notebook off the table. *Asshole.*

"Good morning, class. Before we begin, we have some new additions to our year." He gestured toward the door. "Transfer students from our sister academies!"

Avery twisted her pen in between her fingers, looking at the intricacies of the stained-glass window beside her while fighting to keep her eyes open. Anything was better than watching the lucky bastards who strolled through the door.

She had applied for a transfer out of Caerwyn two years ago, but her mother denied it. She never thought that nepotism would work against her.

Felix passed out next to her, his belly facing the sky and his mittens stretched out, once again using any opportunity to sleep. It was strange sleeping next to an enemy. Although in some convoluted way, it was comforting. For over a year, she had been stewing in her own presence, a soup of loneliness. Somehow, sleeping next to her enemy had resulted in better sleep than she'd had for the last year. Was that fucked up? Probably.

Maya nudged her, forcing her to look back to the front of the class.

Her heart stopped for a moment as her gaze landed on the tallest one in the group. He was sporting a shit-eating grin. Her jaw hung open.

Felix, not cat Felix, stood in front of the class wearing a Caerwyn uniform with a Cheshire Cat smile plastered on his face and a black ferret on his shoulder. No ears. No tail. No sign of being a shifter at all. But it was unmistakably him. She looked back down at cat Felix, who somehow also had a shit-eating grin plastered on its face. She put her hand down on the cat, and it looked and felt like a normal cat, but when she looked closer, she saw the swirling patterns, a dead giveaway.

It was made of shadow. She looked back at him, her jaw still slack.

He eyed her from across the room, smirking, before tapping his chin with his finger. She clamped her mouth shut.

That rat bastard.

A group of girls murmured, craning their necks to get a better look. He sent them a devastating smile, his fangs no longer there. They gasped like the damn goddess herself had blessed them. If only they knew.

Standing next to the witches, he was a colossal mountain next to them. It wasn't unheard of to be so tall, but it certainly drew attention. They were meant to be lying low. What the hell was he doing?

"Students, please welcome the transfer students," Councilor Delis announced. "I'll leave you in the capable hands of Professor Bran. If you need anything, you know where to go."

She was the nicest of all the councilors; her demeanor was always warm and inviting. Avery often went to her rather than her mother when she needed anything.

The transfers found their seats, including Felix, who took the empty seat a few away from Maya and her. He pointedly didn't look at them, preferring to smirk at the girls sitting in the front row.

Jealousy festered in the pit of her stomach before she starved it of its oxygen and shoved it down to the deepest parts of her. She would not be jealous of a shifter. Maya looked over her shoulder, giving him a look.

Felix looked back at them, giving them a polite smile, before looking back to the front and settling comfortably in his chair. He was far too good at playing pretend. He played a familiar and a student. There wasn't a single hair on his stupid head that she could trust.

"Stop staring, little witch. You'll start drooling."

She rolled her eyes, ignoring the little comment. The man was designed to get under her skin. More than that, he was getting bolder. The question still played on her mind, though. Why the hell had he shown up looking like a witch, in uniform and all?

She sent that thought down the bond.

A small smile tugged at his lips. *"Wouldn't you like to know,"* he replied. She didn't jump at the sound of his voice in her mind this time. It almost felt like it was meant to be there.

"I would actually."

"What are you going to give me for telling you?"

"I have nothing to offer you."

"I could think of many things you could have to offer." He

looked down at her chest. *"I'm looking at two of them right now."*

"You're disgusting."

The professor interrupted their chain of thought sparring. "Today, we will be going over the basics of pulling magic from your bond." Some students groaned before the professor only raised a hand to silence them. "This year will demand greater precision in your magic, and you will need to pull from your familiar faster and better than before. Everyone, please follow me to the lab."

Pale autumn light filtered through the stained-glass windows of the laboratory. Wooden tables were strewn with open textbooks and medical tools while the hum of students chattering in the background continued.

Felix was several paces behind her, his eyes boring into the back of her head. Since they had become bonded, she was acutely aware of him at all times, something that was necessary for a witch and a familiar pair—with Felix, it was a giant pain in the ass. She wanted nothing more than to be oblivious to his presence.

Students filed in next to tables, and Avery took her usual spot, waiting for Maya to fill in next to her as she normally did.

But of course, of *fucking* course.

"Is this spot taken?" Felix said. The sound of hearing his voice out loud in public was far more disturbing than she thought it would be.

Avery turned to the shifter, cocked her hip, crossed her arms, and looked up at him with a scowl on her face. "It is actually."

He gave a polite smile; on the outside, it would look like he was nothing more than a gentlemanly student. But the words that came out of his mouth were anything but. "Move the fuck over before I make you."

A traitorous blush crept along her neck. She wouldn't risk

making a scene, not when she was already so scrutinized for her performance. Begrudgingly, she took a step back.

"Good girl."

She bit her tongue; there were so many things she wanted to say out loud that would not go over well with the professor, the first being *cockhead.*

Maya raised an eyebrow at her as she passed, to which Avery only shrugged as her friend went and found a place with one of the girls from the swim team.

The fake familiar Felix had conjured, a black ferret, played with a pen on the table, while Avery's fake familiar, who should have been Felix, slapped at it like a mouse. Even their shadow collars made noises.

"Why are you doing this?" she said into his mind.

"God forbid a man want a little independence."

Huffing, she gave up. Nothing serious ever came out of that man's mouth. Everything was a goddess damn joke. How they were ever going to unbind each other was a mystery only the goddess knew.

Speaking of the goddess, the tree played on her mind. The more she reflected on it, the more she thought it was almost impossible that it was truly Cerituen. It seemed too convenient. The golden key Felix had retrieved, and its engraving was another riddle that she hadn't yet figured out.

Felix's voice slithered through her. *"You seem unfocused. Are you thinking about me again?"*

"You fucking wish," she said, out loud.

Shit.

She looked up, her mouth slightly agape. Every single person had turned around to stare at her.

The professor stopped mid-chalk, turning slowly to look down at her through his glasses. If looks could kill, she would have smashed into a fine enough powder that one could snort like cocaine.

"Miss Alarch? Something to share?"

She dropped her shoulders, making herself as small as possible, fervently wishing that she could materialize in another plane of existence. The sound of Felix's laughter filled her mind.

Nineteen

Felix

The look on her face was *priceless*. He wished he could frame it. It was the cherry on top of the plan he had haphazardly thought out this morning. The witches' constant proximity was starting to grate on him, especially after he had been caught last night. He needed a way to move around without suspicion. Students had cover. Ergo, he was a student. Simple math. Never mind that he stood a head taller than every witch in the room and was far older than any student here.

Already he was pulling unwanted attention from the women in the class. Their giggling and staring, and worse, the whispers of the filthy things they would do to him. He had exceptional hearing, and they had an exceptional lack of subtlety. Truly, he didn't blame them; even with his best features glamored away, how could they stand to be in front of such a handsome specimen as himself without acting accordingly?

But the only person he was interested in hearing from at the moment was silent.

Her lips pursed into a hard line, glaring at the innocent

shadow beings on the table. So she was pissed. Fine. He could work with that. It was what he wanted all along, anyway, to not be reminded of her existence. Yet for some reason, it annoyed him that she was annoyed. And yes, he needed a better term than annoyed, but with the way she had his head frazzled, a dog could probably eat alphabet soup and shit out a better sentence than him right now.

"Healing the self," Professor Bran started, pulling their attention to him as he scratched his salt and pepper beard, "is one of the most important skills a witch can have before they enter the field." He cleared his throat, pausing for effect. "Before you can repair another body, you must understand the mechanics of your own."

He stopped at a student's station.

"The first stage of healing requires you to locate the wound with your awareness, not your eyes. Your eyes will lie to you. Your magic will not. A healer who cannot do this for themself is a healer who will kill her patients."

The little witch looked down as the professor's gaze landed on her.

"After all, how can you expect to help others if you cannot help yourself?"

Felix watched the teacher continue to move around the room, etching his face into his mind for when he eventually got around to killing him for the whole collar thing.

"Begin," the professor declared.

Metal clinked against wood across the room in a cacophony of noises as each student picked up a myriad of medieval-looking torture devices that were splayed out on the desks. He wondered what they could possibly use them for when healing was the main priority in this class.

They rolled up the sleeves of their uniforms, only to slice a thin line with a scalpel down their forearms. Blood welled to the surface, staining their palms. They moved in tandem as if they were spelled to do so. Some visibly winced, others didn't even blink.

So that was the reason. This was how they taught healing? It seemed extreme even for him. Surely there were better ways to learn than this. But it was a testament to the witches just how little they cared for the sanctity of magic. Their bodies were only tools, a vessel in the pursuit of power. It was how they always had been.

"Feel the wound, feel how deep it goes, feel the way the body rushes to save itself even if it's futile," the professor said with a tad too much passion. "The body is a marvelous thing, but magic is the true marvel. It can heal everything *except* the wounds of the heart, which are often the most painful."

Felix rolled his eyes at the Shakespearean performance the professor was putting on; he *knew* Bran was a wet blanket at parties.

"When you have located the true injury, channel from your familiar, and imagine you are an artist, and the wound is your canvas."

Good god, he was insufferable. A few students sent tentative looks to their familiars. A crow ruffled its feathers. A small serpent wound tighter around its witch's wrist as they started to heal their wounds. Felix shoved his sleeve up and dragged the blade down as rivulets of hot blood seeped from the wound. But before the blood could even drop, the wound knit itself shut. He narrowed his eyes on his arm and then did it again. The wound opened and closed just as quickly.

What the fuck? Unease wove through his gut; this was not normal. Not even close to normal.

Usually, it took at least a minute for anything to start healing, and complex wounds took even longer. Even something as minor as a paper cut wouldn't heal for at least a minute. He really hated paper cuts, though; they had no business being so painful.

It wasn't even the speed that bothered him the most. It was that he didn't even need to think about it. Before, it took intense concentration; now it was automatic, like his body knew what he needed before he could tell it.

Felix looked to where she had taken the scalpel, her face as pale as a cat that had dipped its face in milk as she stared at it, the shiny reflection glinting against the clinical light hanging above their station. She hovered it just above the crook of the elbow, her small hand trembling. Would her body heal as fast? He wanted to find out.

Her breaths quickened, becoming shallow with each one. For a second, he thought she would pass out when the professor's gaze landed on them, his beady eyes looking her up and down. Shreds of panic found their way down the bond, tightening Felix's chest.

This was going on too long. Felix reached for her, but she slapped his hand away.

"I can do it," she said.

One second of contact was enough to send a current of electricity running up his arm, the world narrowing to the two inches of skin where they connected, and he became suddenly, painfully aware of everywhere they *weren't* touching.

Usually, when someone touched him, it was repulsive. Even when he fucked someone, it would be with his shadows, never laying a hand on their bodies. He couldn't remember the last time he'd wanted to. The last time he'd let someone close enough to try. Until her. Until the little witch summoned him, and apparently, he left everything about himself back in London. Each day that passed, he became something more unrecognizable, a shifter who craved a witch's touch.

The witch still hesitated.

Felix rolled his eyes. "Any day now."

"Shut up," she snapped back, her brows furrowing. "Give me a second."

To be fair, Felix did wait a single second before he wrapped his hand around hers, pushing the knife into her fair skin. He told himself it was a necessary touch to keep up appearances. She didn't wince as the knife slid down her skin.

The professor nodded, turning his attention back to the other students.

Felix's gaze wandered back to her, something he found himself doing more often than not as the days went on. He blamed it on his cat instincts, the way he saw it, and what he told himself so he could sleep at night, was that while threats surrounded him, he had to stay vigilant. She was a threat, so he had to keep his eyes on her. Completely normal behavior that had nothing to do with anything else.

Felix licked his fang, resisting the urge to bend down and lick it all up. Why the hell did her blood taste so good? He expected her to look away from the cut, or worse, faint. The color still hadn't returned to her face. She forced herself to look at the wound, to hold her eyes there even though he could tell she so desperately wanted to turn away.

A flicker of respect took him by surprise. Most would turn away. She didn't.

She had, however, forgotten to breathe.

"Breathe, little witch," he said into her mind.

A controlled noise escaped her, like she was pretending she had been breathing normally this whole time.

"Why do you care?" she said, her gaze meeting his.

"Because you are no use to me passed out."

"Right." Even through her sarcasm, he watched as her chest rose and fell, taking deep breaths at his command. A sense of calm replaced the bothersome panic that had been filtering through his walls before.

"Good girl, just like that."

Something else flickered down the bond at his words. Something he vehemently ignored lest he get a boner like a fucking teenager. The bond flared to life in his chest, its golden tether searching for its other half. As if she felt it too, her eyes flicked to his, lips parting in recognition before both of them took a step away from one another. A stony wall wedged between them. It was only the bond. And that was all it would ever be.

The professor looked down at the pair, judging their progress through his thin spectacles. All the others had closed their wounds. The only one left was the little witch, her blood dripping slowly onto the floor as she hid her arm from the rest of the class. The professor gave her a disapproving look, as if he had caught a child awake during nap time and moved on without a word, nose plastered high to the sky.

Felix ran a hand through his hair, something knotting in his stomach. He had not only caused the wound, but the humiliation along with it.

Laughter broke out behind him, stealing his attention. Two students, one of them with the wolf that sniffed his ass the other day. A growl rumbled through his chest. They were not laughing at him; they were laughing at *his* witch.

"I guess even with a familiar, she's still useless." The guy with the shaved head looked like a boiled egg he would happily crack open. He would Humpty Dumpty that motherfucker. The other one was obnoxiously pretty, a golden halo of hair sitting on top of his pompous head. Felix's eyes zeroed in on his notebook, where he had written his name on the front like a child.

Julian.

Any coherent thought flew out of Felix's mind, replaced by a choking rage threatening to overtake him. His shortened fangs ground so hard into his teeth that he thought they might break. *She is mine. Mine. I am the only one who gets to laugh at her, touch her, hurt her.*

The monster within him stirred, taunting him as his vision narrowed towards the smug smile resting on Julian's face. The words weren't even directed at him, or that loud. But Felix heard them perfectly, and from the way her shoulders tensed, so could she. It was suffocating to be in a room full of people and unable to do anything about it. Felix's nostrils flared as a violent heat rose within him, his pulse reverberating in his skull.

"The only thing useful about her is her cunt." The boiled egg smirked, smacked Julian's chest, and he laughed as if he had just heard the greatest joke of his mediocre life. "At least you got a taste of it before she went all weird."

That was it. He was going to fucking kill them.

His vision bled red, and his jaw clenched as his fangs lengthened to rip their stupid heads off. He almost shifted right there, damn the consequences. The monster continued to stir and throw itself against his ribs, demanding release, screaming for blood.

Mine. Mine. Mine. Mine. Mine.

The word rang through his skull. This was *his* witch. He would make them regret her name ever leaving their lips. Claws threatened to come out, the tips of his fingers darkening and lengthening, black bleeding into the tips. He curled his hands into fists tight enough that the sharp ends dug into his palms, his blood joining hers on the floor.

A low growl escaped him before her hand found his, her fingers pressing flat over his skin. The moment she touched him, Felix's entire body went rigid.

Such a small touch, enough to send a shock clean through him and pull him out of the trance and haul him back from whatever edge he'd been about to throw himself off.

"Don't," she whispered. "They're not worth it."

Oh, they were worth it. Unfortunately, she was right about staying quiet. He ground his jaw, willing his fangs to retract before he felt the need to use them again. Slowly, his vision cleared, and the laboratory came back into focus. The world still turned, students chattering away while they healed themselves or cooed over their familiars. He didn't dare look back at the *boys.* He could only control himself so much. They had no idea how close they had come to having their heads removed from their bodies. In any other setting, city or room, there would have been nothing left of them to identify. He would have enjoyed it. But never say never. Their time would come, just like the goddamn professor who waltzed over to their station. An interruption, Felix was choosing, very generously, to treat as a reprieve rather than an insult. Felix yanked his hand away from her, not missing the slight flicker of hurt that found its way onto her face.

"Everything okay here, Miss Alarch, Mr. uh?"

"Sukacok," Felix replied through gritted teeth. "Transfer student."

She couldn't help the snort that left her nose, earning a glare from the teacher.

"Interesting last name."

"It's Russian."

He was only half-lying; his real last name was Sukachov. His mother was Russian. But Sukacok was an unfortunate nickname that had stuck since he was a child back at the den. And it felt good to have a little revenge.

The professor turned his shrewd brown eyes onto the little witch, eyeing the cut. "You used your magic?"

"Yes," she said meekly.

"It didn't work?"

"Obviously, you old cunt." Her voice slipped into Felix's head, making it his turn to snort, earning another glare from

the old cunt. He didn't think she meant to project that, which made it even funnier.

"Yes, sir," she said instead. Part of him wanted to teach her how to have a backbone, the other part of him wanted to use the professor's backbone as a ladder to go pick some apples. The only sounds that followed were the silent weight of her disappointment settling over the room and her blood dripping in time with the clock.

"May I be excused to go to the healers?"

"No," he said coldly. "Miss Alarch, what did I say at the beginning of the class?"

"To help others, you must help yourself."

"Exactly, and you would only be a burden to the healers with more pressing matters than something that will heal on its own."

She flinched. Felix's jaw ticked.

"Let the pain and the scar be a reminder that failure is not tolerated in Caerwyn."

She swallowed, clearly holding back tears, before she nodded toward the professor. Felix's shadow cat hissed at him. Good kitty.

There was something about an old man with a superiority complex through the roof that made him want to pummel it back down to the ground, regardless of species. Shifters were brutal, but even they knew you didn't break someone before they'd learned to stand.

Twenty

Avery

The sun was setting as the dreary day drew to a close. Fog swallowed the spires in the distance, and the lamps created a blurry mirage of light. Felix walked beside her, puddles splashing under their feet as they climbed the long stairs. Halfheartedly, she held a hand above her face to shield herself from the rain, but the drops still battered it. Felix especially had a displeased look on his face, which only brought a smile to hers. A cat that hated water. At least he was consistent. Even his shadow familiars looked unhappy, though she couldn't help feeling sorry for them and their sad little faces.

Blood still dripped from her jacket, leaving a pitiful trail that washed away with the rain. Only now had she gotten around to the brilliant idea of putting pressure on it. She dropped back a step, carefully placing a hand over her sleeve where the wound was, wincing as she clamped down around it. The sound was enough to stop Felix in his tracks. Hands in his pockets, he turned from a couple of stairs above, looking down.

From down here, he looked almost otherworldly against the darkening sky. Even when he pretended to be normal, his features were unsettling—like those of a deadly yet beautiful predator. And when he looked at her, she didn't know whether to run or get on her knees and accept her fate.

Her instinct told her to apologize for the holdup. She told her instinct to shut up. He'd caused the goddess-forsaken wound, so he could wait while she tried to stop it from bleeding. Holding his gaze, she gritted her teeth and clamped tighter.

Rolling his eyes, he descended until he stood one step above her. The rain had drenched him, his white school shirt completely see-through, the fabric clinging to his muscles. Where he had undone some buttons, his bare skin steamed when a drop of rain found itself on his chest. Never in her life had Avery been jealous of a drop of water.

"You need to heal that," he deadpanned, cocking his head as his pupils constricted to slits. The feline manner of him was something his human form couldn't shed.

Lips trembling from the cold, she tried to make a sassy retort. "Don't you think if I could have done that, I would have already?"

The corner of his mouth lifted as he shook his head. "Follow me."

This wasn't a brilliant time to refuse help, but somewhere in Avery's mind, it was the perfect time to throw a tantrum.

"No. I'm sick of following everything you say. I'm not your dog."

His smile only grew. "Are you disobeying me, pet?"

"Ugh, gross, I'm not your pet."

"Are you not?"

She took a step closer, the rage building enough to take a daring poke into his chest with her good hand. But being the wall of muscle he was, he didn't move an inch.

"Listen here, you overgrown furball, I am not *your* anything, and I'm not going anywhere with you." She jabbed his chest again for dramatic effect, but this time he caught it. His large hand wrapped around her finger and pulled her closer. So close that his warm breath fanned her face. The bond purred in her chest. She didn't dare look up, her sudden confidence already halfway out the window.

A blinding pain overtook her as Felix wrapped his hand around her forearm and squeezed. The pain made her dizzy, but unfortunately for her, her body had other plans. Part of her liked it. Some sick, masochistic side of her sparked to life between her legs.

Felix went still. Without releasing her, he raised his free hand next to Avery's head. She flinched at the sudden movement, and a flicker of hurt ran down the bond, so quick she thought she might have imagined it. But Felix didn't stop, eyes darkening as he pushed strands of wet hair out of her face, with such a gentle movement she hadn't thought him capable of.

Her lips parted at the contact, the touch sending an electrifying ripple through her body, masking the pain he was causing her wounded arm.

"If you won't follow me, I will take you anyway." Felix threw her over his shoulder like a sack of kitty litter.

The world tilted as her stomach pressed against his shoulder, and he carried her to goddess knew where.

"Put me down, you Neanderthal!" she yelled, pounding on his back. At least there was no one around to witness the sheer embarrassment of being manhandled. Was this how he felt when he was a cat? No wonder he had shifted when she dumped him in the bath.

A chuckle rumbled through him, the sound vibrating through her and spreading warmth into her core. "Not until I take a look at that wound." Felix took the stairs two at a time before rounding the railing and taking the path down to the lake. He didn't listen to her protests. He didn't even put her down until he went between the curtain of a willow tree. The fog was so dense, the floating lilies were barely visible. The canopy of the willow was thick, a green wall between them and everything else. Avery swallowed.

He threw her from his shoulder, and she felt her back hit the tree. Before her head could crack against it, his hand moved behind her so that it cushioned the impact.

Her heart beat wildly against her chest. Despite the cold, her body burned; her trembling had nothing to do with the temperature. Fear? Anticipation? She couldn't pinpoint what was happening to her. But this time, she didn't want to run.

"Wha—" she started, the words dying on her tongue.

"Take off your blazer, little witch." Hand leaving her head, he crossed his arms.

She furrowed her brows. She wanted to obey, oh goddess, how every part of her wanted to obey.

But the word that came out was, "No."

His grin went feral, fangs elongating as he ran his tongue across them. "Take. Off. Your. Fucking. Blazer."

She shuddered at the power in his voice. This time, she didn't protest. Slowly, she took off her blazer, watching him as he watched her strip it off her wet body. Her breathing quickened, and she told herself it was her body's way of compensating for the cold. Looking down, she could see her shirt was see-through, the black bralette she had decided to wear this morning completely on display, the white sleeve red now.

Felix didn't break eye contact with her, even as she heard students hollering close by.

"Shirt. Off," he bit out. It almost sounded painful for him to talk right now.

She shook her head, mouth gaping at the brazen request. "Make me."

Too fast for her to react, his hand shot out and grabbed

her face, squeezing her cheeks. Using his pinky, he traced the line of her bottom lip, a growl rumbling from his throat.

She inhaled sharply, the ache between her thighs growing.

He spoke low. Almost low enough that she couldn't make out what he said through the rain. "It's almost like you were created to torture me, Avery."

The sound of her name tumbling from his lips had every nerve coming alive just to respond to his voice. She didn't move. Felix's pupils dilated, wide, then narrow, as if he were fighting against his own nature. Claws extending, he ripped a line down the front of her shirt while she held her breath so her skin didn't catch the tip of it. Her nipples puckered through the bralette, displaying her body's betrayal to the beast in front of her.

But he didn't stop with the shirt. He tore through the bralette like paper, exposing her breasts to the cool air, breath hitching at the sight of her bare skin. The illusion he had flickered, his ears and tail slipping through. His tail wrapped around her leg as his shadows came out.

"Put your hands up."

"What are you going to do?"

He didn't wait to answer; he grabbed her arms and pinned them above her head as shadows followed, wrapping themselves around the tree like a rope, securing her to it. They even plastered themselves to her ankles, spreading her legs just a bit further as Felix let out a dark chuckle, her wound long forgotten. She expected it to scream in pain, but instead it started to hum, the pain subsiding into a delightful warmth.

He moved closer, his body almost close enough to press against her. And shamelessly, she wanted the pressure, wanted him to fill the aching space between them. She tried to move against the shadows, bucking her hips as she did.

"So *eager*," he said, a *tsk-tsk* sound reverberating through her mind.

Shadows pulsed against her, as Felix's grip burned against her still-wet skin. Her heart quickened as the air thickened between them, his face so close that she thought he might kiss her again. Instead, his mouth found her neck, and he inhaled deeply, his broad shoulders expanding with the movement before he ran his tongue up the column of her throat, sending an exquisite wave of shivers down her body.

The bond sang between them, until the edges blurred, until she couldn't say where she stopped and he started. It felt *so* right. If it was forbidden, if it was wrong. Why did it feel so fucking good? She didn't want to question it anymore; she wanted to succumb to it, to let him pull her into the depths of his depravity, wherever this level of pleasure lay.

Fangs grazed the sensitive spot on her neck, pulling a soft moan from her lips. She wanted him to bite her, to feel those fangs on her, and the tension in her body coiled even tighter as she arched against his mouth. He bit down hungrily, his fangs sinking in. Pain and pleasure bled into one, setting her nerves alight. It would leave a mark, but she didn't care. She wanted so much fucking more. It was like he was injecting poison into her veins, corrupting her every cell to want him. But it didn't matter; her body was *alive*. The bond thrummed in answer, a drumbeat in her chest that spread through her ribs, her arms, her fingertips, as if whispers of magic roared to life.

A gasp tore from her as he palmed her breast with his massive hands, his claws like knives, threatening to cut.

"No," she whined as he moved his mouth away from her neck.

But it didn't last long. He took his hand and guided her nipple into his mouth as he sucked, the cold no longer a problem. She *burned* at his touch, her body running a sick fever for this shifter. He pulled back for only a second before she watched him using his fangs to pierce a hole through her nipple. She jerked at the sharp pain before he took it into his mouth again, ravishing it like it was his last meal. The tension in her core wound higher and higher as he lapped at her breast. Was she going to come just from him touching her?

He moved onto the other nipple as she watched a shadow weave its way into the hole he had left with his fangs, creating a solid bar. She bit her lip, hard enough to draw blood, to keep from crying out. She shouldn't be enjoying this as much as she was.

"Look at you." His voice roughened. "Just begging for someone to put you in your place, little witch."

"Felix," she breathed out. She was, for one merciful moment, completely empty of everything. Nothing else mattered but the two of them below this willow tree.

His body stiffened. As if she had just reminded him of whose nipples he was sucking on. The cold rushed between them as Felix took a step back, shaking his head out of the spell she must have put him under. His tail lashed behind him, chest heaving to catch a breath. Shame scalded Avery's cheek as she watched the man who devoured her turn away in anguish, his jaw clenching.

The shadows fell away gently like tattered ribbons; the only one to stay was her new piercing. Her breath rose and fell in time with his, their heartbeat still synce through the bond. Tears threatened to fall from her eyes as she folded her arms over her chest, the cold seeping into her bones.

Yet there was no pain where she expected it to be. She pulled her arm out, and where there should be a cut, there was nothing, not even a scar.

"Did you...heal me?"

Felix whipped his head toward her, his brows knitting as he looked. Taking a step toward her, he grabbed her arm and then looked up at her, a rare look of surprise flickering over his face. "Shifters cannot heal others, witch."

Understanding settled over her, tingling her skin. "Holy *fuck*, I have magic."

Twenty-One

Felix

Felix's eyes widened as he stood in front of his bonded witch, a sense of awe swirling in his chest. She had used magic. *His magic.* The moon shone over her in dappled light, shadows of the tree crawled over her topless form as if they were worshipping her. Felix looked to the stars lest he be tempted again. The meager sliver of control he'd been clinging to had already slipped. It always did with brats who needed to be put in their place. This little witch was going to be his undoing. Her arms shook from the cold, and something within him fought to warm her, cover her. The urge died as he shoved that instinct down and turned it into a snake that coiled within him, ready to strike.

"You took something of mine without permission, little witch." His lip curled as he spoke.

Shifters couldn't heal others. It was impossible; it was why the humans needed the witches. Shifters were made to be beasts, for violence and protection. Witches were meant for restoration. Somehow, she had tapped into his magic and made it her own. Like he was a goddamn familiar. *No.*

"*Your* magic?" she protested.

In one movement, he grabbed her arm and, for the second time that day, made her bleed. She tried to jerk it free, but he only grabbed tighter, earning a hiss as blood poured down onto the forest floor. Its sweet scent enveloped him; he couldn't hold back any longer. He needed to taste it again. He licked it clean like some sort of deranged beast.

He wiped the blood from his mouth and sucked it off his fingers. "Heal it."

"I don't know how."

"You did it once, you can do it again."

Her lip quivered slightly, but it was enough that knots formed in his stomach, something that might've been regret, causing it. Somewhere over the last few days, he had started to hesitate, to think about the pain he caused before he caused it. That wasn't like him at all. He was a blade, and she was dulling his goddamn edge. He should've hated it. Hated *her.* She may have been the one bleeding right now, but his fucking heart was bleeding more.

Avery fluttered her eyes shut, and something tugged at the bond. The blood on the ground started to vibrate, ripples violently moving through it.

Every muscle stiffened. *What the fuck?*

It was small at first, almost unnoticeable. A gentle pull on the bond. Then all at once, a rush of ecstasy flooded his system, unlike anything he had ever felt before. His knees almost buckled, power thrumming within him as he saw the golden threads of their bond weaving around them like trails of fireflies. It took everything in him to stand upright. He barely managed to lean into the tree and look down at the witch whose wound was healing. More than that, he was only inches from her face, and the need to kiss her pulsed through him as she parted her lips, beckoning him forth.

Worst of all, it felt natural. Like this was what was meant to happen. It made no sense, *none* of this made any fucking sense. Only shifter mates had a bond, only witches pulled power from their familiars. Whatever was happening between them was unholy. For a moment, he almost let her have it. Let himself be a vessel for her use, his body begging to give in to her.

The bond purred in his chest, its appetite ravenous for the little witch. It wasn't sexual, exactly, though there was something undeniably intimate about it, like he was opened, exposed—like she was reaching inside and touching something no one should ever touch.

Magic poured from him, rushing to fill the empty spaces inside her, pieces of a puzzle destined to fit together.

No. *No.* He was *not* a familiar. She was not his mate.

Every rational thought recoiled as his body lapped up the connection. He grabbed his head, clawing at his mind and drawing blood, the hot rivulets running down his face.

No.

He clamped down on the connection, imagining himself severing the line. He pictured himself cutting the golden thread, burning, disintegrating it—anything to make it fade into nothing.

If only it were that easy.

Avery continued to siphon, the wound closing even further. Her eyes moved back and forth under her lids as if she were stuck in a trance. With each passing second, he felt his power draining. Was she using it? Stealing it? Channeling it? It didn't matter; his magic was leaving him, pouring into her as if she were a bottomless pit, a river that refused to be dammed. He wouldn't let this little witch take any more than she already had.

"*AVERY*," he screamed her name into her mind.

Shadows erupted around him, but it wasn't him controlling them anymore. The shadows, the ones that had obeyed him for years, started to slither around him, a golden thread inside them pulsing in time with their heartbeat. His breathing became ragged, shoulders moving up and down as if he had scaled a mountain. Never in his life had he been so powerless.

The shadows caressed him, like a lover's kiss. But what confused him was that if she had control, why not hurt him like he had hurt her? Why not use them against him? Instead, they continued to encircle them, wrapping them in a blanket of power. Worst of all, it felt *safe*. Instead of fighting, he gave in, letting her invade him like no one ever had.

He towered over her, close enough to see the pulse fluttering in her throat. What little control remained was sliding into full collapse. What was one more slip? His gaze dropped to her mouth, and he closed the distance. Before their lips could meet, the connection severed. Avery's eyes snapped open.

He didn't move. "How did you do that, witch?" Felix tried to keep his voice controlled despite the tightness in his chest.

"I have no idea," she whispered.

Frustration bubbled up through him, and he took a step back. Once again, he was left with a string of questions, stumbling around in the fucking dark like he was about to be blindfolded and fucked.

And at the center of it all was the witch. She was everything he couldn't control, and that scared him more than anything.

Avery's family didn't say a word to each other as they ate. The only sounds were the crackle of the fire and metal scraping on plates. It was slightly depressing, to be honest. This is how they lived? It was so different from what he was used to back at the den. Every dinner was rowdy and full of laughter. A pang of sadness went through him; as much as he liked being alone, he missed his den.

Candlelight flickered along the patterned wallpaper, thorned flowers twisting around different beasts. It was fitting for the family, except for his little witch.

Compared to Avery, her family looked like vipers sitting around the dark wooden table. She looked nothing like them. Avery was innocent. Doe eyes rounded and large, and her hair falling in soft brown waves. Her family's eyes, however, were deceptive. Still blue, but a viciousness lurked on the edges. Their bone structure was severe, black hair as straight as swords. All three of them put his teeth on edge.

Felix remembered the matriarch's name as soon as he saw her. Eleri Alarch, the High Councilor, had been in some of his mission briefings. Her posture was rigid, as if someone had shoved a fire poker up her ass and left it there.

Avery's sister, Wren, was the same. They were dangerous creatures, the power rolling off them palpable enough that he could almost lick it. Eleri had been pushing her witches into shifter territory, trying to find what, he wasn't sure. What was worse, though, she ignored him, seeing him as a regular familiar in his cat form. He still wasn't over how much it irritated him. So instead of being a good familiar, he resorted to being as obnoxious as possible.

Felix sat within striking distance of Avery, close enough to intercept if anything happened. Like her own personal guard dog, well, guard cat. He also sat close enough to her food so that a few of his hairs made their way into her pumpkin soup. A small revenge for earlier, but a satisfying one.

Delicately, Eleri stabbed her braised chicken, each cut making his fur prickle. It didn't stop him from trying to steal a piece of chicken from Avery's plate, though. The food piled high on the table had his mouth watering, even though he had just eaten an hour ago. Why was it always goddamn chicken that tempted him? He wondered if Avery was made of chicken, and that's why she was simply irresistible. He pawed at the plate, trying to steal a piece and run away with it before Avery slapped his paw away. *Rude.*

"How dare you come between a man and his chicken?" he said into her mind.

"You're not a man right now, are you?"

He narrowed his eyes at her. "*Touché, witch.*"

"Gwyn, darling, how are your studies?" Eleri said, her voice so cold it could have frosted the windows.

Gwyn practically glowed under the attention, blue eyes shining under the candlelight. "Exceptional, Mother. Professor Salin says I'm advancing faster than any student he's had in decades."

Avery choked mid-swallow while Gwyn sent her a scathing look.

"As I would expect, you're well on your way to receiving the first familiar of your year," she said, sporting a smile that withered toward her eyes. Then, her gaze slid to Avery, head tilting like a viper.

"And, Avery, how are things now that you *finally* have a familiar?"

The scrape of silverware died; the sisters also turned their full attention to her now. Avery swished her wine glass before taking a long sip of the merlot. "Fine."

"Fine," Eleri repeated, the word turning sour. "Care to elaborate?"

Felix's ears flattened. The urge to claw her eyes out was pulsing through him in time with his thumping heart. The goddamn bond made something as simple as an insult set his teeth on edge.

Gwyn spoke for her, fork twirling between her fingers. "I heard you couldn't even heal a basic cut. Professor Bran was telling Mother all about it."

Wren lightly slapped Gwyn on the shoulder as a warning rather than a reprimand.

Avery ignored her. "So you know?" she asked her mother.

"Of course, I know, Avery. I know everything that happens in this school."

Felix's claws extended slightly, rumpling up the tablecloth. The urge to hiss built in his throat. Avery's mother obviously didn't know everything, otherwise he wouldn't be here right now.

"It was nothing," Avery said, her shoulders slumping forward in order to make herself seem smaller. Felix wanted to slap some sense into her. If he knew anything about her, it was that she was more resilient than she seemed. She had stood up to what was supposed to be her mortal enemy, but her mother made her crumble. He supposed parents had a way of doing that to their children, grinding them down until they believed the enemy was themselves.

"It was an embarrassment," her mother said, taking a sip of her wine. "You're as useless as your aunt was."

Avery swallowed the insult and lowered her gaze. He had never wanted to punch a middle-aged woman more than he did now. Gwyn smirked as she pretended to move around the food on her plate, while Wren said nothing.

"Mother—" Avery started.

"Enough." The word cut through the air. "I won't have your bumbling excuses. I've heard enough of them already."

Wren cut in. "Perhaps we could get Avery a tutor? Someone to help her outside of class?"

Gwyn snorted, and Avery only became smaller, tears

burning in her eyes and her breathing starting to pick up. Panic spidered down the bond and wrapped around Felix's ribs.

"Breathe, little witch, remember what we talked about before."

Avery's gaze cut to him, and she took a deep breath.

"No. She won't get special treatment for her shortcomings," her mother said, talking about Avery as if she weren't even in the room.

"Another breath, Avery. You passing out won't help you get out of the situation."

Avery snorted a laugh before immediately covering her mouth. If Felix could smile right now, he would, like the cat that got the cream.

Finally, her mother looked at her. "It's sink or swim, darling." There was nothing motherly about the way she said it.

Felix started to lick his paws in a way to act natural rather than letting the growl rip from his throat like he wanted to. Despite the bond screaming at him, it would take a bit more than that to get him to shift.

Eleri cleared her throat, finally choosing to acknowledge his existence. "Avery, get your familiar off the table."

That would do it. Felix stopped mid-lick to let out a hiss, his tail lashing hard enough to send the salt shaker toppling off the table and skittering across the ground with a crack.

All eyes snapped to him. Including the dust bunnies holed up in the corner.

"Please don't make this worse than it already is," Avery pleaded.

He sighed as much as a cat could. *"Fine. But I'm doing this for you, not because your ghastly mother demanded it."*

A smile ghosted across Avery's mouth. Felix leapt down, wound between her ankles, then sprang onto the mantel above the fireplace. This had a better vantage point, anyway. He eyed the oil painting of her mother's face and considered his options. He contemplated knocking it off the mantel, but he thought better of it. Who hangs a painting of themselves anyway? Felix was slightly narcissistic—he knew he was handsome—but that was just straight pathological.

Eleri stared him down, suspicion swirling in her eyes. Instead, he held her gaze, not backing down like a good little pet, and straightened his spine. Just for good measure, he let out a little hiss. In case it wasn't already abundantly fucking clear.

"Felix," Avery mentally scolded him. Damn. Why was that kind of hot? He had always been the dominant one in bed, but for her...maybe he'd let her try. Only for Avery, though.

Her mother's jaw went tight. "Interesting."

Avery cleared her throat, pulling back the attention. "Mother, I—" Her voice trembled.

"For the love of god, woman, stand up for yourself."

To his surprise, she lifted her chin. "I will be a healer before I graduate. Then I will leave to join the others in the field."

Silence fell upon them, the tension almost choking the room. Even the smirk fell away from Gwyn's face.

"Leave?" Gwyn said, her voice high-pitched in surprise. "Why would you want to leave? Caerwyn is the safest place for witches; the human territories are crawling with shifters."

Oh, sweetheart, if only you knew.

"I'm sure I will be safe. I haven't heard of a random shifter attack in years."

Wren laughed. Dammit. Wren was *just* growing on him. "You cannot seriously be that naïve. Shifters are animals; they're dangerous. My entire career is eliminating them so you can have that type of opinion, Avery." Her voice grew heated.

"In London, there have been five witches killed this week by shifters."

His crew had been busy since he was gone; good for them.

Avery stiffened at the words.

Felix jumped in before she spiraled. *"We only kill them if they have breached the policies in the treaty."*

Avery's mother held up her wine glass, peering into the red liquid like a crystal ball as the firelight reflected off it. "The world is dangerous, Avery," she said, eyes returning to her least favorite daughter. "Which is why the council is working on something, something that will protect more witches against the shifters."

Eleri's gaze swept over Felix.

She fucking knew. She knew he was a shifter.

"What kind of protection?" Gwyn asked.

Eleri's smile was as wicked as a witch. "All in good time, darling. The council will make an announcement when we are ready," she said simply.

She had to know something about the missing shifters. He would bet his left nut on it.

Eleri stabbed her fork into the chicken with far too much force. "They have run rampant for far too long; someone needs to put them in their place." She paused. "Especially after what they did to your father."

Both sisters froze, forks halfway to their mouths.

Wren's eyes went wide. "Mother!"

"Are you saying a shifter killed our father?" Avery's voice wobbled.

Fuck.

Twenty-Two

Avery

A shifter killed him.

Gwyn's face drained of color. "What?"

Avery's chest constricted, the panic coming back in full force. The room blurred in and out as memories crashed over her, the grief lashing her with a fresh wound.

Her mother rested her glass on the table. She told her it had been a heart attack. That he died in his sleep peacefully. Instead, he died frightened, *in pain*, fucking alone, bleeding out somewhere.

"Avery." Wren reached for her.

She jerked back from the table, chair legs scraping against the wood. She stood, head dizzy. "You knew. You both knew, and you kept it from me."

"You were young."

"Bullshit, I was older than Gwyn was." Avery turned toward her sister. For once, Gwyn was silent, looking down at her plate.

Her mother clucked her tongue, as if she was being defiant, as if she was being *irrational* like a child throwing a tantrum.

"Sit down, we're not finished."

"What else is there to talk about?" Avery spat out.

Wren chimed in. "We don't know that a shifter killed him," she said almost quietly. "His body was never found."

Avery gaped, flickers of hurt piercing her already tender heart. "What did we bury then?" Her voice cracked, tears bleeding into her eyes as she slumped back in her seat.

"An empty casket." Her mother's voice was flat as she picked cat hair off the table.

Avery's nails dug into her palms. "How do you know he's dead?"

"Our intelligence suggests he is." She stated it like it didn't matter that her husband could be somewhere out there. Her *father*.

"But—"

"Avery," she said. Her eyes snapped up to Avery's, the finality in her tone brutal. "If your father were alive, he wouldn't have left you to grieve for the last year."

A bitter smile pulled at Avery's mouth, the tears finally falling.

She got up from the table, not bothering to look back as she stormed out of the room.

The hallway blurred. Her teeth sank into her bottom lip, hard enough that she tasted copper. The pain was grounding, real, something to hold onto when everything else was spinning apart. Rain slammed into her the moment she stepped outside, the sky crying with her. The guards called after her, but she didn't stop, didn't slow. She ran through the garden paths, her feet slipping on the wet stones, the rain indistinguishable from the tears on her face. She ran until her lungs burned, until her legs screamed, until she physically couldn't push herself anymore.

She didn't know where Felix was. Didn't care.

Moonlight turned the grand oaks to towering shadows.

Almost subconsciously, she had come back to the same spot that had started this all. A choked sound came out of her as she took shelter under an oak tree across from the statues, her back slamming against the bark as she slid down to the ground and tucked her arms around herself. A cavern cracked open in her chest. The feelings that she had been burying deeper and deeper down rose to the surface, as desperate as someone who was drowning clawed their way to breathe.

Her breaths came in shallow gasps, each one doing less than the last. Her limbs tingled, and her body flushed cold as the panic crested far past the point where she could talk herself down. The edges of her vision darkened, her head swimming as she became ravenous for air. She surrendered to it, let it almost pull her under.

It had been years since she'd had a panic attack.

Through her blurred vision, she saw the silhouette of Felix in front of her, not the cat, but him, his sleeves rolled up, the rain drenching his shirt as he crouched in front of her. One look from him and a sense of calm washed through her before the panic snatched it back again.

Avery tried to scramble back. "No! Get away from me."

"I'm not going anywhere, Avery," he said, voice gentle, rain dripping from his hair.

She pressed her palms against her eyes, the pressure doing nothing to stop the tears.

"You're a monster; all your kind are," she said, the words coming out strange and distant, as if they didn't belong to her.

He visibly flinched at that one. "Yes," he said.

Shadows appeared at her side, slithering across the forest floor like snakes. But they weren't coming from Felix, she realized.

They were coming from *her*, bleeding out of her in wispy tendrils. Felix must have noticed them too, because she saw his surprise as he tracked them across the ground.

"Your kind murdered my father," she spat, not caring about the implications of standing up to a shifter. How stupid had she been to trust one of them; if only she had known earlier. Now she was fucking bound to one. A sickness rose in her throat, tightening it even further.

"Probably."

The confirmation broke something in her. Her breath hitched as a sob tore from her throat. She folded in on herself, her arms wrapped tightly around her ribs because she was going to split apart, she was going to shatter into a thousand tiny pieces next to the very thing that broke her.

For a moment, the shadows were calm. Then they exploded outward. Tendrils of darkness writhed through the rain, lashing against the tree trunk, coiling around her arms. The shadows twisted and snarled, feeding off her grief and rage, growing darker and more violent with each breath.

Felix's eyes went wide, watching her detonate in front of him. She tried to stand, but her legs gave out. The shadows surged higher, blocking out what little light remained. They were going to consume her. She was going to drown in them.

She sensed that he was closer, moving through the darkness that lashed like a tornado around them. The shadows recoiled from him slightly, as if recognizing him. Warm hands pressed on her shoulders.

She froze. "Don't."

Felix's grip tightened, the sensation of his fingers taking her away from the confusion of her mind, for just long enough to remind her that he was there. Something she had wished for her whole life. She didn't have to drown alone for once.

"You need to breathe." He crouched in front of her, close enough that she could see the tension in his jaw. "Look at me."

"I can't." The shadows lashed out again, one tendril striking the tree so hard the bark splintered.

Felix caught her wrist, his grip a tender force.

"Yes, you can. Breathe with me."

She shook her head, gasping. Black swallowed the edges of her vision, pulling her under the surface. The shadows were spinning faster now, a vortex of darkness and rain and grief, and she couldn't—

"Avery—fuck—"

The world tilted. Her body went limp as the darkness came to collect her. The last thing she felt was Felix's arms catching her before she hit the ground.

WARM WATER LAPPED AT HER THIGHS AS HER consciousness returned. Avery's eyes fluttered open. She was in a bathtub? Her bathtub, back in the dorm. The water was murky but warm, almost hot, as steam curled in wisps around her. Her clothes were gone, but someone had left her in her undergarments. Candles flickered along the walls, the bath catching their golden reflection. She ran her hand through the warm water, trying to remember how she got here.

"Warm enough?" he said.

She jumped as she saw Felix next to her, the water cascading over the edge.

"Goddess, you scared me."

He didn't say anything. His shirt was still damp and clinging to his frame. At least he still had pants on. Silently, he raised a washcloth, running it over a piece of mud on her arm.

The tenderness of it caught her off guard.

"If you want me to leave, I will. Just say the word," he said.

The words sat on her tongue; she even opened her mouth to say them. *Leave. I don't want you here.* But they didn't come. They died in her throat as Felix moved closer and reached up to her chin, wiping away the dried blood from where she had bitten through her lip. She stared at him. His eyes caught hers, something unrecognizable flashing through them before he looked away, his jaw tight. She had called him a monster, but is this really how a monster would act? Regret twisted her gut as she grimaced at the memory.

Felix tilted his head. "What are you thinking about?"

"I'm sorry," she said.

He paused, dipping the cloth back into a separate bowl of water before continuing to work down her arm. "You have nothing to be sorry for."

She did. She had no way of knowing if a shifter had killed her father, or if he was even dead. Pain tugged at her chest as she thought about him. One thing her mother had said had been right at least. If he were alive, why hadn't he come back? Why did he leave her? Death would be easier to accept. The alternative, that he'd chosen to stay gone, cut deeper.

The mud came off in small chunks, small scrapes, and scratches, revealing themselves.

"You don't have to," she started.

"Yes, I do." His jaw tightened. "You were covered in mud and blood and half-frozen. I wasn't going to leave you like that."

She swallowed, as if it could force down everything her mother had just served her.

"I'm sorry," she choked out again.

"Avery," he said, brushing wet hair from her cheek. "Don't ever apologize for something that isn't your fault. You are far crueler to yourself than you have been to me."

That was enough to push her over the edge. Fresh tears spilled over her as a sob racked her. She tried to wipe them away, but they kept coming. Her whole body shook. From the dinner, from the rage, from the aching loneliness that has lived inside her for so long.

Because she just wanted someone, anyone, to fucking hold

her and tell her she wasn't broken for feeling this way. More than that, she wanted the warmth of someone who wouldn't leave her when she did.

Somehow, Felix knew. To her surprise, he stepped into the bath with her, clothes and all. He sat down across from her, dragging a sound from her that was half-laugh, half-sob, as he pulled her into his arms, surrounding her like a barrier against the harsh world.

"You're getting wet," Avery said.

"It's nothing."

She cried into his chest. Into the arms of a shifter.

"You—a shifter—might have killed my father," Avery whispered, almost as if to make it real, but even saying it out loud, she didn't quite believe it.

"As your kind killed mine." He said it so low that she thought she had misheard him. She froze, her breath catching until his hand stroked her back, a steady presence just as her father had been when she was small.

"I understand," he said softly.

And for the first time, she believed that someone really did understand her. The words gutted her, flayed open her defenses as her composure completely splintered. Lost, she buried her face in his chest, her body shaking with the force. He only held her tighter. She had spent years building barricades, but she was so fucking tired.

For the first time in years, she didn't feel so alone.

Twenty-Three

Felix

Felix watched as Avery had spent the last couple of days hibernating from the world, waiting for the grief in her chest to settle from a roaring river to a lake. He knew it well.

Unfortunately for him, though, she threw herself into swimming and dragged Felix along with her. He had *not* taken kindly to being splashed with water; in fact, he had never quite been so murderous. During the quiet nights, they sat by the fireplace as they tried to decipher the riddle on the key. And when she had been sleeping, he had snuck out to scour the grounds for any sign of missing shifters, for which so far, there had been a grand total of fuck all. This irritated him to no end because he was a hunter, yet he couldn't catch a scent of a damn thing.

Even worse, when he came back from hunting, he always fell asleep on the bed as a cat, but in the mornings, he would wake up wrapped around Avery, tail and all. His body had betrayed him. Secretly, he had started to look forward to it. He should stop. Pull back. Sleep on the fucking couch. He never did.

Tonight, though, was another more serious matter. Avery was going on a *date*. She had canceled on Callum for the last few nights, and tonight, he wouldn't take no for an answer, and he bribed her with chocolate ice cream. The bastard knew her weakness.

Felix pretended to watch hockey, but he couldn't take his eyes off the reflection of Avery as she shimmied into a tight black dress. *Fuuuuuuuuuuuuck*. He groaned inwardly. It was a slip of a thing, and the neckline showed off her perfect tits. Tonight was going to be a struggle not to remove Callum's eyes from his goddamn head.

Finally, Felix turned his head; he needed her in full line of sight. "That's what you're wearing on your date?"

A blush crept along her features. "Yes...What's wrong with it?"

"You're wasting it on a witch," he said, doing nothing to hide his grumpy tone.

"I am a witch, Felix."

Before she could register what was happening, he was up and across the room, towering above her. Even in her heels, she had to tilt her head up to look at him. She tried to look mad, but it only made her look more adorable.

His eyes raked her body, dragging slowly up and down, taking in every beautiful inch of her. Every part of him screamed to lock the doors and occupy her in other ways. And with the way Avery's scent changed, he was so fucking close. The bond thrummed between them, feeding off each other's arousal until it was painful.

"Cancel your date. We have better things to do," Felix said, gritting his teeth.

"Like what?"

"Like solving the riddle."

"Let's give it a rest for one night." She went to check her phone.

"So you can give fuckface a chance?" he bit out.

"Creative."

"I try." A hint of something flashed across his face before he could stop it.

"Oh my goddess," Avery said, scoffing. "You're jealous."

Fuck. He said nothing. He only crossed his arms over his chest, then seamlessly shifted into a cat.

Avery rolled her eyes, muttering to herself, "Men will do anything but talk about their feelings."

Padding toward her, he wound his way around her ankles and rubbed himself up and down her legs with his face. For someone who hated touch, he was sure touching her as much as he possibly could. What the hell was wrong with him?

"What are you doing?" Avery asked.

He didn't answer, only continued to rub his face against her leg.

"You're going to get cat hair on my dress."

He sent a dark laugh down the bond. *"If you insist on going out, your fucking scent will be unrecognizable. I'm going to make sure every last inch of you smells like me."*

Felix watched as Avery sipped on her fourth glass of red wine that night, a blush climbing over her features, like the ivy that crawled along the wooden beams. They sat at a corner table at the back of the pub, the short stone walls decorated by chandeliers of candles and chains, and a gentle folk tune played in the background. Felix perched in the middle of the table next to the bread basket while Callum's fox lay on the floor like a good little bitch. Well, technically a vixen rather than a bitch, but he digressed.

Felix returned to staring at Callum, making sure that every time he so much as leaned forward, his glare was the only thing the witch was thinking about. It kept working, so instead of saying something smooth, Callum would bumblefuck his way through a pickup line. Honestly, it was the most fun he had all week. That was a lie, actually. Surprisingly, being around the witch had been far more fun than he imagined. They had debated for hours whether pickles were necessary for a good burger. Then it had spiraled into what shade of red was superior. Felix said bright red, like the fresh blood of a witch, to which Avery responded, *that is barbaric and not nearly as sophisticated as maroon*. He had made such a compelling argument that Avery had ended up trying to smother him with a pillow. A valiant effort on her part.

Callum reached across the table for the breadbasket before flinching back as Felix faked him out with a swipe, only to lick his paw instead. Callum was right to flinch, though; he wouldn't hesitate to bite a finger again.

The enforcer cleared his throat, still side-eying Felix. "You look beautiful tonight."

Avery hiccupped, pressing the napkin to her face to hide the obvious blush that deepened.

Felix internally rolled his eyes. *"Avery, please have some standards for a man's compliment, that is the bare minimum."*

"Shut up," she said, her speech ever so slightly slurred.

"Oh, sorry."

She shook her head. "No, I meant like shut uppp, you too."

"Terrible save," Felix said into her mind.

An awkward laugh escaped Callum as he ran a hand through his hair. Felix supposed he wasn't terrible-looking; he had broad shoulders and a chiseled jawline. Felix decided his was better, obviously.

Avery slumped her head on her hand, her blue eyes twinkling in the low light. Through his cat sight, he saw her perfectly. Perhaps a little too perfectly. He was attuned to her every movement, even something as small as her pupils dilating when she looked at him wouldn't be missed.

"How are you and your familiar getting along?" Callum said, trying to change the subject.

Avery grimaced a little before putting on a pasted smile. "Great! Nothing unusual at all."

Dear god, kill me now.

Callum's eyes softened as he looked over her. Another rumble of jealousy coursed through Felix's chest, his tail lashing and threatening to land in the pasta sauce. Then Callum did the unthinkable. Covered her hand with his.

"So...I've been thinking."

Could have fooled me.

"I really like you, Avery."

Avery's eyes went wide before hiccupping. Even with the jealousy, the second-hand embarrassment started creeping in instead. Felix cringed internally, his mouth pulling so that his fangs showed. What he would give to chew on an exposed wire right now.

Avery's brows furrowed, her mouth slightly opening. "You...like me?"

"Well, yeah, you're stunning, and you remind me of my mother," Callum said, picking at his pasta like crows did roadkill.

Oh, *brother*. Had the man never heard of Oedipus?

"My parents had an arranged marriage, and they both ended up sitting on the council. Not that I'm saying we should be married straightaway, but I think if you gave me a chance, we could be like them?"

Avery's jaw opened wider and wider. "Callum, I—"

"It's fine, you don't have to answer now," he said, putting on a subtle pout that surely Avery saw right through? Right?

Callum looked back at Avery, whose eyes softened at his obvious manipulation.

Nope, absolutely not.

He had to put a stop to this. Using his paw, Felix knocked over the glass of wine sitting on the table and spilled it onto Callum's crisp white shirt, the red spreading over his abdomen as if he had just been stabbed. And honestly, Felix wished he had thrown a knife at him instead.

Callum cursed as he jumped back, the wine dripping onto his pant legs. A smug smile tugged at Felix's lips, his fangs completely showing as the enforcer tsked at his white shirt while Avery tried to hide her tipsy giggling behind a napkin.

Callum sighed. "Do you want to get out of here?"

"Absolutely," Avery said, swaying slightly as she stood.

Wait, no! That's not what Felix wanted. Why didn't he want to go home to change? Did the man have no dignity?

The night air bit at Felix's nose as they stepped outside. Wind whipped through the trees, tumbling orange leaves around their feet and paws. Callum, ever the chivalrous man, draped his jacket over Avery's shoulders. Perhaps next time, he would sneak into Callum's room and piss on it.

"I want to show you something." He held out his hand, and Avery took it with a wobble. Now she was just doing this to spite him. There was no way Avery would actually have an interest in this belligerent oaf.

Callum led her down a cobblestone path still damp from an earlier rain. The pine trees became denser while fog rolled around the ground. It almost made Felix and the fox look like they were swimming. The fox tried to play, taking strikes at Felix before he finally tackled it and put it in its place. Another degrading memory that was going to keep him up at night.

"My father always said that the strongest unions are chosen." Callum's voice carried to where Felix was lagging a few paces behind.

Avery stumbled slightly on the uneven stones. The wine

was clearly affecting her coordination, though it had never really been great, from what he had seen.

"That sounds depressing," she said.

"Does it?" Callum said, gripping her elbow to steady her. Felix's claws extended, making it sound like he was tap dancing on the stones as he walked. He could just kill the witch. There was no one around. Who would see? He would happily tap dance on his corpse.

"The council matched my parents. Together they became the youngest council members in history."

"So romantic," Avery muttered.

"I think it is, actually." Callum's grip tightened on her elbow, and Felix's ears flattened against his skull. "They built something greater than themselves."

Avery rubbed the back of her neck, her nervousness traveling down the bond like bugs he desperately wanted to shake off. "Right."

"Your parents' marriage was arranged, right?"

Avery stiffened at the mention of her dad, looking around like she wanted to escape. A spike of grief came down the bond, hitting between his ribs and taking his breath away. By some miracle, Callum noticed and didn't press her further.

They continued to walk in silence until the trees seemed to thin and stop in a line. There was no clearing; instead, there was a large green hedge with an arched iron gate in the middle. Avery looked up at it, stumbling backward.

"Easy there." Callum laughed. "Maybe we should sit?" He guided her over to a bench outside the hedge. The wood was old and rotted, moss crawling along its planks. Hopefully, it broke under Callum.

"What is this place?" Avery asked.

"It's a maze—my father actually took my mother here on their first date. When I had a dream about it last night, I knew I had to take you too."

Felix clawed at the dirt, stretching his back as he tried to shake the irritation coursing through him. The cold mud did nothing but piss him off more. Cold paws were the worst.

"Callum," Avery said, pulling the jacket around herself as the fog floated around their feet. Felix's whiskers twitched, picking up something in the air that made his hackles rise.

"Can I tell you something?" Callum's voice became gentle. "My mother tells this story about how nervous she was the first time they had dinner together. She spilled soup all over herself."

Avery let out a laugh. "Really?"

"Really," he laughed. "And my father just handed her his napkin and told her a joke to make her feel better. Just like tonight."

Just like tonight? Felix's ears swiveled forward. Was this asshole seriously comparing Avery to his mother again?

Callum smiled at the memory. "They weren't in love at first. But they built their life together. Something strong." He paused. "The thing they had most in common, though, was that they were ambitious, and it made them unstoppable."

"That's... nice," Avery said.

"It is." Callum turned to look at her. "They always tell me that love is a choice. That real partnership is about choosing someone who makes you better. Someone you can build a life with."

Felix involuntarily gagged like he had a furball, earning a glare from Callum while Avery only stifled a laugh behind her fingers.

"I know this might seem sudden." Callum reached out, taking her hand delicately like a doll he would break. "But I've admired you for years, Avery. Since we were kids. You're brilliant and funny, and you don't give yourself nearly enough credit."

"Just a reminder he said you reminded him of his mother." He purred as he felt her confusion rippling through the bond.

"I think we could be good together," Callum continued. His thumb brushed over her knuckles. "Really good. I could help you with your studies. My family has resources and connections. And you, you'd make me better too. You always have."

"I don't know what to say."

"You don't have to say anything yet." His smile was hopeful. "I just wanted you to know how I feel."

"I..." Avery started. Her voice still carried the slight slur of wine. "I need time to think."

"Of course." Callum squeezed her hand. "Take all the time you need."

They sat in silence for a moment, the night stilling along with their conversation.

"You're shivering," Callum said softly. He shifted closer, arm moving to wrap around her shoulders. "Here."

Felix's vision narrowed at the contact. The warmth that should be his, not this preening peacock's He shouldn't be jealous; he had no right to be, but with Avery, he was a frog in boiling water. And soon he would be absolutely cooked.

"Better?" Callum asked.

Avery nodded, but Felix felt how uncomfortable she was through the bond. She didn't want this. Her body was rigid, tense. He could see it even from here, the way her shoulders had gone stiff. She didn't pull away, though.

Enough.

He jumped on the bench, meowing and forcibly wedged himself between them, using his small body to pry them apart as far as possible. God, his dignity had flown so far.

"Your familiar is uh...attentive," Callum said.

Avery snorted. "Yeah, something like that."

"I really do care about you," Callum murmured. Turning

toward her, his free hand came up to brush a strand of hair from her face. "I have for so long."

"Callum..."

"I know you're scared. I know everything feels uncertain right now." His touch lingered for a second too long, and every fur on Felix's body stood up. "But I promise, if you give me a chance, I'll show you what we could be."

Time slowed as Callum leaned in slowly. Giving her time to move, to protest. His eyes started to close, lips parting slightly. Oh, this fucker was really going to do it. He was really going to kiss her.

Avery hesitated.

Do it. Knee him in the balls. Headbutt him. Something!

She didn't. Time slowed as Callum puckered his lips toward her. Not on his furry watch. She was far too nice to do anything. Felix surged his anger through the bond, pushing it all into Avery.

In a split second, Avery's hand came up and connected with his face. The slap rang out across the clearing was the best sound he had ever goddamn heard. A moonlight slap sonata, if you will. Felix purred loudly. He had *never* been proud of a witch. This was a first.

"Are you serious?" Avery said, turning toward Felix, her voice laced with anger.

Oops.

Avery went to smooth it over but before she could, Callum stood up suddenly, burying his face in his hands. "I am so sorry, I completely misread the situation."

Felix purred even louder as a little bit of blood fell from Callum's nose.

Callum looked around, embarrassment flooding his face. "I should go. I'm sorry."

He started to turn around, then stopped. "Oh, my jacket?" he said, before turning around with an open palm.

Avery raised her eyebrows at him and shrugged off his jacket as if she were shaking off a bug. And with that, the clueless oaf did a ding-dong ditch and left Avery gaping and shaking her head as she watched him walk away.

Once he was out of sight, Felix shifted to his human form. A shit-eating grin plastered onto his face.

"Don't even fucking start, Felix," she said.

Twenty-Four

Avery

He left her in the woods alone at night. Without his jacket! *Fucking nice guy, my ass.*

Who did that? Even *if* she rejected him, he should have at least had the decency to walk her out of the goddamn woods. She supposed she had slapped him, though.

And *fucking* Felix, filling her with rage enough that she did slap him. Cat stew sounded fucking wonderful right now. She couldn't blame it all on him though, she still didn't hold back. Maybe deep down she did want to slap him. She felt bad until he asked for his jacket back. Rejection always showed the true color of men, even if it came in the form of a slap.

Somehow, she wasn't surprised. After all, you can't spell disappointment without men.

Avery swiveled on the bench, the alcohol making everything blurrier than it should be, and took stock of her surroundings. She was in the southern woods; that much was obvious. Towering pines crowded her rather than the grand oaks of the northern woods. Their tall canopies swayed against the clear night sky, the moon illuminating the trawling fog in silver.

"Are you okay?" Felix asked, wrapping her in a shadow sweater. Her breath caught in her throat as the new piercing vibrated at the contact, like it was beckoning the other shadows forward.

That was the last thing she expected from him. His grin had dropped, brows furrowing with concern. "I'm sorry you had to deal with that." It was a simple sentence. But it showed far more care than Callum did. Even with all the pretty words from before. They meant nothing when he left a girl alone in the woods. Never mind that she went out there on her own volition and was perfectly fine. It was the principle, dammit.

She sighed, rubbing her arms to warm them. "It's fine, it wasn't the first time."

"Give me names, baby," he said, a lethal edge creeping into his tone.

"Did you just call me baby?"

Felix cleared his throat. "Must have been the wind."

She was drunk. But she wasn't that drunk. She ignored him and most definitely ignored the fluttering in her stomach at the pet name. Why hadn't Callum had that effect on her? He was everything she should want. Handsome, stable, *boring*. He would give her everything her mother wanted for her in life, everything that mattered to a witch: power, stability, children. Was it strange to want none of that? To want to experience life before it becomes predictable?

Felix crossed his arms, and her traitorous brain seemed to have migrated between her legs. The moon illuminated the defined veins popping out of his arms—thanks moon, she was definitely a girl's girl.

She could woman up and admit she wanted him to fuck her. Maybe it was the alcohol talking, but alcohol had a way of bringing up one's deepest desires. And drunk Avery got what sober Avery wanted. If he was poison, so be it; she was going to drown in it.

But before she could decide to make a move, something else caught her eye. Fishing out her phone from her purse, Avery turned on the flashlight and scanned the iron gate. Ivy grew around its wrought iron poles, covering most of the surface. The only thing really visible was a keyhole.

"Holy shit," she gasped. "Felix, come here."

In an instant, he was behind her. He could have taken a step to the side, instead the cold of her back was suddenly warm, his body not touching, but inches away. Avery tried to ignore it, but the scent of him was overwhelming. She really showed an amazing amount of restraint, and someone other than drunk Avery should acknowledge that.

"What is it?"

The damn rumble of his deep voice wasn't helping. She wondered what it would feel like against her pussy.

Dammit, focus, Avery, she told herself as she eyed the gate.

This had to be the place the riddle meant. *Twisted lovers surround her:* ivy. *Circling an aching hole that has yet to be filled:* a keyhole. *If you want to find what you seek, open her legs and slip inside her waiting labyrinth:* a maze!

It was so stupidly simple she wanted to slap herself. She had completely forgotten this place even existed. When she was a child, they used to use it for Spirit Night, but no one could ever reach the middle. The thing was huge.

"Do you still have the key?" she asked.

"Yeah, I do." Felix fished it from his pocket.

Where does it go when he shifts? Does he have metaphysical pockets? Because as a woman, that would be so helpful. She would never have to carry a bag again. Just fish out her lip balm from the void. Never to be lost again.

"Put it in the hole."

"At least take me to dinner first, kitten."

Avery waited until he finally sidestepped around her, the cold rushing in between where the heat had been. She already missed it. Putting the key into the lock, he turned it, and a click sounded.

Hope jolted through her body. This had to be it. The iron squealed as it opened, one half of the vine-covered gate swinging inward.

Felix gestured toward the gate. “Ladies first.”

Avery pressed her lips together. “Coward.”

When she went to walk in front of him, he grabbed her shoulders, his claws grazing her collarbone. Her heart rate skyrocketed as he leaned close. His breath was hot against her ear, sending goose bumps skittering over her body.

“I was joking.”

After an hour or so, and with much bickering, they finally made it to the inner part of the maze. While Avery had been correct a few times in her directions, her stubbornness had led them back to the same hedge at least three times. At that point, she made the executive decision to surrender her directions to Felix, who led them to the center in five minutes flat. *Cocky bastard.*

“If I weren’t drunk, I could have done that,” Avery said, crossing her arms as he walked through the arched entrance. She was sobering up, but she neglected to mention that fact.

Felix didn’t reply; she figured he was still brooding from when she had called him a little bitch.

“Felix?”

He didn’t answer. Annoyed now, she followed his gaze to something in front of them, his eyes narrowing.

In the center of the maze stood a statue of an unknown figure, a man carved from marble, body sculpted to perfection. Massive wings like those of a dragon sprang out from the back of him, horns curling atop his head. In a strange way, he reminded Avery of Felix. Or maybe it was the abs. Probably just the abs.

"What is it?" she asked, voice dropping.

"That's the shifter god. Arawn."

She stepped closer to the statue, running her finger along the base where moss had claimed it as its own. "Why would witches have a statue of your god on Caerwyn?"

"Your guess is as good as mine, little witch."

The funny feeling returned to her stomach at the nickname. She hated to admit it was growing on her. That he was growing on her. But the gnawing question about why the witches had a hidden statue of the shifter god on their island quickly replaced it. The plinth looked familiar, similar to the one that was cut away near where she did the ritual. "I think I've seen the plinth befor—"

A vine burst from the moss at the base of the statue. Felix grabbed her collar and yanked her away from it, putting his body between them. More vines shot up, climbing to the top as they wound their way around Arawn's legs, his torso, and stopping at his neck. Wolf's milk bloomed along their length, huge yellow petals peeling back to show gold stamens.

The flowers pulsed. Light gathered in their centers, spilling out in rhythmic waves like a dozen tiny hearts beating in sync. Every flower opened at once, their petals coming together and apart like mouths taking their first breath.

"When spirits writhe and reach their peak, their mouth will open, hungry and yearning for you to come inside. Only then will the final truth reveal itself."

The voice layered over itself, a chorus that came from every flower at different pitches, the old language rolling through the clearing in an otherworldly echo. The sound crawled up Avery's spine.

The goddess.

Felix's shoulders dropped, but his hand remained on her arm, his grip firm.

Avery turned the riddle over in her mind, looking up at the moon as if it would whisper the answer.

Spirits writhing and reaching their peak, a crude metaphor for Spirit Night. It had to be. The veil was at its thinnest at midnight.

The mouth? It could only be one thing.

As the answer clicked, a smile formed on her face. "The midnight cave on Spirit Night."

Despite the tides, the midnight cave always seemed to open at the strike of twelve. She had been there once or twice, but apart from the magically disappearing water, it was just a cave.

A smile tugged at Felix's mouth as well, before he seemed to catch himself and frowned instead, trying to look like he was a fearless predator. In reality, he looked like an overgrown itty-bitty kitty, or maybe he had just grown on her more than she thought.

"Am I really so predictable?" the goddess said in her chorus of flowers.

Avery chuckled. "It was a pretty easy riddle."

The flowers let out a witchy cackle that rang around the leafy walls, scattering birds from within the hedge. Felix's ears flattened against his skull, his tail giving a single irritated lash. His grip on her arm tightened, then released entirely.

"Hmm, smarter than I thought," the goddess said. "I have a few more tricks up my sleeve, though."

Not ominous at all.

"Like what?" Felix said.

The flowers chuckled, golden pollen falling from their stamens. "That's for me to know and for you to find out, my little kitten."

Avery snorted at the demeaning nickname while Felix glared at the flowers. Payback was sweet.

"You could be what I have been waiting for," the goddess said. "Let us see if you can live up to your own potential."

They exchanged a wary glance between them. What the hell did that mean?

The goddess's laughter shook the maze, and the flowers started to breathe, expanding and contracting like lungs before they shot out clouds of shimmering glitter that drizzled on them like golden snow. Avery, more curious than her cat counterpart, held out a hand to catch the pollen. It landed softly, gently resting on her and shimmering under the light.

Pollen floated around them, dusting them in a fine layer of gold. She tipped her head back and closed her eyes, letting the tiny particles catch on her face, a childlike joy spreading through her. For just a moment, the world fell away.

"It's beautiful," she said.

When she opened her eyes again, her gaze landed on Felix, who was already staring.

"It is," he said, not looking at the pollen.

Her heart stumbled, missing more than a few beats. Gold dust clung to his dark hair, the pollen settling in the hollow of his throat. His eyes gleamed with something she couldn't quite decipher. A beautiful riddle just waiting to be untangled. And by the fucking goddess, she desperately wanted to.

She laughed again, feeling more giddy than usual as she watched it make Felix into a glittery beacon, not an inch of him spared. What a strange situation they were thrust into. She never would have chosen it for herself. But wasn't that the beautiful thing about life? The paths that you least expected, even the ones you detested, always led to something extraordinary, if for only a moment. And this was that moment.

A shifter and a witch, bound by fate, and she wouldn't want to be anywhere else.

Pollen swirled around them, dancing and shimmering in the light as Felix took a step closer. She didn't move. Didn't take a step back. His hand came up and cupped her cheek, her heart hammering like a bird against its cage.

Using his other hand, he grabbed the waist of her dress and pulled her forward until she was flush against his warm skin. An inch, that was all it would take for her lips to meet his. Every part of her wanted to. She was sick of pretending like she hadn't spent the better part of the last week thinking about the kiss beneath the oak. She wanted it all and *more.* For once in her life, she wanted to be selfish. To do what she wanted.

Felix stumbled back, claws extending with a pained groan. Avery's blood ran cold, the hairs on her arm raising as if subconsciously detecting danger. Something was very, *very* wrong.

Shadows grew around him instead of shrinking as he continued shifting. His face snapped and snarled, as if he were trying to stop the transformation.

"Run, little witch," he said, voice demonic and hungry.

But the voice wasn't his. It belonged to something else entirely.

Terror locked her body as she realized what was happening. Taking a step back, she tripped on a root and fell backward onto her ass. She crawled away, ignoring the pain of the rough dirt dragging against her skin as Felix's features hardened into something predatory, mouth grinning wildly like a man who wanted to hunt, and she was his prey.

Fuck fuck fuck fuck.

Felix grabbed his head and dropped to his knees, a strangled snarl escaping him. When her back hit the hedge, and she couldn't move any further, she froze like a mouse in front of a cat. It was a terrible habit of hers.

Every limb went limp. For some reason, her body debated fighting or flighting and had decided to be utterly useless. Would playing dead work? Probably not. All she could do was watch in horror as his limbs lengthened and bones cracked and stretched into shadow.

His voice slammed into her mind, Felix's voice, not the thing's.

"AVERY, RUN! I cannot hold it back any longer."

Felix's body morphed into something inhuman. Shadow swallowed him whole, reshaping him into something with a cat's build and a skull for a face. A monster. All the blood drained from her face as she finally heeded his warning. Finally, her legs unlocked, and she scrambled to her feet and hit the ground with all the force she could muster, pushing herself forward and back into the maze.

Dark laughter echoed, sending goose bumps skittering across her skin as she ran for her life.

"Keep running, little witch, because if I catch you, I'm going to fuck you," the monster said.

Dear fucking goddess. Why the fuck had the goddess done this? Did she want to see how fast she ran? Panic clawed up her throat. She didn't want to find out what the monster meant by that. Her legs burned as she pushed herself further, walls of leaves bleeding past her vision. She didn't remember the way they came. A wall of green interrupted her. Dead end. *Fuck.*

The monster's voice rumbled through her head. *"I can scent him on you, witch, and I'm going to make sure that I fucking rub every inch of you to get his scent off and replace it with mine."*

"Five," the monster said.

He was counting down. Her stomach turned over, fear

twisting in her gut. Her shoulders moved rapidly as she fought to catch her breath. No time to stop. Keep going. Keep fucking going. Blood roared in her ears. Her muscles bunched, every instinct shrieking one word: *run*.

The walls blurred around her, and her thighs screamed, slowing her down while the cold wind of the late night sliced her cheeks. Her lungs burned. She didn't dare look behind her.

The walls became denser, the moon struggling to light the way through the maze. But she didn't stop. A low, foreboding purr rumbled through the maze. The vibration sent a bolt of unwanted pleasure through her core. She choked on a sob of horror and humiliation, stumbling on a root. Rough bark scraped the skin from her palm as she broke her fall. *No. I will not fucking die here.* Clambering to her feet, she pushed off and ran.

"Four."

Dead end.

"Three."

Dead end.

"Two."

Dead fucking end!

"One."

No. No no no no. Her legs gave out. She caught herself against the hedge wall, gasping and shaking. But the sound of heavy footfalls behind her pushed her harder, despite the stitch in her side, despite her vision spotting, despite the purring coming closer. Something dark blurred past, forcing her to move sideways, but a hulking form of shadows already blocked her path, so she banked left. The shadows shifted to seal every other escape.

There was nowhere else to go.

Eight feet of pure nightmare stalked toward her. The skull

almost looked like it was smiling, a sadistic grin that promised pain.

She went still. It moved like a cat—one careful paw in front of the other, the purr vibrating in every bone. Even her piercing vibrated along with it. The pleasure made bile rise in her throat even as her nipples hardened.

"Found you," it said. The voice was like a rapacious symphony, begging her forward with its predatory rhythm. Shadows poured from its form like smoke, its tail swishing back and forth.

Avery pressed herself into the foliage, praying for a gap, a door, anything. Every time she tried, roots moved to block her path. Her body went hot and wet despite the terror freezing her lungs. She wanted to scream at herself, at her traitorous cunt for responding to a monster. Tears pricked her eyes as it kept creeping closer, its movement so animalistic.

Her body tensed under its gaze, her legs starting to shake.

"Please," she said.

It cocked its head at her words, examining her in a feline manner as she begged the beast not to come any closer. But it didn't stop. Didn't relent its violent pursuit. Her heart raced so fast she thought it would beat out of her chest. As it came closer, she saw his eyes within the skull. They looked so much like his. Was he still in there? It had to be worth a try.

"Felix, you don't want to do this," she begged him.

"Oh, but little witch, I have been waiting to ravage you since the moment I saw you," he said before turning his nose to the sky and inhaling. *"I can smell you, smell how much my mate wants this."*

The word *mate* reverberated around her mind. No time to unpack that. On instinct, she pressed herself as far as she could into the wall and bit into her tongue hard enough that she tasted blood.

Tendrils of shadow grabbed her ankles and wrists, hauling

her into the air. All the air left her lungs as her body hung suspended. The tendrils pulled so fiercely she half-expected her limbs to rip loose. They hoisted her higher until she met its eyes, glowing hazel and green.

"Going somewhere?" The words carved into her mind. Her breath caught; even if she wanted to scream, she couldn't. The tendrils tightened and loosened like a living vise around her. A whimper escaped her lips, sending a wave of pleasure through the bond, not hers, she realized with horror. It was the monster reveling in her fear.

It spoke again. *"My mate's blood tastes delicious."* The voice sent shivers down her spine. Heat bloomed deep in her belly, and she hated herself for it, hated her body for responding to fear like this. Blood roared in her ears, the rational and completely sane part of her screaming *run, run, run*. But there was nowhere to go. She wanted to look away, but her body didn't let her, eyes rooted to the undulating shadows. More tendrils emerged from the creature, extensions of pure darkness racing toward her.

Avery started to babble. "Felix, what are you doing?"

"Enough words, little witch."

The protest died as a tendril shot into her mouth, snapping her head back. She screamed against it, the sound muffled by the wriggling darkness in her throat. She gagged, choking on them, even as her pussy clenched. The more she fought, the more he hungered.

He jerked her head upright, forcing her to watch as tendrils snaked around her legs, arms, and stomach, soft yet solid, pulling a moan from her that only made them tighten more. The monster's pleasure collided with her fear, a foreign sensation that made her want to flee and lean in at once. Another burst of heat sparked under her skin. One tendril slid under her dress, coiling around her ribs, the others starting to play with her taut nipples, the piercing vibrating quicker. She rolled her eyes back at the feeling of it. It shouldn't feel this good. A possessive squeeze brought her back to reality as she choked on the invader in her throat.

A purr ripped through him, and his grip tightened. *"Look at you, such an innocent witch. Yet you're enjoying this, aren't you?"*

She shook her head frantically. *Liar*, her body said, slick and aching. The tendril beneath her ribs teased until, without warning, it *ripped*. Fabric tore, her dress falling apart in tatters. Cold air lashed her exposed skin, raising goose bumps. Her nipples tightened painfully as shadows wrenched her arms wider, displaying her bare chest, pulling an involuntary moan from her lips. The exposure made her want to curl into herself, to hide, but the shadows held her spread and vulnerable.

Its purr shook the maze, a deranged sound. *"I wonder if you're wet for me, little witch. Wet for a monster."*

Avery shook her head defiantly, refusing to acknowledge the dampness between her thighs. It was wrong, but she wanted *more*.

Another tendril slipped beneath the shreds of her dress. She bucked against her restraints, trying to press into it, her sanity out the window as lust clouded her vision. A dark laugh resounded through her head as a tendril hooked her underwear, shredding it with a single pull. Leaving her exposed to the night. To Felix. To *it*.

She clenched her thighs, too late. Air kissed her glistening flesh, the moonlight betraying her arousal.

The monster went still. Then it laughed. *"Oh?"* A tendril traced her inner thigh, slow and hungry. *"You little liar."*

A shadow paused just shy of where she throbbed. *"Is this why you stopped running? Because your cunt aches for this?"* it said.

The tendril ripped from her throat, trailing spit. She

thrashed, but shadows held her spread and vulnerable. "Fuck you," she choked out.

"You'd like that, wouldn't you?" The tendril dragged upward, collecting her wetness and hovering threateningly close. A moan tore from her. The tendril rose, poised before her lips with her own slick. *"Open up, witch."*

Defiant, she twisted away. Another tendril fisted her hair, holding her still as it forced itself back into her mouth. *"Taste yourself. Taste the monster your cunt is dripping for."*

Goose bumps pebbled her skin as it fucked her throat. She gagged, the sound feeding the gluttonous monster before her.

A warm tendril curled around her piercing, squeezing just shy of pain. Its hot tip flicked her nipple until her back arched. A broken noise escaped her, half protest, half plea. Heat burned through her, and she couldn't tell where her desire ended and his began.

"You hate this, don't you?" His laugh ripped another shiver from her. The voice alone threatened to unravel her. More shadows embraced her: one squeezed her throat, another wrenched her thighs apart, calves pressed to the back of her legs. Shadows vibrated near her sensitive bundle of nerves, teasing her pussy.

Closer, she thought wildly. The monster snarled its approval. She wanted his touch. Almost said please. She bit her tongue bloody to keep from begging, a metallic taste filling her mouth.

Her blood. Avery's eyes snapped open. No, she wouldn't let the monster take control of her. Not now. Not here. When she fucked Felix, it would be because the man in him was begging for her. And she was going to be the one to bring this cat to its knees. She knew he was in there. He had to be.

Tasting the blood on her tongue, she imagined pushing back against the bond, taking control of the shadows. For just a moment, they hesitated. But it was enough. Enough to prove that she could.

Avery pushed her magic into the bond again, this time putting everything she had behind it. It slammed into Felix, again and again. The cat skull gnashed and fought against the invisible predator. Her limbs threatened to give out, to fold under the weight of it. The monster was powerful, but so was she. And it was time that she fucking believed that.

One. Last. Push.

Her magic surged into it, and the shadows retreated back into the monster, dropping her on the ground, pain springing through her knees as she landed. But she didn't stop. She bit deeper into her tongue, almost like her body knew she needed the blood, and continued to push and push until the very monster itself was bowing to her.

Was this what the goddess meant? What she wanted her to find? Her shoulders heaved up and down, her chest burning.

She really did have magic. It wasn't a fluke. Finally, she was fucking worth something in the eyes of the witch world. How sad that this is what it had to come to, just to be somebody. To have a place. And they'd go back to hating her if they knew her power came from a shifter.

Slowly, the monster retreated.

All that was left of him was a man on his knees, his head hung low.

Twenty-Five

Felix

Confusion swam in Felix's mind as the world came back into focus. The mossy ground bit into his knees as he looked at his hands, his bare thighs, his naked torso.

Fuck.

The monster had come out.

Green walls still towered above him. So, he was still in the maze. His head throbbed as he grasped at memories, trying to figure out what had happened only moments ago. *Avery*. Where was Avery?

His breath caught as he saw her, almost a mirror of himself. Her pale skin glowed in the moonlight, and what was left of her dress, not much, hung in shreds that shifted with each breath.

She looked wild. She looked *beautiful*. And he had no right to look upon her if he had been the one to do that to her. Guilt grabbed inside him. Had he done that? The monster never let him remember. Sometimes that was for the best.

Avery moved, picking herself up off the ground and storming toward him. A little slither of fear gripped his chest. Felix scrambled to his feet before she came up to him like he was a red flag and she was the bull, bare-ass naked and furious enough to gore him.

She poked him hard in the chest. "You ruined my only dress, you behemoth."

Really, that was her first concern? "If it's any consolation, you look far better without it."

A blush formed over her face as she crossed her arms over her chest. "Explain yourself."

"About the dress? I think you know what happened to that, kitten."

"No. The giant-ass shadow-cat-monster you just became," she hissed, voice dropping like someone might hear them.

"It's complicated," he said, subconsciously mirroring her and crossing his arms. It wasn't that complicated; he could be an itty-bitty kitty or a big scary kitty. Did he scare her? Obviously not enough for her to run away.

"Try me."

"All shifters have a monstrous form, little witch. It's powerful, but hard to control, and often burns us out for a few days," Felix said. His monster was now locked away once more and sulking.

Her face softened. "So now you can't use magic?"

"Temporarily, yes."

She chewed at her lip, a bit of blood dripping from her bottom lip. He resisted the urge to wipe it away.

"And why was my magic able to stop it?" she questioned.

The air around him stilled. "What do you mean?"

"I mean, when I pushed my magic into you, you went back to normal."

What? That was new. Usually, his form would just tire itself out. It had never been forcibly shoved back into its box somewhere inside him. Every damn day, there was something new with this witch. With this bond. If only he had been able to control it himself.

"I'm sorry I lost control," he said.

She smiled. "It wasn't you; it was the damn goddess and that stupid pollen."

"Still," Felix said, jaw grinding. "The monster is a part of me."

The goddess had invoked his monster form, but he had given over to it. Hadn't resisted its pull. And now he had done god knew what to Avery. And how the hell had she forced him out of it? Was that what the goddess meant about their potential? It was a dangerous power if witches could force shifters to their knees.

Avery opened her mouth, but a sound cut through the clearing. The steady beat of dragon wings. Without a second thought, he grabbed her, put a hand over her mouth, and dragged them toward a shadowy part of the hedge. She squirmed against him, her scent mixed with his, flooding his nose—what had he done to her? Because it smelled like sex. And it was fucking irresistible. But now was not the time to act like a total creep and shove his nose in the crook of her neck like he so desperately wanted.

Muffled annoyance came through his hand, but he didn't let up. He also ignored the way that Avery seemed to perfectly fit against his body, and how easy it would be to bend her over.

The wings grew louder until he heard a dragon landing. Finally, Avery stopped squirming, her breath coming a bit faster as she realized what was happening. Hooves followed, clattering from the forest's edge.

An enforcer's voice rang out. "This is where the shifter signature came from, Commander."

Fuck. His monster form must have triggered the wards. He had just painted a target on both of their backs.

Slowly, he let go of Avery. She turned toward him, and just in case she was going to say something, he put a finger to his lips.

"That's my sister," she said into his mind.

"I'm aware. It's also an entire squad of enforcers."

"What are we going to do?" Her voice climbed higher, laced with panic.

He had no magic. No weapons. No fucking plan. What bad luck was following him right now? Probably karma from the hundreds of witches he had killed and had most definitely cursed him far into the afterlife. It was fine. This was fine.

"Search the maze!" Wren's voice rang out through the clearing.

Fuck. He had left the gate open like an amateur.

Avery whispered through the bond. *"I know something I can do."*

"Avery, no."

"Run," she said, echoing what he had said only minutes earlier.

Absolutely the fuck not. Before he could reach out and grab her, she was already gone, running out through the maze.

He bolted after her, gravel crunching under his bare feet. And just before she could get to the entrance, he caught her. Felix slammed them both into the hedge wall, branches scraping.

"What are you doing!" Avery screeched down the bond.

"You will not sacrifice yourself for me, little witch."

The gate squeaked open. Almost instinctively, he reached for his magic and stopped cold. The well was full. Impossibly full, as if his monster form hadn't just burned through every drop. He didn't have time to dissect it now. Later, he would, as well as Avery's complete disregard for her own safety.

He cloaked them in shadow, blending them in with the surrounding night. The high of the chase still hadn't subsided, even if he hadn't been a conscious participant; the feeling of it lingered. Avery's sweet scent told him she hadn't shaken it off either. Fuck, it drove him crazy.

An enforcer walked into the maze, Wren on her heels. The blazing rifle drenched the green walls in a glowing pulse, stopping just short of their hiding spot. But they would need to move soon.

The enforcers crept closer, and with their every step, Avery's panic spiked through the bond.

"Now is not the best time to panic, kitten," Felix murmured, forcing his breathing to come out slow and hoping it was enough to calm the bees swarming inside of her.

"You think, dickhead?" Her nails clawed into his skin.

He smothered a smile, but after a few seconds, her breath fell into line with his, her heartbeat following a beat behind. They were far more entwined than he ever knew.

His grip tightened, a warning. *Don't be stupid*. She had thrown herself in harm's way for him. Willingly. A tail-lashing lecture was in her near future. Unless she had been running to tell her sister about the shifter in the maze. *No*. He didn't believe that for a second. It was what he would have believed last week. The realization wrapped around his throat. She had tried to *save* him. A terrible way to do it, but it was the thought that counted. This little witch had created cracks in his armor, and it was so close to shattering.

The enforcers were within arm's reach, almost close enough for Avery to reach out and touch. Both of them held their breaths, becoming as still as the statues in the maze.

A familiar hadn't followed them in here yet, thank whatever god was listening. The moment one did, those noses would find them in seconds. *Think, dammit.* They were sitting mice here.

The enforcers passed, including Wren. Felix's shoulders barely began to drop before another group appeared at the gate, this time with familiars in tow, a dog and a fox.

Fuck. They were intent on finding them.

His shadows slipped into the hedge, winding their way

through dense foliage. There wasn't a tangle of branches or anything stopping them from going through it. It was his only option.

"What are you doing!" Avery said.

He put his hand around her mouth to make sure she didn't make a sound. *"Trust me, little witch."*

Pulling them into a sea of green, he made each movement carefully so as to not make any noise. Out of all the things he had survived, a rustle of leaves would not be his goddamn end.

His shadows carved a peephole. Clear. Just one squad off in the distance that was too far to matter.

"Stay close to me," he commanded.

For once, she obeyed, hands clinging to his arm as they emerged from the bush. He clothed them in shadow, blending into the night. They kept moving, kept going until the tree line that bordered the campus was in sight.

Almost there. *Almost ther—*

The ground shook.

A black dragon took a step forward, its giant head swiveling toward them in a serpentine manner.

"We're going to die," Avery screeched into his head.

"Stay very fucking still."

The dragon did nothing but stare, its gaze boring into them. There was something off about it, like it recognized them even cloaked in shadow.

Voices in the distance had his ears swiveling. A squad was moving this way. They needed to go, *now*. Felix tugged at a frozen Avery, keeping his eyes firmly locked on the beast just in case it changed its mind. But it didn't. The dragon followed their movements, delicately sniffing the air and doing nothing to alert its owner. Did it want them to escape?

Those golden eyes watched until the forest swallowed them whole.

THE OAK DOOR OF THE DORM SHUT BEHIND THEM, and the tension sizzled between them like water on coals.

Felix had kept his mouth shut the entire walk back. Why had she tried to do something so stupid? He wanted to fuck some sense into her. *Shake*, he meant shake.

He ran a hand through his damp hair, which he swore hadn't been dry since he'd been summoned to this wretched island. Her dorm room, on the other hand, had become a sense of safety he didn't expect. A gentle breeze lifted the curtains, and the fire nursed its final embers. It was the only place he didn't have to pretend. Or maybe it was just her.

Deep down, he knew. Avery was far more than any ordinary witch. She had heart. Probably too much. The other day, he had almost killed a spider until she got between them, and calmly put it outside, sending it on its way with a care package of a moth that had died naturally.

Or maybe, he had gotten it wrong. Not all witches were as bad as he thought they were. It was a betrayal to even admit that. But watching her now, sitting by the glowing fire, denying it was getting harder. She'd put herself between him and the enforcers without hesitation. He wouldn't forget that. Ever.

But as much as he appreciated it, he was still angry. *He* was the one who should protect her. He would make sure she fucking knew that.

Felix's tail lashed back and forth. "What was that?"

"What was what?" Avery said, batting her eyelashes.

"*Tsk. Tsk.*"

The fireplace crackled beside her, but he could tell the heat had nothing to do with the way she was blushing right now. Even her makeshift shadow clothes tightened at his presence.

"You know what you did, little witch." He took a step.

Throat bobbing, she held her ground, holding her chin up high like a defiant little thing. Oh, what fun he would have in breaking that. It had been over a week now, a *week* of her scent driving him mad, watching her mouth move and imagining it elsewhere, every goddamn instinct screaming at him to mark her like she was his mate.

A step closer. Then another. Until he was close enough that he could see the candles flickering in her eyes, their bodies only inches away. He cocked his head. "You take my magic without my permission."

"Your permission?" She scoffed, getting up from her knees to face him.

"You don't listen when I tell you to stay put."

"Because I wanted to help you, you stupid cat."

Smiling faintly, he made sure his fangs were showing. He was going to ruin her.

Taking another step, he pressed into her space. "You consistently talk back."

Instinctively, she retreated, flattening herself against the wall as he caged her in.

"You live to disobey me, Avery."

He raised a hand to her face and unsheathed his claws. Avery didn't dare breathe as he pressed the back of his claw to her face, cold and rough against her fervent skin. Achingly slow, he moved it down to her neck, her pulse throbbing against its tip. One wrong move and it would slash her jugular.

The next words came out as a whisper as he leaned into her. "Disobey me one more time, Avery, and tell me to stop."

The edge in his voice gave him away. He wanted her to say it. But Felix was right about one thing: she would disobey him to the end. She wouldn't give him the satisfaction.

Though her body had other ideas. She squeezed her thighs together, a subtle movement, but one that didn't go unnoticed. His eyes fluttered shut. *Fuck, he could smell her.* Her scent sent every rational thought out the window. He wanted to pin her down and fuck her until she couldn't walk. He should stop, should walk away. But he couldn't, not when she looked like a fucking goddess in her own right. Freckled skin so supple and soft, and features so perfect, it was like she was made for him specifically. Carved from a dream.

His tongue flicked over his fangs, and he only wished it would be somewhere else. He couldn't hold back any longer. Finally, he dragged his claw down and down, until it brushed over a nipple. A breathy moan escaped her.

Using his magic, he called away the shadows that clothed her. They fell as fast as his inhibitions.

For a moment, he just stepped back, his breath hitching as he looked at her. Nipples pebbled, one still gloriously pierced with his shadow standing to attention. Begging, no, pleading with him to taste her. How could he resist that? There were so many ways that he could ravage her. Usually, he was a patient shifter, but *fuck*, this little witch would be the death of him.

His gaze dropped. Dripping, she was dripping for him. He crouched, and Avery watched him, heavy-lidded, as he took his claw and ran it through the puddle she'd spilled onto the ground. He rose from the floor and brought his claw to his mouth, licking her slick juices from the ridges. *God, she tasted so fucking good*, like cinnamon and honey. His thumb pressed against her bottom lip until it gave. Carefully, he slipped his claw past her teeth, making sure not to cut anything soft. The needy whine she let out almost had him spilling right there, and if that didn't work, then the way Avery's pupils dilated until her usually bright eyes were almost black would send him over. *Fuck.*

Shadows threaded around her neck, forming a collar. Just for the fun of it, he made a heart-shaped tag with '*property of Felix*' engraved on it. Another shadow connected it, almost like a lead. She had collared him, so he would collar her, too.

He stepped back, smirking, and tugged. The collar forced her to her knees.

Tug.

She didn't move.

Tug.

Defiant little thing.

Tug.

Finally, with a glare, she crawled toward him like a cat.

With the way her arousal snaked down the bond, he shouldn't stop. *She was enjoying this. She wanted him to take control.*

He led her to the armchair. In one swift motion, he picked her up and dropped her into the armchair with a surprised yelp. Candlelight flickered over her form, illuminating every curve that he would ravish. So much skin, so little time. Then, before he could second-guess it, he sank to his knees. Shock flashed through her face, like she hadn't expected him to do that. And with anyone else, he wouldn't.

"Open your thighs for me, Avery," he commanded.

She hesitated, which prompted him to stop and ask, "What's wrong?"

"I've just never had anyone do that for me."

His eyes darkened, a growl building in his chest. "You've been with others, yes?"

"Yes," she said meekly.

"And not one of them has eaten you out?"

"No," she admitted, shuffling awkwardly.

"Oh, little witch, I am going to fucking ruin you for any other *boy*."

Her breathing stopped. Using his claw, he nudged her legs apart until she was spread wide, putting her body on full display for him. Pink flesh slicked with her heat, so swollen and needy. The little witch was so vulnerable, and all fucking *his*.

"You have such a pretty pussy." It was an understatement; he was fucking entranced by it. "Do you like the sight of me on my knees for you?" Using the back of his claws, he carefully spread her cunt, stretching her out until a moan tumbled from her lips.

So she liked being exposed? *Naughty kitten.*

He stuck his tongue out. It was barbed, just like his cock.

"Will it hurt?" she asked, eyes widening as she looked over the ridges.

Felix chuckled. "They're not as sharp as they look. It will feel good." He moved closer to her thigh, resisting the urge to bite.

"I promise."

Twenty-Six

Avery

The first stroke of his tongue had her almost collapsing forward. It wasn't gentle. The barbs dragged over her clit, rough, wet, and *so fucking good*. Her entire body locked up. She couldn't breathe. Couldn't think.

And just when she thought it couldn't get any better, he groaned like a man starved, and she was his final meal. She would die just from the noise alone.

A shifter on his knees for her, enjoying this maybe even more than she was. A muttered curse was all she could manage to get out.

And then, he *sucked*. A fervor spread through her veins as he ravaged her, his rough tongue working over her sensitive bundle of nerves. Her fingers dug into the armrest, which creaked under the contact. He didn't stop. She might have been embarrassed if she could form a coherent thought, but all she felt was white-hot pleasure coursing through her. Every second, the coil within her tightened, ready to release.

But Felix wasn't done. A purr vibrated through his body and went straight to her clit. Her world narrowed down to the sweet pressure building between her legs. She tried to say something, anything, mostly *don't fucking stop*. Instead, it came out as garbled blabbering as her eyes rolled back into her head.

Her hips bucked, but he didn't stop purring. His hand pressed down on her stomach, pinning her to the chair. She was trapped under him, spread open, completely at his mercy, and good fucking goddess, she wanted more.

Like he could hear her pleas, she felt a claw push its way inside of her, stretching her tight pussy. There was no sharp edge, nothing painful about it. Her body clenched around it, trying to pull it deeper, and he made a sound against her that was somewhere between a laugh and a growl.

"You want to fuck my claw, Avery? Say please." His voice was animalistic.

Any fight had already left her and fluttered out the goddamn window. She didn't care. "Please."

It was enough for him. He started to move. Thrusting deep with a remorseless rhythm. Her moans became louder, and her hand moved without thinking. Reaching down, she slid her fingers into his soft black locks, needing something to anchor her before she flew out the window too.

He went still.

For a second, she thought she had done something wrong. But then, her fingers brushed the base of his cat ear, just barely touching the dark fur. He shuddered. Actually shuddered, a full body tremor that she felt between her legs.

Oh.

Her fingers moved higher, tracing the edge of it. Even just the slightest touch had his hips jerking forward. She did it again. Rubbed the soft inside of his ear with her thumb, and his whole body went rigid. Hot breath ghosted over her soaked skin as he panted and trembled, this powerful, dangerous shifter falling apart beneath her, because *she* had touched him.

He pumped his claw into her faster, his tongue merciless

in its pursuit of her climax. She climbed higher and higher. Until it was almost too much, his mouth, his claw, the thought that she alone could make him unravel. Her legs shook, walls clamping around his thick claw that curled inside, which hit *just* the right spot. She tumbled over the edge and shattered. Stars scattered around her vision as wave after wave of delirious pleasure coursed through her. Her teeth sank into her lip, biting it so hard that blood filled her mouth.

When she opened her eyes, her dorm had disappeared. In its place was a room of shadow. The walls moved, shadows curving and twining their way around each other.

"What are you doing?" Avery whispered.

"It's not me that's controlling them, little witch."

Her throat tightened as she sat up against the chair. The shadows responded in kind, pressing in toward them the more anxious she got.

"What the fuck is happening?" she asked Felix, her eyes darting across the room.

"Eyes on me." His deep voice was a slight reprieve against the rising wave of panic, but still not enough. Avery's breathing picked up, nails digging into the chair as the wave threatened to drag her under and drown her.

A gentle touch on her chin brought her gaze back to him. The corners of his mouth lifted. "You're okay, little witch, I have you."

Somehow, even though her mind hadn't caught up just yet, the words were enough for her body to loosen. Finger by finger and limb by limb, the fire that had overtaken her quietened to just a simmer.

"Good girl," he said.

And just like that, something different entirely surged through her. A blush crept over her face, and Felix licked one of his fangs.

"Will I shoot out shadows every time I have an orgasm?"

Felix chuckled. "Only if I make you cum so hard that you bleed."

"I didn't mean to." She watched them out of the corner of her eye as the shadows still moved, restless things that seemed far too alive. "How do I stop?"

"Why would you want to stop?" Felix said, positioning himself between her legs so that his face was level with hers. *Goddess, he was beautiful.* His eyes were a sea of emotions, ones she so desperately wanted to be privy to.

"It's your magic now, too," he said quietly. "I can teach you how to use what you're taking from me."

"My teachers said—,"

"Your teachers," he spat, "don't know shit about real magic."

Her pulse kicked up. "You want to teach me?"

"I want..." His thumb brushed across her lower lip, smearing the blood. He almost seemed like he stopped himself from saying what she so desperately wanted him to say. "I want you to be able to protect yourself."

A curling disappointment unraveled in her chest.

Felix cocked his head, almost like he could feel it too. "And maybe," he started, "I want to see what you can do with it. For science, of course."

A smile spread across her lips. "Of course."

"Close your eyes," he said walking to the couch, his voice dropping into something dark that sent warmth pooling low within her. "Find the bond."

Avery closed her eyes, searching for where the magic welled inside of her, the thread that connected her to Felix. Blood pulsed through her veins, like it was imbuing her with its power. "I can feel it."

"Good, now imagine the shadows are like extensions of your body."

Listening to the soothing sound of his voice, she did as he

asked. Shadows materialized, worming tendrils pooling from a black void on the floor. They danced around her ankles, slithering and curling their way up her leg, leaving a warm tickling feeling in their wake.

She was no longer frightened of them. Instead, she giggled at the feel of them caressing her. She imagined them climbing higher up her thigh, and they followed suit. They really were listening to her. Did shadows count as elemental magic? It didn't matter; it was *her* magic now. Witches didn't usually have elemental magic; controlling shadows would instantly shoot her to a top spot in the school. The only other elemental magic user she knew of at the school was Wren. She didn't care about any of that anymore. Not grades. Not her future. How could she when she was bonded to a shifter, and a goddess was making her solve riddles? Something was changing. And it wasn't just herself.

Felix's breathing got heavier from across the room. Slowly, she opened her eyes to meet his, and she was surprised to see a burning ache that mirrored her own. Her heartbeat rose with the throb between her thighs, as his shadows kissed and caressed her inner legs at her behest.

"I want you to use me, Avery."

Goddess. The way her name slid off his tongue was fucking divine. Shivers climbed down her spine. It was almost embarrassing how easily she was affected by him. Enough to send her desire rising even higher, but it still wasn't enough; she was aching, greedy for more. The shadows responded in kind, tying themselves around her wrists and her ankles, and lifting her off the ground. A squeal came from her lips, and she almost let them drop.

"Let them play, Avery," Felix said, his husky voice dropping even lower. The bond hummed with pleasure. Whether it was hers or Felix—she couldn't tell. The more days that passed, the more the line between them blurred.

The shadows clasped themselves around her legs, like she was kneeling on the ground, but instead, she was floating in the air. The others wrapped themselves in her hair and tied her arms behind her back. She was completely bound. Completely exposed to him. He stood up, just to admire her like a piece of art in a museum. He walked around her, the shadows pulling her hair so her head tilted back in line with his cock.

His shadow clothes disappeared before her eyes, leaving him as naked as she was. The tip of his cock glistened, hard and veiny and so fucking hot. A flutter of pride went through her that she could have such an effect on him.

"Please," she whined. She was so close to his cock. She tried to move closer, letting out a little whimper when he stepped back. He was teasing her. Asshole.

"Not yet, little witch." He walked away from her, leaving her suspended in his shadows—or were they hers now? She couldn't tell who was controlling them at this point. All she knew was they felt fucking amazing. Felix sat on the couch, palming himself as the shadows around her started to move again.

She panted, the blood pooling in her head as the shadows contorted her tighter. Goose bumps erupted over her skin as more tendrils started to explore. One swirled and tightened around her left breast, the tip of the shadow devouring her nipple as it fondled and played with it. A moan left her lips. It was more careful around the right nipple where Felix had pierced it, flicking delicately. She squirmed underneath the shadow's touch as it continued to caress.

"You're doing so good, kitten." His voice came from everywhere and nowhere all at once. *"Don't be quiet. Moan for me."*

She heeded his command, letting out the moan she had been desperately holding back.

"Good girl."

Fuck. She opened one of her eyes, watching Felix out the

side of it, watching him stroke himself to *her*. Excitement blasted through her that *she* had done that to him, gotten him so hard that he couldn't help but stroke himself.

A shadow licked her pussy like a long tongue, taking all of the glistening wetness with it, before it held it up like a trophy for Felix to see.

"Fuck, little witch, you're so fucking wet for me."

Another moan ripped from her throat. Missing the contact of the shadow already. She didn't give a fuck how needy she was for him. She wanted more. She wanted to be fucking filled.

As if the shadow heard her, it came back to dance around her entrance. Licking its way up and down as it slickened itself against her sensitive bundle of nerves. She almost begged for more. Begged for him. But that thought was cut off by the shadow somehow wrapping itself around her clit and sucking on it. She jerked against the hold, a hitching breath tearing from her throat as it worked her folds. "Fuck."

"Already shaking, little witch?"

She let out a gasp as the shadow tightened. Her thighs were indeed shaking, but she wouldn't let him have the satisfaction. He already had too much of her. She murmured something incomprehensible instead.

"Use your words," Felix said, smirking.

Oh goddess. She wanted more. She wanted him inside her. Principles be damned. She let out a breathy, "Please."

He let out a pleased growl that reverberated around the room. Another tendril slipped around her neck, choking her ever so slightly, heightening the pleasure as the shadows continued to suck on her needy clit.

"You're so pretty when you beg." He let out a dark laugh. "Do you want more pets? All you need to do is ask."

Her pleasure rolled in waves, higher and higher until she thought she might burst. Other tendrils played at her entrance, stretching her cunt so wide that her slickness started to drip on the floor like a gentle stream.

"Fucking beg for it, Avery."

"Please," she begged him.

"Please, what?"

"Please fuck me."

That was good enough for him. The tendril shifted and took on the shape of a cock before burying itself inside of her, filling her hole to the brim. Before a scream tore from her throat, another one slithered inside her mouth, cutting it off before she could alert the whole dorm to what she was doing. The shadows worked in tandem, thrusting and fondling her as she rode them in front of a shifter. Ragged moans came through her as they worked her higher and higher, each thrust sending her closer to the edge.

He sent another one inside of her. Then another. "No more...I can't," she said. She felt so full that she thought she might explode.

"You can take another one, kitten, just one more."

He slid another one in. She thought it would be painful, but it only felt that much fucking better.

She heard Felix working himself closer to his release. The sound of his hands running up and down his shaft. His gentle moans.

"Felix, I'm going to—"

"Come for me, Avery," he commanded her.

She obeyed. That was all she needed. She arched her back, toes curled as her world shattered around her. A climax crashed over her like a wave of exquisite pleasure. She writhed and convulsed against the shadows. Her tight pussy contracting around them as she trembled against the shockwaves.

But the shadows didn't stop. Not until she turned her head to watch Felix, her breath rapid along with her heart.

And at the end of the tether, she felt him. As needy as she was. As ravenous as she was. Their breaths timed up, hearts syncing in beat as she felt a wave of his pleasure running down the bond. His eyes opened and locked on hers as he fell off the edge, his cum spurting and leaking out of him like a glorious volcano. All the while, not once did he take his mismatched eyes off her.

If this was supposed to be forbidden, then why did it feel so right?

Twenty-Seven

Felix

In the non-weirdest way possible, Felix loved to watch Avery sleep. The slow rise and fall of her chest, the slight part of her lips. He was utterly bewitched. It was the only time he had to really look at her, without the voice in his head telling him he should look away. That looking too long would mean wanting things he couldn't have. He looked anyway.

Each night, Felix memorized the clusters of freckles splattered over her skin like paint on a canvas. Some would find them imperfections, but he loved that out of all the people in the world, only one person looked exactly like Avery. That she had freckles that only she had. And now he knew the taste of her. But it wasn't enough. He still didn't know what her lips tasted like. They had kissed once already, yes, but he didn't pay attention the first time, and now he wished he had.

Leaving her to sleep, Felix swiped her phone and stepped out of her dorm into the hallway in his human form, wearing the Caerwyn uniform. Only a few stragglers remained in the halls when he passed, most too focused on their own business to give him more than a glance, including Callum, doing his usual duty of standing by the bottom of the stairs. It took everything in him not to slam Callum's head against the stone stairs for what he did.

Callum didn't deserve Avery. But Felix wasn't sure if he did either.

Even now, she was only upstairs, but there was an incessant pull that led him right back to her every time. At first, it was annoying. Now? He would be empty without it. What a cruel thing life is. To give a taste of heaven and then rip it away. When it came to it, he didn't know if he would let it go.

He shook his head. She was distracting him, *again.* And she wasn't even here. He had spent long enough working on the riddles, and there was still the blaring question that Ciro had left him with the other night. Shifters kept going missing, and every road led to Caerwyn. And with the way Eleri had looked at him at the dining table could have been coincidental. When his gut told him something, he listened to it.

Felix traced the path back to the council tower where Avery had taken him for dinner, and using his shadow cloak, he slipped past the guards unnoticed. The main hall was grand, with towering spiral staircases and vaulted ceilings. Paintings of previous councilors lined the walls, their eyes following him as he clung to the edges where the flickering candlelight didn't reach and climbed the staircase.

He would start in the suite where they had dinner. That seemed the most logical first step. Hopefully, Avery's mother wasn't there, but more than likely, she hid her secrets like a goddamn dragon hoarding gold. Which was a harmful stereotype to his dragon buddies, but to his credit, he had seen them literally hoarding gold in the caves below their den. There were some instincts nature could never break.

Halfway up, small gusts of dust blew in like tumbleweeds, blocking his path. He could have stepped over them easily, but instead, Felix stopped in his tracks. They weren't just any specks of dust. They were goddamn dust bunnies.

Crouching, he gave one of them a pat on the head before they hopped toward him, making circles around his legs excitedly before running off. Change of plans. He was going to follow the little creatures. Was following a dust bunny a bad idea? Probably. But they had been helpful before, so he trusted his gut screaming at him to follow it. It had kept him alive this long. Curiosity wouldn't kill him this time, bitches.

The creatures led him down the stairs and then down another spiral staircase that led deep into the underbelly of the council tower. The space became so small that Felix had to duck his head to avoid the basalt walls carved out of the very earth itself. Moss hung from the cracks, the air becoming thicker the lower they descended. Nothing made a sound, not even his heavy footfalls.

At the bottom, a large arched door ended the path. When he walked closer, he noticed an engraving of Cerituen defeating his god, Arawn. The goddess was sending her two dogs onto Arawn while holding a spear over him as he begged for his life. Felix was no artiste but the door didn't look as ancient as it made itself out to be. Its color was too uniform to be weathered naturally. But what the fuck did he know? He was just a cat in a witch's world. Nothing worked like it should have.

Ignoring it, he went to open the door. But before he touched it, the dust bunnies squeaked at him with an alarm he hadn't thought they were capable of.

The fuck?

Felix's hand jolted back, and lo and behold, a faint shimmer of a barrier was up in front of the door.

A ward.

He had gone through many in his time; witches had a habit of warding their apartments against shifters, but he always got through them. There was only one barrier he couldn't get through back in London. And he absolutely didn't let it get to his ego that a shimmery wall stopped him. This one was the same, blood rippling through water.

Purely out of spite, he sent his magic into the ward. Usually, he felt some sort of resistance. Some sort of pushback against him. He would need to strain to pull it apart, limbs shaking like a shitting dog.

But this one was far too easy. It split almost instantly for him, creating a doorway just wide enough for him to grab the handle, open the door, and step through before it snapped back behind him.

Ego restored. He was the best.

Still, the little inkling in the back of his mind knew that something in him had changed. His magic had changed. His goddamn heart had changed for the little witch he had left sleeping in the dorm.

Inside, the space opened up to a carved cave, the black walls swallowing the light. Even with his superior eyesight, the room was like a void. As far as he could tell, there was no one here, but that didn't stop his senses coming alive as if there were. Grabbing Avery's phone from his pocket, he turned on the flashlight and followed the wall until he came to a shelf-like structure carved into the very basalt.

Looking closer, he realized they were animal statues.

Hundreds and hundreds of animal statues.

The room tilted.

Why the fuck would witches have a room full of animal statues protected behind a barrier? Dread crept into his chest like it was rotting. The further he moved along the dusty shelves, the more that rot spread.

A griffon, a selkie, a pegasus, and a basilisk. Were they familiars? Were they just statues?

No. That would be the easiest thing to believe, but deep

down, *he* knew. The cloying scent of magic almost confirmed it. It invaded his senses, an involuntary gag taking over him. There was far more magic in this room than just the barrier.

Felix held his hand up to one of them, the magic radiating out of it so palpable that his fingers started to shake. He moved his hand closer, and closer, almost touching before a sharp pain tore through him. He pulled his hand back, pain lacing through it. Another fucking barrier. How had he not seen it? He held his trembling hand as it numbed from the shock, a stifled groan slipping from his mouth.

Voices wandered down the hall. Felix's cat ears pricked up, trying to pinpoint the sound.

Instinct kicked in, and he darted to a dark corner, willing his body to shift. But it didn't come. He couldn't even use magic to hide himself. It was the last confirmation he needed. This room didn't keep shifters out. It kept them in. Imprisoned in fucking statues like experiments in a goddamn jar. Killing them would have been kinder.

Bile rose to his throat as he pressed himself into the cold stone. He knew witches were sick, but this was far beyond that. What the hell were they keeping a full army of shifters in their basement for? He had to tell Ciro. Had to get off this island before they found him and imprisoned his ass in some ceramic cat statue. It *would* be the prettiest one on the shelf, though.

When he heard the voices fade away, he grabbed Avery's phone and took pictures of them with shaking hands. Not statues. Them. Hundreds of lives trapped in stasis. Ciro would undoubtedly believe him, but it helped to have proof. Even with the photos, he still wasn't one hundred percent sure.

His head pounded from the stale air, or maybe just the massive headache that witches always seemed to give him. Why couldn't they just be normal and not some villainous cartoon rubbing their hands together? After he sorted this out, he was going on a vacation. For a moment, he let himself imagine somewhere warm and sunny, no water, Avery splayed out naked on the bed. Perfect.

For a moment of bliss, the thought carried him happily back through the barrier. It parted for him again with no questions. Unfortunately, the thought of his little witch opening her legs like a meal wasn't enough to keep his mind from spinning about the literal shifters kept underground. Eventually, he knew he had to leave. He couldn't keep playing a pet for the rest of his life. He needed to get back to the den as quickly as possible. Something splintered in his chest at the thought of it, of leaving Avery.

The thought that consumed him the most, though? How would Avery react? Every part of him wanted to tell her. To protect her, even though he shouldn't. And wasn't that just the story of his life right now? He shouldn't. But by *fucking* god, he desperately wanted to.

Coming around the corner of the stairs, he nearly collided with a body that blocked his way.

"Sorry," Felix said, trying to slip past the person's shoulder.

"What are you doing here? Students aren't allowed down here," a voice said.

Felix's eyes snapped up to Wren, standing on the staircase with her arms crossed over her chest. Her and Avery's eyes were almost exactly the same, but that was where the similarity ended. Seeing them on the street, he would never think that they were sisters. Wren reminded him of a panther, whereas Avery was a fluffy kitten. His kitten could still leave scratches, though.

"I was looking for a bathroom," Felix said, lazing against the stone wall.

"There are no bathrooms down here."

"Well, now I know that," he said, trying to shove his way

past the enforcer who didn't budge. He took a step back down, making her feel like she had the upper hand.

"What's your name?" The authority in her voice would have shaken a lesser man.

"Felix, transfer student."

"Last name?"

He didn't think she would appreciate being told to go suck a cock. Oh, how he wished he could.

"Solav."

She narrowed her eyes at him. Every bone in his body could tell that she didn't believe a word of it. His nostrils flared in frustration, a subtle movement, but one that Wren caught anyway. She was far more perceptive than any witch he had met. Neither of them moved, both predators circling each other.

Eventually, Felix moved aside and put a dazzling smile on his face. He would yield this time for the sake of cover. Next time, she wouldn't be so lucky. Avery probably wouldn't like him killing her sister, though. Ugh. Every decision he made revolved around the little witch now.

Wren didn't take her eye off him until he was out of sight. When Felix heard footsteps going down, he finally let out a breath. Was she going down to the room full of shifters? Did she know? Did *Avery* know?

Felix wasn't a man of doubt, not by any standard, but maybe he had been too believing that she would just accept him. Maybe he had been a fool. Maybe the bond had made him stupid. Shifters were everything they were taught to hate, to kill.

Was it so hard to believe that the whole family was in on this?

It wasn't.

The seeds of doubt started to sprout like a poisonous ivy, weaving their way through every interaction they had. Every moment. Avery seemed innocent, but how much of that was a mask? Had this been her plan all along? His father had underestimated a witch, and it had gotten him killed.

He wouldn't let the little witch do the same. Even if it meant walking away from the only person who'd ever made him feel *something.* Even if it meant ripping out the bond and letting that emptiness swallow him whole once again.

The witches would never win.

WHEN FELIX CAME BACK INTO THE DORM, IT WAS FAR past midnight.

Avery still slept soundly, a small patch of drool on her pillow and a fluffle of dust bunnies curled up by her head. They were lucky she didn't have allergies. Despite everything, Felix chuckled at the sight. It was that easy to make him melt around her. He was so completely, utterly fucked.

Before he had met her, he had wanted nothing more than to be alone. People would tire, bore, and frustrate the living fuck out of him. At the end of the day, he would beg that everyone just go away.

But with Avery, for the first time in his whole goddamn life, he wanted her company more than his own. He wanted to fall asleep with her. Wake up with her. He wanted to spend every fucking waking moment in her presence. Most of all, he wanted her.

Funnily enough, his father had told him the exact same thing over dinner one night. He explained to Felix what it felt like when a shifter met the one person in the universe who was made exactly for them. A gift from Arawn. Perhaps it was just the bond, but Felix couldn't blame it on *only* the bond now. This was all him. All his catastrophic fucking mistake.

But still, something held him back. Until he knew for sure, he still had one finger holding onto that cliff.

Running a hand through his hair, he dialed the number he had used to call Ciro on before. Maybe he needed a reminder of home. Maybe Ciro could talk him out of how stupid he was being. *You like a witch?* Oh, how Ciro would fucking laugh. They were our mortal enemies, and no one hated witches more than Felix. And he still did hate witches, just not Avery; she was a fatal exception.

The line didn't ring; it just made a beeping sound like the call failed. He tried again. The same thing happened. What the hell?

Opening up the messages, he tried to send the photos of the statues. *Status undelivered.* Again. *Undelivered.* Again. *Undelivered.*

Pricks of ice dotted through his body. Did someone know? Did something happen to Ciro? His whole den could be under attack by the witches, and he didn't even know. He was letting them down, only thinking of himself, whipped by a fucking witch. A lot more than whipped now.

There was no way he could do this alone. Break whatever spell was on those prisons. He needed to get off this goddamn island. Come back with a whole army, or something, anything. The hardest part of it all, though? He didn't want to leave without Avery.

A warm hand gripped his wrist, stealing him away from his thoughts. When had she even gotten up?

Felix twirled around, meeting her tired eyes as she rubbed at them with her other hand.

"What are you doing?" she said sleepily. "Are you okay?"

That was the moment that broke him. Those three little words were enough to have his mouth moving before he could stop it.

"I found something."

Twenty-Eight

Avery

I FOUND SOMETHING.

Avery's heart dropped at the words.

She blinked at Felix in the dim light of her dorm, hand still wrapped around his wrist. His pulse hammered against her fingers, which probably wasn't a great sign. Gently, he let go of her and sat on the bed, shoulders slumping forward. Whatever it was, it had him shaken enough to display it. This was not good.

"What did you find?" Avery asked softly.

He pulled out her phone without answering her. Opening up the photos, he swiped to the bottom and turned it around. Unease curled through her spine as she looked. Rows of animal statues on a shelf.

"What are they?" she asked, scared of what his response would be.

"Shifters."

Her mind stuttered. "What?"

She waited for him to say that he was joking. But it didn't come.

"Hundreds of them, trapped in statues." He swiped to

another photo, and then another. Each time, the dread coiled tighter. "The entire room was warded ten times over."

Avery's hand started to shake. So many questions blurred through her mind. Who? What? *Fucking* why? Her heart pounded in her chest. She wasn't built for this kind of information. If it was true, everything would change. Especially now Felix knew. The fragile truce between the two species would break.

"Where?" The single word was the only thing she could get out.

"Beneath the council tower." He ran a hand through his hair, exhaling deeply. "Dust bunnies led me there."

Avery's lips parted. "The goddess led you there."

"I think she wanted me to see it." Felix looked pained. Maybe this was an apology from the goddess for the maze. But why would the goddess help shifters? She was always depicted to hate shifters. It was in their teachings, in the fabric of their society.

Her legs gave out. She sank onto the bed next to him, bent forward, arms wrapped around her ribs because her chest was caving in, collapsing under the weight of it all. A natural part of her wanted to doubt him. He was a shifter, after all. If she hadn't summoned him in the first place, she might have thought this was all an elaborate ruse. But with everything they had already been through, it felt impossible to fake. She desperately wanted to believe him. For this to be real. Not the shifters imprisoned. *But them*. Whatever they were. Whatever the bond had made them. Nothing in her life had made sense more than this. Yet, everything else around her made little sense. Shifters imprisoned under the council tower? It was downright diabolical.

"Who do you think's behind it?" she asked.

Felix gave her a look like he was pleading with her not to say it.

"No," Avery whispered. A fracture formed in her chest. Her nails dug into her arms, hard enough to leave marks. The pain grounded her for half a second before the panic swallowed it whole.

"It's the only person who makes sense, Avery."

"Why?" Her voice broke. "It can't be her."

"You heard what your mother said at the dinner table."

Her mother was a bitch, but this was beyond evil. Trapping shifters in statues? And for what? Wouldn't she just kill them? Avery pressed her palms against her eyes to stop the tears that threatened to fall.

"What are you going to do?" It was a stupid question. She already knew the answer.

"I have to get them out." Felix's jaw ticked. "But I can't do it alone."

She understood what he was saying without him actually saying the words. He had to leave. To go back to London. It was not like he could stay here forever anyway. Every day that passed, he got closer to being caught. It wasn't safe for him. Yet, every part of her screamed to be with him in every moment. The bond thrummed between them, and she felt his concern bleeding through, his alarm spiking as he watched her unravel. That made it worse. Because he was here, witnessing her fall apart over what her mother had done to people like him, and in two days, he'd be gone and she'd never see him again and hundreds of shifters were trapped in stone and her mother was a monster and—

"What about the bond?" She hated how small her voice sounded.

His voice came out emotionless, but his eyes gave him away. "We have two days until the final riddle. After that, the bond will be broken, and I will leave."

Avery flinched. She pressed a hand to her chest, as if she could physically stop her heart from falling out. Her throat tightened, another wave of panic threatening to drown her. This time, though, she swallowed it down.

Something unrecognizable flickered across Felix's face. But he didn't say anything. There was nothing to say. Only the grim reality that was before them. Any future they could have had in tatters because thousands of years ago, two sides decided to hate each other.

A simmering anger built her walls up instead. At him. At the goddess. At the unfairness of it all. He had fundamentally changed something within her. Her magic, yes. But so much more than that. Far more than she should have allowed. What happened when something so tangled couldn't be undone?

It didn't matter. Not really, when hundreds of people were trapped in statues. Not shifters. People. She had to help in any way she could, regardless of what she wanted.

A sad smile pulled at her lips. "And until then?"

His features softened. "We pretend."

"To do what?"

"Pretend we could have had a chance."

MAYA BURPED AS SHE PASSED THE BOTTLE BACK TO Avery. Their weekly ritual had been delayed due to *things*. But Maya hadn't minded.

Avery felt a sad guilt as she took a swig, then gave the bottle to her best friend. They used to tell each other everything, or at least she had told Maya everything. The need to tell her about the past few days was eating her alive, probably one of the reasons she was avoiding her best friend. Avery wondered how Maya would react to finding out that shifters were buried underneath the council tower. Not that Avery would tell her. She was already putting her friend in danger by even being here, in the same room as a shifter.

Felix had promised not to touch her. And he had been peacefully watching from the bed as he said he would. Some part of her knew that he wouldn't do anything. That somehow, despite what he was, she could trust him. Which was insane, trusting a shifter. But she did. If you had told her two weeks ago that she trusted a shifter more than her own family, she would have called you insane. But this was her fucked-up reality. Drinking was the answer.

Avery sent a smile over to him as she took another swig from her turn of the bottle. Even in cat form, he made her stomach flip. They had turned off the TV ages ago, and the warm, tipsy feeling filled her veins. Halfway through the reality show, they migrated to the floor where Maya draped her legs over the couch backward.

"Does your familiar always stare like that?" Maya asked, giggling.

"Yeah, he does."

"It's creepy. I mean, mine is always around, obviously, but he doesn't just like, stare." Maya looked over fondly to her crow, throwing him a piece of popcorn that he gracefully caught midair.

"He sleeps sometimes."

"I'm glad you got a familiar, but I'm sorry it's that one." Maya snorted.

Avery made a fake gasp and hit Maya lightly with the back of her hand. "He's just...attentive."

Felix's amusement rumbled through the bond. He was far more than just *attentive.*

Maya raised her eyebrows and then looked away. She was smart; she definitely sensed something was wrong with him. Maya had always been able to read Avery like a spell book; she could see through her bullshit before Avery even opened her mouth. Luckily, the alcohol probably dampened that worry.

Who would ever suspect that a shifter was in their goddess-damn dorm room?

"Have you decided what you're going to wear to the Spirit Night party?"

Spirit Night. Ugh. That was right. There was always a massive party during Spirit Night; they went together every year. Even after Avery's dad died, she didn't skip it. It wasn't a fun one, but she still went. And they had to solve the final riddle. And break the bond. Avery drank from the bottle to fill her chest with a burning that drowned out the other feelings threatening to bubble to the surface.

Two days. That was all they had left.

"I haven't had anything made yet. I was thinking of just wearing the same costume as last year." Avery said.

"Boooo, that's so boring," Maya said, pouting and putting her thumbs down before sitting up on her elbows. "Also I knew you were going to do that, so I had something made for you to match."

"Maya," Avery said, throat tightening. Maya had commissioned a costume for her. While Avery had spent the week lying to her face. Goddess, she really was a horrible friend.

"Avery," she warned. "I'll surprise you on the day."

She smiled softly, putting her hand over Maya's and squeezing, which squeezed her heart just as hard. "Thank you."

At least she would still have her.

Maya smiled back and then brushed her off. "Ugh, enough mushiness, come on, you know I hate that."

There she was.

"Okay, let's play a game. You have to answer the question or take a drink," Maya said.

Avery did not like where this was going, but agreed. "I'll start."

"Best hookup?"

"You better say me, little witch, or I'll be offended," Felix said through the bond.

Avery made a gesture that her lips were sealed and took a swig from the bottle. It was not like she could say the shifter currently on the bed.

Maya's mouth hung open. "You sly little wench, I knew you had been seeing someone!"

"What!" Avery squealed. "How could you possibly know that?"

"Well, for one, you just confirmed it with your reaction. Two, you would have just said Julian, because that was your tried and true answer before."

Fuck. She had her there.

A rumble came from Felix's throat. *"Really? You went back multiple times to Julian and his punchable face?"*

"Shut it, it was a mistake."

"Mistake-ssss," he said.

Avery ignored him and turned her attention back to Maya. Her cheeks burned. This conversation had veered into dangerous territory, and she needed to steer it somewhere, anywhere, else. "Okay, yes, fine, I'm seeing someone. But I can't say who yet."

"No need." Maya held up her hand. "I already know who it is."

Oh goddess. She knew. Panic ripped through her, every muscle locking up. This was a trap. She was wearing some sort of recording device and was trying to call her out. The theater in her mind played it all out. Enforcers dragging Avery to the council chamber in chains or publicly burning her at the stake like her ancestors. Felix turned to ash.

"It's that transfer student, isn't it?" Maya said, raising her eyebrows over and over.

Avery blew out a breath, the panic draining so fast she felt dizzy. She got it half correct. More than half. Just missing a slight, tiny, crucial detail that she hooked up with a shifter. "Guilty," she said through her teeth, an awkward smile plastered on her face.

"I knew it!" Maya said, getting up like a wobbly doe and pointing a long finger at her. "Why didn't you tell me?" she said with a twinge of hurt in her voice.

Because I can't! She wanted to scream. Instead, all she said was, "I'm sorry."

Maya's eyes softened. "You know you can always tell me anything, right? I'm not going to judge you."

If only she knew. Bile rose in her throat, whether that was from the alcohol or the guilt; her stomach was churning.

"Do not tell her," Felix said into her mind.

"I know," Avery smiled, answering them both, but she didn't meet either of their eyes. She wanted to tell Maya everything; she wanted someone other than Felix to talk to about this insane week she had lived through. To set her head straight. Or at least be able to just talk about it. It would just be so nice to say: *hey, I summoned a shifter with blood magic, bound him, and now I'm dreaming about fucking him into tomorrow. Oh! And mother is keeping hundreds of trapped shifters underground. Pass the whiskey?*

Avery was never good at keeping secrets. And the whiskey was absolutely not helping. She was the type who it physically hurt not to tell someone something. But even if she did tell Maya, and by the grace of the goddess, she didn't turn her in or run screaming, Maya would be in danger.

"He's sooo hot though," Maya said drunkenly. "I just knew by the way he eye-fucked you in class that he had the hots for you."

"Yeah, he's pretty cute."

"Cute? Later, I'll show you fucking cute," Felix said low, earning a shiver down her spine.

Her stomach fluttered at the promise, heat pooling low in

her core. The memory of his mouth, his shadows. The way he had touched her was divine, like he was truly worshipping her. She had come so hard she had seen fucking stars. It seemed hard to imagine it could get better than that, but something told her that they had barely started.

Avery needed to change the subject. "Okay, my turn. Weirdest thing you've ever done?"

Maya put her hands on her face and tilted her head in embarrassment. "Nooo, you're gonna judge me."

Avery choked on her whiskey as she drank it, laughing, some of it coming out of her nose. "Trust me, I will be the *last* person to judge you for anything." Not when Avery's secrets had secrets.

"Ugh, fine, just because I do not want to get more drunk than I am already," Maya said.

Surely it couldn't be that bad? It was Maya. Apart from the drinking, she was practically a saint.

"I..." she stumbled, "I read a lot of erotica."

Avery shook her head. "You...you whore!" she screamed jokingly. "Burn the witch." Avery pretended to flick water on her to cleanse her of her sins while Maya giggled.

"Come on," Avery said. "It's not that weird; I read it all the time."

"Do you now?" Felix said into her mind.

"Oh my goddess? Really? How have we never talked about this?"

"Okay, but *what* do you read?" Avery asked her.

It definitely wasn't shifter porn; not everyone was as much of a degenerate as she was.

"I would never ever do this in real life, and obviously they're, like, super bad."

Oh my fucking goddess.

"But I read a basilisk shifter novel recently, and I have *never* been so turned on in my life."

Avery squealed so loud that Maya had to tackle her and put a hand over her mouth lest they be found by the wicked housemother. Once Maya released her face, Avery also confirmed that she, too, read shifter porn. They ended up lying on the ground, laughing so much together that tears streamed down their face, and every time they stopped giggling, one of them would start up again.

Maya raised the bottle in a mock toast. "To reading monster porn and making questionable life choices."

Avery clinked her bottle against Maya's. "To questionable life choices."

United in shifter smut. Could they ever be better friends?

They drank, and for a moment, everything felt almost normal. Like they were just two friends, drunk in a dorm room, talking about ridiculous things that didn't matter. She had a familiar, a best friend who cared about her more than her own family did, and she was finally getting the hang of magic. For a minute, she just let herself bask in the normalcy—a false dream that everything worked out the way it should have. It was a nice dream. But like any dream, reality doused her in its cold waters.

"You have a cute laugh," Felix said into her mind.

Maybe reality wasn't so bad. But it would never be this. Her heart ached when she thought about her future, and really, there wasn't one. Not after what Felix had told her. She and Felix would break the bond, he would leave back to wherever den he came from, and Avery would once again be magicless and alone. Maya would probably grow distant, and witches hardly ever left the university, let alone the island. She would try, fail, and while Maya would succeed at something, eventually they would lose contact, and her family would disown her for daring to try. They probably already should. Her mother trapped shifters in statues, and Avery was lying on the floor, drunk, in love with one. The Alarch family legacy in full fucking bloom.

Suddenly, the tears of laughter turned sour. Luckily, Maya didn't notice, too lost in her own world of her drunken dreams. Avery blinked back the tears that had carved their way down her face so many times; if they were cuts, they would have scarred.

"Little witch, are you okay?" Felix asked gently.

She shook her head against the floor. Next thing she knew, she heard the sound of paws hitting the ground and the sound of nails coming across the wood. For a moment, Felix only looked into her eyes, his mismatched gaze staring into hers as she turned her head to face him. Felix headbutted her, rubbing his feline face against hers, and a sad softness swept through her.

Maya's breathing evened out; she always seemed to fall asleep in Avery's room.

Felix didn't say anything. He didn't have to. Somehow, he knew. Maybe he felt the same. No matter how entangled they became, they would always be cleaved apart in the end. So instead, they just pretended. Pretended that day wouldn't come.

Felix stepped his paw on her and positioned himself on her chest. As he lay down, he made some biscuits on her skin. Avery scooped him in close and cried into his fur. He didn't make a move, didn't say a thing, and as much as she knew he despised water, he let Avery cry onto his coat.

Twenty-Nine

Avery

Avery nudged Maya awake enough to convince her to go back to her own room. They had stumbled their way through the hallway, and Avery had tucked her in.

When Avery came back into the dorm, Felix leaned against a wooden beam, looking so effortlessly handsome that she had to take a shaky exhale just from looking at him. A smirk graced his face, and the silver light caught his jaw in such a way that made him look more god than shifter. Not that she would ever tell him that, his head would get so big it would simply float away.

"I have something to show you," Felix said.

"Oh?"

Grin widening, he pushed the window up, the night air prickling her skin and rippling the fire in its hearth.

Avery's eyebrow shot up. "You wanted to show me that the window opens?"

She really shouldn't taunt him so much. Don't bite the hand that fingers you, or whatever the saying is.

"Funny." Felix grabbed the top of the pane and hoisted himself out of the window onto the ledge outside in one fluid motion. Damn his cat-like grace. Avery was more akin to a foal than anything. When she was a child, she attempted to climb a tree and was barely a foot off the ground before falling and breaking her arm. Heights had never really been her friend since.

Crossing to the window, she leaned out far enough to see him balanced on a stone ledge barely wider than his boots. "What are you doing?" she hissed under her breath.

He held his hand, waiting for her to take it. "Do you trust me?"

"No," she said too quickly.

He leaned back in, close enough that she could see the mischievous glint in his eye. "Liar," he said, and grabbed her hand anyway.

She didn't resist. Didn't snatch it back. She let him pull her over the sill and onto the ledge with him. The wind whipped through her hair and bit through her thin clothes. It was *fucking* freezing. But that wasn't the worst of it. Stupidly, and against all logic, Avery looked down over the ledge and gasped. Why was the ground so far away? It was far enough that her stomach dropped and her fingers clamped around his. Felix caught her chin, tilting her face up to meet his instead of the drop below.

"I have you," he said simply. But it still made her heart jump.

Even if he didn't, she would make damn sure that he came off the ledge with her for putting her in this precarious situation in the first place. She was not a cat and would most definitely land on her head instead of her feet.

Felix's grip tightened even more as he led her across the ledge to where two slanted sections of the roof met. The black tiles overlapped enough that they weren't completely vertical, but they were still fairly steep. What was his plan here?

He gestured upward. "Climb."

"Are you insane? I'll fall."

"The only way you're falling is for me, little witch."

For a moment, that made her pause, heart lurching in her chest. The truth was she had already fallen. Far fucking further than she ever wanted to. Would he fall too?

The rustling of the trees filled the silence before she could scramble her thoughts back together. "Shut up. I'm not climbing that."

Felix's fangs glinted in the moonlight. "Oh, but you are."

Before she could argue further, he grabbed her, one moment she was on the ledge; the next, she was splayed against the roof tiles, clinging to them like her life depended on it. Because it did. "Felix!" she whispered harshly.

"I'll be right behind you."

Goddess, strike him down. Actually, wait until I'm back on the ground and then strike him down.

Taking a deep breath in, she reached for the next tile up, fingers finding the lip where they overlapped, and hauled herself higher. The rough ceramic bit into her palms, but it kept her from looking down.

"Good girl." Felix's voice purred through her mind.

She ignored him, but her body had other ideas, sending a shiver running down her that wasn't from the cold. Stupid horny body. Stupid climbing cat. She would not help him down again if he got stuck.

True to his word, Felix climbed behind her, acting as a cushion if she fell. It was the least he could do, but it still didn't make her feel any better. Though she had to admit, as the adrenaline kicked in and her muscles burned with the effort, part of her was enjoying this. Or maybe she was still drunk. Thank fuck Felix was there to catch her.

His voice came from just below her. *"Keep going until you reach the top, and you'll see it."*

A few more feet and the view opened up. The familiar

lantern tower of her dorm rose beside the roof. She had seen it from below, of course, its tall stone arches were hard to miss. Up close, though, the arches seemed to pierce the very sky, reaching up to the stars like they wanted to touch them. And underneath, a circular platform ringed the tower's base that was impossible to see from below.

Carefully, she hoisted herself onto the flat ridge where the roof peak converged, then crawled across it on her hands and knees because standing seemed like asking for certain death. Felix followed closely behind her, standing, hands in his pockets like he was strolling the goddessdamn promenade. Show off.

Reaching the platform, she lowered herself down, boots hitting the stone. When she turned around, the view stole her breath right out of her lungs. Caerwyn spread out below in every direction, the whole island visible from this height. Lights from the town and university dotted across the rolling hills, the sea beyond dark and infinite. A desperate need to know what was beyond clawed at her. If only she could go with Felix. But there was no place for a witch in a den.

Felix landed beside her with barely a sound, and she twirled on her heels to face him. "I can't believe you made me do that." She slammed her palms against his hard chest and barely moved. "I hate you. I hate you so fucking much."

"Is that right, kitten?" He smirked, clearly enjoying the contact between them.

"You're a beastly oaf, a thorn in my side, you *dog.*"

His smile only widened at the blatant insults. "I could do this all day, kitten."

"I could have died." Her voice cracked on the last word, embarrassing, but there it was.

The smirk vanished. He took a step closer to her, closing the distance between them. The space between them became electric, like he was pulling her closer without even trying. "I wouldn't have let you fall."

Except they both knew what went unsaid. Would that still be true later? When the bond was broken, and they were enemies again? She pushed those thoughts out of her head, labeling them for a later Avery problem. Because just for one night, she didn't want to think about the future, as much as her mind demanded it to be heard.

He exhaled hard through his nose. "Let me show you something else."

Taking a few steps back, his eyes never leaving hers, he moved to the center of the platform and crouched, pressing his palm flat against the stone. Light bloomed under his hand, thin golden threads that raced outward like veins, climbing the arches and spreading across the tower's roof. Slowly, the stone roof started to fade, translucent at first, and then gone as if it never existed. Only the arches remained, framing a view of a sky so clear and vast it seemed like a painting. Her lips parted as she took in the night.

She started to lower her gaze, but Felix's fingers found her chin, tipping it back up. "Keep looking," he said.

At first, nothing changed. Then a streak of light, so fast she almost missed it. Another followed. Then three more. Within seconds, the sky was full of them, hundreds of shooting stars streaking in every direction like the cosmos had caught fire.

"It's the dragon's fire," Avery said.

An almost childlike smile came to Avery's face. It was beautiful. She hadn't seen it since she was a child. Her dad had been the one to show her; he took her up to the highest hill in Caerwyn, and they had pointed at the stars long after she should have been in bed. Since then, she had avoided it. Avoided the pang of grief that would have gone through her.

But standing there now, she felt none of that. Perhaps in caging her grief, she had lost more than just letting it fly free.

When her eyes wandered back to Felix, he wasn't looking up but staring straight at her.

She wanted to squirm under his intense gaze; instead, she held her ground. "At least that's what they told us."

"We were told the same." His voice came out quieter than before, laced with the same grief that festered within her. "I watch it every year."

He went to open his mouth again before stopping, deciding against whatever he was about to say. She wanted to press him, to find out every little thing about him. But the pain ran down the bond; it was something she knew all too well. Instead, she just sat with him. Sometimes it was all that was needed.

"My father and I used to watch it together." An unguarded smile formed on his face, like he was recalling the same memory that she had. "But I'm glad I get to watch it with you."

Out of the corner of her eye, Avery spotted movement near the base of one of the arches. Felix followed her line of sight as they both watched a fluffle of dust bunnies doing *something*. They maneuvered back and forth, gathering dust from somewhere and wriggling around the floor until she realized that they were trying to spell something.

N-o-w k-i-s-s.

Oh my goddess. Of all the things.

A laugh broke her line of thought, before a gust of wind swept away their hard work, sending specks swirling around the tower. Even the goddess seemed desperate for them to have this. To take what little time they had left.

Felix's hand came up slowly, giving her time to pull away. He hesitated for a moment as if she would pull away. But when she didn't, his palm curved against her cheek. Her lips parted at feather light touch. She couldn't look away even if she wanted to; she was utterly transfixed by him. And when he moved his calloused thumb across her lips, she couldn't stop the gasp from tumbling from her. Every nerve came alive, yearning to be joined with his.

For a heartbeat, he just stood there, thumb resting at the corner of her mouth as if thinking about something. Time ticked by agonizingly slow, her heartbeat roaring in her ears before she heard the two words that broke her.

"Fuck it," he said.

The first kiss was gentle, tentative; his mouth barely brushing hers like a test. As if he were asking her *is this okay*. She wanted to tell him that it was, that everything he did was just perfect. But before she could answer, Felix's lips crashed into hers like a man starved. Despite the cold, a wildfire spread through her, consuming every thought that this would never work. It burned and burned as he deepened the kiss, but still it wasn't enough. She needed him, needed his touch, needed him to hold her. Not just now; she needed him for longer than just this second. Until she was bleeding and raw. Until he left marks on her that would still be there in years to come. If he was a cut, she desperately hoped it scarred.

Still, their bodies didn't touch. That gap between them existed. Wide enough to remind them that this would never work. Even the very wind itself was determined to push them apart, roaring through them like a tunnel. But Avery never listened to the weather; instead, she embraced it. How many moments would she miss for the fear of something out of her control?

Gently, Avery put her hand up to the nape of his neck, sliding her hand between his collar.

He jerked back like she had burned him, putting more distance between them than was necessary. His breaths came ragged, shoulders moving up and down with the effort. Everything gentle about his expression had gone. He looked like a cornered animal, eyes wide and searching hers.

"I'm sorry," he said, taking another step back. "I can't."

Her chest constricted as his hand started toward his throat, then stopped. She wanted to reach out to him, to tell him it would all be okay. Instead, she gave him space as he dropped into a crouch, running a hand through his hair.

She kneeled across from him, close enough that if he wanted to reach out, he could.

Each one of his breaths came faster than the last as he fought a war in his mind. She didn't know what memory had him by the throat, but she recognized the shape of it, knew what it looked like when the past dragged you under. Her chest flooded with anxiety, but she realized quickly that it wasn't hers; it was his.

"Breathe," she pushed the word down the bond.

His eyes snapped up to hers, wild and full of emotion swelling within him. Avery closed her eyes, taking a deep breath of her own, and pushing her feelings of calm down the bond, just as he had done for her. She didn't tell him it would be okay, or that things would get better, or that this would be over soon. She said none of that; she only held him without touching him. Just being there was enough for his breathing to start evening out.

When she opened her eyes, he was staring right at her. "Thank you," he said simply.

It was the least she could do when he had done it for her so many times. And while she could usually claw her way back to calm on her own, having someone else there while she worked through the emotions herself, helped. She'd been alone long enough that admitting she needed that felt like weakness. But she did need it.

"When I was young..."

"Felix, you don't have to."

A tentative silence filled the air, and for a moment, she thought he wouldn't say anything.

"When I was eight, a witch killed my father as he slept."

The breath rushed from her lungs.

He swallowed before he continued, like he was trying to push it down far enough down that it couldn't hurt him anymore. "So I ran to his room, but by the time I got there, it was already over."

An unfamiliar feeling tore through her. A vicious urge to rip apart the witch that had done this to him. To his father. This time she couldn't blame it on Felix; it was her own rage. And when a single tear slipped from his eye. That small drop of water was large enough to crack open something she had repressed for so long. If the witch was still alive, they were dead.

Felix cleared his throat, blinking back another tear. "At that time, I still couldn't shift at will. I couldn't protect him."

"You were a child," Avery said.

"I know. My father hadn't even gone cold before—" He took another deep breath. "She grabbed my throat with both hands. Squeezed. Like I was an insect. Maybe she thought she'd killed me. Maybe she just didn't care. Either way, she left me there on the floor next to my father's body."

Avery opened her mouth to say something, but the words didn't come. What could she possibly say? There was nothing that would make this okay. Nothing that would undo what her people had done to him.

"I'm not telling you so you'll feel sorry for me." His eyes snapped to her, still fierce and defensive after all this time, still so afraid of being pitied that he'd rather be hated. "I'm telling you because you put your hand near my throat and I—"

He didn't finish.

Avery stood there and watched him in the starlight. He wasn't a monster. Just a boy who'd watched his father die. The real monster was the witch who'd murdered a man in his sleep and then choked a child for the crime of existing.

"I'm not going to hurt you," was all Avery could say. The only thing she knew for certain.

As quick as a switch, his face softened. "You couldn't if you tried."

There he was, back to being an asshole.

"I take it back," she said, fake lunging forward. But he caught her wrist mid-motion and pulled, dragging her forward until their knees touched. Felix closed his eyes, took her hand, and placed it gently on his neck. A shaky exhale left him as her palm stretched out across it, his pulse fluttering underneath her touch. She moved slowly, just in case she spooked him. At first, she only moved a thumb across his neck. He didn't stop her. Then, using her fingers, she traced the line of his jaw. Then, the lines of his face, committing them to memory as if they would disappear. Soon, they would. She worked her fingers into his hair, running her hand through his soft, inky waves and then to the base of his cat ears.

"Is this okay?" she asked.

"Mmhmm." He shivered, and when his eyes opened, they were dark, pupils blown wide, darkness sweltering through them.

His hands found her thigh, and he pulled her forward until she was straddling him. The length of him was already hard, pressing against the thin fabric between them. Felix moved his fingers achingly slow, tracing her edges before undoing the buttons of her blouse. "Is this okay?" he asked, mirroring her question from before. Already caught in a daze, she nodded, throat too tight for words.

He pulled the blouse off her shoulders, letting it fall behind them. Then her bralette. Then her skirt. He ran his hands, his real hands, all over her body. He left a burning path, tattooing her skin with his touch, feeling every divot and crevice.

"Please," he said in a hoarse whisper. "*Please* kiss me."

It was so gentle that it almost broke her. He'd told her once he'd never say please to a witch. And here he was, begging *her* to kiss him. It wasn't even a question; she indulged him, their mouths devouring each other as if they were stars colliding. Her heart beat against her ribs, so dangerously close to exploding.

The sound made something in him snap. Her panties didn't stand a chance; he tore through the fabric like it was paper, adding another pair to the growing count of underwear he'd destroyed. She didn't mind, as the pleasure was always worth it. His shadow clothing fell away like smoke, leaving him as bare as her, the last barrier removed between them as she pressed herself against him. Never in her life had something felt so right. That every inch of skin and muscle and bone was born to intertwine with hers. How had she ever thought they weren't meant for this? Her body knew his like they'd been made to fit together.

Out of breath, she placed her hand against his chest, pushing him back for just a moment to see this beautiful creature in all his glory.

His cock twitched under her attention, and—

She froze.

Holy shit, his cock was *barbed*.

The shaft looked normal enough, thick, veins visible along its length. How had she not seen this before? Likely far too distracted by his other talents. But when he pulled the skin back, it revealed another layer beneath it with small barbs.

A soft laugh made her look back at him, her mouth slightly agape. Felix cocked his head, studying her, clearly entertained.

"Will it hurt?" she asked.

"Only if you want me to hurt you." His smile turned feral. "But no, it will only enhance your pleasure."

As if to prove his point, he grabbed her ass and pulled her flush against him, and ground his cock against her core. The barbs dragged against her, an obscenely delicious pressure in all the right places, and...fuck. A strangled moan slipped from her throat.

She couldn't help it; her hips rolled, chasing that friction. The barbs caught against her clit with every movement. He was right, it didn't hurt, it felt fucking amazing. Better even than his tongue.

The sound Felix made was guttural, and his claws slid out, points pressing into her skin, not breaking it, but reminding her who was touching her.

Still, she didn't slow down; she ground against his shaft until she felt sweet pressure building and building. It wasn't enough, not nearly enough. She so badly wanted to feel him inside of her. To feel full of him.

"Felix, please, I want you inside of me." The words came out as a desperate plea.

"Soon, I promise, little witch."

Instead, she felt the ghost of his tail, sleek fur brushing up against her *other* hole. A gasp ripped from her throat as Felix retracted his claws and brought his fingers between her thighs, before two of his fingers plunged into her pussy without warning. She speared herself onto them, chasing *more*.

His fingers plunged in and out, the obscene wet sounds filling the space between them. When she opened her mouth to cry out, his other hand was there, two fingers pushing past her lips and pressing down on her tongue, muffling the sound.

"You're taking them so fucking well, kitten. I fucking love how you grind against my cock." His voice was rough in her mind.

She kept riding the waves of pleasure until she was almost there, almost at the fucking edge.

The whine that tore from her throat was pitiful. His laugh in response was dark, pleased. Bastard. She was going to kill him. Right after he made her come.

"Please," she moaned.

"Please what?"

"Please fucking fill me."

"You dirty fucking witch." His tail circled her ass once more, mercilessly teasing her before it tested the tip of her tight hole. The stretch was unfamiliar, almost too much before her body adjusted to it. But when a thumb came down on her clit, all coherent thoughts fled her mind.

Words left her mouth, but they weren't words anymore, just sounds. *So fucking full. I feel so fucking full.* Her body lit up, almost combusting.

Utter bliss rocked through her as everything moved all at once. His tail in her ass, his fingers in her pussy, pumping in and out, his fingers filling her mouth. In and out. In and out. She was going to shatter.

He used the fingers inside her to pull her forward, grinding his barbed cock against her again. He brought her closer and closer to the edge, until she tumbled over it. A silent cry came out of her mouth as she completely came apart around him, pussy clamping down on his fingers as she shook. Pleasure racked her body in waves, her grip finding Felix's hair and gripping on for dear fucking life.

"Fuck, Avery, that's my good fucking girl."

Felix shuddered beneath her, and she felt the hot spill of his release on her stomach.

Their hearts pounded together as she collapsed forward onto his shoulder. The dragon's fire continued to rain down across the sky.

How the fuck could she ever let him walk away?

THIRTY

FELIX

"REALLY, A WITCH? HOW ORIGINAL," FELIX SAID TO Avery as she spread out her costume on the bed. From what he could see, it was a little black dress. The pointed hat sat beside it, the brim slightly bent at its tip. A pitiful growl rumbled in his throat at the thought of the others looking at what was his. He had planned to attend as Avery's familiar, but in that dress, he would dress up as a brick wall to block any wandering eyes. Even worse, at the back of his mind, his instincts tingled that something bad might happen. Perhaps he could tempt her to stay with a tongue party instead. What a shame that they would miss it.

Avery scoffed at his comment. "Well, that's what Maya chose for Spirit Night, so that's what Maya gets."

She was hiding it well, but a flicker of sadness came down the bond. It really was a shame Maya was a witch; she reminded him of his sister. They would probably get along. If things were different, a different world, he would have even invited her and Avery back to the den. What a fucking fantasy that was.

"Why do you call it spirit night? Isn't it just Halloween?" he asked.

Avery fake-gasped. "How dare you?" she said. "They are *nothing* alike."

Felix gave her a look. And she couldn't keep up the facade.

"Okay, there are a lot of similarities, but it's what we've always celebrated here. The ancient witches of Wales called it Nos Galan Gaeaf, which means night of the winter calends. It is essentially our New Year."

"And what will you do at this party?"

"Well, in witch fashion, there will be a bonfire, lots of drinks, and fraternizing between students." Avery wiggled her eyebrows.

Felix's eyes darkened at the word *fraternizing*. Over his dead fucking body. The image alone of some drunk asshole feeling her up in that sexy costume that no witch or shifter alike deserved to see had his blood boiling. "I'm coming with you."

"You can't. You don't have a costume."

"I can just make some devil horns with my shadows."

"No. That simply won't do." Avery tapped her chin, calculating some diabolical plan he was sure, before she clapped. "I have an idea."

Felix groaned and flopped back onto the bed as Avery went to rummage through her closet with far too much enthusiasm. Before he knew it, she emerged from the closet holding what could only be described as a costume straight from a porn set. A maid's outfit, complete with ruffles and an apron that wouldn't cover a damn thing.

"Absolutely not," Felix said sternly. He was pussy-whipped, but no one on earth could make him show up to a party in that.

Avery gave him a sour look. "Geez, what crawled up your ass and died?"

"You did."

"You wish."

He rose from the bed and closed the distance between them in two strides. Avery gulped and took a step back, but he could tell she secretly loved it. The sweet aroma of her arousal was already filling the air, the cute way her pupils blew out. It was un-fucking-bearable. He needed to taste it. They had time, right? Just a little taste.

A knock interrupted them. God *fucking* dammit. Something about this night was off.

"Avery, it's me!" Maya said.

Felix quickly let the shadows reshape his clothes into a uniform, camouflaging his tail and ears and created Lucky the shadow cat that went with Avery to the door.

Avery gave him a look that screamed, *what are you doing?*

"What? She already thinks we're fucking."

She glared at him. "Fine."

Avery opened the door for Maya, let her in, and gave her a hug that made his own heart squeeze just a bit. God, how soft he had gotten. Already, Avery had rubbed all the edges off of him.

The crow saw him first, giving him a squawk that made Maya stop short. "Oh...hey!"

"Sorry, I should have warned you he was here," Avery said.

"It's all good, the more the merrier! It's Felix, right?" Maya said.

"Yeah, and you must be Maya?" Felix asked faux politely.

"Yep!" she said, popping the 'p.' Her crow cawed again on her shoulder, obviously sensing the danger as she got closer to Felix. "You can hold this." She thrust a bottle of whiskey into his hands, smiling before spinning toward Avery and mouthing something to her that he couldn't quite catch.

"What did she say?" he asked.

"That's for me to know and you to find out, bitch boy."

"Careful, kitten, you'll get a spank for that."

A shiver of arousal ran down the bond that had him grinning like the cat that got the cream.

"We were just discussing Felix's costume for the night," Avery said, her voice dripping with mischief that made him want to grab her and kiss that smug little smile off her face. He groaned, running a hand down his face.

"Oh yeah? What is it?" Maya asked.

"Well, he said he didn't have anything, so I offered him last year's costume."

Smart little thing, she was backing him into a corner to wear a damn maid outfit. He could say no. He should say no. Both of the witches stared at him with a hopeful expression, grinning ear to ear.

"That would be perfect! All you need is cat ears and a tail," Maya said.

Avery choked on a laugh, but not for the reason Maya thought.

He smiled, trying his best not to seem like an asshole in front of her friend. "Great!" he said with fake enthusiasm while Avery laughed all the way to the bathroom to get ready.

He was absolutely not wearing the maid costume.

The maid costume was rather tight. And short. He had to make shadow pants, just so he didn't flash his ass toward everyone. Only Avery was allowed to see "his beautiful buttocks," as she put it so kindly.

Girls could be evil sometimes. The way they both ganged up on him and wore him down was merciless. Avery even pulled out the *no touching her boobs for a week* card. Evil.

They sat on a log near an enormous bonfire that Avery had called a Coelcerth while the sun dipped below the horizon. Tonight was the night when they were meant to go to the midnight cave. Both of them had avoided talking about it. If the final riddle really did break the bond, then...

No. He shook his head. It was better this way.

Avery held a red cup before she downed the dregs of the mysterious punch that had been passed around. He had to admit she looked positively scrumptious tonight. It was simple, but *fuck*, it turned him on. Students lazed around the fire, some throwing stones into it.

Felix's brows furrowed. "Why are they throwing stones?"

"It's tradition, you write your name on it, toss it into the fire, and then if it's not there the following morning, you'll die within the next year."

"Delightful," he said, face blank.

Maya and Avery chuckled at him, and he had to stop himself from joining in.

"How have you been going with your magic?" Maya asked her.

"Really good," Avery said.

They had been practicing, *actually* practicing. Avery was a natural when it came to controlling his shadows. Last night, she had managed to heal her arm on purpose this time. Most importantly, though, Felix wanted to make sure she could defend herself in case something happened.

Guilt gnawed at him. Severing the bond would leave her alone and powerless for any of these witches to hurt. But he couldn't stay here. Something in his chest tore as he thought about leaving her. He couldn't imagine the pain when he actually did. What would it feel like not to have Avery on the other side of that thread?

Instead of unpacking it, he took a sip of whiskey, the burn numbing the pain for one blissful moment.

The harsh caw of Maya's crow jerked him back to the present. Firelight danced over Avery's frame, and she tipped her head back, laughing at something Maya said. Felix smiled, committing the scene to memory. Just in case.

The little witch was only inches away, but he was aware of every one of them. She turned her head toward him, a slight haze of alcohol flushing her cheeks pink. The golden sun warmed their backs as much as the fire did their front, but the heat rising within him had nothing to do with that. He couldn't help himself; he raised his hand and tucked a loose hair behind her ear.

"Can you two get a room?" Maya said jokingly. He had to admit that Maya was growing on him. *Maybe some witches weren't so bad.*

Avery laughed, a blush deepening across her face. "Do you mind getting me another drink?" she asked him.

"Sure."

Am I her bitch now? If he was, he kind of liked it. He knew he was a cat, but if she wanted him to be her dog, he would bark instead. Woof.

Felix walked past students enjoying themselves to the music that floated through the trees, bass thumping under laughter and the crack of the bonfire. Some danced and grinded against each other, others just talked amongst themselves. The smell of burning pine swept through the forest, but still, he could never shake off Avery's scent. He knew there was only one logical explanation for that. But somehow he still didn't want to admit it to himself. It didn't matter anyway. She was a witch. He was a shifter. Their worlds could never collide. No matter how desperately he wanted them to.

When he reached the table with the punch, he filled the cups with the shimmering liquid that seemed bottomless no matter how much had been taken from it. Piles of students congregated around the table playing some sort of drinking game. A girl on the end watched him looking him up and down. Oh no. Time to leave. Before he'd taken two steps, the same drunk girl materialized in front of him, wobbling on her heels.

"Oh my goddessss," she slurred. "I loveee your costume, how did you get the ears and tail to look so real?"

A physical repulsion went through him. Sure, she was pretty enough. Didn't matter. The thought of anyone else touching him, *being* with him, made him want to hurl. The girl batted her hazel eyes at him, waiting for a reply while his tail swished behind him.

"Magic," he said gruffly.

"Righttt," she said, moving to touch his arm before Felix sidestepped her, putting the punch table between them and walking away.

Still, the drunk girl's irritating voice came through the trees. "I can't believe he didn't want me," she whined.

"Don't worry," a familiar male voice said. The voice stopped him dead in his tracks. Felix melted into the shadows behind a tree and poked his head out. Julian fucking Ainsworth. Of course it was. "He's fascinated by that magic-less slut."

A spark of rage lit in Felix's chest as he gripped the cups, claws going right through them. The liquid stained his hands like the blood he was about to spill. Walk away, Felix. Walk the fuck away.

"I need to take a piss," Julian announced.

Nope. This was just too perfect. Who was he to question the divine timing of the goddess? Felix stalked the witch as he walked deeper into the forest next to the shimmering black lake, fog rolling off it as if it were steaming. The sound of the party faded into the background the further they went. The way Julian stumbled told him the idiot was drunk already. He wouldn't be able to kill him yet, not with everyone around to find him. Maybe he could make him piss himself a little?

Not even the twigs snapped as Felix followed behind him like a shadow, the thrill of the hunt filling the void that had been left there for so long since he came here. The only taste he had was his monster hunting Avery in the maze. How he wished he could remember it. This was what he was made for. What he lived for. At least he had, before Avery had come along. Even the slightest picture of the little witch in his mind had him misstepping onto a branch that snapped harshly under his feet.

Luckily, Julian was far too drunk to notice as he leaned a single hand against a gnarling oak far from the party. With his other hand, Julian unzipped his pants, and the sound of a stream hitting a tree filled the air, steam rising in the cool night.

Felix moved up behind him, towering above the disgusting excuse for a man.

He reached out, claws unsheathed. So *close* to impaling them through his neck. He had missed the sweet gurgling sound his victims made. But where was the fun in that? He had barely gotten started. All of his senses came alive, his monster sharpening his hunter senses. The worst was the stink of Julian's god-awful cologne and sour breath. Felix slinked back behind the tree and sent out his shadows to pull his pants down to the ground.

Julian stumbled and caught himself against the tree. "The fuck?"

He tried to pull his pants up again to no avail. Felix's shadows had pinned them. It was entirely immature, but Felix was only three in cat years, so it checked out. What is life without a little silly?

Without any sort of warning, Julian bent over and showed

him where the sun didn't shine. Ugh. Gross. Did that man even wash his ass? He was betting he didn't. Time to go.

Crunching leaves made his head snap to the tree line. Quickly, he faded into the shadows as a familiar face walked out next to Julian as he zipped up his pants and jingled his belt.

What the fuck was she doing here?

Avery appeared through the trees, spotting Julian. "Oh shit, sorry," she said, immediately averting her eyes. "I was looking for Felix."

Ah, shit indeed, she followed the bond here.

Felix could have announced himself, but there was something that told him to hide in the shadows. They had been practicing her magic for long enough now that she could defend herself. She could handle Julian. He was sure of it. Putting down a dog like him was the confidence booster that she needed. His muscles coiled anyway, ready to move the second she needed him.

"It's fine, nothing you haven't seen before, sweetcakes."

Bile rose in Felix's throat as his lip curled, fangs lengthening. The nickname alone was enough to send a fresh hit of rage surging through his veins. Someone should recommend superglue as lip balm to him.

"Don't call me that." Avery's voice came out flat. She seemed more bored with the conversation than anything.

"Why? Brings up too many memories?" Julian moved into her space, swaying slightly, but Avery didn't even flinch. Such a feisty kitten. He liked this side of her.

"Traumatic ones, yes."

"Oh, come on, don't be like that, you used to like it when I—"

"When you what? Couldn't find the clit?" Avery quipped.

Burnnnn. You got this, little witch. Once again, Felix was begging that she kick someone in the balls. Did he need to send her anger into her again? No. She needed to do this on her own.

"Did Felix come this way or not?"

Julian's face instantly dropped, the snide smirk turning sour. "You're wasting your time with him. He's no one."

These were the witches he knew. The ones that were obsessed with power and nothing else. Julian would grow up to be dangerous. Felix's tail lashed behind him in the dirt.

Avery raised a brow. "Opposed to you being *someone*?"

Julian took another step toward her, and Avery backed herself up against the tree. *Come on, little witch.*

"I'm someone who can make you feel much better than he can." Another step. "I know your body, sweetcakes. I know *exactly* what you need."

Avery, unlike Felix, did actually gag, to which Felix had to cover his mouth to stop the laugh coming from his throat.

"You know how hard it makes me when you talk back." Julian laughed, dipping his head before his arm shot out and gripped it around Avery, pushing her flush against the tree. In a split second, he had his hand gripped around her breast, squeezing it and shoving his rat face into her neck while his other hand had made its way up Avery's skirt.

"Fuck off, Julian!" Avery shouted. Shadows that weren't his own wrapped around Julian's body, but the witch was too drunk to notice.

Felix tore across the clearing. He grabbed the mop of Julian's blonde hair and ripped him off his little witch. Julian's hands went up to his head as Felix gripped hard enough for him to feel the witch's scalp trying to detach from his head. He dragged him along the dirt as he kicked and screamed and smashed his face into the nearest tree. It was fitting; the only wood he was getting tonight was a face full of bark.

When he pulled Julian back, blood trickled down his face. Felix almost wished the witch still had his cock out so it would experience the same pain. He stopped for a second as he saw Avery's shadows climb up Julian's legs and tighten around his balls. *Great minds think alike.*

The rage dripping from her features was the most beautiful thing he had ever seen. *Let it out, little witch.*

"What the fuck is this?" Julian screamed again. "My father is the chancellor! You and that bitch will be expelled!"

Felix's smile went feral, eyes slitting. Finally, his shadows materialized, imbuing him with power as they slid along the ground like fog. Sweet recognition poured over the witch's face as he realized the very thing in front of him was no student. It was a monster in a maid's outfit.

"Shifter," Julian breathed out.

Avery had sunk to her knees, watching the scene before her play out. Instinctively, Felix sent one of his shadows out behind him, covering her eyes so she couldn't watch.

Before Julian could scream for help, Felix plunged his face into the bark again, again, and again, the lovely sound of crunching bones into bark like music to his ears. Finally, he stopped making noises. Felix dropped the witch on the floor with a thud, his face more a squished peach than witch. On the bright side, the tree had a new hollow for the owls to nest in.

"Is he dead?" Avery asked, her arms shaking a little.

"As a dodo," Felix said. "Dodo's deserved far better than him, though."

Carefully Felix walked over to Avery, putting himself between her and the body so she didn't see the carnage of what he had left behind. She didn't flinch away from him like he expected. Instead, she leaned into him more, using his body as a means of safety.

"You didn't have to kill him," she said calmly, far more calm than anyone near a maimed body should be.

"I did," Felix said simply. "There is no world where I

would let anyone touch a woman like that and walk away. If I had time, I would have taken him finger by finger, limb by limb, stuffed his own cock in his face, and see how he liked it."

"Thank you."

"Don't thank me for this."

The thumping sounds of paws hitting the ground had him pushing Avery behind him before the griffin hit the ground. It postured itself like it was going to charge, pawing at the ground. Its claws were as big as his goddamn head. *Fuck.* He had forgotten about Julian's stupid familiar. It let out an ear-piercing screech, loud enough to attract attention. Felix hissed back at it, his ears flattening against his head.

"Wait!" Avery said. "Don't attack it."

Felix looked behind his shoulder at the little witch. "Why the fuck not?"

She stepped out from behind him. "Just trust me."

Every part of him screamed to yank her back behind him. To protect her. How hypocritical that in mere hours, he would be leaving her anyway. He ground his teeth together. Was there another way?

Slowly, Avery approached the griffin. It ruffled its golden feathers, lowering its head as it watched her come closer. "Easy," she said, her voice soft. The griffin dug its talons into the earth, making a snapping sound with its beak.

Felix couldn't help the low growl that came out of him. One that the griffin matched.

"Stop," Avery said, not turning around. "You're scaring it."

"It's scaring me," Felix muttered.

The griffin let out a low trilling sound. Avery took another step. Close enough now that Felix's entire body tensed, ready to drag her back if the thing so much as twitched wrong.

And then Avery put her hand on its beak. *Goddamit.* Her and her bleeding heart. But, to his surprise, the griffin leaned into it. Letting out a soft keen, it sat on its paws and folded its wings into itself.

"It's okay," Avery whispered. "You can go home now."

The griffin's eyes fluttered shut, and its form began to shimmer. Gold light bled through its form like splintering cracks in a wall. It stood, wings spreading wide, and Avery stepped back.

The light grew brighter. Warm on Felix's skin even from where he stood. The griffin looked at Avery one last time, something almost like gratitude in its eyes.

Then it was gone, light scattering into nothing.

Avery stood there, hand still raised. The forest settled back into silence.

"What the fuck just happened?" Felix said.

Turning, she smiled at him, not an inkling of sadness in her features. "It returned to the goddess. As all familiars do."

"So...that was normal then?"

"Very."

"Aren't you sad?" Felix said, confused, considering she cried over an ant she accidentally stepped on last week.

She furrowed her brows like she didn't understand the question.

"About Julian? No. About the familiar? Well, there's nothing to be sad about. It's returned to Cerituen's plane to wait for another witch."

He understood it now. It was kind of beautiful. Shifters believed in something similar for their own kind. Maybe everything he had been taught about the afterlife was true. It was hard to doubt when a literal goddess had been fucking with him for the last week. He should really stop cursing the gods so much.

Felix gently pulled her in for a hug. The gesture was as much for her as it was for him.

“What do we do with the body?” she mumbled into his chest as he stroked the outside of her hair.

“I don’t want you to worry about that,” he replied. While he held her, Felix’s shadows picked up the body and tossed it far into the lake. That was a *later* problem. By the time it washed ashore, he would be long gone.

Felix took Avery’s hand, guiding her back to the party as if nothing had happened.

THIRTY-ONE

AVERY

FELIX KILLED SOMEONE.

He killed *Julian.*

But the feeling that ran through Avery wasn't fear. Not even close. Perhaps she could blame the drunkenness, but deep below the whiskey haze, she knew that wasn't the case. Sparks prickled her skin, racing from where Felix's hand touched hers. It should have repulsed her, should have had her yanking away from a killer's grip, but instead she relished it. How could she ever let him go when it felt this good?

Felix guided her out of the woods. A misting rain fell from the sky, the world around her unfocused apart from the man in front of her. The maid costume was gone—discarded in the lake with Julian. Avery's mouth went dry as she watched water droplets cascade down Felix's bare chest. The way they caught the firelight, sliding down his ribs and disappearing below the waistband of his shadow pants, was almost hypnotic. A shifter. A killer. It was what the witches thought of them. And what she should have too. Julian's walloped head, or what was left of it anyway, still haunted her mind. But she didn't feel a lick of remorse. It was strange, considering she felt bad about crushing an ant. The ants, she would feel bad for. They were innocent. A man who tried to take what he couldn't have? He should be crushed and pummeled into the ground. Even the ground didn't deserve that level of filth.

The Coelcerth warmed her chilled skin as they moved closer to the party. Students spun around the bonfire, some tossing their stones into the flames, others grinding and forgetting the world around them. How she wished she could. Out of all the damn witches, why had she been chosen for this life of danger? She was built for bed, not for beheading. Regardless, she wouldn't change it for the world. Because she had met Felix. And that made it all worth it.

"We should go to the cave," he whispered against her ear, a delicious jolt of electricity down her spine.

But she didn't want to go to the cave. Not yet. She wanted to stay here with him. Bonded to *him*. He wasn't a shifter to her anymore. He was just Felix. The man who had taken care of her in so many ways. So instead of letting him drag her away, she fought against his hold just to pull him into her, the fire warming her back and him flush against her front, an intoxicating heat she wanted no escape from. If she was going to burn, this was the way she wanted to go up in flames.

His eyes darkened as he gripped her body tightly, as if he knew exactly where to place them to drive her crazy. Avery started to sway to the music, Felix following in her footsteps. Despite his height, his forehead found hers as they moved to the beat, her body alive next to his. She felt him everywhere. His chest against hers, his thigh pressing between her legs, breath ghosting along her lips. It was too much, and not nearly enough. The world around them didn't matter, the riddle didn't matter, the fact that her mortal enemy had been where she had found her sanctuary. None of it mattered.

The music swelled, and with it, Felix dipped his head even lower and gently, ever so gently, bit her bottom lip. A moan tumbled from her, and Felix responded in kind as he sucked harder, the rumble of a purr vibrating against her body. The sound traveled through her, igniting every nerve. She knew shifters could be dangerous, but never in this way. More than ever, she craved the danger in front of her, like teetering on the edge of a cliff. She knew that only a single word from him calling from below would have her falling over the edge.

But for right now, she stayed firmly on that edge, enjoying the blissful moment before everything changed. In the way he held her, it was like he felt the same. If he let her go, she would simply disappear.

"Please don't kiss me again," he said, voice pained.

"Why?" she whispered against him.

He exhaled deeply like he was trying to steady himself. "Because if you do, I might not be able to stop."

"I don't want you to stop."

Their lips almost collided. So close. But instead, he flipped her so her back was against his chest. He laughed darkly, tilting her chin with his hand so she watched the others just as lost in their own dances as she was.

"When I finally get to kiss you the way you deserve, no one will be allowed to watch. You are mine. Mine to touch. *Mine* to watch. You are an angel that is undeserving of the eyes of mortals."

A fire burned through her at the possessive rasp in his voice, the promise threaded through every word. Her pulse hammered in her throat where his fingers rested, and she wondered if he could feel it, if he knew exactly what those words did to her.

"We need to go," he said, a solemn tone in his voice.

Instantly, her face fell, the cold finding its way between them. Her body begged and pleaded to go back to him. But it wasn't just *her* body that wanted that; it was *his*, too. The bond made sure that both of them knew.

Still, he pulled away.

"Felix, wait," she said.

He turned on his heels, his stare so intense she thought she would simply disappear beneath it. The words were on the tip of her tongue; all she had to say was that she didn't want to break the bond. The words stuck in her throat. What right did she have to ask him to stay, though? To ask him to be bound to her, to live in danger of getting caught every second? As much as she wanted to be with him, she cared about his life more than for it to be tangled with hers. And what a fucking tangle it was. So, against every fiber of her being, she let the wind steal her words away.

"Let's go," she said, smiling, letting go of his hand and walking toward the cave.

The cave entrance was near the north woods, close to where Avery had originally performed the ritual. How fitting—it would end where it started. It had only been less than two weeks, yet her whole life had changed.

They walked past the statue of Cerituen and the plinth that had been cut clean, where pines gave way to the cliffs of Caerwyn. A set of stairs was carved into the very cliff face itself. The stone was worn smooth by wind and salt, treacherously slippery in the dark. Avery moved down first, keeping one hand on the rock wall, feeling the damp algae slick beneath her fingers. Dust bunnies wove between their legs, almost tripping Felix as he walked behind her, muttering curses at the little things. Did they disintegrate in the water? She didn't want to think about it. Waves crashed against the moonlit stairs, sending the spray high enough to cover them with mist. She didn't even need to look back at Felix to feel the annoyance coming from him. The lower they went, the higher the tide rose.

They stopped at the lowest step, waves breaking on her ankles. Felix stayed on the step above, a nervous jitter coming through the bond that, for once, wasn't hers. Turning around, she saw Felix's face recoiling as he looked upon the inky depths of the ocean. The cave entrance was at least fifty yards away, the mouth of the cave still partially underwater. They still had time until midnight.

"We're going to have to swim to it," Avery said.

Felix looked toward the water, then back at Avery, his jaw tight. She had never seen the man be truly afraid of anything. Even when he was stuck in the tree, he was still sassy; now, he was just... silent. An 'O' formed on her lips as the realization took hold of her.

"Are you afraid of the water?" she said.

"No," he said too quickly.

Avery narrowed her eyes at him. "Then what is it?"

"I can't..."

"Can't what?"

"I can't..." He licked his fangs.

Finally, he closed his eyes and huffed out a breath. "I can't...swim."

"Oh." Avery raised her eyebrows in disbelief.

"Yeah. Oh."

Avery fought the urge to laugh; it was almost poetic—a cat that couldn't swim. "Do you at least know how to doggy paddle—well, cat paddle?" An almost laughable thought came to her mind of Felix paddling in the ocean with his head barely above water. She shouldn't laugh. She really shouldn't.

"Funny."

She bit her lip to keep the smile from forming. "It's the only way to get across."

"I know," he said, resignation in his voice.

Avery could tell he was truly nervous. Out of all things that would best him, it would be the ocean.

As if nature wanted to remind them just how mighty she was, a large wave came up and drenched them both in icy water. It hit like a gut punch, stealing all the breath from her lungs as her already tight dress became heavier with the cool water.

Still, the water dripping off Felix's brow onto his bare chest was enough for Avery to let a giggle slide out. His long tongue came out to catch the drop. Felix looked less than impressed.

"Do you trust me?" Avery said, echoing his words from before, holding out her hand for him to take.

"No," he said, but she knew he didn't mean it, as his hand slid into hers.

Avery gave him a reassuring smile.

"Just don't let go of me, okay?"

She squeezed his fingers, looking over the moonlit water that thrashed against the rocks. Even with his body weight, she was a strong swimmer, and would be able to guide him through the water. "On the count of three, we jump," Avery said, a wicked smile forming on her face. "One—"

She pulled him into the water.

Her stomach lurched as the frigid water swallowed them. Cold pierced into her bones like knives, her muscles seizing. For a heartbeat, she couldn't think, could only feel the shock of it as they were suspended beneath the waves, the calm beneath the storm. It was rougher than she thought, the waves pushing and pulling them towards the rocky edge. Currents tugged at her dress, trying to twist her around. She kicked hard, fighting to orient herself in the churning dark. It was violent and beautiful all at the same time. The force of it tried to separate them, but she clung to him and pulled them upward.

Their heads broke the surface, Felix gasping desperately for breath. He flapped and flailed, trying to swim, but instead pulled them under the water again. His weight dragged her down. Water filled her mouth, her nose, and panic spiked through her chest before she kicked harder, hauled them both up.

"Felix!" she managed to scream before he yet again pulled them under the surface.

Once again, she pulled them up and grabbed a hold of his face, shaking it. "For the last fucking time, calm down! You'll drown us!" she yelled over the roar of the waves.

For a moment, he calmed on the surface, at least. She felt his legs thrashing, trying to keep his head afloat. His chest heaved against hers, his eyes wide and wild.

"Shift!" Avery yelled at him.

"Why?" he said through gargled breath.

"Just trust me."

He gave her one last look, as if he was about to die, and he was memorizing her face for the final time. It took Avery all of her willpower not to slap him.

Felix shifted into a cat, looking like a soggy rat as she scooped him into her. She winced as his claws dug into her shoulder and onto her scalp. Finally, he settled on her head, like a very fashionable cat tail hat. But her arms were free, and she wasn't getting kicked or dragged under the waves.

A piercing yowl wailed in her ear as she swam toward the entrance of the cave and fought against the dark waves while Felix's tail obscured her vision. Hopefully, all this splashing around didn't attract the sharks. Felix would never even look at the water again. The silver moonlight lit her path, almost as if the goddess were guiding her towards it. She even saw dust bunnies riding the waves. So they *didn't* disintegrate.

The water became calmer as she swam into a deep pool cut off from the rolling waves, the sudden stillness disorienting.

Gigantic rocks shot out from the water and formed a protective barrier between them and the force of nature, the sound of the waves quietening. She could only just touch the bottom by the time they reached the entrance.

She had been here before. It was a well-known spot on the island that only the strongest swimmers could get to. She and Wren used to jump off the cliffs and swim into the cave at midnight, much to the chagrin of her mother, who, in hindsight, only cared about Wren's safety; she was sure.

They had come right on time. Despite it being called the midnight cave, it actually opened up a bit before that. The top lip of the entrance became visible as scarlet water bled out from the cave, mixing with the blue like an artist's palette. She forgot how beautiful it was; it was truly a wonder of the island. It almost made sense that this would be where the final riddle would be solved. There were always rumors that this was where the ley lines converged on the island.

Avery waited until the water came low enough to fit her *and* her new hat underneath the mouth. Dust bunnies dived under with them, swimming into the cave. She ducked, holding onto Felix with one hand and using the slimy top as a guide with the other.

Moving through the tunnel, she noticed that the water that touched her created luminous ripples cascading outward, as if it were alive. That was new. The deeper she went, the more heated the water became, almost like a natural spring. All the cold left her body, replaced by a delightful warmth.

At the end of the tunnel, it opened up to an enormous cavern. Every other time she had been here, it had been pitch black. She and her sister had fumbled around in the dark with flashlights for hours just to find their way back out before the water swallowed the entrance once again.

But this time, she could see *everything*. Her lips parted as she looked around. Slowly, she watched as every inch of the cave walls lit up red, twinkling like a night sky. Even the plants that hung from the ceiling were a brilliant crimson color. It was another world entirely.

She waded through the water until her feet met a soft bed of sand, like silk beneath her feet.

Time to get this hat off. She gently coaxed Felix into the water like she had weeks ago in the bath. The memory brought a soft smile to her face. He clung to her hair, taking some of it with him as she lowered him towards the water. "You can shift back now."

Felix made a displeased hiss as his paws met the water. For a moment, he flailed as she held him afloat. Then he shifted, looking exactly like the day she met him, wet and pissed off. This time, she wasn't scared. This time, his eyes had softened just a touch. She slid her hands over his chest, the red glow of the water reflecting in his eyes. As much as he hated getting wet, he looked so handsome when he was absolutely drenched. Water streamed down his face, dripping from his hair onto his shoulders, making his skin gleam in the strange light. Avery let out a laugh as she moved a piece of his hair from his face.

"See? Not so bad, is it?" she teased.

"You terrify me," he said softly, so quiet she almost missed it.

"A magicless witch scares a shifter? Someone call the news."

"You are not magicless anymore, not with me."

For how much longer? She wanted to ask. But she didn't. Instead, she looked away from him, not able to keep the emotion from drenching every feature. It was futile. He knew. He always knew. He caught her chin and brought her back to face him, cocking his head.

Despite her mind telling her not to, the words tumbled from her lips. "What happens when we break the bond?"

Felix swallowed, as if he were hesitating. "Do you want

that?" he asked. The tone in his voice had a fracture forming in her chest.

"I..." Avery hesitated. She knew what she wanted. She wanted him.

Without him, she had no magic. She would go back to being useless, or at least she would be by her mother's standards. It wasn't about the magic anymore, not really. She had gone her whole life without magic; she could survive without it. But the thought of not being bonded to Felix?

That bond was her now. Woven into her skin and bones. It was a far scarier reality than being magicless ever was.

But when she opened her mouth, nothing came out.

A sad smile fell onto Felix's face.

No, say something! Her heart screamed at her to fix it, to tell him not to break the bond, for them to figure it out. But before she could speak, Felix was kissing her. He didn't ask for permission; he took what he wanted and stole her breath along with the last string of her heart that was still holding onto a world where she could live without him in it.

"Just one more," he said, stealing a quick kiss before pulling away. It must have been close to midnight. Close to when the goddess would break the bond.

An unspoken feeling bloomed between them that they would be bonded until that time. And they were going to fucking act like it.

"One more," he said.

He didn't waste any more time. A fervent heat overtook them as his lips found hers again. It wasn't delicate by any means; he was hungry. No. *Ravenous* for her. Their tongues twisted over each other, his rough one playing with the soft parts of her mouth. Nerves sang as Felix devoured her with the savageness of a man who had nothing left to lose. Nothing else would ever feel this good again. She was absolutely sure of it.

His hands tightened around her waist as he pulled her

closer, goose bumps exploding over her skin. She wrapped her legs around him as he walked them back through the glowing water to the cave wall, the water lapping at their waists. Her back met the cold stone, but she didn't care, not when this man was in front of her.

Hands explored her body like he couldn't get enough of it, grabbing and pulling, desperate for her to be closer. His shadow pants fell away, dissolving into the water and forgotten entirely. Not long after, her dress was coming over her head, flung somewhere she didn't care. All she cared about was that every inch of her was touched, and even still, it wasn't enough.

He tore away again, his eyes burning into hers. "Fuck my pride, fuck everything. I want you. No, I fucking need you, Avery."

Her heart soared at the words, flooding her with warmth and need. Because she needed him, too. It wasn't a question anymore. The bond whipped between them, wild and untamed, demanding that they collide. That they meld into one.

"Come back to the den with me," he said, softer this time. "Please."

He wanted her to come back to the den with her?

The vulnerability in his gaze broke something in her. How could she say no?

Before she could answer, his claws raked against her ass—not hard enough to cut, but enough to make her gasp, taking any sort of coherent thought away from her. The scrape of them against her skin sent shivers racing up her spine, making her arch into him. Using his shadows, he slid down her panties, careful not to shred them this time.

Goddess, how she needed him to touch her. Mind, body, spirit, and pussy, the holy quadrinity needed him. Impatient, she rubbed her bare mound against his hard length, the barbs creating the perfect friction. A moan tumbled from her, echoing around the cave. The water swelled around them, the tide coming and going in a gentle lapping motion. The red glow pulsed brighter with each wave, turning everything dreamlike. He held her hips back, so she couldn't do it again. A frustrated groan escaped her.

Using his tongue, he made a *tut tut* sound. "Good things come to kittens who wait, little witch."

True to his word, he positioned her just at the tip of his cock, using his smooth head to rub against her clit. *Fuck, it felt good.* Slowly, he tested the entrance, pushing just between her folds. She took in a hitched breath as it did, straightening her back against the stone wall. His hands grabbed at her skin, desperately clawing like he was restraining himself.

"Please," she whimpered.

That was all it took. A simple *please.* He looked up at her, their eyes meeting for one suspended second. But he didn't look away. Even as his cock speared into her.

A scream tore from her throat as he filled her up, stretching her inner walls to just the edge of pain. It was almost too much, the fullness pushing deep into her pussy. Her body fought to accommodate him, stretching and adjusting around him. But when she did, it was fucking incredible.

And when he moved, she felt the glorious barbs gripping into her walls, heightening the pleasure tenfold. It should hurt, but for some reason it didn't. It just made everything feel so much fucking *better.* She had never felt anything like it. He slid out slowly, much to her protest. She didn't need to wait much longer. A needy moan slipped from her lips as he guided her down onto his length. Each withdrawal left her achingly empty, each thrust filled her so completely she thought she might shatter. The water amplified every sensation, the slick slide of skin on skin, the way he stretched and filled and claimed her.

Out of the corner of her eye, she saw shadows come out to play. They wrapped themselves around her breasts and squeezed her nipples.

Felix let out a grunt. "You can take it, kitten. You're doing so well."

A savage need pulsed through her at the praise and the edge in his voice that said he was barely holding on. Did she really have such an effect on him? It was addictive. Just to test her theory, she moved one of her hands through his hair, and almost instantly his whole form shook with the contact. Avery moaned, arching her back into the rock wall. He took advantage of the angle, tongue scraping, circling the peaked flesh, before his fangs scraped across them. At first, she thought he was about to pierce her other nipple. Actually, she welcomed the idea. Instead, he latched his mouth onto her unpierced nipple, continuing to drive himself deeper and deeper.

She looked up, praying it wasn't midnight yet so this could last just a bit longer.

Long fingers squeezed her cheeks, forcing her to look at him.

"If you look away from me again, I'll stop."

If they had time, she would have done it just to see what he would do. Her thighs clenched around his waist, pulling him into one long, deep stroke that had her so close to coming. Another breathy whimper escaped her—but she didn't look away. She held his gaze, watching his honey and green irises contract and dilate as his lips parted around a moan. She committed them to memory. How was this going to be the last time she would be this close to him? It couldn't be.

More than the obvious lust between them, something else was happening. With each thrust, she felt more of herself pour into him, and more of him seep into her. Shadows shot out from her, intertwining with his, as if they were a physical manifestation of their souls becoming one. The bond sung between them, alive and growing.

A sort of frenzy overtook them. His rhythm grew erratic and desperate as he pounded into her. She could feel it through the bond, the primal urge not just from him. But from her. It was impossible to ignore. The urge to claim and mark him in a way that didn't make sense to her right now.

He hesitated for just a second.

"Don't you dare fucking stop," she said fiercely.

Something wild flashed in his eyes, the last thread of his control snapping.

"I need to—I'm sorry." Felix gave over to it and sank his fangs into her shoulder, and at the same time, the barbs inside of her turned into spikes, hooking into her flesh. Pain flared through her for only a second before a delirious pleasure replaced it. The room blurred, while the lights dimmed and flickered in time with their hearts like crimson starlight. Her body hummed, every fiber of her very being electrified as Felix bit down even further. She didn't register the blood running down her back, nor did she have any control over what she did next.

Instinct took over. She bit him back, sinking her little canines into his skin, driven by the same primal need as him. Blood filled her mouth, the metallic taste of it gliding over her tongue. Felix shuddered under her, a purr rumbling through him, which only made her bite down harder, a feral desire surging through her. Magic flooded her veins, and with it, a merciless onslaught of ecstasy took her over. It was like her body was gone, floating above somewhere else. This was what they were made for. For this single moment. They were too deeply entwined, too deeply embedded in each other for anyone to ever pull them apart. Goddess help anyone who tried.

Felix thrust deeper, groaning as she felt the base of his cock begin to swell. Yes, goddess, *yes*. He ripped his mouth away from her shoulder, blood coating his lips. He was feral. He was beautiful.

"Mine."

The single word shattered her, thrusting her back in her body as she finally combusted, the orgasm ripping through her like a wildfire. Felix roared, hard enough to shake the walls of the cave as his cock swelled even more, his release spilling hot into her core.

Small rocks tumbled from the ceiling, splashing into the glowing water. The entire cavern shook like the island itself was responding to what they'd done—and maybe it was.

He thrust in one more time and held himself deep as the knot swelled fully, stretching her past what she thought possible, locking them together so completely she could feel his pulse inside her.

Felix's head rested against her chest, their breath heaving together. She ran her fingers through his wet hair. For one blissful moment, they just embraced each other.

"I'll come with you," she murmured into his hair. Somehow they would get out of here. There was nothing else she could do. There wasn't anywhere in the world he could go that she wouldn't follow. They needed to leave the cave before the goddess could break the bond.

His breath warmed her chest as he murmured against it. "If you think I would have let you go now that I have you, you would be very wrong. Your goddess herself would have to tear you from me, and even then I would fight her to my dying breath."

Felix lifted his head, eyes relaxed and drowsy, roaming her body. Already, the heat returned to her.

But then, he stilled. The color drained from his face.

"What is it?" She swallowed, looking down at her body, at her arms.

Oh shit.

Black marks almost identical to Felix had appeared. The marks spiraled up her arms, across her collarbone, down her ribs, and legs. She studied her arm, calmer than she should have.

"What are they?" she asked.

Felix swallowed. "They're mating marks," he said, his eyes roaming her body in disbelief. "You're my mate."

The walls started to shake.

Thirty-Two

Felix

The cave was going to collapse, but at least Felix would die inside of Avery. What a way to go. Knotted inside his *mate.* The marks confirmed it.

Mate—it was a word that swirled around his mind. It was the only way to describe his connection to Avery that made sense. Nothing had ever felt more right. She was his, and not even the goddess could take that away. At least he hoped anyway. Panic flooded his system. *Avery.*

Using his body, he covered Avery from the loose rocks falling from the cave's roof; sharp fragments pelted his back, bouncing off and plopping into the water. Lights pulsed in an erratic rhythm. Then, as fast as it came on, it stopped, plunging them into darkness.

Fuck. It was the goddess. It had to be. Felix held onto Avery tighter, as if holding onto her physically would stop the magic from tearing them apart. His eyes tried to adjust to the dark, but he couldn't see anything. It was as if someone was intentionally blinding him.

"What's happening?" Avery's voice quivered.

"I'm not sure, little witch," he said, hackles raising. His

knot eased, and he pulled out of her in preparation to fight the invisible force that wanted to separate them. One day soon, he would knot his mate completely, staying there for as long as he goddamn liked. Well, as long as Avery wanted him to. Felix's shadows shot out, covering them like armor.

The blood from where they had bitten each other seeped into the water. It absorbed it like a hungry mouth, making its own river before it branched out across the wall like an intricate spider web with its own beating heart.

Slowly, the unnatural starlight died down to embers, plunging them into the dark. He didn't let go of Avery. Not a fucking chance. He placed his head against her, realizing her chest wasn't moving.

"Breathe, little witch."

She shuddered out a deep exhale. "I'm your mate?"

The lights exploded again, blinding him for a second. Felix rarely flinched, but this time he did, fear and adrenaline racing through him as he waited for his eyes to adjust to the brightness. And when they finally did, he saw a familiar face.

"Bingo!" the goddess said, cackling manically to herself. Just like the tree, she had carved herself a face, this time out of rocks.

Felix rolled his eyes. "Fucking hell, you scared the shit out of us."

"What's the point of life if you don't terrify people just a little bit?" The goddess smiled and the hairs on his arm stood up. The last time he had seen her, she had sent him into an uncontrollable frenzy. If that happened again, he would kill her. Somehow. The goddess peered around him, as if actually looking for his good bits in the water.

Wait. "Were you watching us the whole time?" Felix snarled.

"Perhaps." The goddess laughed. "It would have been rude to interrupt. And what a show you two put on!"

"Oh my goddess." Avery pressed a hand over her face.

"Yes." The stone face looked insufferably pleased with itself. "Exactly."

For a moment, there was silence. Avery tightened her grip on his arm, and her anxiety rushed through him. He knew exactly what she was about to ask, and he desperately needed the answer.

"Are you going to break the bond?" she asked.

The goddess let out a bellowing laugh, enough to shake the cave again, more loose stones falling from the top. "You really think I would go to all this trouble just to break you up? This is the most fun I've had in centuries."

"So..." Avery said, confused. "You're not going to break it?"

An unnerving smile pulled at the goddess's lips, the stone cracking with the force. "Just the opposite. You are mated for life under my *very* watchful eye, the first witch-shifter mate bond in thousands of years."

Felix swallowed. "We aren't the first?"

"No, sorry, you're not *that* special," the goddess said. "But I'll show you this."

Confusion threaded through him as the goddess faded away, stone returning to normal. For a moment, they just stood in the darkness, waiting and watching. The longer it went on, the more Felix primed himself to fight. Who knew what the goddess had in store?

"Look," Avery said, pointing to the corner. A figure with massive horns and jagged tail swishing behind it bloomed out of the darkness, made entirely of red starlight. It walked across the cave wall, footsteps silent, each movement leaving trails of light that faded into the stone.

"A dragon shifter," Felix whispered, mesmerized by the display. It stood there, looking left to right as if it were searching for something or someone. Another figure emerged from the other end. Swirls of magic danced around them, curling and flying across the wall. A pointy hat materialized on the other figure's head. It was a little on the nose, but it got the point across. Most definitely a witch then.

Slowly, the two walked toward each other, their hands reaching out. They circled each other for a few turns, inching closer. Their magic twisted together before they did, spiraling in loops that reminded Felix of dragons dancing.

And when their hands finally touched, the cave erupted. Their aura of stars intensified, cascading off the walls and into the air in mighty swirls that he could feel pulsating on his skin. Involuntarily, his body tensed. A bit of PTSD from the pollen. The goddess wasn't going to make him turn again, would she?

Felix looked down at his mate, the recognition clear in her face. The bond flared in his chest, responding in kind to the magic cascading down above them like a shimmery waterfall. She took his hand, their own power answering the call and threading through their veins.

But the vision playing out before them wasn't done.

Dozens more figures appeared on either side of the pair. They moved like a swarm, grabbing the pair as they reached out for each other, wrenching them apart, even as they desperately tried to claw their way back. Pain flared in Felix's chest. Was the goddess foreshadowing their own demise? Or was it something else? The mobs disappeared without the witch and shifter for only a second before running back into the middle in a violent clash of bodies and magic. It was silent, but he could hear their mouths opening and screaming as the fight became a massacre.

The cave went dark again, swallowing the violence in its stone.

"What does it mean?" Avery said.

The goddess's face returned, the stone contorting in ways

it definitely should not. "Did you not watch the movie I played you? I worked hard on that."

"Explain," Felix said gruffly, not caring that he was in the presence of a goddess who could probably wipe him out before he even blinked.

The goddess sighed, as if disappointed in their lackluster detective skills. "Your god is gone. I do not know where. I have spent a very long time looking." The stone face showed nothing, but something in the air of the cave pressed down. "A god without their mate does not function as they should. Neither, it turns out, does their creation."

"Those figures were you and Arawn." Avery's voice came out quiet. "Your separation. That's why."

"That is why," the goddess confirmed. She looked away wistfully, as if recalling a painful memory. "You were never meant to hate each other. You were meant to be more powerful together than you could ever be apart. You were meant to be mates." A pause. "Your people chose to go in another direction."

"You let it happen," Felix said.

Avery grabbed his arm, but he didn't take it back.

The goddess looked at him, her stone face unreadable. "I did. I may be a goddess, but my mate is gone, his power with it." She sighed longingly. And for the first time, Felix understood her. Avery was his mate—what would it be like to lose her?

"I also try to respect your free will, to a point." Dry amusement returned to her expression. "Although you all seemed to run with it a bit too far, you seem very comfortable hating each other."

"Thousands of years of war," Felix said, his jaw clenching so hard he thought his teeth might break. "Witches and shifters dead."

If she could have done something, then why didn't she? If

this was what shifters and witches were made for, then why had they been kept separate for so long?

"Felix." Avery's hand pressed harder on his arm. A warning.

"I am not offended," Ceritu en said. "He is not wrong. I have always been here, but I have been limited to what I can and can't do by forces much greater than me." The goddess paused. "Because my mate is gone, I must conserve my power for when it matters."

Felix tried to believe her, but truly, it was hard to take a talking rock seriously. He wouldn't be surprised if somehow this had all been a hallucination. Although he hoped to god it wasn't. The only thing more painful than losing Avery now was never knowing her at all.

"It is up to you now. Everyone will try to separate you again, but mark my words, I will find Arawn, and this world will be whole once more. But I cannot do it alone; the hatred has gone too far."

As the goddess faded away, Avery came around the front of Felix, wading through the water to get closer to her.

"Wait! Why me? Why us?" she asked.

The goddess looked down on her, not in judgment, but with respect. "Your lineage is powerful, Avery. What runs in your blood has the ability to change the world. Unfortunately, some in your family have used that for nefarious purposes."

That checked out. It basically just confirmed that Avery's mother was behind the shifter kidnappings. But if the goddess knew more, he needed to find out. "What do you mean by that?" Felix asked.

"I cannot say more."

"The statues?"

"Nope."

"Helpful." Felix's face fell.

"I try." She shrugged, the rocks cracking as she did.

But Avery wasn't done with the questions. "Why did you choose Felix?"

"He has a nice ass," the goddess said candidly.

Felix blinked. Really? That was all he had going for him?

The goddess laughed. "No, I'm just kidding. He's your fate. It was written long before you were born. You will change your fellow shifters."

Fate. As if he had never had a choice at all. It didn't matter now. He was glad it had let him here. To Avery. The other stuff he could really do without, but Avery, he could not live without. But to be honest, the gods' affairs were of no concern to him, whether there were many or one, or where his god had gone. All that mattered was Avery and undoing the steaming shit pile the gods had left for them.

He took a deep inhale, focusing on what he could control. The shifters in his den hated witches as much as they had before he had met Avery. But they didn't have a choice anymore; he would shove Avery's love down their throats, and they *would* change their minds. At least about her. For the other witches, he wasn't so sure.

The goddess cleared her throat. "I'll leave you with a final riddle." She paused for dramatic effect. "The council sucks, don't trust them."

Avery gave out a disappointed huff. "That's a terrible riddle."

"I will still be here watching." The rocks cracked as the goddess smiled. "Specifically, I will be keeping an eye on you both because you are absolute freaks in the sheets."

"Ugh, gross," Avery said. Heat crawled up Felix's neck. A literal divine being was commenting on their sex life. Outstanding.

And with that, the face faded into the cave wall, leaving only bare rocks. The cave was plunged into darkness once again, the only light coming from the ripples as they moved. The silence felt louder than the goddess's voice.

Felix's heartbeat thundered in his ears, but Avery touched his arm, and it was enough to bring him back to the here and now. Her hands tangled in his, sending shivers up his spine. Somehow in the last hour, her touch had become even more divine. More intense. He would never get sick of it.

"My mate." He moved his hand to cup her face. "My marks look good on you."

They really did. The way they moved over her soft skin utterly mesmerized him. How was it possible that she looked even more attractive now? A primal urge surged through him, his monster satisfied with what they had done. *Mine.* The word echoed through him.

"Do you think they grow every time we do it?"

Felix hiked Avery out of the water so she was straddling him, their noses almost touching. "There's only one way to find out."

Avery giggled as Felix pushed them against the rock wall and buried his face in the crook of her neck, her intoxicating cinnamon scent filling his head with desire. He wanted to bite her and mark her again, keep her where no one could ever reach her but him. But if he knew anything about Avery, she was not a bird to be caged, not on this island, and certainly not by him. He would follow her into hell if that was where she led him.

But he had to make one request. "Let's go back to the den tonight," he murmured against her neck, not caring if he sounded desperate anymore. He just wanted her safe. She was far too good for this world. Far too good for him. Did it make him a terrible person to love her? He didn't care. Call him selfish, but fuck, he would hide her away if it meant no one would lay eyes on her again.

Mine.

Avery stiffened in his grasp, and Felix lowered her into the water, the cold rushing between them. "What is it?" he asked, as if he didn't already know.

"It's just..." she started, and his heart sank.

Had she already changed her mind? After everything, would she reject him here and now? The seconds stretched out far too long.

She chewed her lip. "Getting off this island is all I ever wanted. But I'm also scared to leave my world behind, and to enter a den of shifters who quite clearly would want to murder me."

"I would never let anyone hurt you," he said, brushing her wet hair away from her face. The shifters would accept her, or he would tear them apart limb by limb until they did.

A tear slipped from Avery's face, and Felix gently thumbed it away. "I just want to say goodbye to everything I have known, before we run away."

As much as it pained him to see her cry, his heart soared instead. She *did* want to come with him. He was so happy that he wanted to start purring. Instead, he pulled her into a hug. The way she breathed against him was a feeling he would never tire of. Their hearts beat as one, as she fit perfectly beneath him.

Carefully, she kissed the crook of his neck, and he didn't even flinch. He never had craved someone's touch as much as he did hers. Never thought that a witch would be the one to undo the damage one of her kind had inflicted in the first place. How ironic that things that hurt the worst could sometimes be the greatest source of love.

"Felix," she said breathlessly, but not because she was overcome by emotion, but because he was literally restricting her breathing.

"Sorry," he said, loosening his grip only marginally. "I can't help it."

He didn't know who started laughing first. But just for that moment, everything was perfect.

The tide was low enough now for them to walk on the rocks rather than swim back through his most treacherous enemy, the sea. His hatred for deep waters had now overtaken witches. The beach was a close third, because not only did you wake up with sand everywhere, even in your crack, but it was also close to the ocean.

The grains of silver sand crunched beneath their feet as they trudged along it. The wind howled loud enough that it set his teeth on edge, almost as if it were trying to warn them of something. He would prefer it to be quiet, so he could actually hear if danger was approaching.

They only had to stay on this godforsaken island long enough for Avery to say goodbye.

His shadows did their best to protect them from the bite of the wind, clothing them from head to toe. The only person who was allowed to bite Avery was him.

"How are we going to get off the island?" she asked, raising her voice so it wasn't drowned out.

"I have my ways," he said, walking backward to face her and wiggling his eyebrows.

Avery snorted. "I've tried to get off the island at least a hundred times, but I've never actually made it through the wards."

"But you've also never had a handsome shifter by your side to break them." He winked.

She rolled her eyes. "My savior."

"I have an idea. But you might not like it."

Before he could even open his mouth to explain, the sound of wingbeats cut him off. Dread snaked through him as he looked up to the sky. The fucking dragon. Its large body descended downward with alarming speed. He bet his left nut it was Wren. But that wasn't all; more creatures descended from the clouds—a pegasus, and a couple of griffins. *Fuck.*

There was no time to run. Any one of those creatures could catch him. The dragon alone would make a roast dinner out of him.

Shadows pooled at his feet, but he didn't bother hiding them. If they were descending with so many, they already knew. His tail whipped behind him, adrenaline pumping through his body. All his senses sharpened, ready for a fight he definitely couldn't win. That didn't mean he wouldn't try, though.

The little witch's hand shook as he took it into his, gripping it tightly. Her fingers trembled against his, pulse hammering so fast he could feel it through her palm. But she didn't let go, even as her sister's dragon hit the beach with a thump. The impact shook the ground. Sand exploded outward, the wind whipping it around.

The unit descended all around them, encasing them in a circle as he pulled Avery into him. Over the hill, a handful of enforcers' rifles glinted. Yep, they were fucked. He was strong, but he couldn't take down an entire unit out in the open.

Calmly, Wren jumped off her dragon as it bowed its head for her. He didn't know why, but the very movement made the blood boil in his veins, seeing its blind obedience to a witch. Felix still had far to go before he didn't meet every witch with visceral hatred.

"Shifter," Wren hissed, holding her rifle up.

"Guilty," Felix said, a feral smile pulling at his lips. He made sure his fangs showed.

"Step away from it," Wren said, not talking to him.

Avery let go of his hand.

Thirty-Three

Avery

Avery moved in front of him. There wasn't a chance in hell she could do anything to protect him, but it was the thought that counted. Never in a million fucking years did she think she would be lying down to be a sacrifice for a shifter, but here she was.

Wren didn't take her eyes off the shifter, her gaze fixed on the threat. "I'm not asking, Avery. Move away from it now."

Avery didn't say anything, only held her head up high. It was almost sad how much Wren sounded like their mom. They had been close once. Not anymore. Not after she had become an enforcer and the spitting image of her mother.

Wren made a signal with her hand, and the sound of cocking rifles rang over the crashing waves. Tension rippled through the bond as Wren came two steps closer, enforcers following closely behind. She could feel Felix priming himself for a fight, her body doing the same. For the first time, the shadows didn't feel so far away, like they were at her beck and call, simmering just under the surface and ready to strike.

"Don't," was all she said to Felix. As much as her sister was a bitch, she didn't want her to get hurt either. There was a way

to come out of this without bloodshed. Because that was what it would be.

"Do you have any idea what you are standing next to? What this looks like?" Wren said, venom dripping off every word. But her sister had a tell, the slight clench in her jaw told her it was a front, that fear was driving her more than anything. Avery didn't blame her for it, though. Her mother and every other person on this island had shifter hatred drilled into them since they were children. Untold stories about how dangerous they were.

"I know what it looks like," Avery said, trying to keep her voice even despite the tremble in her arms.

Wren blinked, gripping the rifle. "Then you understand why I have to do this."

"Please, I'm begging you to let us go."

Wren laughed coldly. "Leave? Avery, listen to yourself. Where are you going to go with a shifter?" Her demeanor showed a crack for only a second before it went back to its practiced mask. She never used to wear it, not much anyway, but since she became a commander, since her father had died, it had become a permanent fixture on her.

"The shifters killed our father," she said, devoid of any emotion.

She held her sister's gaze. "He could still be alive."

"Don't be stupid. Shifters have killed so many of us, and you're standing there having a fucking stroll with one."

Avery flinched, but she didn't let the doubt take root. She knew it looked like she was spitting on her father's empty grave. But what she didn't have enough time to explain was, well, *everything*. The bond, the bunnies, the goddess, the statues. That everything wasn't what it seemed, and that she had bet her life on Felix, several times over. But there wasn't enough time. Her throat felt tight, words scraping out as she spoke. "We have it all wrong. Shifters are not who you think they are."

Behind her, Felix said nothing, but she felt another thrum of power surge down the bond, a crackling force ready to unleash at any moment.

Disgust flickered along Wren's face, her eyes hardening. "I will not let one of them take another one of my family away."

Avery's heart dropped, a conflicted flicker going through her. Her sister did care, but it was too late. Avery knew what she was about to do. Time seemed to stop, the beach deadly quiet as Wren sent out the command. "Take the shifter!"

"No!" The word tore out of her as chaos ensued around her.

The enforcers moved.

But Felix moved first.

Shadows exploded as the monster inside Felix formed into a beast as large as the dragon. It let out a deafening roar, bullets slicing through its limbs. No matter what they thought. It was still Felix. Her mate. She had to stop this. Had to stop him from being killed. But before she could do anything, a whip of darkness flung Avery into her sister.

No.

Pain flared up her side as she landed in the cold sand. The impact knocked the air out of her lungs, while bullets continued to whistle past her as she took wheezing breaths.

"What are you doing!" Avery said to Felix through the bond.

"You will be safe with her. I will hold them off for as long as I can."

Shot after shot rang out. She saw it unfold in slow motion. Shadows moved everywhere, piercing enforcers like spears and tossing their limp bodies into the ocean, the inky depths claiming their souls. Magic burned her nostrils so much that she wanted to claw it out.

Her sister's hand wrenched Avery's arm, pulling her off the sand. "We're leaving."

With surprising strength, she got on her knees and pushed Wren back a few feet. Shock plastered on her sister's face, as if she didn't think Avery would fight back. Well, she was sick of being predictable. Sick of being underestimated. Sick of being drowned by the weight of others. It was about time she clawed her way to the fucking surface.

"Stop this! You don't understand," Avery said, rising up from the sand.

"I understand perfectly," she snarled.

Using her fingers, she felt for the mating bite on her shoulder. When she found it, she sank her nails into it. Pain radiated out from the wound. But she didn't care. She kept going until hot rivulets of blood ran down her chest. Avery called forth her shadows. They listened to her, because they were hers. This was her power, and no one, not even Felix, could take that back from her anymore.

First, she formed her shadows into wisps that left every part of her exposed apart from her lady bits. Because goddess forbid a powerful bitch not want her hoohaa out on display. The mating marks glowed gold on the edges, lighting paths around her body. And with the way Wren's face dropped, her sister had seen them immediately.

Wren's eyes went wide. "What—" She stopped in her tracks. "What have you done?"

"You should have let us explain."

A bitter laugh escaped her sister. "It has you fooled. It's a hunter, Avery. It's not a pet, or a friend, or whatever you've told yourself it is. They are our *enemy.*"

Just for a moment, a seed of doubt placed itself within her. Wren seemed so certain that what she was doing was wrong. Years of the academy whispering that she had been made into a fool. Then, she thought of Felix putting his life on the line for her, of the goddess, and for fuck's sake, herself. She knew her heart better than anyone. And she burned that seed to fucking ash. "Then what am I now?"

Wren swallowed, signaling something behind her. The dragon lowered its head next to her sister, growling at Avery. Heat radiated off its scales as if it were brewing fire in its throat.

"Enough," Wren spat. She gripped her wrist, but Avery was faster.

Already raising her hands, she reached for the well of power within her. Magic gathered in her palms, a crackling electricity racing through her veins before she threw everything she had from pure instinct. Shadows burst out, whipping her sister back into the leg of her dragon. Its head snapped back, roaring up at the night sky in pain before shaking its head, its long neck swaying with the motion. The recoil slammed through her arms, leaving them shaking. She'd never channeled that much power before, hadn't known she could.

Avery didn't run immediately. She watched as Wren picked herself off the ground, making sure the blast hadn't killed her. But it had royally fucked her up. Blood flowed from her temple, sand all in her uniform and hair, face twisting into fury.

As much as Avery liked her newfound power, she did not want to stick around for the butt of her sister's rage. Too late. A deranged smirk spread across her sister's face. *Oh shit.* Yep, she had pissed her off. Time to go.

Avery scrambled through the sand toward Felix, who was still thrashing shadows in every direction. Many enforcers were either dead and crumpled on the sand or missing. The few that were left were quaking in their boots. It wouldn't be long before more enforcers came.

Felix spotted her from across the range, hesitating for just a second. It was long enough that the enforcer shot out a bullet, its path leaving a blazing trail across the monster's form. But it didn't hit, only bounced off his form. Fury ignited in his eyes as his head snapped toward the enforcer who shot at him.

The monster cast out its shadows, wrapping around the rifle, crushing the barrel inward and forcing it up towards the enforcer's face, while another shadow pulled the trigger.

The head exploded, chunks flying across the sand.

Avery gulped at the gruesome sight, at the bodies scattered on the floor. Was she really doing the right thing? Her stomach flipped. But it didn't matter now; it was done.

"We have to go," she yelled into his mind, hoping desperately that it would reach him. This was only going to end one way. Felix may be more powerful, but these were trained enforcers; their only chance was to run before more came.

The monster only roared as more shots rang out, and Felix put himself between them and her. *"There is nowhere to run, little witch, we must fight."*

It was then that she realized. She wasn't talking to the monster. Felix was conscious in there. It wasn't some mindless beast. He was choosing to stand there and die for her.

Out of the corner of her eye, she saw her sister raise her hands.

Fuck.

"Run!" she screamed at him.

Felix turned around, looking her dead in the eye. Like he was memorizing her face for one last time. *No. Please run. You stupid fucking cat!*

Flames lashed out of Wren's palms, the rifle long discarded. They raced towards Felix, trailing in the sand before engulfing him in a wildfire, wrapping around his legs like vines. He let out a deafening bellow, trying his hardest to break the binds. The sound cracked her chest right open. It was futile. Avery watched as they flew over him like ropes, forcing him to the ground.

Something caught her from behind, not Felix's shadow but the cold grip of an enforcer. Warded handcuffs bit into her wrists. She looked behind her to see Callum's face, his expression unreadable as he forced her to the ground, her knees taking the impact. She wasn't even surprised at that stage. Of course, it was him. The last few hours had her soaring and only to crash right back down. Numbness seeped through her, protecting her from losing her shit entirely. There was still a chance. There had to be.

A blast hit her chest, snapping her head to the floor as Felix roared out. The enforcers worked in tandem, creating a ward that she hadn't seen before. He thrashed against the flames, his shadows slowly dissipating, getting picked up by the wind as if they were merely smoke.

The ward came from below, a complex pattern spewing flaming strings and tangling Felix in its web. The magic that had felt so alive only moments ago had died to a strangled whisper. Four enforcers surrounded him, holding up their hands to control the ward's movement. How many shifters had they captured like this? How many had her mother imprisoned?

The monster had gone, leaving only Felix kneeling on the ground, his body trembling as he still fought the wards that restricted his every movement. Avery looked around desperately, searching for something that might help. Anything.

Goddess please, she begged. *Do something!*

But she was only met with silence.

The goddess was still a bitch then.

Felix's chest moved with haggard breaths. When his eyes found Avery's, he stilled, face softening. *"I'm sorry I could not protect you."*

He was apologizing. He was kneeling in a binding ward

designed to torture shifters, surrounded by enforcers ready to kill him, and *he* was apologizing to her. This was all her fault. She had done the ritual. She had made him be her familiar.

Rage ignited in Avery's chest as she thrashed against the hold. Callum didn't let her move an inch as she watched her sister cross behind Felix. It couldn't end like this. Not when she had just found the one person who made her feel alive again.

"This is for your own good," Wren said, looking Avery directly in the eye, and put a hand onto his head before he slumped forward into the sand.

Thirty-Four

Avery

She *knew* this school had fucking dungeons.

The salt rusted bars snarled upwards into a stone roof as Avery sat on the floor of a jail cell. Cold stone bit into her thighs, and rats scurried across the back. The only light was the flickering of candles and a tiny barred window that led to nowhere but ocean. Beside her in another cell, Felix lay unconscious. But he was breathing, that was all that mattered.

They had dressed them in brown prison clothes, which she was sure did a good job of hiding the bloodstains of whoever they tortured down here. There were still dark patches on the floor that she didn't want to think about. If they ever released the shifters, was this be where they would keep them? What did they do with them when they came out?

The muscles in her spine went rigid as footsteps echoed through the cells. Out of the corner of her eye, she saw Callum appear, holding a glass of water.

Callum seethed at her—he had been the one to put the cuffs on her. To walk her down like a prisoner. At the end of the day, he was only doing his job. She would like to think that he would at least hear someone out. All these people who claimed to love and care about her, only to abandon her when she really needed them. It wasn't surprising anymore. But just maybe, he would help her. If she played it right.

"Callum!" Avery said, pretending with all her being to be nice to this fucker who had left her in the woods without a jacket. But his usually bright complexion darkened, his face as stony as her sister's.

"Here," he said, shoving a glass of water through the bars at her, some of it spilling over the rim. The gruffness in his voice belonged to a stranger. The fox at his feet whined, as if it wanted to come to Avery to say hello, but was unable to do so.

She took the glass of water and downed half of it, leaving the rest for Felix. She made sure the water dribbled down below her neckline and postured herself in a way that her prison clothes showed off her curves. Any integrity had fallen through the floor the day she met Felix. She didn't give a fuck anymore. "Do you think you could let me out?" Avery said, batting her eyelashes. It was a slim chance, but a chance nonetheless.

Callum laughed in her face. "If you think I would go anywhere near a shifter fucking whore, you'd be sorely mistaken."

She couldn't hide the disgust crawling over her face. "Really? Shifter fucker? How creative." Still, it didn't mask the hurt crawling up her chest, and the heat prickling behind her eyes. The man before her was no longer her friend. It hit her like whiplash. Goddess, he had practically proposed the last time they were together.

The shiny regalia on his uniform was polished, down to his shoes, the candlelight reflecting off it like a mirror as he turned to walk away. Instead, he twisted on his heels and pointed a finger towards Avery. "We could have been something. Both of our parents sit on the council. We could have been a power couple."

It took everything in her not to laugh. "So you never really wanted me, just my seat."

"Your sister made it clear that she would never be interested. So you were the next best thing."

Ahhh. There it was. Always an ulterior motivation. It was easy to lose trust, especially in this world where people seemed to go out of their way to ram a cock down your throat. Still, she wanted to love them, trust them, even when everything was begging her not to. Was that courage or stupidity? She supposed she had to live to find out. And by the fucking goddess, she wouldn't die in a dark, damp hole.

"You really know how to make a girl swoon," Avery said flatly.

Disgust twisted across his face as he turned away, walking close to the iron bars, far too close. In a split second, Felix shot out his arm, grabbed Callum by the collar, and slammed his head against the bars. A sickening crack rang out. Felix was awake and fucking *pissed*.

"There are many ways to be fucked by a shifter," he said, voice laced with rage.

When did he wake up? His morning voice was sexy. *Not really the priority to be thinking about right now, Avery.*

The hit didn't knock Callum unconscious, at least not yet. The fox growled and snapped at the bars, trying to get to Felix.

Now that was how to make a girl swoon. But Avery still raised her hand for Felix to stop.

"Please, don't hurt him."

He really did deserve it. Avery had seen enough bloodshed tonight, though.

Felix glared at the enforcer. "Can I at least take his eyes?"

"No."

"Fine," he said, settling for spitting in his face and pushing him back against the wall with a thud. The enforcer ran like a puppy with his tail between his legs, his fox bounding after him.

Felix stumbled backward, clutching his shoulder, blood seeping from his sleeve.

"You're hurt," Avery said, going to the bars that separated their cells.

"It's just a flesh wound."

"Let me look at it."

"It's kind of sexy when you order me around." A smirk pulled at his lips, but she could still see the hurt he was masking. The breaths he took were shallow and pained, and he gripped his arm like he was holding the very thing together.

"Shut up and come here."

"Reoww," he purred.

Avery only rolled her eyes as he moved closer to the bars so that she could reach between them to touch her hand to his shoulder. He winced at the contact as she touched it and tried to draw on the well of power like she had practiced. She searched deep inside herself, but nothing came when she called upon it. It was like she was empty. Even her mating marks had faded. Like she had been a few weeks ago.

Again, she reached for that dark current inside her—nothing. Nada. Fuck all. Frustration bloomed through her.

"Try using your magic," she bit out.

Lifting up his hand, he tried to summon a shadow. Again, nothing happened. "There must be some kind of ward against magic down here," he said. Felix looked around, sensing something she couldn't.

Avery's chest crumbled inward like loose rocks as she took stock of the situation. In the plainest of terms, they were utterly fucked.

A smile curved across his face, slightly obscured by the bars. On what seemed like instinct alone, his hand reached out for hers like he could sense the panic that was threatening to overtake her once again. Even though the bond seemed to be suppressed, he still knew her.

This time, she swallowed her own anxiety down, closed her eyes, and took a deep breath through her nose, smelling the fresh pine of Felix, mixed with pungent damp stone, until the churning sea inside of her calmed.

"Good girl," Felix said.

The words sent her mind into a frenzy. How was she so easily affected by him? She loved the praise. *No.* She loved him. She *fucking* loved him. It had been that way for longer than she wanted to admit.

Felix winced as he pulled her gently into the bars and wrapped his arms around her. A warmth spread through her despite the cool metal keeping them apart. He planted a soft kiss on her forehead. She wanted to laugh at the irony. In her whole life, she had never felt safer than she did now.

"I'm sorry," Avery said, choked.

"Why?" Felix said, only holding her tighter.

A tremor worked through her bottom lip as she tried to hold back the burning tears threatening to fall. "If you'd never met me, you would have been safe."

"Avery." The sound rumbled through his chest as his hand stroked her hair. "Did you know, before you, I was lost, so completely fucking lost. If I had never met you, I would have lived every life searching for you. Thank you for putting me out of my eternal misery."

If her heart were a garden, a thousand roses would have bloomed. At first, she thought he was a weed, a thorn in her side; now she would do anything to be suffocated by those vines.

The clacking of boots had Felix's ears swiveling in their direction. Avery shifted closer to the bars, her spine straightening as if pulled taut by an invisible thread, her body recognizing the footsteps before her mind could place them.

And when she saw who rounded the corner, she understood why. Her mother, dressed in full decorated enforcer attire, with medals that shone in the low light.

A feral growl ripped from Felix's throat, the sound echoing through the stone walls and vibrating through her bones.

Her mother let out a cold laugh.

She felt an icy fury come down the bond as if it were her own, rushing through her veins. Felix slammed himself against the bars so hard that dust fell from the stone ceiling, falling on the high councilor.

Her mother only raised her eyebrows as if he were some unruly kitten and brushed the dust off her shoulders. Unbothered, she walked with her hands behind her back, stopping at Avery's cell. "Now, what should I do with you, my *daughter*?"

"Let us go?" Avery suggested almost hopefully. Worth a shot. Maybe somewhere in her mother's heart, she might hold some love still for her own daughter. Doubtful. Very, very doubtful.

"Your dear *familiar* just killed twenty enforcers back there, plus the chancellor's son."

Avery breathed out. "That's how you knew...Julian's body."

"I knew far before that; I just didn't know the extent to which he was awake. He has become more trouble than he's worth, I'm afraid."

Avery furrowed her brows, confused by the statement. But then, realization slammed through her with the fury of a ram. *Oh, fuck no.*

"You see, that book you picked up was meant for Gwyn. You were meant to be a dud and fade out of existence as quietly as your aunt did, like your father did. An unfortunate stain on an otherwise great lineage." She leaned against the wall, not an inch of remorse on her still face. "The best thing I ever did was get my sister committed for blood magic. Your father thought he could be with *her* while he was married to me...And when she got pregnant, well...That's when I knew, I had to get her out of the way."

"You put your own sister into Anoddun while *pregnant*?" Avery said. How did she end up with someone like her as a mother? She was more deranged than Mother Gothel.

"Happily." Her mother smiled coldly. "We are better off without them."

"Don't speak about them that way," Avery quivered. That poor child.

"Color me surprised when you managed to summon a shifter and bind one without my help and without a statue."

Felix growled with deadly force, vicious enough to make the room rumble violently. Her mother didn't even flinch. But it was the confirmation she needed. The statues. The missing shifters. It all made sense. They were fucking *binding* them to witches. Her mother smirked, as if she saw the realization dawning over them. Was the goddess in on this? The goddess knew. Avery was absolutely fucking sure of it from what she said, or didn't say, in the cave.

"Why would you want Gwyn to be bound to a shifter?" Avery asked. Despite her newfound power, her voice was meek. It always was around her mother.

"Because, as you may have noticed, even someone as untalented as you could be granted power beyond your means. Just look at what your older sister has done with it."

Shock flashed through her. "Wren?"

It wasn't possible. Wren could be a bitch, but she wasn't that heartless. Could she? And if she knew...

No. Wren wouldn't, if only out of pride in her own abilities. If that made her naive, she didn't fucking care. She knew her sister. No matter how far they have drifted apart. Or at least, she thought she did. "Does she know?" Avery sputtered.

"She knows enough." Her mother shrugged. That was not an answer.

Avery's rage got the better of her before she could stamp it out. It ripped through her like a wildfire. Why would her mother do this? To her. To Wren. To Gywn. "Wren would never agree to this."

"You underestimate your sister's hatred," she said simply, dusting off her hands as if shaking off the guilt with it. How could someone be so indifferent? Was she a psychopath? A praying mantis in a skin suit? By the way she held her arms when she walked, she wouldn't be surprised.

Her mother walked back to the edge, away from Felix's palpable rage. "Now, how did you manage to summon a shifter without trapping them in a statue, and *how* is he allowed to shift?"

"Don't answer her, Avery," Felix said, his voice laced with warning.

Her mother rolled her eyes. Purple lightning shot out from her palm, lighting up all over his body like a spider web and paralyzing him almost immediately. A scream tore from his throat before his knees made a sickening crack against the cold floor. Avery could only watch in horror as he convulsed to the point where he couldn't hold himself up.

She whipped her head back to her mother, who seemed far too pleased with herself, the lightning reflecting in her eyes. "Answer, or I won't stop until it kills him."

His eyes found hers, and to her surprise, they were swarming with fear. It was the first time she had seen him truly scared. A sharp crack went through her chest at the sight. *"Don't...answer,"* he said through the bond.

There was no information worth his life. No world worth living in without him in it. No world worth being left alone in a world that had finally, briefly, made sense for one fucking second.

"I did the ritual like the book said!" she said quickly, the words tumbling out in a desperate rush.

"The one you stole from my office?"

"It was in the library."

Her mother narrowed her eyes as if she didn't believe her. Purple lightning arched from her mother's fingers, slamming into Felix with a sound that Avery never wanted to hear again. She saw how he closed his mouth, trying desperately not to scream, but he couldn't hold off. When he finally let it out, it was like an animalistic roar rather than anything that should come from a man.

"Make it stop." She wanted to cover her ears, to block out the sound of the man she loved being electrocuted. "Please fucking make it stop!" The words came out broken, nearly a sob. She couldn't breathe past the crushing tightness in her chest.

Her mother tilted her head at Felix convulsing on the floor, as if he were an experiment rather than a living being. By the grace of the goddess, she let the lightning die out.

"How did you do it? What ingredients did you use?"

Avery's eyes raced back and forth, her mind scrambling through the ritual steps even as her eyes kept darting back to Felix. "Wolf's milk, sage, candles, bones, and—" She paused. "Blood."

"Apple doesn't fall from the tree, does it? Blood and wolf's milk, Avery, really? You're just like her," she spat. "How could you manage to be a more spectacular fuckup than you already were?"

Felix threw himself at the bars, desperation overriding sense. Her mother didn't even need to look at him. The lightning hit him again, and this time Avery felt it, singing her nerves alive along with his. Bile raced up her throat as his back arched off the ground, violently trembling as she held up her hand to keep from vomiting.

"Bad kitty," her mother said, voice dripping with venom. "The ingredient was meant to be wolf's *bane*." She laughed softly to herself. "So that's how you did it."

"Don't say anything about the goddess," Felix pleaded into her head, voice fractured from the pain. She could only look at him for a second, could only take the sight of him on the floor for that long without breaking entirely. Her hands shook, rage and terror warring in her chest until she couldn't tell them apart.

A pegasus appeared next to her mother with a crack of lightning. Did it just fucking teleport in here? Its black coat was as shining and gleaming as her mother's boots. Its nostrils flared, steam coming out.

Wait. *No*, it couldn't be.

"You...you have a shifter too?" Avery wobbled. Disbelief caved in her chest. Her whole life was a goddess-damn lie. What was real? She tried to pick it apart in her head, going over every memory she could in such a short time. Had her father's wolf been one too? She didn't want to know. It would be too much.

"Of course." Her mother smiled sweetly, but Avery didn't miss the deadliness behind it. Finally, fucking finally, her mother stopped shocking her mate. Felix's chest heaved as he dragged in air, his whole body trembling, and Avery could see the burns mottling his skin, the way his hands shook as he tried to push himself up. Running to the bars, she reached out to him, grabbing his hand.

Her mother's lip curled in disgust. "And that is why you were never meant to have one. You are far too delicate. You would have been cut like a daisy, darling."

Avery's fist balled at her side, nails digging into her palm hard enough to draw blood. "Being kind in a cruel world is not a weakness."

"You are just like your father." A pitied look crossed her face.

Avery wanted to rip it off her. As long as she was nothing like her mother, she was doing well in the world.

Her mother sighed. As if this whole thing was nothing more than an inconvenience.

"Luckily for you two, you have presented a unique opportunity. It has been tiresome trapping shifters, and quite dangerous, actually. But Avery, you have done something useful for once, shown us a way to summon them straight from the source." She clapped her hands. "And I'm sure we can find a way to make your shifter back into his docile state, while you keep all the power."

She held back a scream. She wanted to do what Felix had done, grab her by the throat and smash her head against the bars. Instead, she swallowed the violence. "I won't let you."

"It's funny you think you have a choice. Either way, you'll probably die afterwards."

The words hit her like a gut punch. Stealing all the air from her lungs. "You'd... you'd kill your own daughter?"

"You were never mine to begin with," she said, looking her up and down with a sneer on her face.

Avery's heart dropped through her chest. "What?" She didn't like the picture that was forming in her head, but she had to ask. "Who's my mom?"

"Really? Still haven't put it together?" She tutted with tongue. "*You* were the baby."

Her aunt? Alys was her mother? She stumbled backwards, one hand flying to her mouth. As if she could physically hold the grief threatening to tear her apart.

"Your father made me swear on the goddess that I would take care of you, or he would leave. He did anyway in the end, but at least I got Gwyn. *Finally*, I can get rid of you."

The bars between her and Felix felt like miles now, an

unbridgeable distance, and her knees hit the stone floor hard enough to split the skin. But the pain didn't matter; it was nothing compared to the gaping wound her *mother's* words had torn open. The tears came then, burning down her face as they sat in the dark, both of them broken in so many ways.

And with that, the person she always thought was her mother turned away, her clinking medals fading with her boot steps.

THIRTY-FIVE

AVERY

A CREEPING NUMBNESS HAD SPREAD THROUGH HER like rot, her own body protecting her from everything she had learned over the last few days. It was too much for one person to carry. Felix had checked in on her throughout the day, trying his best to reach out to her. It wasn't fair to him to shut down. But it was all her body had allowed her to do. It was all she could do.

It was strange to think that her real mother could be in a cell not too far from here. Wrongly imprisoned by someone she thought was her family. She wondered if she was still there. What was she like now? Was there a way to get her out? She wanted to know, but even the thought of it was too much to deal with right now. So instead, she shoved it down, not ignoring the pain, but simply letting it be, to let it sit without consuming her. That was a power within itself, a lesson she had perhaps learned too late.

Moonlight shone through the small window while rain pattered against the stone walls, the familiar scent of Caerwyn wafting in from between the bars. Felix slept soundly on the stone floor of the cell, chest rising and falling soundly as if he were in a bed. Cats could really sleep anywhere.

The shuffle of boots of enforcers had come and gone, leaving them with nothing but meager sips of water. Even the sound of the rain outside had Avery's mouth watering. The enforcers watching them were the council's personal guard. She had dinner with them a few times. Watched their lives as they grew up through the academy. How many were in on this? Or did they even know at all? She supposed she didn't blame them. How could she when a month ago she would have thought the same? A witch hiding a shifter in plain sight. A danger. A disgrace.

Her mother, or not mother now, wouldn't want this to get out. A single tear slipped down her face, and she stifled the sob that racked her body, trying not to wake Felix. An ache went through her, one that nothing but time could fill.

Soft fur brushed up against her ankles. At first, she thought Felix had somehow shifted. But when she looked down, there were dozens of dust bunnies surrounding her, hopping around her ankles in circles.

"Hello there," Avery cooed at one, her voice croaky from dehydration.

She gave the one on her ankle a scratch on the head before it broke off and scurried towards the wall, the rest of the fluffle trailing after it like a horde of rats. What were they up to?

Avery turned around on her knees, watching them as they started to form a line at the bottom of the wall. Then, more dust bunnies got on top of one another, forming a structure.

"Felix," she hissed, picking up a stone and throwing it at him to wake him. It bounced off his skin, and he sat up almost straight away, alert and disheveled. His hair was flat on one side and tousled on the other, lines of stone etched into his face. Must have been a good nap. Bastard.

When he came to, he immediately caught the movement

of the dust bunnies and furrowed his brows at the little beings. Scooting closer to the bars, he examined them through long lashes, ears piquing curiously. They watched them create stack after stack, reaching higher than they should have.

At last, the final bunny made its way to the top. They had made a pyramid of dust bunnies at least four feet high. What the fuck were they doing?

Then, the top dust bunny started to *gnaw*. She saw crimson ripples moving like waves through the stone, and she realized what they were doing.

"They're breaking the ward," Felix said, his jaw slackening in shock.

Slowly, but surely, the hole became bigger, the dust bunny literally consuming the ward in the bottomless pit of its stomach. When the hole got big enough, the other bunnies started joining in.

"Smart little fuckers." Felix smirked.

Avery couldn't help the smile that came to her face. Despite it all, with Felix by her side, she felt invincible. She didn't want to test that theory, though, so hopefully they didn't get shot in the process of getting out of this damn prison.

As quick as they came, the bunnies disappeared into dust, floating through the air and going goddess knew where. Probably off to make some more nests somewhere.

Tentatively, Avery called on her shadows, reaching for the well inside of her. She felt the magic pooling within her, answering her pull. It wasn't as strong as it should be. But they had done it. The bunnies had broken the ward.

"Can you use your magic?" she asked Felix.

Felix held up his hand, as if to test if a shadow would come out. But after a few seconds, he only shook his head. That explained it. Her other half was still warded.

Fuck. She had to break him out old school.

Using her sharpest tooth, she bit the skin of her arm hard enough to draw blood. The ruby drops ran down her skin, imbuing her with power. The warmth spread through her veins, through her very being. A shudder went down her spine, and goose bumps lined her arms. The feeling was addictive.

Felix watched her from the cell, eyes darkening as he looked upon her. "I can feel your power from here, little witch."

She didn't know what that meant for her. But there was no time to dissect it.

Using her shadows, she sent them out, carefully guiding them to the metal bars at the front. They looped around the iron, and using all the force her form could physically muster, she wrenched them apart. The bar of metal not only moved but shattered completely.

A small chuckle came from Felix.

"What?" she asked.

"Nothing," he said, shaking his head. "You're just the most incredible woman I have ever met."

A blush crept up her neck and spread along her face. "Stop distracting me."

"Never."

Rolling her eyes, she stepped over the shattered iron bars, ducking her head so the top ones didn't scalp her. What a painful way to go that would be. After all this trauma, just to be impaled on some shitty bars. She'd rather die impaled on Felix's cock. The image played in her head, distracting her as her foot hooked around the iron and she stumbled forward into the wall. Goddess, maybe he did distract her even when he wasn't even trying. Stupid handsome cat.

"See?" he said, smirking wildly.

"Shut it, shifter."

She recovered herself, dusting the dirt off her prison clothes as a means of soothing the sting of embarrassment.

Turning on her heels, she saw the shimmer of a ward on Felix's side still active. Couldn't the bunnies have eaten through his, too? Why did the goddess seem to half-ass everything? Half-assed riddles, half-assed truths, half-assed bunny ward eating.

"Have you ever broken a ward?" Felix asked her.

She shook her head, the anxiety crawling back up her spine.

"Listen to me carefully. Using your magic, concentrate on a single fine point, and send everything you have through it."

"What if I hit you?"

"You won't," he reassured her.

Closing her eyes, she formed her shadow into a needle, the tip thinning and placing itself right next to the ward. The sound of Felix's feet hitting the stone told her he had moved out of the way. So he was afraid of her hitting him. She swallowed the lump in her throat, wishing desperately for the tightness in her chest to go the fuck away. It always came at the worst times.

"Little witch, it's okay, I believe in you."

That stopped her for a moment. He believed in *her*? Tears welled behind her eyes, threatening to fall. The last person who said that was her dad, over a year ago. She knew she should believe in herself. That she shouldn't need the validation from others to know that she was worthy. That she was capable. But was it so horrible to have someone start the process for you? When life had beaten you to a pulp, to have someone believe in you until you could believe in yourself? Sometimes that was all we needed.

Power laced through her fingertips, blood rushing downward towards the shadow. And when they touched? Avery sent everything she had into the ward.

It was silent. Then black shadows spidered through the ward's magic faster than her eyes could keep up with. Felix took a step back, pressing himself into the corner of the cell as if he knew what was about to happen.

Avery yelped as everything shattered. The wards, the bars. Splinters of magic and iron and stone went flying around them. She only saw it for a second before a cloak of darkness surrounded her. Shadows, she realized—a barrier made out of them.

Clamoring footsteps echoed down the hall. Enforcers drawn by the noise. But when the shadows dropped, she didn't see the enforcers. She saw Felix. He rushed up to her, gripped her face between his hands, and kissed her until she couldn't fucking breathe.

The footsteps got closer. But they didn't care. Felix pushed her against the wall as their tongues danced around each other. It had been mere hours since they touched, but it felt like a lifetime. The bond flared between them, shadows curling around them as they devoured each other.

"Oi!" A voice rang out.

It didn't last long.

Felix never broke the kiss, but out of the corner of her eye, she saw a shadow wrap around an enforcer's throat and take his head clean off. It tumbled to the ground, spurting blood across the floor. Part of felt awful. Did that enforcer have to die? The other part only cared about who was touching her right now.

Goddess. Was he going to take her right here?

The sound of another set of footsteps had their heads turning.

Callum stood there, fury raging in his eyes as he looked between them and the head on the ground. Before Felix could send a shadow out, Callum had already taken off.

"We need to go," Felix said breathlessly, but he didn't let

go of her. Didn’t stop gazing into her eyes. The green and brown of his eyes were blazing so intensely she thought they might burst into flames.

She nodded, pushing him away because she knew he wouldn’t be able to do it.

“He’s going to send for backup,” Avery said.

Felix smirked, lacing his fingers through hers. “Then we’d better go home.”

The council tower bell clanged through the forest, each peal drilling into Avery’s skull as trees blurred past. Her boots slipped on wet moss, bark scraping her palms when she caught herself against a trunk. They had made it out of the dungeon with little interference. Avery’s calves burned, but she didn’t stop. Didn’t slow. *Fuck*, she hated running though. Behind her, Felix’s footfalls matched her rhythm, his breathing nowhere has haggard as hers. She could feel his attention darting to every shadow, every crack of a branch, waiting for the enforcers to close in. For better or for worse, nothing had stopped them. But Callum had rung that bell. Callum knew they were gone.

What was the plan here? Sprint until her heart exploded? Until they hit ocean or ran out of island? She shoved the thought down. One crisis at a time.

The trees gave way to the clearing—moonlight puddling across the wolf’s milk meadow. Rain hung in the air like sullen mist, dampening her face, and soaking through her prison shirt. The frigid wind sliced her cheeks as each step carried Avery moved closer to the place that had started it all. Once again. She had ended up right back here. How poetic.

They slowed next to the statue of Cerituen, the cut-away plinth beside it now more obvious than ever. It was Arawn, the shifter god. How many centuries had the witches spent erasing the island of its history, literally carving away every trace that witches and shifters had once stood side by side?

Felix's tail lashed behind him; he was deep in thought. Likely, his train of thought was *how the fuck are we going to get off this island?*

"How the fuck are we going to get off this island?" Felix said.

Called it.

Avery smiled to herself, trying to hide how out of breath she was from the run. Her lungs burned, face dripping with sweat. It was funny how quickly you could know someone when they were meant for you.

"I could hot-wire us a boat?" he suggested.

"Do you know how to do that?"

Felix looked to the side. "I could figure it out."

Avery sighed. Even with all his amazing qualities. He was still a man.

The sound of heavy wingbeats had their necks snapping up towards the sky. A black silhouette of a dragon blocked out the moon; it was only for a second, but it was long enough for them to know that they were, once again, *utterly* fucked.

"Go!" Felix shouted at her.

They bolted back toward the tree line. Branches whipped at her face as they plunged back into the forest, ducking and weaving between trunks. But there was only so far they could go. This whole side of the island was cliffs, sheer drops that plunged straight into ocean. She could already hear the waves smashing against rock somewhere ahead, the raging ocean ready to swallow them whole.

"Fuck fuck fuck fuck fuck fuck." Felix's inner monologue made its way to her head. It would have been funny if they weren't being chased down by a fucking dragon.

The trees thinned out, the forest floor turning to a

meadow of wolf's milk, and beyond that—nothing. Just the sound of the ocean roaring up from below, confirming what she already knew. There was nowhere else to run. Nowhere to go but over the edge. Why had they even run this direction? She knew this was a dead end. But something had called her here. Something always pulled her back.

Before they could double back, the ground bucked beneath her feet, the impact so violent that every flower shook like they themselves were frightened.

The dragon slammed down in front of them, claws gouging deep craters into the earth. Wren sat on top of the beast, the glinting rifle already trained on Felix.

Every instinct screamed at her to run. Something in her was compelling her to go forward. To try to make her sister understand, even if she had imprisoned them before. Out here, though, it was just them. Maybe that changed things. Maybe Avery could make her understand. Even if they had a different mother, Wren was still her sister. At the very least, she had to try.

She took a step forward. Felix caught her wrist, and she whirled to face him.

"Don't," is all he said. His nostrils flared, emotion swimming in his gaze that he didn't try to hide. Fear for her. Fear for him.

She pulled her wrist free as gently as she could, holding his gaze. "Trust me, it's my sister."

"Avery," he warned. *"Please, I can't lose you, too."*

The words wrenched her heart, like he had just reached inside and squeezed. Still, she turned around and didn't look back. Somehow, she knew this was the right thing. It had to be.

Wren slid off her dragon, boots thumping onto the ground, never taking her rifle off Felix. As she closed the distance between them, she saw the ice in her sister's eyes, dark circles running under them. Her hair was dark and lifeless. So, she was sleep-deprived and pissed. Lovely. Her sister always struggled with no sleep. It always made Avery wonder what she had seen. How much did she know about the council? It was enough to keep anyone up at night.

"Wren—" Avery started.

Wren cocked her rifle, cutting her off. "You have three minutes before this place is swarming with enforcers."

Avery swallowed hard, looking down the butt of the rifle. Her sister was ruthless with shifters. If Felix so much as twitched, Wren would pull the trigger.

For a moment, she froze, her mind going blank. How did you even start a conversation like this without sounding insane? *"Hey, sis, the council's been lying to us for centuries, and also Mom's evil?"* Every version sounded deranged.

Wren took a step forward, gripping the rifle harder. "Avery, now."

"Our—your mother isn't who you think she is," Avery managed to get out.

Wren narrowed her eyes.

"They've been lying to us. Trapping shifters in statues and bonding them to witches."

"Who?"

"The council. It's a long story."

"Try me," Wren hissed.

"You wouldn't believe me if I did."

Wren's nostrils flared. "Two minutes left. Tell me, or I pull the fucking trigger."

Anxiety flared through her, her pulse hammering in her ears as she tried to get the words out to explain.

"Okay! *Okay.*" Avery took a shaking breath. But she still couldn't stop what came out. "Mom is bonded to a shifter. *You* are bonded to a shifter, like I am."

"That's...that's not possible," Wren said. "This isn't the time to joke," she said, white-knuckling the rifle.

Anger swirled through Avery, her whole body tensing. She could even feel her shadows demanding to come out. All they needed was a bit of blood. "For once in your life, can you trust me?"

"Do you know how insane you sound?" Her voice wavered.

"Yep. Quite aware."

"Then you can understand why I'm a touch bit skeptical that you're telling me the dragon I've had for years is a *shifter.*"

"Tell me one thing then." Avery swallowed past the tightness in her throat. "How did you do your ritual?"

"It doesn't matter."

"You used blood?"

"I said it doesn't matter," Wren hissed.

"You're smarter than this. There's a reason only certain families get elemental powers."

Her lips parted, just for a second, but Avery saw it. Wren hadn't known. She genuinely hadn't put it together.

Just to drive the point home, Avery bit her tongue, the metallic taste of blood seeping into her mouth and coating her tongue. Shadows crawled along the ground and twisted up her legs. Wren took a step back, her eyes going wide and finger hovering over the trigger.

"I don't have a familiar, Wren. How do you think I have these powers?"

Wren furrowed her brows, looking between her dragon and Avery. "Who told you this? The shifters?"

Avery scratched the back of her head. "The goddess," she said, the sound going up at the end. Yep, she truly sounded insane.

Wren scoffed, disbelief rolling off her face. "Are you

fucking serious, Avery? The goddess? She's a figurehead, a *deity*. She means nothing in the real world."

"I wouldn't piss her off—"

As if on cue, the wolf's milk flowers started to breathe, closing in and out just like they had in the maze. Avery recognized it almost immediately. Her stomach dropped. The goddess. She was doing this. Wren stared at the meadow, color draining from her face as she watched the flowers pulse in unison. Even the dragon took a step back. Ley lines lit up along the meadow, beating like they had their own heart. Perhaps it was the goddesses. The earth her body, the ley lines her veins.

"Enough." She looked down the scope of the rifle. Avery stepped directly into the rifle's line of fire, blocking Felix.

"Move," Wren commanded.

"Not until you let us go."

"Why would I do that?"

"Because you know something's not right. "

Wren's jaw clenched, her grip shifting on the rifle.

Shouts erupted from the tree line, boots and paws thudding against earth, familiars snarling and snapping. They were closing in.

"*Please*," Avery begged.

Wren's rifle trembled. "I can't, I'm sorry."

Pollen burst from the meadow, spiraling up in thick golden clouds. For one suspended moment, it looked almost gentle, just pollen drifting on the wind, catching the moonlight.

Avery just smiled. "I told you not to piss her off."

Then the world exploded into gold. The air turned thick and shimmering, pollen so dense it choked the light and obscured the view of the approaching enforcers. The dragon inhaled deeply, nostrils flaring wide, drawing the pollen deep into its lungs. Its eyes flooded black, pupils swallowing the color whole.

Oh *fuck*. Was she about to get fucked again? Had she ever read dragon smut? She made a mental note to revisit it later. The only fucking thing she needed to do right now, though, was fucking run.

"Witches," a deep and furious voice said into her mind. Wren stilled as if she had heard it too, all the blood draining away from her face. The beast roared so hard the ground shook. It was the dragon's voice. And it was a goddamn shifter.

"Time to go, kitten." Felix's voice came into her mind.

Avery didn't stick around to find out. That was a Wren problem now.

Gunfire cracked behind her, bullets hissing past her head, thudding into the ground and spraying up clods of wet dirt.

She ran for Felix in the distance. Where the fuck were they going to go?

Bullets continued to ring out around them. Behind them were a hundred enforcers and whatever the fuck Wren's dragon had become. Ahead was nothing but cliffs and the ocean. She had understood why the goddess had brought her here now. But was she going to actually help them get away? Surely she wouldn't be that helpful.

The enforcers pressed forward, their familiars coming up behind them as shots rang out. They ran as far as they could, stopping just at the edge of the cliff, rocks falling away at their feet. Felix threw up a wall of shadow, but a single bullet threaded through the darkness. Avery saw it tear through the shadows, saw it embed itself in Felix's chest with a *thunk*.

The scream that tore from her was no sound a living being should make. It didn't even sound like her. *No.*

The shadow wall collapsed, like a curtain falling. On the other side, Callum kneeled with a rifle. *Motherfucker.* Avery didn't think. She didn't need to. Blind fury overtook her, her shadows bursting out of her at a speed nothing could keep up with. In an instant, they found their target. They wrapped around Callum's throat and squeezed. Squeezed until the fucking light faded from his eyes. Consequences be damned. She was never coming back to this wretched island unless they fucking buried her here.

When she turned back, Felix wobbled, clutching his chest, and fell off the cliff.

Thirty-Six

Felix

Felix never really believed in Anawn. But the only way he could describe what he was seeing was an angel. *His* angel. Avery.

His vision went in and out as he looked at her fading away. *God, she is so beautiful.*

Pain laced every breath he took, but it was eased by even just the sight of her. He wished he could pause time, just so he could have this moment just a little bit longer. To look at her, to hold her, to *love* her.

What a cruel world this is, to rip love from him just when he had found it.

Maybe in the next life, little witch.

Thirty-Seven

Avery

"Jump!" The word threaded through her head. She didn't know where it came from. Didn't care. Didn't stop to question it. She followed it. Jumping after Felix into the dark abyss.

It was funny. She never thought she would literally be falling for him.

The drop had her stomach lurching into her throat. Somehow, she wasn't anxious. Her mind stilled as the wind screamed past her ears, tearing at her clothes and hair. She fell, and fell and fell. So close to Felix that she could almost reach out and touch him.

At least they'd die together. At least he wouldn't be alone.

The last thing she saw was a massive talon coming down on top of her.

All the wind was knocked from her lungs as the enormous claw clasped around them, the impact jolting them upwards into its grip. Her body almost crushed against Felix's as talons the width of trees caged them in. Each wingbeat sent them swaying, and Avery braced her hands against the rough scales to keep from being thrown into him again. The sound of the gunfire and ocean grew fainter with each second, leaving only the sound of its wingbeats. Her hands shook, adrenaline coursing through her body that had nowhere to go.

Holy shit. They had lived. Somehow, they had gotten out. Had they passed the wards?

"Wait! The wards!" Avery shouted upwards, her heart dropping.

"These puny wards are no match for me, witch, do not insult me like that." The dragon's voice was strange in her head, foreign compared to Felix.

Felix.

A rattling cough jerked her attention back to him, blood spurting from his mouth onto his chest and the scales around him. Absolutely fucking not. He was not going to die here. They had been through too much just for him to die in the cradle of a dragon. Using her shadows, she ripped off the prison shirt.

Fear like Avery had never felt before sliced through her, like a thousand cuts all over her body. Fresh tears burned a path down her face. Some insane part of her tried to smile, mouth trembling with the effort. "It's going to be okay. I promise," she said, hovering her hand over him. A small lie, one that would help them both. She rifled through her mind, pinching out any healing knowledge she could. She needed to stop bleeding.

Using one of Felix's claws, she sliced her leg. It was ironic that to stop the bleeding, she must bleed herself. Something about that had to be poetic.

Her magic flared to life, and she pulled from the well inside of her, trying her best to concentrate on pulling the bullet out. Using her shadows, she fashioned them into tweezers and carefully pulled out the bullet. Felix's breath came rapidly as he looked like he was trying not to scream. Then she focused on knitting the skin's surface together. A dust bunny hopped from goddess knew where and sat on his chest, ripples of magic coming from its paws. *It was helping. The goddess was helping.*

Her hands shook as she worked, power stuttering and fading out as Felix's consciousness did. The dragon's claw kept swaying, Felix kept bleeding, and she couldn't get her breathing steady enough to channel properly. He winced as she worked, taking shallow, pained breaths.

After a few minutes, she managed to stop the bleeding. Still, his skin was deathly pale. There was something wrong with this wound. Something that was killing him from within. But there was nothing more she could do.

Another cough stopped her for a moment. Felix raised his good arm, his clawed hand finding her face. She leaned into his hand, where she should have felt warmth, but it was cold and clammy instead. A sudden sob racked her body. *It couldn't end like this. Please, goddess, don't take him from me.*

He opened his mouth to speak, but only a croak came out. He wasn't even strong enough to speak. The tears flowed freely, falling and mixing with the residual blood on his chest. When she looked back up at him, the stupid cat had a smirk on his face.

"I love you, Avery."

He loved her? Her breath caught in her throat, her chin wobbling as she spoke. "No, you don't get to say that now." A tear burned down her face. She barely got the next words out. "When you're okay, you can tell me again."

The smirk fell away from his face as his eyes rolled back into his head. Quickly, she put her ear to his chest. Not dead. Just unconscious. But he was barely holding on.

She didn't let go of Felix's hand as it dropped.

Using her free hand, she covered her mouth to keep the scream from coming out. Frustration, fear, love, hate, everything swirling through her like a violent hurricane. It was too much. It was all too fucking much. Her body threatened to shut down again, too numb. But she wouldn't let it.

"No, you stupid cat, death will not do us fucking part!" she yelled at him. "Please go faster, Sparky!" she beckoned the dragon.

"It's Kai."

More than an hour had passed, but somehow Felix was still holding on. Each minute felt like an hour. Avery's world became the rise and fall of his chest. She'd tried healing again, but whatever was lodged in his chest rejected her magic. She hoped this was only one of his nine lives.

The dragon started to slow, so she lowered Felix's head and tried to stand up. Her legs protested, stiff from an hour of kneeling on scales, and she had to grip the talon for balance as the dragon banked into a turn.

Twinkling lights and skyscrapers came into view. She immediately knew the London skyline, the human territory. For only a moment, every worry was left behind as she looked at the cityscape. All those late nights in her dorm, researching neighborhoods and imagining a life beyond the island's reach, and here it was. She never thought it would be like this, though. In the clutches of a dragon and mated to a shifter.

How life could change.

Her ears popped from the pressure as the dragon glided lower and lower. The city gave way to darkness until he was soaring over the English farmland.

He was close to landing. She braced herself against the dragon as he touched down, his limbs shaking with the effort.

Slowly, he opened his claws, gently laying Felix onto a green and sprawling lawn. A gentle breeze brought the smell of fresh flowers and rain.

"We are here, witch." The dragon's rough voice shocked her as it came through her mind.

They were at the den. Felix had made it this far. The dust bunny hopped away and ran off into the night. Had she just introduced an invasive species? Oh well, really not her biggest problem right now.

When Kai moved his large talons away, the sight before Avery took her breath away. It was a gigantic mansion. Green ivy clawed up the pale stone walls, which were dotted with floor-to-ceiling windows. Warm lights spilled out from them, illuminating perfectly manicured hedges and autumnal garden beds teeming with life. Large stone walls surrounded the building, with ornate gates in the middle. Beyond the gates was a dense forest of oaks and pines, completely secluding the house from the outside world.

"Thank you," Avery said to him.

"Don't thank me yet, witch."

Slightly ominous. Thanks, dickhead. Why did no one ever say what they meant?

But he was right to warn her.

Another dragon touched down next to Kai, shaking the ground. It was a wonder they didn't set off earthquakes every minute.

This dragon's scales were a glistening opal, and the warm lights from the mansion made them look almost golden. The two dragon heads moved like they were talking, which they likely were, but it wasn't a conversation Avery was to be privy to.

Were all dragons so rude?

The new dragon transformed in front of her eyes, scales retracted into skin, wings folding into their shoulder blades. A giant beast becoming, well, a giant man.

Man was putting it lightly. He was as tall as Felix, if not taller. Everything about him seemed absolutely lethal. Even his jawline looked sharp enough to cut. Long white hair flowed down to his waist, and poking through the sides were the tips of pointed ears. Atop his head were twisting white horns with gold jewelry pierced in them, while golden tattoos shaped like fire covered the rest of him, like the very flames licked at his skin.

And he was stalking toward them, anger written into every feature. *Shit. Fuck. Shit. Fuck.* That was not a nice-looking lizard.

Avery took a step back as the man crossed the lawn in four strides. "What did you do to him, you fucking *witch*?"

"Don't..." Felix's voice cut through the tension, weary and pained. "Don't talk about my mate," he said through choked gasps. She hadn't realized he had woken up. Or how much it must have taken him to speak at all, given the way his face went even paler after he'd finished.

The man's head snaked like a serpent to Felix. "Mate?" he hissed.

"Let her explain...please, brother," he said.

Brother? Like biological or like bro? Didn't matter.

"Help him first," Avery pleaded.

The dragon scowled at her, his lip moving so she could see the long fangs he was sporting.

The man put his fingers in his mouth. Was she about to be turned to ash? She always did want to be cremated.

Instead, what came out was a whistle, so loud that she instinctively put her hands up to her ears to cover them.

One second, the lawn was empty except for the four of them; the next, it was full of shifters, emerging from the shadows, dropping from trees, and some materializing out of thin air.

Goose bumps ran up her arms as she took in the surroundings, her whole body going on high alert. So many shifters. Some were in their animal forms, others looked vaguely human. By vaguely, she meant horns of all shapes and sizes adorned a few of their heads, a basilisk shifter was partially covered in scales, and the largest wolf she had ever seen was glaring at her with yellow eyes. One shifter had antlers that branched up like a crown, another had feathers where hair should have been. The variety was staggering, and every single one of them was looking at her with varying degrees of murder in their eyes. Avery gulped and took a step back, trying her best not to disappear into mist and let the goddamn wind take her where it wanted.

A smaller—still taller than Avery—cat shifter, in her human form, ran up to them, planting herself right next to the dragon shifter who had whistled.

"Oh my god, Felix," she said, worried, before the lines of her face etched with anger. "What did you do to him, witch?"

Avery's nose wrinkled as she said the word *witch.* Such a terrible insult, at least call her a cockwomble or something creative.

"I would never hurt him," Avery said plainly, dropping to her knees and grabbing his hand.

"Get away from my brother!" she shrieked before the dragon pale-haired shifter held her back. She snapped her head up to him. "What are you doing, Ciro? Why are you protecting her?"

"They are bonded," Ciro said. "Felix called her his mate."

The cat shifter's eyes widened, flitting between them as if she could find evidence of it on the surface. "It's not possible."

Before Avery could show the cat shifter her mating marks, something shifters would respect, Ciro barked out orders. "Take him to the infirmary; he's been hit by a suppression bullet."

"But," the cat shifter said.

"That's an order, Eimi. Now," Ciro commanded.

Eimi scowled before signaling over a few other shifters,

who carefully lifted him up off the ground as he winced in pain. Avery twitched, as if to yank him back from the shifter's clutches, but he was in safe hands here. She had to respect the shifters. Each sound he made took a few years off her life. She would never forget the memory of him falling off a cliff.

Avery went to follow them before the dragon, Ciro, stood in front of her. "You're not going anywhere, witch."

Oh dear. She nodded. What else could she do, balls-deep in shifter territory? She was alone and surrounded by people who would tear off her limbs for fun. Felix had been taken from her. What were they going to do with him? Would he be okay? They had been through so much. She had to trust that he would. Hopefully, the worst of things was behind her.

Ciro turned and didn't have to say anything as he walked away; his mere presence beckoned her to follow him.

Colossal arched doors welcomed their presence; the architecture was built to accommodate those of large stature. She was sure it would fit a dragon through them if they really tried. The doors themselves were wooden, intricate carvings of different shifter forms displayed artfully. It was so different from Caerwyn, which was still beautiful, but something about this place was far more homely than the island ever felt.

Instead of dark features, the building radiated light even in the middle of the night. When she walked through the door, delicate furnishings and plush comfort greeted her over the hard chairs she was used to. Deep sofas to sink into and art that filled you with joy instead of horror. It took everything in her not to gape. She was no stranger to opulence and wealth, but something about this place felt alive in a way Caerwyn wasn't. Magic teetered on every surface, brooms moving themselves past the floor, lights dancing along the walls; the magic wanted to be here. This place was meant to be lived in. The floors were a polished dark wood; not even a single creak sounded as they walked along them. Avery found herself wondering how old this place was, how many generations of shifters had lived here.

They went past what she assumed was the foyer and up a set of stairs that curved to a grandiose dining room. A modern chandelier hung from the ceiling, throwing dapples of light over a long table that could seat more than thirty people. Grand floor-to-ceiling windows overlooked a sprawling, shimmering lake and rolling hills of forests dotted with leaves of russets and golds, almost silver in the moonlight. The view was stunning enough that Avery forgot to be terrified for approximately five seconds.

"I didn't think shifters lived like this," she said out loud.

"Where did you think we lived? Filthy basements and tunnels below the city?" Ciro said, the deep voice making her flinch when she realized who was next to her.

"Yes, actually." No point in lying about it now. That was exactly what she'd been taught, what every witch believed: they were scavengers, barely better than animals.

Ciro rolled his eyes, crossing his arms over his shirtless body. Even though Felix was the most handsome man she had ever seen, she couldn't deny that this shifter was a close contender. He was *obscenely* attractive. His golden eyes pierced her in a slightly chilling manner. *And* he had tattoos. *Smash.*

"Sit," Ciro said, voice gruff.

She did so, knowing it wasn't a nicety. Though the chair looked comfortable, she perched on the edge of it, ready to run if necessary. Not that running would help her in any way, shape, or form.

He leaned on the table, his talons clacking against the wood. Avery stilled in the way a deer does. Even with powers, she still had the survival instincts of a peanut.

"How the fuck did you bond to my brother?" he said. She still didn't know if he was his blood brother like Eimi, but something in her told her it wasn't the time to ask. *What happens if two different shifters mate? Is that how the griffin happened?*

Avery wasted no time catching him up on what had happened over the last few weeks, excluding the obvious details of his brother sticking shadows up her butt. She told him of the bonding, the goddess, and what the goddess had said about their history. About the statues, about her not mother. About the mating—not the fun parts. He listened without interrupting, expression unreadable, and Avery couldn't tell if he believed her or was simply waiting for her to hang herself with her own words.

Ciro didn't say anything when she finished, but the slight clench in his jaw gave him away.

He took a seat at the head of the table, finally meeting her at her level. "Mates have been a part of our history for a long time, but I have never heard of one between a witch and a shifter."

Avery pulled back her sleeves. The dragon's throat worked as he looked her up and down, taking in the visible mating tattoos that he could see on her arm. For a second, a flash of surprise came across his face, which somehow was more frightening than his anger had been. She and Felix were truly the first witch and shifter mates.

Ciro poked and prodded her with question after question. Trying to squeeze every last bit of information out of them. She probably should have been more careful with what she said. But truly, she didn't care. They were keeping shifters at Caerwyn, binding them to witches against their will. She wanted to help them.

"And you're saying after you mated, he could control his monster?" Ciro asked.

"Yes."

"Interesting," was all he said. Avery didn't know why she waited for his words that wouldn't come. This dragon wouldn't trust her as far as he could throw her. Which was ironic because he could throw her, very, *very*, far.

"When Felix is awake, I would like to hear it from him." Ciro stood in one graceful movement, chair scraping back across the wood floor.

"Mark my words, witch," he said, turning to the window. "If you have tampered with his mind in any way, I will peel off your fingernails one by one, rip you limb from limb, and feed you to my pet fish. Is that clear?"

"Crystal," she squeaked, smiling to hide the pure terror climbing over her features instead. Not that it mattered, he could probably smell that she was one jump away from pissing her pants.

There was nothing left to say after that. Ciro didn't dismiss her. He briefly talked to Kai. *Talked* was a stretch, given they were just nodding at each other, obviously having a conversation in their heads. So, Avery just sat in awkward silence and waited for Felix to be awake.

Thirty-Eight

Felix

The world came into focus as Felix opened his eyes to a familiar ceiling. He ended up here a lot. He had never bothered being careful when he hunted, mostly, but he'd had fuck all to be careful for. Until now.

The stale, sterile smell burned his nostrils. He blinked rapidly as his eyes adjusted to the dark, the only light coming in through the starlit window.

"Avery?" he croaked out. His throat was unbearably dry as he tried to sit up, a flash of agony going through his chest. He gritted his teeth and sat himself up. The pain threatened to pull him under, making him see stars. *Inside.*

That wasn't good. That was, in fact, spectacularly bad.

Instead, he focused on the bond, pulling him like a rope toward her.

He was in the den. And Avery was here too.

Oh *fuck.*

Using all his strength, he wrenched himself off the bed with considerable effort. But instead of going upright, he flopped onto the floor. *Fucking gravity.* The cold tiles hit his back, knocking all the breath from his lungs. For a moment, he just lay there. Defeated. In agony. A long, pained groan escaped him like a deflating balloon. What had his life come to?

Avery.

The thought of her alone was enough to have his body preparing to move. She was a witch in enemy territory, and he hadn't been there to explain, to protect her, to do a single fucking useful thing. The thought of Avery, his *mate*, in danger made him feral. Adrenaline coursed through him. Using the bed as leverage, he yowled as he brought himself to his feet. If his legs gave out again, he'd crawl the rest of the way on his belly if he had to. The room tilted as he forced himself forward, navigating by pure instinct as he followed the thread that connected him to her.

He shoved his way into the dining room, slamming into the door with his good shoulder. The impact sent a fresh wave of agony through his chest, but he'd endured far worse, and none of it mattered if Avery was in danger.

Ciro stood near the window, the dragon shifter's head whipping around at the noise. But Felix didn't care about him right now. Avery sat only mere feet from his friend, and when her gaze locked on his, relief filled her face. Thank fuck. She was alive, she was *here.*

She ran to him and instantly put her arms around him, squeezing him as hard as the little witch could manage. His body screamed at him, but he didn't care that it fucking hurt; all he cared about was that she was in his arms. He kissed her forehead and breathed in her scent of cinnamon and honey and home. Ciro's face was stony as he looked him up and down. Still, Felix could read him like a book. The dragon was undoubtedly wondering what the fuck he was witnessing. Felix didn't do physical affection, and he certainly didn't do it with witches.

Warm light flooded the spinning dining room. How long had he been out?

"You always know how to make a dramatic entrance, brother," Ciro said, turning to face them. "Shouldn't you be horizontal right now?"

Felix flipped him off with his good hand while still hugging Avery, which made Ciro chuckle. But almost on cue, his legs stumbled forward into her, and only her surprising strength kept him from face-planting into the floor. When had she gotten strong? Felix likey.

He should most definitely be horizontal with the way his head spun. Fucking magic bullets, they were designed to lodge themselves into their target. His injury would heal. The skin had already knitted back. But the poison that flowed through him would sap him of magic for at least a month. Luckily, the bullet had missed anything particularly vital, but it had still done plenty of damage. They were a bitch of a thing to heal, and they still hadn't found the antidote.

Avery guided him over to a dining chair and gently lowered him into it before taking a seat on the chair beside him. He hated feeling so powerless, but with Avery next to him, it wasn't all bad. Her hand found his under the table, fingers threading through his, and some of the pain eased in his chest, replaced by a delightful warmth.

An unfamiliar dragon shifter walked into the room. On instinct, Felix rose quickly, his hackles raising as the world tilted violently. He was in no state to fight, but his body primed anyway. His tail whipped across the table, sending a glass clattering to the floor.

"God fucking dammit, Felix, sit down," Ciro said. "This is Kai, he's the one who saved you."

He blinked twice at the dragon, trying to focus despite the world threatening to fall out from under him. The dragon's skin was bronze with long dark hair plaited down his back. He shared the same golden eyes as all dragons did. Black horns jutted from his head, pierced in the same way that Ciro had. Felix didn't sit. "He's bonded to an enforcer."

"I know, dipshit, now sit the fuck down," Ciro said, running a hand through his hair. "I never thought I'd see the day where the pussy got pussy whipped."

Felix lunged towards Ciro, but Avery's hand planted itself firmly on his chest and sent him collapsing back down in his chair. Fuck. This pussy *was* pussy whipped. And he couldn't even pretend to mind.

"Felix is right. He's my sister's dragon," Avery explained.

His golden eyes met hers, blazing with fire. "I am no one's but my own," he said, snarling.

Avery kept her hand on him; without that anchor, he would've gone for the dragon's throat purely for daring to speak to his witch in that tone

"Sorry. I just meant you're bonded to her," Avery said quickly.

Kai's jaw ground. The muscle jumped in his cheek, tension radiating off him. "I was bonded to her years ago against my will, after I was stolen from my home and shoved into a statue," he said through gritted teeth.

Felix had only experienced the dungeon for a day. Warded and kept apart from Avery for too long. What would it be like to spend years? How long had some of them been down there? The thought sent a fresh wave of anger bubbling within him.

Avery's lip wobbled. "Did she know?" The question was quiet. He could tell that she didn't want to believe that her sister was in on it. Although from Wren's reaction back on the island, maybe she didn't. Or maybe she was far smarter than they were giving her credit for. Maybe she was just like *her* mother. Felix was glad his little witch wasn't born from that wretched hag.

"Of course. How else would she have done the ritual?" Kai spat.

Avery sat back, letting out a sigh. "My mot—" she stuttered. "Eleri...is manipulative."

Understatement of the fucking century.

Leaning forward despite the protest from his ribs, Felix added, "There are hundreds of statues below the council tower."

Ciro closed his eyes, letting out a sharp breath through his nostrils, puffs of smoke wisping out. Ciro didn't show it. But he was pissed. Felix knew the shifter like the back of his hand. They had done pretty much everything together. "Fuck. So it is true."

The memory of it still made his stomach turn, bile coming up his throat that he had to swallow down. At least Kai might be able to provide them with some valuable information.

"Are you still connected to her?" Avery questioned the grumpy dragon in the corner.

"Unfortunately. I can feel her on the other side even now, like a fucking splinter I can't dig out."

"She will come for you," Avery said.

Pushing off from the window, Ciro's voice turned hard. "And we will be ready."

Avery's eyes went wide with alarm, darting between Ciro and Kai. "They will obliterate this place. You need to run, or hide, or do something other than face them head-on."

The concern in her voice made Felix's chest tighten. She was trying to protect them, his brothers, his sisters. His den. How had he gotten so lucky?

Ciro grunted, displeased that Avery would even suggest such a thing. "We are far more powerful than you think, witch." The fury in his gaze was unmistakable. "The witches are the ones who will have to run from us."

Avery stood quickly, the urgency in her features palpable.

"You don't understand, if they have been bonded to shifters, they are more powerful than anything you've ever seen before." Her voice carried a hint of desperation as she tried to make them understand the danger of the situation. "My sister is the most powerful witch of my generation, and they're not mates, or even properly bonded in the way the goddess intended."

Felix's hands clenched by his side. They really had no idea. "Avery is right; Wren took down my monster like it was nothing."

It was subtle, but he saw the way Ciro blinked. Stupidly, he was underestimating them.

"She is powerless without me, and I will not give her my magic," the dragon countered.

Felix wanted to shake that goddamn confidence out of him. Kai should know better than anyone what she could do.

"You don't know that she won't be able to force it out of you." Avery's gaze dropped to her hands, twisting together in her lap. "None of this is right. The bond between a familiar and a witch is sacred." She looked back up at them. "I will help in any way I can. But please promise me you will not hurt my sister."

Felix knew that they would never make a promise like that. Shifters kept their oaths, as if they were bound to them by death. After a few moments, Avery sat back down, understanding their silence.

"What about your not-mother?" Felix said, trying to lighten the mood. Perhaps a bit too soon.

"You can hurt her."

He snorted. There was his little witch.

"I'll make no promises, witch, my priority is to free the shifters," Ciro finally said. "If *any* witches get in my way, they will be obliterated."

A flicker of surprise went through Felix; it was more than

he would ever usually grant a witch. Somehow, he knew they would get along. Maybe. At some point.

"It's Avery," she hissed.

Felix clicked his fingers sassily at Ciro, who only rolled his eyes in response.

A ghost of a smile flickered across Avery's face before she squared her shoulders and addressed Ciro again. "I am a healer," she said confidently, before she added. "In training. If that helps at all."

Fuck yeah, she was. She was going to be a great healer, considering how quickly she picked up healing herself and using his shadows. The way she had handled them and fucked herself, and others with them. A natural.

Avery gave him a look, as if she could feel the way his dick was suddenly straining against his pants.

"Can you find a way to nullify the fucking magic bullets they use?" Ciro said.

"I've learned about them in class, so I might be able to," Avery said hopefully. He had full faith in her that she could. The bullets were among the witches' worst weapons against shifters. If they found a way to nullify the effects of it? They'd be unstoppable.

Ciro took a deep breath in. "Fine, you can stay, but you will be escorted by one of us at all times."

"Ciro," Felix warned.

"She is still a witch, mate or not," he said.

"And the fact I can control my monster form, her being able to use powers no witch should have?" Felix said. He supposed he shouldn't be surprised that the sentiment wouldn't change overnight. He was going to convince them. It was worth it. This was what the goddess wanted. This was how shifters and witches should be. Humans still sucked, though.

"I'll believe it when I see it," he said gruffly, still unconvinced.

Felix understood the skepticism. He would've been the same in Ciro's position, would've demanded proof before believing in fairy tales about fated mates and goddess-blessed bonds. It still sounded strange when he thought about it. "The world is going to change, brother, let's make sure we are on the right side of it."

Ciro's arms folded across his chest, a tell Felix had learned to read decades ago, the physical manifestation of knowing his friend was right but being too stubborn to say it aloud. "I will start to contact other dens, see if they know anything."

Felix started to stand, legs shaking with the effort. "I'll help."

Ciro raised an eyebrow at his pathetic display. "Are you incapable of sitting down?"

"Maybe."

Turning his attention to Avery, Ciro blew a hair away from his face. Felix had gotten under his skin. *Hehehe*. It was one of his favorite pastimes. Felix had to bite his tongue to stop from grinning.

"Your first order is to make sure he goes to bed and stays there."

Avery nodded.

The betrayal.

"Fight me bitch," Felix said to Ciro. He might have nearly died, but he still wasn't dead.

Rolling his eyes, Ciro started to walk out the door. "I'd burn you to a crisp, you oversized hairball." Before he left, he stopped behind Avery's back. "Avery, you have my permission to use the spray bottle on him, but don't use the laser pointer for a while; he'll break something."

"Prick." Felix's grumble was halfhearted at best; he was too tired to have a better retort.

A horrified look crossed Avery's face, but soon after, it dissolved into laughter. Felix couldn't help but join her.

Watching her laugh, here in the den surrounded by shifters who should be her enemies, Felix could suddenly see it with perfect clarity, a future where this became normal, where Avery belonged here as much as he did. Too bad shifters and witches couldn't have children together. Just the thought of it sent a delicious shiver down his spine, not because it could happen, but because his monster didn't care about biological impossibilities when it came to claiming his mate in every way possible.

Halfway through laughing, he started to cough. The coughing fit doubled him over, each spasm sending fresh agony dancing through his chest. Avery was on her feet instantly, hands steadying him, worry bleeding through the bond. Maybe bed wasn't the worst idea. Just for Avery, though.

"Felix," Ciro said, clapping him hard on his good shoulder—still sending a throbbing ache through him. "I'm glad you're home."

"Me too," he said, smiling through the pain.

Thirty-Nine

Avery

Felix's room was a couple of floors up, so they took an elevator. An *elevator.* Caerwyn was truly made for torture because nowhere in that goddamn school was a single elevator to be found. The shifters, apparently, believed in basic infrastructure. Point to them.

Whether this would be her new home now, she couldn't say. The shifters clearly hated her mere presence. But she could never go back to Caerwyn. As much as she fantasized about leaving, she thought she would be sadder, but the only thing she missed was Maya. She didn't even get to say goodbye. Maya would just think she had disappeared. Or what if they told her she died? The thought of Maya getting that news and believing it made something twist beneath Avery's ribs.

Guilt wound its way through Avery. There had to be a way to get a message to her. An idea flashed past her mind. What if she wrote fanfiction about her and Felix? Maya had to see it. Now that she knew Maya was on those same websites, surely she would see it. Maybe it could even make some witches more open to shifters. The power of smut was endless. If that was her destiny and duty in life, she would do it with pride.

But for right now, all she focused on was getting Felix down the hallway. He leaned against her, his massive frame almost toppling her over at one point. From what she knew, he couldn't shift until the poison left his system. Even with their newfound power. A single bullet. That was all it took. An inch closer and—she forced herself to stop.

Avery opened the simple door, but what was behind it was far from that.

The first thing she saw was the massive windows, overlooking the orange and red forest below lit silver by the moon. Herringbone floorboards caught by the firelight, flickering away in a massive fireplace, the room warmer than her dorm had ever been. It would be nice not to worry about toes freezing off in the middle of the night again.

In the center of the room were brown leather couches with plush pillows surrounding a mahogany coffee table. Above the fireplace, a TV reflected the flames in its black screen. The whole room was the size of her dorm, and this was only the living room. It smelled of pine and winter, of *him*. Despite everything, it put her at ease. Was this home?

She helped Felix past a modest kitchen into the bedroom to the right. An arch welcomed them in, and when Avery saw the room, she was speechless. The same floor-to-ceiling glass, the same view of stars and trees, but here the bed dominated. It was massive, enough to fit multiple people in it, draped in dark fabric that looked soft enough to drown in. Above the bed, cut into the ceiling, a skylight framed a perfect rectangle of night sky.

"You can change anything you like; this is your home now, too," he said.

So it was her home. It didn't really matter where it was though, as long as Felix was with her. But this was where she would be staying for the foreseeable future. It was everything she dreamed of. She wouldn't lie, though; it needed some feminine touch, but he had done pretty well on his own.

"It's perfect," she said honestly.

Across from the bed, another fireplace crackled, already lit, warming the space with its soft glow.

Carefully, she helped Felix lie down on the bed, a moan of pain coming out of him. He made a come here motion with his damaged arm. His arm needed a sling, just so he stopped fucking moving it. Maybe she could tie him down. Nope. She liked that option a bit too much to entertain it.

Finding the TV remote on the nightstand, she flipped through the channels until she found a bird watching one. When a starling filled the screen, its blue and black feathers bright against snow, she slid her gaze sideways to Felix.

"Very funny," he deadpanned.

He made a chittering sound, the one cats made at birds through windows, and it was so absurdly accurate she almost laughed.

Sitting down on the silk sheets, she was suddenly self-conscious about how filthy she was. They had already dragged in tons of mud that she would have to clean later.

Felix eyed her, instantly picking up what she was worried about. "Don't worry, the maids will get it later."

How did he always know?

"You have maids?"

"Well, not exactly, they're more like magic brooms that *love* to clean."

Another point to shifters, then. Magic brooms and elevators? They were living the life. Now if only she could get her hands on some chicken nuggets.

"Will you be okay if I go take a shower?"

"No. I will simply crumble away into the aether," he said, splaying himself across the bed and doing a fake cough like that of a dying Victorian child. Until it turned into a real cough. Served him right.

"So dramatic," she said.

Before she could get up and go to where she thought the bathroom was, he caught her hands in his, fingers wrapping around her. "Leave the door open," he said.

Something warm unfurled in her chest. She nodded, sliding off the bed to open the door she assumed led to the bathroom. Except she found a closet instead.

"Other one, kitten."

She'd explore the closet situation later; the fact that he apparently owned more than one shadow shirt was a revelation. Opening the other door, she walked into the bathroom. The lights automatically turned on for her, flooding the room with a soft glow. It was the most beautiful bathroom she had ever seen. Once again, large windows dominated the space; in front of them was an enormous bathtub, which was ironic given how much he seemed to hate them, or perhaps it was maybe the fact that she had shoved him in there like a dick with no lube? How did he even stay clean? The mental image of Felix licking his own shoulder like a house cat made her snort, but the alternative, some kind of magical scrubbing charm, seemed equally ridiculous.

The shower occupied the corner, glass-walled, with a rainfall showerhead that she was far too excited about. The same style skylight cut through the ceiling above it. Her dorm room had charm in a cramped, familiar way, but this was something else entirely.

Through the glass, stars scattered across hills that rolled into darkness. How far did the territory extend? Where did the shifter land end, and human civilization begin?

Before she took off her clothes, she looked over her shoulder to see that Felix had a full view of her and the shower.

A hot shudder went through her, a coiling feeling threading through her core.

Felix watched her with an intensity that made her skin burn even hotter.

Slowly, one by one, she finally got to drop the prison clothes. First the shirt, then the pants. She wanted to burn them in the fire, but that would happen later.

She didn't look back, not even to see if he was watching—she knew he was.

Water hit her skin, hot enough to sting against the cold, and she gasped, tilting her head back to let it run through her hair, down her neck, between her breasts, washing the day away. Goddess, it felt so good. Steam filled the space, but not enough to obscure his view of her. Whether it was the temperature or his gaze making her feel dizzy, she couldn't tell.

The shower was the exact thing she needed right now. Pulse quickening, her hands ran over her body; she took her time, let her fingers drag slow enough to leave trails of sensation behind them. Her core started to throb with the movement, and the bond responded in kind, flaring to life in her chest, heightening the desire coursing through her, but whether that was from her or Felix, it was impossible to tell. She loved it, though; feeding off each other's emotions like bloodthirsty beasts, and she was *ravenous* for him.

The steam became so thick that she could no longer see Felix from the shower. Whether or not he could see her show wouldn't stop her. Her hand slid down her thigh, and the touch sent sparks skittering over her.

The other hand moved upwards, exploring her own curves, and made its way up to her pierced nipple. She gave it a gentle pinch, and it started to vibrate, a small moan escaping her lips. Felix's hands came to mind, and the very thought of him sent a fever rushing through her. Her fingers dove beneath her slick folds, finding the tight bud. If she closed her eyes, she could almost pretend it was him, his fingers instead of hers, his palm cupping her breast, his breath hot against her neck instead of steam. She arched into the fantasy, chasing it, her fingers moving faster as her breath came quicker, hotter.

A small whimper escaped her lips as she slipped a finger inside. Nothing, absolutely nothing, compared to the stretch of him, but the thought of it dragged another gasp from her lungs.

Movement outside the door stopped her in her tracks. Was he coming in? No, he hated water; he wouldn't do that. She gave it another breath before she continued. Knowing he was listening, that he could hear every small sound she made, brought her so close to the edge she had to slow down or risk finishing before she wanted to.

"What do you think you're doing, little witch?" Felix said into her ear, the words low and husky. She jumped. How the fuck had he just appeared next to her? Her heart hammered—part shock, part arousal made worse by the way he was looking at her. His pupils had gone to slits, green and amber burning through the steam. He looked her up and down, and everything clenched in response.

"Having a shower." The lie came out breathless, unconvincing even to her own ears.

Felix leaned in. "We both know that's not true." He cocked his head, tail swishing behind him. "Now tell me. What. Were. You. Doing."

She looked down before she answered, and found the hard length of him straining against his grey track pants wet from the spray of the shower. Her breath caught in her throat; she couldn't even speak.

"Answer me, pet," he demanded.

"Touching myself."

He smiled, tongue sliding over his fang. "Good girl." His hand wrapped around hers, her fingers wet from being inside herself. Was he about to? He took her fingers into his mouth, his barbed tongue licking up all her juices in an unbelievably hot way. When he was finished, he kissed them. "That wasn't so hard, was it?"

"I thought you didn't like water," she said, her voice still struggling to get out. Goddess knew her brain wasn't working.

Holding her gaze, he walked into the fall of the water. "There is nothing I wouldn't do for you, Avery," he said, not talking about the shower anymore. "If you're going to get wet, I'd better have something to fucking do with it."

Using his good hand, he wrapped it around her neck and pulled her into a vicious kiss, devouring her the same way she hungered for him. The bond flared within them, moving like a living thing inside of them as they moved in tandem.

Desperately, Avery kneeled and pulled down his track pants, springing his cock out.

"Fuck," she said, her breath heavy. She would never get used to him; everything about him was carved as if he were stone. Every part of him made from a vision only an artist could conceive. His breathing came faster, rougher as he pulled her up with one hand and turned her around, flattening her against the shower wall.

"Your ass is fucking mesmerizing," he said. He leaned in close to her ear. "I'm going to bury myself in you, and you're going to take my knot like a good girl."

Shivers went down her spine as he slapped a hand against her ass cheek, the sound echoing around the room. It only stung for a second, and then turned into a pleasurable burn spreading all the way through her core. "More," she said.

"More what?"

"More, *please*."

Another hand came and clapped against her ass cheek, harder this time, and the impact reverberated through her pelvis, making her gasp.

"When I slap you again, I want you to know what it means."

"What does it mean?"

The next slap landed hard enough to make stars burst behind her eyelids, and she pressed her forehead against the glass to stay grounded.

"You're mine."

Slap.

"You're *fucking* mine."

Slap.

"Say it."

Slap.

"I'm *yours*."

Grabbing her ass, Felix ran his length between her legs, gliding agonizingly slow through her wetness. When he retreated, another whimper tore from her throat. She needed him inside her, not teasing, not almost, but buried to the fucking hilt. A low growl reverberated through her, the glass panes shaking.

But before he could do it again, he let out a groan, not one of pleasure but of pain.

The sound cut through the haze, and she twisted in his grip to face him.

"Did I tell you to turn around?" he said, grinding his teeth, the words coming out strained.

"You need to lie in bed. You're hurting," she said.

Felix's face had gone pale, eyelids barely staying open. This wasn't good for him.

Felix tried to push her into the wall again, but she resisted. "Not until I get my fill of you, kitten."

"You still will," she said, reaching past him and turning off the shower. Taking his hand, she led him back to the bedroom.

Gently, she helped him lie down, wincing every time he

did. The firelight caught every glorious muscle, his gaze so dark it reflected the flames.

Climbing on top of him, she made sure not to put any weight on anywhere that hurt and positioned herself over his erect cock.

"Wait," he said, gripping her before she could sink down on it. "Wait," he whispered again. Concern wove through her; had she done something wrong? Was he in pain?

For a moment, he just stared at her, his features brimming with emotion. "You said to tell you when I'm okay."

Her breath hitched. Was he going to say it?

"I wanted to say I love you. But it's not—"

What? He didn't love her?

"It's so much more than that." He swallowed, a single tear slipping down his face. "Avery, you are everything. Everything I want. Everything I need. I can't even put it into words—"

He sat up suddenly, his gaze blazing into hers. "I love you. I fucking *love* you. I will spend every hour, *every* second, making up for the time our souls hadn't been intertwined."

All the breath was knocked out of her lungs. He grabbed her face between his hands and kissed her reverently, *feverishly*. With the greed of a man who was insatiable. Sparks lit up her body, igniting a wildfire that utterly consumed her. *He* consumed her. She had to break away for a moment. Had to say it back.

"I love you," she said. But it didn't feel nearly enough. Those three little words were incapable of portraying the depth of how much she loved him.

A smile pulled at his lips. *"I know you do, little witch,"* he said into her mind.

She rolled her eyes, pushing him back on the bed. She kissed down his chest, letting her tongue trace the lines between muscle, tasting him. When she reached his hip, she looked up to find him watching her with an expression that bordered on feral.

"Don't," he said, voice raw. "If you put your mouth on me right now, this will be over before it starts."

The confession sent a thrill through her. Next time, then.

Instead, she came back up and gripped his cock, harder than she probably should. She worked him up and down. The moan he let out was fucking depraved. She wanted so much more. Could listen to that sound on repeat and never get bored.

And then, she let it spring forward, only to grind her sensitive flesh against his. She rolled her hips, inhaling the delicious friction that threatened to push her over right there and then. But she wanted him inside of her, and by the way his hand clamped onto her hip, fingers digging in as he guided her up and positioned his tip at her entrance, he wanted the same thing.

Slowly at first, she slid just the head in, moans tumbling from both their lips. Before, when she had sex, she had been somewhat self-conscious, but now? The way she sank herself down on him was downright animalistic. Inch by inch, she took him. Took him until he was fucking buried in her. She was so full she could barely breathe. Every nerve screamed for him.

She was already so close, but this just sent her soaring higher and higher. He thrust into her, in and out, in and out until she felt it getting fuller and fuller inside of her. Waves of pleasure crashed through her each time she felt it swelling with each thrust, the knot forming and growing until she was stretched so tight she saw stars. Just when she thought she couldn't take any more, the barbs hooked into her walls. She cried out from the sensation that flipped from pain to ecstasy in the space of a heartbeat. By the sound of it, Felix was close himself.

"Fuck, Avery, I'm going to—"

Her gaze caught his, and goddess, the way he looked at her. It was enough. It shoved her over the edge, and she took him with her. Her walls clenched around his knot as his heat flooded inside of her, filling her with his sweet cum. It was like falling, like for a second, she was completely weightless, before another thrust of his cock had her coming apart in tatters. The noise she made wasn't witch, human, or shifter. She crashed down, pleasure racking her body with no mercy.

Their breaths heaved together as his knot swelled, locking them together so completely she couldn't have moved if she wanted to. She let herself collapse forward carefully, avoiding his shoulder, until her cheek rested against his chest.

In every way possible, they were tied together, bound by the threads of fate and woven together by choice. When she lifted her head to look at him, he was already watching her.

Her lips curved up. "You're staring at me."

His fingers brushed through her hair, finding a piece and tucking it behind her ear. "And I won't ever stop."

Forty

Felix

He hadn't been lying. The sun rose above the hill and kissed Avery before he could, but he hadn't taken his eyes off her in hours. It was like he couldn't physically rip himself away from looking at her, that if she so much as blinked, she would be gone.

The dawn light crept across the floorboards, the sun coming out as if it were just for her, drenching the room in a golden hue. It stretched over the bed, climbing over her like it couldn't get enough of her either. The scent of cinnamon and honey filled the room, and *fuck*, would he ever get used to it? He didn't think so. He didn't want to. Slowly, Avery opened her eyes, the blue oceans of them glistening in the morning light, catching on him almost immediately. *God, she was so beautiful.*

"You are still staring." She smiled sleepily.

"I am a man of my word," he said. "Why would I look away when my whole world is in front of me?"

And Felix meant every word. Before her, he had been hollow, moving through life like a lifeless husk. If he had a soul before, it was in the ashes, and somehow, she had set it aflame.

His *mate.* And now that he had found her, he would never let her go. Even the gods themselves should be terrified of the lengths he would go to. No matter whether he was alive or dead, he would find her, protect her, and love her. He *fucking* loved her. His *fucking* mate.

"Are you hungry?" he asked.

She nodded, rubbing the sleep out of her eyes.

"Follow me," he said.

Using his good shoulder, he hoisted her up from the bed and clothed her in a big shirt of his and some pants Eimi had lent her. He led her through the house to the dining hall. It was still the ass crack of dawn, but shifters moved in and out of the dining hall, all giving the little witch a wide berth. Her shoulders had crept up toward her ears, her hands fidgeting with the hem of her shirt, and Felix wanted to snarl at every shifter who made her feel unwelcome. But he didn't. Yet.

The dining hall wasn't dissimilar to the one in Caerwyn. It held rows of tables and benches, designed to seat over a hundred people. Vaulted ceilings supported the roof, but the chandeliers had long since been replaced by more modern designs, casting warm light over the room. They took a seat at the back, away from the majority of shifters. Who despite Felix being right next to her, they still stared. A growl rumbled from him, and that was all it took for them to whip their heads away.

A lazy smile pulled at his lips. Not even his den could ruin his good mood. "Don't worry about them, they'll warm up to you."

"It's fine, I can understand why they aren't happy to have a witch in their den."

Anyone who wasn't happy after he was better would be *made* to be happy. But Felix didn't tell her that. She was *his.* Anyone who had a problem with that would have a fucking smile carved into their face.

Felix pulled her against his side and tucked her into the crook of his chest. The wound pulled when he moved, an aching reminder that he wasn't at full strength yet, but he'd suffer worse if she wasn't close.

He inhaled deeply. *God*, her scent, it would drive him mad. He had half a mind to chuck her over his shoulder and ravage her all over again. But he had a surprise in store that he couldn't ruin.

"Where do we get food from?" she asked.

The sound was audible in the quiet between them, and Felix bit back a smile.

"Today it will come to us."

"How?" she said, head tilting.

"Magic," he said, shaking his hands in the air and then wincing from the pain. Fuck. Forgot about the chest wound.

"Stop using that arm, you idiot."

"Make me." He wiggled his eyebrows.

She glared at him, but it had little meaning when he could see the smile pulling at her lips.

Eimi and Ciro came back from the mission Felix had set them on at seven a.m. His sister had been more than displeased to fetch like a dog, but because he almost died, he had some leverage. They walked down the hall, Eimi holding a brown paper bag. Avery's nostrils flared as she tried her hardest not to look like she was smelling the delicious scent coming from inside it, her attempt at nonchalance undermined by the way she leaned forward half an inch. Felix took the bag from his sister and pushed it toward her. Felix caught Eimi's eye and mouthed *thank you*.

Tentatively, Avery took the bag and opened the top of it before crinkling it closed again. "Is this what I think it is?"

Even Eimi couldn't help the grin forming on her face. "Mmhmm, went all the way into London for it."

Like a kid on Christmas, the wonder in her eyes couldn't

be missed as she opened the bag. Her lip wobbled. Was she about to cry over chicken nuggets?

"How did you know?" Her voice cracked. She really was.

"You talked about them in your sleep," Felix said, a warmth spreading in his chest. He'd listened to her mumble feverishly for twenty minutes about the perfect crispy texture, like she was repeating a goddamn ad from memory or something. He'd known exactly what he needed to do. It was then that he realized that they had a shared obsession with delicious chicken. They truly were soulmates.

Avery fished the nuggets out of the bag and held the box like she was carrying a delicate artifact. "You don't know how much this means to me, thank you," she said sincerely, before turning to Eimi and Ciro. "Thank you."

He knew she meant it, every word. Felix watched Avery look at his sister as she had just performed a miracle instead of a fast-food run.

"Consider it your welcoming gift to the den," Eimi said. "Usually, for any other witch, they would be poisoned, but for my brother's mate, I'll make an exception."

Avery looked surprised. "He's your brother?"

"Unfortunately," she deadpanned. "But thank you for keeping him safe."

They smiled at each other, and Felix recognized that particular expression: the girl smile. The we're-going-to-talk-about-you-later smile. Oh god. Were they going to be friends? It was good that Avery would have friends here, but all Felix could think about was every embarrassing story Eimi had kept hidden over the years.

"Now eat them before they get cold," Eimi insisted.

Avery happily obliged, opening the box and looking at the ten crispy golden nuggets and sauce that steamed in the morning chill. They all watched her face light up like he'd given her the fucking crown jewels. Even Ciro couldn't hide the chuckle behind his hand. The scent of greasy chicken hit his nose. He had to admit, they smelled pretty good. Carefully, she dipped the nugget in the sauce. And when Avery took a bite of one? She moaned and rolled her eyes back more than any lick of his tongue had ever done. That chicken nugget was living its best life, and Felix was absolutely, pathetically jealous. It was then that he realized he would live his life a jealous man, of the clothes that kissed her back, the seats that held her, and the blankets that warmed her when he couldn't. Jealous of all the days, hours, and minutes he had spent not touching her. Felix would spend an eternity making up for lost time, and he would love every second. As long as he was alive, she would never have personal space again.

Funny how they always said curiosity killed the cat, well, they had never said how love could destroy one. It had wrecked him completely and built something better in its place. In a game of cat and witch, somehow they had both won. He wouldn't have it any other way.

EPILOGUE

WREN

HER DRAGON'S VOICE, *HIS VOICE*, ECHOED AROUND her mind. It was a fucking shifter.

The rifle jammed as she tried to shoot it, and she grabbed it hard enough that it could snap between her fingers. Her magic wasn't working. And her familiar, the *shifter*, was flying away with her sister and another shifter in its claws.

"Fuck," she muttered under her breath as they disappeared over the hill.

Lowering the scope, she took in the scene around her. Carnage rained, bodies littered the ground, and injured enforcers crawled across the ground, groaning.

"Call the healers!" Wren barked at the stunned enforcer next to her. The young woman stared blankly back at her. She was obviously not high-ranking or had even been an enforcer for very long, given the way she reacted to the blood flowing in a river towards them. Wren felt nothing looking at the gore, had stopped feeling anything about blood years ago, but watching this girl freeze pissed her off. She stepped over it and walked towards an enforcer tending to one of the wounded before he saw her coming and stood and saluted.

Her dragon was a shifter.

She forced the thought out of her mind. No. There had to be an explanation for it. Her mother would never do that. Not after all the shifters had done to them.

"Call the healers," she barked at the enforcer.

"Yes, Commander."

Turning back to survey the damage, Wren took it all in: four dead, maybe five depending on whether the enforcer missing half her leg made it. This was a fucking mess. One that her sister, her sweet, naive sister, or so she thought, had left in her wake. What was she thinking? Bonding a shifter? Letting him walk around the campus? A rare pang of guilt hit her chest as she questioned why she had never come to her for help. Wren knew why. But instead of entertaining that, she quickly buried it and filed it away under something to be unpacked when she was alone in her room. Her face went blank, a practiced mask that she wore in public.

Wren looked over her shoulder, feeling a looming presence sending daggers into her back. Her mother stood in the shadows of the forest, her face as blank as Wren's, but she knew her mother far better than that. The way the lines of expression were hardened, she was pissed.

She approached her the same way one would approach an angry wolf. She lowered her eyes, making sure not to look directly at her mother, and when she was in her mother's immediate vicinity, she knelt. The wet grass soaked through, the coolness grounding her for one needed moment.

"Get up." Her mother seethed.

Fuck. She was pissed.

"I've sent a task force to secure the island; they couldn't have gone far with the wards." They were impenetrable for shifters. Avery may have had power, but nothing that could break through them. The wards should have held. Should have trapped them on the island like rats in a maze. Either someone had inside help, or...

"They're already off the Island, Wren."

What? It took her back for a second, blinking, she tried to hide the shock on her face. "But—"

"They got through them," she ground out.

No. They couldn't have. What kind of magic could do that? Wren looked to the side, a habit she had formed when she was lost deep in thought. *How?*

Her mother sighed, rubbing her temples. "Follow them," she said calmly.

"There could be more shifters on the island. We need to lock Caerwyn down," she said before thinking.

"That's an order," she hissed. "That dragon is too special to lose, your magic is too special to lose, Wren. Gather a task force and go after them."

An uneasy feeling crawled through her. *That dragon.* Not your familiar.

"And Avery?" Wren asked, unable to hide the bite in her voice. Wouldn't that be her first priority? She knew her mother was harsh on Avery, but her mother loved her.

"Yes," she said, gritting her teeth. "Avery, of course. Bring her back here."

Wren nodded and went to walk away before her mother reached out and gripped her wrist, her long nails digging in. Wren didn't even flinch.

"Do not, under any circumstances, believe what they say. They will try to influence your mind like they've done to Avery, to your *familiar.*"

She had never seen her mother so undone. Her hair, usually slicked back, was fraying at the sides, and the bags under her eyes were particularly noticeable. She almost looked afraid.

Wren wrenched her grasp from her mother. "Understood."

Whatever Avery had stumbled into, whatever had made her run—Wren would find it. She would drag the truth into the light by its ears and make everyone involved answer for it. Something about all of this wasn't right. And she would stop at fucking nothing to unearth it.

Want more?

Felix and Avery will return as side characters in book two, which will follow Wren Alarch with *certain* dragon shifter(s). It's tough to let someone else take the stage from Felix and Avery, but fear not, you'll still get short stories and maybe some smutty pictures.

Join my mailing list using the QR Code below to get updates and access to bonus goodies!

Loved Avery and Felix?

Please consider leaving a review on Amazon or Goodreads if you enjoyed A Game of Cat and Witch! Reviews are the most important things to indie authors. Thank you so much again for reading <3

Scan QR below:

Acknowledgments

Readers: From the very first moment I opened my bookstagram account, I knew that I had stumbled upon something special. This community welcomed me with open arms, and helped me grow into the person I am today, and I sincerely mean this: I could not have done it without you. From answering my silly stories, to all your unwavering support and excitement. You are the people making my dreams come true. I have cried, laughed, and bled over this story, and I truly hope you enjoyed it. From the bottom of my heart, thank you so much.

Steph: My editor, but you are so much more than that. Thank you for the countless days, hours, and minutes you have put into me and this book. From the early morning calls to me calling you just to ask questions I have asked 3000 times already. This book wouldn't have happened without you untangling the knot that is in my head and guiding my through. I have genuinely come to love you with all my heart. You are absolutely incredible at your job and an amazing human!!!

Mum: I am so sorry for scaring you with the unhinged sex scenes you had to edit and making you learn what knotting is, but thank you for tirelessly putting in effort to read and edit my book. And for birthing me in the first place so I could be around to put this absolute whack book together. I love you so much, thank you for always being there for me and supporting every deluded idea I ever had.

Gen: GIRL!!!! YOU CAME IN CLUTCH!!! I appreciate

you so freaking much for reading the book with a fine tooth comb and making it infinitely better!! You're an absolutely incredible author, and even lovelier person. Thank you to the moon and back.

Zee: Thank you so much for taking me on so quickly and being an amazing proofreader! I had the time of my life reading your hilarious comments (unless they're about dangling modifiers which hurt my heart a bit). You are amazing!

Betas: @EternalGrimoires @charityslibrary @aislin-canactuallyread @ajs.library @bookishbreez @FairlyCa-treads @readingandrapture @cc.readingjournal @bookbaefae @spicybookfae @chrissareads sweet summer children. My gremlin crew. Thank you for all your unhinged comments and your memes, thank you for reading with such a quick turn around and absolutely devouring the book and already demanding more! But most of all, thank you for giving me the confidence to press publish. I love you all to absolute bits and I know Felix and Avery would do (they have to because I created them).

My agent: AGH ANGIE!!! Love you to pieces!!! You're such an incredible agent and friend. Thank you for seeing my potential and signing me on. Thank you for answering thousands of questions with speed and patience. And most of all thank you, thank you, thank you, for all the tirelessly hard work you are doing behind the scenes and for bringing this book into places it would have never seen without you.

Authors: My fellow authors, thank you for being so patient with my questions, with helping this book get out in the world, and for your support. I.V. Ophelia, Kate Golden, H.M Wolfe, Avina St. Graves, Demi Clorissa (for your last minute formatting ilysm, I would have crashed out), Lexi Davis, Keshe Chow, Bec George, Genevieve Addison, Lauren

Jackson. You're all incredible authors and I appreciate you all so much.

Artists: Thank you to all the artists who have brought Felix and Avery to life. I will always be astounded by the care and love you have for my characters.

Nina: My pa!! Thank you for dealing with everything being thrown at you last minute because I have the organizational skills of a peanut. Love you to the moon and back!!!

Dad: Thank you for helping me chase my dreams. Thank you for being there for me and always supporting me with 100%. Thank you for believing in me. I love you so much.

My family: I love you all so much. Thank you for sharing your excitement and supporting me however you can. I say this with all the love in my heart, but I truly hope you never read this because I will never look you in the eye again. (Except you Mia, the way we thirsted over Geralt should be illegal).

Jesse: My rock. My Babe. My best friend. My pookie wookie smockems. The love of my life. Thank you for being the best partner in the whole goddamn world (Don't care that I'm bias, it's a fact). Thank you for everything you have done. Thank you for all the sacrifices you have made in order to let me chase my dreams. Thank you for being you. I will love you forever.

Bessie. My elderly cat, thank you for letting me cry into your fur whenever I've been overwhelmed.